# Visibly
# Struck

"Steve Kubicek moves seamlessly between Biblical and American history to weave a story line that is both compelling and exciting. The result is an unprecedented examination of the steps and guiding forces behind perhaps the greatest of our founding fathers. This book should be required reading for all, especially those who doubt this great nation was not formed from a divine charter. In God we trust indeed!"

  —Robert Dickie, *President, Crown*

"I felt as if I were right alongside 'Spitz' as he moved to renew his faith in God while witnessing the many acts of Providence that guided George Washington throughout his journey to becoming the father of the United States of America."

  —Ron Long, *Staff Sergeant and Combat Medic in the*
    *TN Army National Guard*

"*Visibly Struck* is a fascinating glimpse into the faith of our first president and how his relationship with God guided his life and our nation. Told in a powerful, entertaining way that was so unique I couldn't put it down."

  —Aspen West Anderson

"Stephen Spitzen seeks to come to terms with God after losing his son and daughter-in-law in a plane crash. While in a coma he returns to the Revolutionary War era. Well documented events show that George Washington believed God intervened in his life and in the formation of the new nation."

  —Patsy Stevens, *webmaster at Garden of Praise and former school teacher*

"Presently people discuss the meaning or intent of our founding fathers about religious freedom or freedom from religion. This book helps to answer that question by showing George Washington's faith, beliefs, and attitude toward the Almighty! Great book!"

  —Tom Voth, *business owner in Houston Texas*

# STEVE KUBICEK

# Visibly Struck

A NOVEL BASED *on the*

TRUE EXPERIENCES *of* GEORGE WASHINGTON

*and* HIS FAITH *in the* INVISIBLE HAND *of* GOD

SUMMIT
PARTNERS, LLC

Published in Burns, Tennessee, by Summit Partners LLC.

Cover Illustration: "Washington and Lafayette at Valley Forge" by John Ward Dunsmore 1907 (Obtained from the Library Congress—public domain)

Design: Lookout Design, Inc. | www.lookoutdesign.com

This is a work of fiction based on the true experiences of George Washington as described in the journals, letters, and documents of George Washington and as purported in biographies of George Washington and other related research materials. Being fiction, the Names, characters, places, and incidents either are the product of the author's imagination used fictitiously within the historical settings and any resemblance to actual persons, living or dead, events, or locales is entirely coincidental, or they are the product of research, historical accounts, and quotations signified where appropriate by the use of endnotes.

Unless otherwise noted, Scripture is taken from the King James Version of the Bible.

Scripture used as chapter headings (unless otherwise noted) and Scripture marked NIV is taken from THE HOLY BIBLE, NEW INTERNATIONAL VERSION®, NIV® Copyright © 1973, 1978, 1984, 2011 by Biblica, Inc.™ Used by permission. All rights reserved worldwide.

Kubicek, Phillip S. (Steve)

*Visibly Struck* / by Steve Kubicek
p. cm.
Includes bibliographical references.
ISBN 978-0-9848426-4-3 (trade paper)
Library of Congress Control Number: 2013933414
Printed in the United States of America

*I humbly dedicate this book
to my own band of brothers*

*With fond regard for
my father, Jim,
my brother, Mike,
and my sons Kraig and Matthew
And in loving memory*

*of*

*Frank Kubicek and Asa Markham, my grandfathers,
and Rick Kubicek, my brother*

*I also sincerely thank my senior editor,
Sharilyn Grayson,
for her significant collaborative contribution to the text and
flow of the story. Visibly Struck would have been far less moving
and colorful without her clever imagination, professional
writing skills, and insightful guidance.*

# Prologue

*"The Spirit then lifted me up and took me away,*
*and I went in bitterness and in the anger of my spirit, with the*
*strong hand of the LORD on me." —Ezekiel 3:14*

A swirling tunnel of lights like a cyclone of stars surrounded Spitz, moving him forward and upward at a speed he couldn't fathom. His dropping, clenching stomach told him that he was moving in a place without gravity faster than he'd ever moved before. The whirling, racing stars dashed him in weightless acceleration somewhere he couldn't see, and for one moment of sheer panic, Spitz wondered if they'd ever let him go.

Then they did. They set him gently down on grass beneath a night sky. Slowly, they withdrew into the safe, ancient pattern of stars that seemed to laugh at him with their twinkling, denying that they had ever transported him so recklessly from his safe, warm library.

He wished he was there now. The tunnel of lights that had vacuumed him out of his favorite room in his own house had set him somewhere cold and unfamiliar. Mist shrouded him so that he could see clearly no more than a dozen yards around him. Trees and stretches of a gravel path appeared and disappeared as wisps of mist passed in front of them. The path led up a hill, where he could dimly make out the shape of a large building with glowing light at the windows.

Spitz turned around and saw the source of a mist: a vast, brown river exhaling into the winter sky like a living thing. The mist rose only a dozen feet or so into the air before it fell, swirling and ebbing, to the grass and trees around him. He knew of no river so wide and deep and resonant anywhere close to him. His panic began to return, and together with the damp chill in the air, it sent a shiver down his spine. *Where am I? Why is it so cold? How do I get back?*

He craned his neck to examine the stars winking and turning so slowly that they looked still. *What's happening to me? How do I make them send me back home?*

But then his head whipped quickly around to face the gravel path leading up from the river, down from the building above.

He heard footsteps.

# Chapter One

*"Has any god ever tried to take for himself one nation out of another nation, by testings, by signs and wonders, by war, by a mighty hand and an outstretched arm, or by great and awesome deeds, like all the things the Lord your God did for you in Egypt before your very eyes? You were shown these things so that you might know that the Lord is God; besides him there is no other."*
*—Deuteronomy 4:34-35*

Aspen Spitzen flopped down among the pillows on the sectional sofa after a full day at the financial office. Her evening chores were behind her. Now she could finally relax and drift into a world of make-believe. Nothing calmed and transported her like watching television dramas with problems so vastly different from the ones she faced every day: so far away and so reliably solved. And Aspen was excited, because tonight she was going to watch the premiere of a promising new show. *Papa would like this series,* she thought. *I wonder if he'll give it a try.*

A year earlier, Aspen had convinced her grandfather, Papa, to allow her to rearrange their family room into a home theater. The new theater room had become her sanctuary in the same way that the home's library had become his. Tonight Stephen Spitzen III, or Spitz as his friends called him, had retreated to his books after dinner just like he did on most evenings. Aspen had known him to camp there well into the night, sometimes even the early morning. She frowned as she thought of him there alone. Although his studies consumed him, they gave him little pleasure. Papa was obsessed with his "case," the one he'd been building since she was nine.

Aspen padded down the hallway to the library and paused while she looked at her grandfather through the glass-paneled library doors. Papa sat at his desk with a computer monitor centered in front of him. The only diversion he usually allowed himself was a game of solitaire. He said it calmed him down and helped him think. If he was playing solitaire so soon after dinner, then he'd hit a thorny patch in his case. Something was bothering him.

She knocked on the door and opened it without waiting for a reply. "Papa? A new TV show is about to start, and I thought you'd like to watch it with me. It's about politics. You'd probably like it." She crossed to his desk and leaned against the wall, waiting for an answer.

Spitz turned his leather swivel chair to face his granddaughter. "I don't think I'm really up for TV tonight. You go and enjoy your show."

"Are you okay?" she asked, frowning in concern.

"I'm fine," he answered quickly, but he rubbed a hand over his forehead and sighed. "I was reading something that bothered me, and I'm trying to shake it loose. That's all."

Willing to listen, Aspen perched on a nearby chair. "What bothered you so much?"

Spitz dithered a minute, and Aspen could tell he was making up his mind whether to ask her to drop the inquiry or whether to hash it out. She drew her knees up and rested her heels on the seat of the chair, arms around her legs. She was prepared to wait.

Spitz saw her posture and grinned before the sadness caught up with him. "Your daddy was stubborn, too," he told her, his grin fading almost as soon as it arrived.

"I wonder where he got his stubbornness," Aspen said pertly, shooting her Papa a look.

"That's fair." Spitz pushed up from his desk chair and went to the wingback armchair by the fire where he usually did his reading and mulling. He retrieved two books: a biography of George Washington and a collection of Washington's writings. He settled back into the chair by his desk and set them down beside the monitor.

"You sure you want to hear this? It's about one of my dusty old books," he teased her. She regularly twitted him about the state of his library with its stacks of books resting on every available surface in an order known only to him.

"You know, you'd enjoy those dusty old books a lot more if you'd let me organize them for you," she told him. "You could actually see what's on the shelves."

"I can see fine," he retorted. "You still want to hear?" She nodded, concentrating. She had a quick mind. Spitz loved that about her.

He cleared his throat and opened the collection of Washington's writings. "You know I'm still on George Washington, and I picked up tonight with his Inaugural Address right after dinner. The chicken was good, by the way."

"Glad you liked it—what's in the address?"

"Well, he goes on at some length about God being the source of all that's good, and—where is it? Here we go, listen to this: 'No people can be bound to acknowledge and adore the Invisible Hand which conducts the affairs of men more than those of the United States. Every step by which they have advanced to the character of an independent nation seems to have been distinguished by some token of providential agency.' And then here, a bit further on, he tells all us Americans that we owe that invisible hand 'some return of pious gratitude, along with an humble anticipation of the future blessings which the past seem to presage.' Can you believe it?"

"I can," Aspen said quietly. "I'm just sorry it bothered you."

Spitz closed the collection of writings, none too gently. "Of course it bothered me, Aspen; how could it not bother me? Here's the founder of the country cringing to a whimsical God like Oliver Twist with his cap in his hand. 'Please, sir, may I have some more?'" Spitz mocked. "And that whole idea of an invisible hand keeps coming up over and over again, no matter where I start in that book. I just can't stomach it. Where was that invisible hand when your mother and daddy needed it? Are we supposed to return pious gratitude for that? Are we supposed to wait humbly for the invisible hand to give us more of the same?"

"Washington was asking for more of a good thing, Papa; you know that," Aspen disagreed.

"But the invisible hand, Aspen—he's saying that God directly intervened to create this country. 'Providential agency' means that God acted. He did something. He didn't just know about it and look the other way while the patriots went to war. Washington is saying that God conducted the whole thing," Spitz said, his voice rising in accusation.

"I know. I believe that. You know I still believe that," Aspen told him.

"Well here's what really gets under my skin. Your mother and father and your granny's death were not a surprise to God. He not only knew the missionary plane would crash, He allowed it to happen. He allowed your granny's heart to burst, too. These things passed through His fingers. Don't you see?"

Aspen waited silently for Spitz to finish, and then she reached for his quivering hand. "I wish you'd give all this up," she said, tears pooling in her eyes.

"I didn't mean to make you cry," Spitz said grumpily. "I'm sorry."

"It's all right, Papa," Aspen told him, squeezing his hand. "I just don't like to see you so angry. It's not good for you. I worry about you."

"You've got nothing to worry about," Spitz told her. "I'm fine."

"You're not, though," Aspen argued. "You spend so much time combing through these books trying to prove your case that you're just worrying yourself to a shred. It bothers me."

"Honey, I wish I could give it up, but it's not that easy. I gave Him years and years of my life. I lost my only son to Him. I can't just roll over and take that kind of betrayal. It's too much. I can't let it go. He's wrong, and I have to show Him so." Spitz sighed. He and Aspen had spoken these words to each other before. Neither of them entirely saw the other's point; so they gave each other grace to keep to their own corners on the issue. After all, the two of them had no one left but each other. They couldn't let a difference of opinion keep them apart.

Aspen gestured to the monitor beside the books on the desk. "Are you going to play another hand?" she asked.

Spitz looked at the cards on the screen. He'd barely read at all before he'd opened the program, and tonight he had won on the third attempt. But the cards hadn't brought him any solace. And he couldn't concentrate on Aspen's show, no matter how sweet it was that she wanted her grumpy old Papa around. "I think I'll read a bit more now that my hackles are already up," he told her.

Aspén walked to a shelf behind her, and Spitz knew before she got there what she had gone to get. The cover had been old decades ago, and now it smelled like smoke. The edges were burned where flames had licked at the gold leaf. But she handled it like it was made of gold all over. She held it out apologetically, knowing she was hurting him.

"As long as you're reading, Papa, won't you try this one again?" she asked.

"That's too much to ask, Aspen. I wish you'd put it away," he said shortly.

"Look, it's no fair having a one-sided argument. If you're going to yell at Him, you should let Him answer you," she said, putting the book gently down on the desk.

"I've already heard everything He's got to say," Spitz growled. "I'm done listening."

"Okay," Aspen sighed. She picked up his other two books and replaced them on the side table by the fireplace near the comfortable armchair. She smiled falteringly at him. "Here are the Washington books. Would you like me to bring you some tea in a bit? I was thinking of making some."

Spitz swallowed a lump in his throat. When had she started looking after him instead of leaving things the other way around? And she was so careful to hide her kindnesses. He was willing to bet some of his dusty old books that she hadn't thought of the tea until she realized that he might like some, that it might soothe his ruffled soul. "Sure, as long as you're up," he said. He settled himself in the wingback armchair and picked up the book of Washington's writings. She cast him one last half-smile as she left and pulled the door shut behind her. She wanted to make sure that her television didn't disturb him. *What did I ever do to deserve a grandkid as thoughtful as Aspen?*

Immediately the thought rankled in him. Gratitude to fate was an unfamiliar emotion by now, and he didn't welcome it. He'd do better to ask the question that had been bothering him for the past seventeen years. *What did my son ever do to deserve that plane crash and that painful, fiery death?*

The answer was always the same: nothing.

Spitz looked up to the wall above one of his bookshelves, where he'd hung a framed assortment of his grandfather's effects. Displayed in the center behind the glass were a quartz wristwatch and a Mason's gold tie bar. Mounted beneath them were other tie tacks and lapel pens which identified the patriarch's trade—agriculture. A variety of small paper documents affixed to either side included the elder Stephen Spitzen's driver's license and voter registration card. In one corner were five playing cards arranged in a run of alternating colored suits, like one would find in a game of solitaire.

Allowing his mind to drift, Spitz pictured his grandpa sitting in his favorite chair, leaning forward over an old, yellowed coffee table. He could see him as clearly as if the old man were sitting across the room. Gramps would hold half a deck of cards in his left hand and grip an unlit cigar in his mouth while he looked down onto the playing surface, deciding his next move in one of his never-ending games of solitaire. A smile formed as Spitz thought about Gramps playing for hours, literally wearing out the cards. Now he was a chip off the old block, playing the same game. The only differences were that he preferred nuts to cigars and an electronic version to a paper deck. Some things never changed, like getting old and playing solitaire. Spitz paused and then altered his last thought.

*Some things never change, like getting old, playing solitaire, and needing justice. I'm not the first to demand it and not likely the last. Philosophers have been searching for justice for centuries. Just like Gramps and his continuous game of solitaire, they've worn out the cards looking. And boy, have they come up with some mixed results.*

Spitz laid out the perennial questions in his mind like worn-out cards, feeling resentful that no matter how he shuffled this deck, he never won.

Did an all-knowing and all-powerful deity really create the world? If He did, then is He alive and active today? If He's active, is He loving and benevolent? If He is an active, all-knowing, all powerful deity, full of love, then why is there pain and suffering? Why do bad things happen, especially to good people?

*Especially to me,* he thought. Emotionally drained and physically slumped in his comfortable armchair, Spitz soberly whispered, "If You are so good and so powerful, why didn't You stop the crash from happening?" How many times had he asked this gut-wrenching question? More than a thousand times, he supposed. In all this time, why hadn't God given him a satisfactory answer? Was God avoiding him? Was God embarrassed or ashamed because of what had happened? Was God hiding from him?

The thought amused him. It was a giddy thought that the creator of the universe was hiding behind a stray meteor because He'd slipped up, really put His celestial foot in it, and He had no answer. Spitz's eyes lit on the blackened Bible Aspen had retrieved. It had fared much better in the crash than his son's body. Rage coursed through him. "You want to answer me? You want to talk back? Here's Your shot. And You'd better take it, because I'm not giving You another one."

He seized the Bible and opened it at random. The fire in the fireplace surged in a sudden glow of sparks as a log split and crumbled. The bright blaze from it danced over the words and split into a bewildering pattern of small, distinct lights that enveloped him top to toe and lifted him right away from everything he had known, as if he had boarded a recklessly careening midnight train barreling through a channel of stars.

The swirl of lights withdrew, leaving Spitz standing on the bank of a river and shivering with the chill mist that rose from it. He could hear that massive, unhurried river moving behind him. The river mist swirled into a general fog that blanketed the land and obscured the shape of some buildings up a hill. He could see lighted windows.

He shook with chill and panic over his unfamiliar surroundings. Then his panic heightened as he heard footsteps and realized that one of those lights was moving toward him.

"Mr. Spitzen," a deep voice said. In front of him, Spitz saw a tall, handsome black man dressed in an embroidered blue woolen suit with breeches instead of slacks. He wore thick white woolen socks to his knees, a heavy, thick-cuffed overcoat, and a white wig below the tri-cornered hat on his head. He carried a lantern. It was the moving light Spitz had seen.

Spitz glanced down quickly. He was wearing a similar outfit, only his suit was brown. "Yes?" he answered hesitantly. *Who is this guy? Why is he dressed like that? Why am I dressed like this?*

"Please follow me, sir," the man asked. He was crying silently, tears streaming unheeded down his broad, chiseled cheeks.

"What's the matter?" Spitz asked him, concerned.

As he led Spitz uphill, the man took a handkerchief from the pocket of his suit coat and mopped his eyes and cheeks. "The general is very ill, sir. You will excuse me, but it brings me very low."

Spitz only had time to wonder who the general was before the fog thinned enough to allow him to see the shape of the buildings before him. He had seen them before, but the last time he had seen them he had been wearing a baseball cap and T-shirt and carrying a camera. He shook his head.

"Mount Vernon," he breathed in disbelief. So the general was General George Washington. *What's going on? Why does this guy want me up at Mount Vernon? Why is he saying Washington's ill when he's been dead for centuries? Am I part of some kind of reenactment?*

"It is a grand house for a great man," the man beside him said. He inclined his head to acknowledge the compliment he heard in Spitz's awe and disbelief. "Have you never been here before, sir?"

"Only once," Spitz said hesitantly.

"I thought you must have been," the man said confidently, "as long as you have known him. He remembers you, sir, as I do."

"General Washington speaks of me?" Spitz echoed, stunned.

"Yes, sir," the man confirmed, "he has been organizing his papers lately with the aid of Mr. Rawlins, and he remembers the triumphs of his youth. He has told me of your courage in several terrible battles that I did not observe closely, being behind the lines."

"He has?" Spitz asked uncomfortably. *He must be expecting another Mr. Spitzen. I've never fought a day in my life. I'm going to get up to that house and be chucked straight out.* "Are you sure you weren't supposed to meet another Mr. Spitzen? I'm Stephen Spitzen; everyone calls me Spitz."

"Yes, sir, Mr. Stephen Spitzen," the man echoed. "Mr. Rawlins called you by name, and I know your face, though we have both aged. You are the man."

★ ★ ★

When Aspen left Spitz's library retreat, she didn't go to the kitchen to brew tea for Papa as she'd planned or back to the television to start her series. Instead, halfway down the hall she stepped into the bathroom. Closing the door to her secret hideaway, Aspen sighed deeply and shuddered. Suddenly, tears of pent-up emotion dripped down her cheeks. Sinking to the floor with her back to the door, Aspen wandered inside the memory of a hurtful past.

That late October seventeen years ago, yellow and red leaves had cascaded across well-manicured grounds where stone obelisks and angels and tablets interrupted the smooth grass. The air was cool with a welcome edge of crispness. But the drawn and whispering faces that seemed to move in slow motion around her were largely unfamiliar. She remembered her nine-year-old hand reaching up to grasp her Papa's. Holding tightly to each other's cold fingers, they had walked away from the graves that held her mother and father. As it had happened then, a dam inside her seemed to burst, releasing with it a river of tears. Pushed to the floor from the weight of the remembrance, Aspen began to heave uncontrollably.

Her parents' funeral was the last time she had seen Spitz pray. And after Granny's funeral, his customary faith soon morphed into deep contempt. When she was still child enough not to know any better she'd asked him once why the two of them never went to church anymore. "God took your mother and daddy away from us. How can I worship Him now? How can I sing? No, honey, God and I aren't on speaking terms anymore," he'd answered, his jaw set. She came by her stubbornness honestly.

But Papa used to have a softer side. He'd taught Bible classes at church for years, and Aspen sometimes came with him carrying a bag of crayons so that she could draw while he spoke. She could still hear his warm voice saying that everyone chose what to believe. Everyone chose by faith to interpret the evidence around them. Some chose to believe that God was who He said He was, and some chose to believe that He didn't exist. Some chose not to take sides. But even that was a choice.

The idea had been new to her then, and she had spent weeks turning it over in her mind. Everyone chose. She could choose. It seemed a heady amount of power for an eight-year-old girl. But in the years since that class, she had come to think differently. Faith for her wasn't a choice. God was real, as real as gravity. She could rage against Him, but she couldn't ignore him. And she couldn't think of Him as being wrong. If He made mistakes or did evil things, then how could anyone tell what was good? Would the word "good" mean anything anymore without Him behind it?

Her Papa didn't think the way she did, but he had known God a lot longer than she had before the accident. She pictured the rift between Papa and God like a fight between two old friends. And she never gave up hope that Papa would patch it up.

She remembered coming to stay with her Papa and Granny for a week while her parents flew to Papua, New Guinea with missionaries. Her mom and dad were going to deliver shoeboxes full of toys and socks and soap and combs and Bibles to the children there. Clutching her brand-new red suitcase, Aspen had been so happy and excited to climb the stairs to the guest room and put her things away. She remembered the last hugs from her parents. Her father had ruffled her hair, and her mother had touched her cheek. They had reminded her to be good and to say her prayers. They had promised to be home in a week.

At the end of the week, Papa had come into the kitchen, where Aspen had been weaving a potholder on a flimsy, plastic loom. He had sat down beside her and taken her hand while he told her that her parents' plane had crashed in bad weather. He had told her not to worry. The Indonesian province of Irian Jaya on the island of New Guinea was mostly mountainous jungle laced with rivers; the trees and water could provide plenty of places for a soft landing. There was still hope. "We need to pray for your mommy and daddy," Papa had said confidently. "They're in God's hands; we all are. We can depend on God's hands."

A week later, the sad news arrived at the Spitzen home. Aspen had first seen it written on Spitz's frightened brow as he hung up the phone in the hall. Full of grief, she, Granny, and Papa had cried arm in arm for an hour that seemed like a day. That day, things had begun to change.

Two days later, her Papa announced his immediate early retirement. Twenty-four hours into retirement, he boldly set out on a trip to recover the bodies of his beloved son and daughter-in-law. Aspen remembered waiting, terrified, for him to come home again. She remembered the way her thin, pale Granny seemed to fade away in front of her while Papa was gone. Aspen had to remind her to eat. Aspen would wake up in the morning and find Granny still in her clothes, having not slept at all the night before. Papa had looked shocked when he came home and saw her so changed in so short a time. Aspen had listened outside their bedroom door as they talked.

Papa had told Granny that the bodies had been burned beyond recognition. There would be no visitation. There was no comfort of a last look. Granny had sobbed in a horrible way that sounded barely human. Papa had given Granny the Bible from the wreckage, and from that moment on she carried it everywhere she went. She never read it; she just held it like a girl with a doll. She kept forgetting to eat. She never went to bed that Aspen saw.

A few short months after the funeral of Aspen's parents, on the 35th anniversary of her son's birth, Granny passed on, too. "Granny went to see her son on his birthday and decided to stay. Can't blame her," Spitz had said with remorseful envy. Aspen heard people at the funeral say that Granny had died of heart failure. Papa told someone there that she died of a broken heart. The loss of her only child had been too much for her.

Aspen had watched Papa anxiously for signs of that unendurable sadness and fragility that had overtaken her gentle grandmother in the last months of her life. But Papa did not grow weak. Mustering as much encouragement as she figured he could manage, Papa had said, "Don't you worry, Aspen. Papa will take care of you." Until she had left for college, he'd faithfully fulfilled his promise. Spitz helped her with school projects and homework, taught her the finer elements of baseball and fishing, and together with her learned to cook. But when she had grown, Aspen followed her father's footsteps into the workforce. He, too, had been a financial analyst at an investment firm. Aspen now worked at a competing firm.

And despite her childhood trauma, Aspen had grown up beautiful and vibrant. Her vivaciousness served as an antidote to the gloomy spirit that would often overtake her Papa. But even her jovial attitude didn't erase the deep bitterness that the back-to-back funerals had etched into his soul.

As Papa and Aspen both aged, their roles reversed. No major event occurred that required her leadership. It just happened over time, like osmosis. So though Aspen would have been a great catch, she showed little interest in dating and proclaimed absolutely no interest in marriage. Every bachelor at her office knew so from experience. How could she walk out on Papa after all he had done for her? How could she just abandon him and start a new life with someone else?

But her stated intentions did not stop Spitz from playing the role of matchmaker. He often made up excuses to introduce young men to her. Once he even encouraged a potential suitor by purchasing symphony tickets and a restaurant gift card. Though Aspen had enjoyed the evening, she soon broke off the young man's advances. Maybe one day she would date seriously, but not now.

However, matchmaking was not enough of a distraction for Papa. Soon after Granny's funeral, he began to soothe his heartache through a new pursuit: his case. "I'm an old man on an old mission," he would tell her. And with his heart apparently welded shut, he doggedly pursued his quest to challenge the notion of an all-seeing, loving God.

Roused from her memories, Aspen thought she heard Papa's voice thundering down the hall. She wondered what he had found to make him raise his voice like that. She got up quickly and splashed water on her face to hide the traces of her tears. She wiped her face on the hand towel, put on her cheerleader's smile, and opened the door to the hall. Leaving the bathroom, she heard the sound of objects falling and glass breaking. An alarm sounded in her heart.

"Papa, are you all right?" she called as she ran down the hall. When Aspen reached the library, she found Spitz lying face down on a rug near the fireplace. Broken glass from a lamp had scattered across the wood floor. Spitz was holding the burned Bible with his left hand. Like a pillow, the Bible was wedged underneath his head.

"Papa, what happened?" Aspen wailed. She patted her Papa's cheeks and felt his neck for a pulse. Then she frantically called 911 and simultaneously called to Papa over and over to answer her and not to leave her.

★ ★ ★

The long night passed in a swirl of activity for Aspen. After the paramedics came, she raced behind their wailing siren to the hospital. There, she anxiously paced through the waiting room until someone came to tell her that her Papa was stable but comatose. She spent that night alone. She hadn't known who to call in the middle of the night.

Now Aspen was lying exhausted in the hospital recliner next to her grandfather's bed. Her morning thoughts began swirling and fluttering like the fallen leaves in the stormy day outside. How would she manage her work schedule? She'd left a barely coherent message last night for her boss, Bernie, telling him not to expect her today. She had enough vacation time to cover a few days here at the hospital. But time off wasn't what was worrying her.

The firm had been expanding, and Bernie had hinted several times that maybe Aspen couldn't handle the work. Her native stubbornness had kicked in, and she had assured him each time that she was up to the task.

He didn't need to worry. She would work nights and weekends to make sure that everything got done. She couldn't imagine the shame of losing her job, let alone the empty terror of having absolutely nothing to do.

She looked at the clock in the corner of the room and saw that it was after seven. Bernie might be in the office by now. She tried the number, and it rang straight to voicemail. But it was late enough in the morning that she could decently call his cell.

"Hello?" his familiar voice answered. Aspen heard a horn honking in the background; he was driving.

"Hey, Bernie—it's Aspen," she said, wincing. Her night of indulging in tears had left her sounding like she had the flu. "Did you get my message?"

"Sorry, kiddo, it's been a bear of a morning; I was going to check them at work. Are you calling in sick?" Bernie asked, sipping his coffee noisily at the end.

Aspen was not offended to be called kiddo. The men in the office were interchangeably buddy, sport, champ, chief, and bucko to Bernie. Being called kiddo was getting off easy, as far as Aspen was concerned. "No, I'm not sick," she began.

"Great! I really need you here. I'm transferring in a new guy, and I need you to show him the ropes. God forbid I should have to leave him with Randy," Bernie said dramatically.

"I'm sorry, Bernie, but it's going to have to be Randy. My grandfather had a stroke, and he's in a coma," Aspen explained, purposely speaking calmly and dispassionately to keep the tears at bay.

"Oh, man—oh, no, kiddo, I'm sorry to hear that. That's terrible news. Hey, don't you worry about a thing," Bernie backtracked. "We'll get the new guy settled in just fine. You know, this actually works out great, because he can have your desk while he's learning the ropes. His hasn't come in yet."

"So there's a new guy," Aspen said, trying to sound light and unconcerned. "Does this mean that I'm out of a job?"

Bernie laughed. "You're really funny, kiddo. I've been telling you and telling you that you need help, you can't handle everything alone, but do you listen to me? Obviously, you do not. Seriously, though, that was a good laugh. So tell me, how long are you at the hospital? I mean, are we looking at a couple of days, a week, or what? Talk to me."

Aspen glanced nervously at Spitz, who lay so still and far away in the bed beside her. "I don't know, Bernie. I haven't really gotten to talk to anybody who knows anything for sure. I don't want to leave him today, though. I'll call you as soon as I know anything."

"Good. Okay. I can work with that. For now, I'll hand the new guy to Randy and hope for the best, and I'll call you this afternoon if I don't hear from you," Bernie said.

"Okay," Aspen told him. "Oh, Bernie, before you go—what's his name?"

"The new guy? He's Wilson Rawlins. I hope I don't have to call him Wilson; it'll feel like I'm talking to a volleyball," Bernie joked. "Do you remember that movie *Cast Away* with Tom Hanks stranded on an island with no one to talk to but the volleyball? And he named it Wilson for the manufacturer's label? Oh, that's funny."

Aspen laughed politely and told him goodbye, and then she hung up. She did not feel better. The new guy was going to be sitting at her desk, using her computer, and looking at her framed photos. Maybe he would be a terrific analyst. Maybe he would get along really well with all of the other guys in the office. Maybe Bernie would decide he didn't need her after all.

She noticed that she was chewing on a fingernail and put her hands firmly in her lap. Then Aspen turned around and gazed despondently at her beloved hero. Just last night, Stephen Spitzen stood a strong, vibrant, and determined man, full of life and energy. Now, he was lying prostrate. *But he's not lifeless; at least he's still breathing,* Aspen admitted to herself. *Thank God.*

She pondered. When was the last time she had thanked God for anything? Should she? She might believe in God like she believed in gravity, but she paid about as much attention to Him as she did the fact that she didn't fly off the planet. To thank Him for sparing her grandfather seemed appropriate, but awkward after so much silence. She tried it. *Thank You for sparing him.* Her words seemed to hover and then disappear.

She studied Papa's face and remembered it twisted in anger the night before as he talked about those long-ago deaths. "It passed through His fingers," he had accused. And she had had nothing to say, because she agreed with him. God had allowed her parents to die, just as he'd allowed Spitz to fall. It was all part of a plan. *Not that I particularly like this plan,* she thought dourly.

But still—Papa had given her a wonderful childhood. She'd had school friends with two parents who had less adult attention and involvement than she'd gotten from him. If her parents had to die, what came after was the best possible outcome for her. She thought of her grandfather mentioning Oliver Twist. Aspen hadn't grown up in an orphanage. She hadn't been starved or abused. She had been comfortable, even spoiled sometimes.

But now if she were left alone, what would she do? How could she face going back to that empty house? Papa had been the center of her world, the one stable pillar. What would she do if that pillar fell forever?

She didn't realize she was crying until she saw a strong, brown hand holding a tissue out to her. She looked up into kind brown eyes in a plain, strong face above a tall body wearing nurse's scrubs. Then she wordlessly took the tissue and pressed it to her nose and eyes.

"Thank you," she rasped after a moment.

"Is he your father or your grandfather?" the nurse asked.

"My grandfather—Papa," Aspen answered.

"You two are close?" the nurse guessed.

Aspen nodded. "He's all I have. He raised me."

"I could tell. Those aren't angry tears. It's hard, seeing some folks in here who have been at each other's throats for years. They feel confused, sitting up with someone while there's still so much bad feeling. But you, you just want your Papa back. I know."

Aspen began to cry again, and the nurse put a long arm around her. "It'll be all right, sugar. You don't have to worry. This man is in God's hands."

Aspen looked up quickly into the nurse's face, searching it. Why had she chosen those words? "Papa used to say that we are all in God's hands; it's funny you should say that."

The nurse picked up Spitz's chart and began checking it against the machines surrounding the bed. "He doesn't say it anymore?"

"Not for a long time now," Aspen answered.

"That doesn't change God's hands, you know," the nurse said.

"Whether we believe they're there or not, they're there. And God has His hands around your Papa right now."

"How is he?" Aspen asked. She craned her neck to peek at the chart.

"He's stable, and that's good news," the nurse answered.

Aspen let out a long, shuddering sigh and sat in the chair where she'd spent a good deal of the night. "I've been so worried."

The nurse turned around and looked at her. "You didn't sleep at all last night, did you?"

Aspen shook her head. "I couldn't."

"I'm Angela, by the way," the nurse offered.

"Aspen Spitzen," Aspen answered, managing a half-smile.

Angela put the clipboard back in its holder on the door and folded her arms. "Aspen, you need to sleep, and you need to eat something, too. You don't want your Papa to wake up and find out you've worn yourself away to nothing crying by his bed, do you?"

Aspen shook her head. "I just didn't feel like I could leave."

"I understand. I would have felt the need to stay, too. But one of the blessings of having skilled nurses working day and night is that it gives you some relief, too. You can leave him with us. We can call you if anything changes," Angela reassured her.

Aspen considered the nurse's statement. "I do need something to eat," she said, "and a shower."

"Aspen, take my advice. Go get some fresh air. Go home, rest, and get some food. Trust the nurses to watch your grandfather and take care of him," Angela suggested.

"I will. Thank you," she smiled. And then her brow wrinkled in concern. "But when should I come back? When will he be better? What do I do about work?"

"These things take time," Angela told her, placing a hand on her arm. "You should do what you normally do. Go back to work; sleep at home. Come back for regular visits to see your Papa here when you can. I can't tell you how long he's going to be here, sugar, because it's different for every patient. Some come back to us in a few days, but others take weeks or months. The sooner you get back to your life, the easier it will be for you to handle things with your Papa if he doesn't come back to us right away. But we're waiting for you, Papa," Angela said, turning to the man on the bed.

"He can hear us?" Aspen said hopefully.

"No one knows for sure, but a lot of doctors think that he does. I think it will help him come back to himself if we speak to him like he can hear us," Angela explained. "I saw on the chart that his name is Stephen?"

Aspen smiled. "Call him Spitz; everybody does. He won't know who you mean if you call him Stephen."

"Spitz, then," Angela agreed, turning around to make a hurried note on the chart. "You hear that, Spitz? I'm sending Aspen home to get some food inside her and sleep. She'll be back to see you in just a little while."

"Tonight?" Aspen asked.

Angela shook her head and patted Aspen's back. "If you come back tonight, you'll end up sleeping in that chair again. Come back tomorrow. If you're going back to work, why don't you come for lunch? I can get you something from the cafeteria so that you don't have to waste time stopping on the way."

Aspen agreed and set up a time with Angela to come back the next day. For the first time since she'd found Papa on the library floor, she felt a sense of hope. Was it really possible that Papa would recover? The doctor she'd seen last night had given her little assurance and was very hesitant to predict how long Papa might linger in a comatose state. "He has a strong heart," was the most promising thing he'd said.

But now the prospect of food and rest and her Papa's eventual recovery had cheered her. She thanked Angela, kissed her Papa's cheek, and left the room. And once she left the front doors of the hospital, she paused in the crisp air and took a deep breath. She smelled fries and burgers and saw a drive-in across the street. *Perfect,* she thought, *Papa's favorite*

# Chapter Two

*"Why do you complain to him that he answers none of man's*
*words? For God does speak—now one way, now another—though*
*man may not perceive it." —Job 33:13-14 NIV*

As the façade of Mount Vernon loomed large before him, Spitz fell silent and braced himself to enter the house. He paused on the front porch and looked into the lighted hall beyond. Three men stood huddled in conference together, their backs to Spitz.

Noticing his absence, the man who had fetched Spitz turned around on the step. "Mr. Spitzen," he prompted, gesturing for Spitz to enter.

One of the men in the huddle heard the name and looked up. "Spitz, you came," he said warmly, coming to Spitz and shaking his hand. "Rawlins told me you would, but knowing the nature of your business and your international travels, I doubted you would receive a message. Have you retired?"

"I retired years ago," Spitz answered warily, wondering how this man knew that he had traveled for work.

"I am glad to see you again, even in such a sad place." The man lowered his voice, and he glanced briefly and sadly upstairs. "Few know how gravely ill George is. If the news were known, we would have a flood of well-wishers hurrying him to his grave."

"Should I leave?" Spitz asked. He felt uncomfortable both at being recognized by a complete stranger and at intruding during such a delicate and important time.

The man laid a hand on his arm to detain him. He was a stout, red-faced, grey-haired man with large, capable hands. "No, no—you don't count among the common flood. George will want to see you after he rests a little while from the last bleeding. In the meantime, I must take you to Rawlins. The man was quite specific—he wanted to see you before you talked to George, straightaway when you came into the house. Do you know him?"

Spitz shook his head, relieved to be able to admit that he didn't know someone. "I've never met him, but I've heard of him before. He's the Rawlins who's organizing General Washington's personal papers?"

"Yes, he is," the doctor said. "Colonel Lear is curating the military papers. Come with me; I shall introduce you to Rawlins." As he left, the two other doctors stopped him. "Doctor Brown and I are going back to him now," one said.

"Fine, fine," the doctor leading Spitz said, "I'll join you momentarily."

Spitz walked behind the stout doctor into an enormous library that made his at home look like a few rickety bookshelves. Tall shelves lined the walls, interrupted only by the windows and the door and an impressive desk. Matching calfskin stamped with silver letters bound each book on those shelves. The tall desk topped with a glass-paned cabinet stood in one corner. An inkpot, quills, blotter, and paper stood neatly ready on the writing surface below like soldiers at attention. A cheerful fire burned in the hearth opposite the door, and before it stood a pair of chairs with elegantly curved legs and wings to their backs. Between them was a delicate table on which rested a single book. A blue Turkey carpet covered the floor from the chairs by the hearth to the door where Spitz stood.

*Maybe I should let Aspen have a whack at my library at home after all,* Spitz thought as he breathed in the order and peace of the room. *If she saw this place, I'd never hear the end of it.*

"Rawlins," the doctor called, striding to one of the wingback chairs. "Here is Mr. Spitzen come to see you."

A head with hair in a neat, straw-colored pigtail leaned around the wing of the chair, and then Rawlins stood and strode to Spitz. "Thank you, Doctor Craik," Rawlins said, and Spitz looked sharply at the man who had escorted him. He'd read that name over and over again in his biography of Washington at home. Rawlins saw the look on Spitz's face and subtly shook his head just once.

Taking the cue, Spitz stuck out his hand and said, "Pleased to meet you, Mr. Rawlins. I heard you were expecting me."

"I have been, Mr. Spitzen," Rawlins confirmed. "I desire your help with some of General Washington's correspondence which I have been recording in a book for him."

"I've heard so," Spitz agreed. He sensed somehow that Rawlins knew what was going on and might be induced to tell him.

Craik put a solid hand on Spitz's shoulder. "I am sure that you will be able to help Rawlins a great deal, considering that a number of these letters will not be new to you." He spoke like a man sharing an inside joke.

Spitz wished he got it, but he didn't have a clue. "Thank you, sir," he said soberly.

Craik sighed. "Your sorrow does you credit, Spitz. It is a grim business, watching so dear a friend suffer. You will understand my feeling when I tell you what he said when I came to him. I took his hand, and he pressed it and told me, 'I die hard; but I am not afraid to go.'"[1]

Spitz did not know what to say. He stammered, "It—it's just like him."

"His courage has not deserted him at this last hour," Craik said. "It is a lesson to us all. Well, Spitz, I will send for you when Rawlins has obtained the assistance he needs. Rawlins, keep him as short a time as you can. I do not know how long the general may remain with us."

Craik nodded to them both and left. Rawlins walked quietly to the library door, peered outside for a moment, and then shut it noiselessly. He put out an arm to the wingback chairs by the fire, inviting Spitz to follow him, and sat back down. "I am sure that this night has been a strange one for you so far, Spitz, appearing here and being recognized by people who seem strangers to you."

Spitz sat down beside him and felt grateful for the warmth of the fire after the chill fog outside and for finally being understood. "Strange doesn't even begin to describe it. Can you tell me what's going on? Is this some kind of a reenactment? Why am I here in these clothes? Why does that man think he's Doctor James Craik? Why does he know me?"

Rawlins tilted his head as if to examine Spitz while he chose which question to address first. "You are here because this is the place where you will listen."

"Listen to who? Listen to what?" Spitz asked, leaning forward.

"Earlier this evening, you said, 'You want to answer me? You want to talk back? Here's Your shot. And You'd better take it, because I'm not giving You another one,'" Rawlins quoted in his calm scholar's voice.

Chills crept up Spitz's back. "How do you know that?"

"He told me," Rawlins said.

"He—who's he?" Spitz asked, scared.

Rawlins frowned. "Really, Spitz, need you ask?"

Spitz leapt up from his chair. "This is a dream—a bad dream. I was reading Washington's biography, and I fell asleep. You're not here. I'm not here. How do I wake up?" He paced around the room, frantically examining the windows before he remembered the door.

But by that time, Rawlins had placed a detaining hand on his wrist. "You are not asleep, Spitz, not really."

"What's that supposed to mean?" Spitz demanded. "What's going on?"

"Sit down, and then we will calmly and reasonably discuss what I mean and what is going on," Rawlins ordered.

Spitz stood in the middle of the room, considering making a break for it. But some inkling that Rawlins was the key to the whole thing stopped him. He sighed wearily and stalked back to the armchair. "All right, I'm sitting down. Now tell me in as few plain words as you can manage what's happened to me."

"You dared God to answer you, and mere moments later, you suffered a stroke." Spitz opened his mouth to interrupt, but Rawlins held up a hand to stop him. "Please—let me speak. The stroke is not a punishment for your question. It was going to happen all along. You have a weak spot in one of your arteries just here," Rawlins said, tapping a spot on his own head. "But God is taking the opportunity of your illness to answer you. So you are here; I should say that your soul is here. Your body is at Sacred Heart Memorial in intensive care. The staff is moving you right now from the emergency room."

"I'm a vegetable now?" Spitz asked hollowly. "Are you telling me I'm paralyzed or dying?"

Rawlins shook his head. "I do not know. I only know that you have suffered a stroke. I know neither how well you will recover nor if you will recover at all. I only know why you have come here at this moment and what you must do next."

"Aspen," Spitz remembered suddenly. " If I'm in the hospital, she must be worried sick. Poor kid - what'll she do without me?"

"Your granddaughter is a beautiful and exceptionally intelligent young woman with a promising job and no mortgage or school debt left to pay. Are you truly worried about her?" Rawlins asked, examining Spitz again.

"Of course I'm worried about her! I'm all she's got left after God took her mother and daddy," Spitz snapped. "You may think I'm irreverent with the way I dared Him to answer me, but He's the one who's wrong. He took them and left that poor girl with no parents. I have every right to demand an answer for that."

"Then we have a single aim between us," Rawlins answered briskly, rising and walking to Washington's desk in the corner. He unlocked the glass-paneled doors above the writing surface with a large, tasseled key. He withdrew two books and carefully relocked the doors.

As he walked back, Spitz recognized one of the books. The blood drained from his face. "Not that one," he objected. "I won't touch it."

"It is part of your answer," Rawlins insisted compassionately, handing him his son's Bible with its burnt and crumbling cover. "And so is this." Rawlins handed Spitz a slim volume that was bound in calf like the rest of the books in the library but unstamped with any silver letters. When Spitz opened it, he saw that the pages were blank.

"What is it?" Spitz asked warily. Any solution that involved poring over his son's Bible was already unappealing. He was considering telling Rawlins that he didn't want an answer after all; he'd just go to the hospital and wake up and begin rehab.

"This is your journal. You are going to observe Washington and write what you see," Rawlins said, gesturing to the blank pages.

"Upstairs? But he's dying; what could I possibly see?" Spitz complained.

"I am confident that you will see something worth recording when you join Dr. Craik upstairs," Rawlins assured him. "But you must begin further back than this moment if you are going to see what General Washington saw. You must begin much further back if you are going to see the invisible hand of God for yourself."

"I'm going to see His invisible hand?" Spitz echoed incredulously. "I don't believe it."

"Tell me so when you bring these pages to me full of what you have seen with your own eyes," Rawlins demanded. "But I believe in that hand and in its benevolence, as do the general and Doctor Craik and thousands of the most venerable, truthful, sage men alive now. You are here to watch and to listen and to record. You have demanded evidence that God is powerful and good and loving. You have mocked the man dying upstairs for believing in that evidence. Now you will walk and fight and ride beside him, seeing what he saw. Then you may tell me whether he is mistaken in his strong belief."

Rawlins spoke with such confident gravity and passion that Spitz felt cowed. "All right," he agreed hesitantly. "I'll watch and listen and write it all down. I'll do it. Where do I start?"

"You start with my commission," Rawlins answered more calmly. "Colonel Lear, General Washington's personal secretary, has seldom left his side since early this morning. The few times he has left, he has written in his journal to preserve a record of this day," Rawlins picked up the book which had been lying on the small table when Spitz entered. He thumbed through it to the last entry. "It is nearly seven now. A few hours past, Lear spoke to me as he wrote the general's words in his diary. Here they are: 'I find I am going, my breath cannot continue long; I believed from the first attack it would be fatal. Do you arrange and record all my late military letters and papers—arrange my accounts and settle my books, as you know more about them than anyone else, and let Mr. Rawlins finish recording my other letters which he has begun.'"[2]

"The other letters—those are his personal letters; I read about that," Spitz said.

Rawlins nodded and closed Colonel Lear's diary. "General Washington wrote often to his friends and family. Though he was guarded and politic in his military correspondence, his family letters are less reserved. I have been assisting him for nearly two years now to choose certain of his letters from the thousands here in this library to be recorded for posterity."

Spitz waved the information away impatiently. "I already know that. What do his letters have to do with my assignment?"

Rawlins stood and walked back to the tall desk in the corner. "Some of those letters are your stepping stones. They are the trail you will follow through Washington's life." He stooped over the desk and retrieved a tiny key from a secret compartment, and he used it to unlock a drawer above the writing surface. He removed a sheaf of papers from the drawer and brought them to Spitz, handing them to him.

"These are Washington's letters—his own handwriting?" Spitz marveled, leafing through them, turning them over in his hands. "They're priceless!"

"Not all of them are in his handwriting. He regularly used aides-de-camp to pen them." Rawlins flashed a brief, secret smile, one that reminded Spitz of the way Craik had looked earlier. "But these letters are ones the general chose for me to record last night. It was the last thing he did on this earth."

"Why was he so worried about these letters?" Spitz asked.

Rawlins frowned. "He was not worried. He simply knew what must be done and did it. Lear told me what he said to Mrs. Washington when he came so late to bed. I have it by heart; he said the same words to me often. Mrs. Washington, knowing how ill he was, admonished that he should have retired to bed early, instead of sorting papers all night. The general responded, 'I came so soon as my business was accomplished. You well know that through a long life, it has been my unvaried rule, never to put off till the morrow the duties which should be performed to-day.'"[3]

Spitz pressed him. "And these letters—were they so important because Washington knew he was dying?"

Rawlins paused and sat again. "I believe that the general did know he was going to die. With this foreknowledge, he worked late into the night to select a few last documents to be copied into the book. I hope that this point confirms in your mind how important the project is to Washington." Rawlins looked at the letter Spitz held and said, "The general wants citizens of future generations to know of the signal and manifold mercies and the favorable interpositions of Almighty God in the course and conclusion of the revolutionary war. He appeals to all Americans to remember these signal favors with thanksgiving. Stop now, and read the letter in your hands. Perhaps you will better understand the general's perspective once you have read this letter to Major General Nathanael Greene."

Spitz noticed the date at the top of the letter: February 6, 1783, just months after the British signed the preliminary Articles of Peace and withdrew. Spitz read silently until he came to a paragraph that struck him, and then he re-read it aloud. "If Historiographers should be hardy enough to fill the page of History with the advantages that have been gained with unequal numbers in the course of this contest, and attempt to relate the distressing circumstances under which they have been obtained, it is more than probable that Posterity will bestow on their labors the epithet and marks of fiction; for it will not be believed that such a force as Great Britain has employed for eight years in this Country could be baffled in their plan of Subjugating it by numbers infinitely less, composed of Men oftentimes half starved; always in Rags, without pay, and experiencing, at times, every species of distress which human nature is capable of undergoing."[4]

When Spitz sat in silence after reading that paragraph, Rawlins leaned over and placed his finger on a phrase. "'The epithet and marks of fiction,' he says. The general has feared that men would make a legend of him while he lived, venerating his person instead of tending to their hard-won liberty, and for that reason he left the collation of his papers to late in his life. But now he wants them published so that every American can see the hand of God at work fashioning their nation. Washington wants to insure that future generations do not perceive as fiction his private and public assertions that he and the whole country were protected by a divine hand, guided by the fingers of Providence, and upheld by the firm grip of Almighty God."

Spitz turned over a few more letters, and then Craik's name at the top of a page caught his eye. He looked at the date: March 25, 1784, three months after Washington had resigned as commander of the army. He read aloud again when a paragraph caught his eye.

"I will frankly declare to you, my dear doctor, that any memoirs of my life, distinct and unconnected with the general history of the war, would rather hurt my feelings than tickle my pride whilst I lived. I had rather glide gently down the stream of life, leaving it to posterity to think and say what they please of me, than by any act of mine to have vanity or ostentation imputed to me...I do not think vanity is a trait of my character."[5] Spitz waved the paper in Rawlins' direction. "So it would hurt him to have a memoir published while he was alive?"

"Look at the qualifying phrase," Rawlins corrected. "He wanted to be remembered only as part of the war, only as an instrument in the hand of God used in concert with other instruments."

"Why? Why was that so important to him?" Spitz asked, putting the priceless papers back on top of Lear's journal. "Why was he so convinced that he was in the hands of God?"

"You will see why," Rawlins told him, picking up the papers and returning them to the drawer.

"Don't I need those?" Spitz asked, following Rawlins to the desk.

"You will see a few of them again when you need to see them," Rawlins told him.

The men heard the sound of a woman weeping outside in the hallway. Rawlins looked at Spitz and then opened the door. They saw a maid rounding the corner into a room across the hall, weeping into a handkerchief as she walked. Rawlins pulled the door closed again and sighed.

"This day has passed so slowly and in such grief for the whole house, though my own sorrow is keenest to me. At sunrise, Lear sent for me to come and bleed the general. To lower a knife into the arm of that man was the most fearful thing I have ever done, and though Mrs. Washington and I begged him to let only a little, he insisted the thing be done thoroughly. I let half a pint." Rawlins sighed again. "Craik and the other doctors have bled him twice more, and the general has taken what medicine he can with his throat so swollen. He is in such pain that Lear must help him move, even to turn over in his bed. To be in this house and to know that the master of it suffers such anguish is more than most of us can bear."

"Did you really think that the bleedings would help?" Spitz asked dubiously.

Rawlins smiled ironically down at Spitz. "I have the questionable advantage this day of hindsight, an advantage I did not have on the day I lived it first. Remember this as you live backwards, like Merlin. The men around you will only know what the age permits them. Your purpose is not to stand before them as a prophet and tell them the future. You will be with the general to watch and to learn, not to speak. Promise me that you will restrain yourself."

"I promise," said Spitz.

"Then it is time for you to go," Rawlins told Spitz, retrieving his journal and Bible from the chair Spitz had left and handing them to him.

"I'm leaving now?" Spitz asked. "Isn't Washington about to die? Isn't Craik sending for me any minute now to get me to see him?"

Rawlins clapped a reassuring hand to Spitz's shoulder. "My friend, time can be a very tricky minister; let it serve you well, and to the benefit of those you love."

Spitz looked around him. "So how does this work? Do you have a time machine behind one of the bookcases or something?"

Rawlins laughed quietly and shook his head. "You forget on whose orders you travel. All times are now to Him. Do you really think that sending you where and when He pleases is so difficult for Him?"

Almost against his will, Spitz looked down at his son's Bible. Though there was not a breath of wind inside the room, the pages began to turn rapidly, as if a breeze blew them. In the fireplace, a log shifted. Its blaze bathed the whole room in a heightened glow. Impossibly, through the ceiling, the stars descended once more, gleefully encircling Spitz and dissolving the library into a whirl of light.

★ ★ ★

As Aspen entered her home, midmorning sunlight streamed through the windows. The unusual quietness seemed surreal. However, one look at the library confirmed that she wasn't dreaming. Glass from a broken lamp lay strewn over the floor. One of the chairs and the spindly table both lay on their sides. Aspen closed the glass doors to the library and sighed. Before she could tackle this mess, she needed a bath.

As she soaked in the tub, she thought of how much her life had changed in less than a day. Yesterday at this time she had been trying to convince Bernie yet again that she could handle the extra clients alone. Bernie had known all along that he was transferring someone else to their branch, but he hadn't said a word. He'd probably planned some elaborate joke. He had probably planned to pretend to fire her or Randy or both of them and then crack up laughing as they began to pack their personal things. Or maybe he was going to make the new guy come in half an hour early and sit at one of their desks without telling him what was going on, just so he could see a reaction. *Poor Bernie, robbed of his joke,* Aspen thought.

She wondered how she'd get along with her new coworker. Wilson Rawlins: the name sounded old. He'd probably be close to Papa's age, a bald and thin and stooped old hand brought in to whip the young pups into shape.

If he was old, she still had hope. He was probably close to retirement anyway, then; he wasn't young and hungry. The biggest threat she saw was a young man desperate to prove that he was more experienced and efficient than a female coworker, a young man with an ego and an attitude and the brains to back them up.

She sighed and closed her eyes, scolding herself. *Stop imagining things, Aspen. Bernie didn't sound like he wanted to fire you this morning. Call him when you get dressed, and tell him you'll be there in the morning. Everything will be fine.*

That last thought made a sob rise in her throat. How would the fact that she still had her job mean that everything would be fine? How could she even think of things being okay with Papa so sick?

She remembered him lying so still in the library as she hovered over him, shouting alternately at him and the 911 operator. She remembered the weak pulse in his neck and the flood of relief she'd felt when she found it. For a moment there, she had thought that he was dead. She had felt completely alone.

*Enough,* she thought. *I have cried and worried and grieved enough for one day.* She slid down in the tub to let the water cover her head and block even the faint sounds of the old house popping and creaking as it adjusted to the autumn chill. Then she pushed back up, got out, dried off, and dressed quickly. She had a job to do before she could finally sleep.

Aspen walked into the library and again surveyed the mess in front of her. She stooped first to pick up the old Bible which had last served as Papa's pillow while he lay unconscious, waiting for the paramedics to arrive. She also gathered the two old books on Washington that her grandfather had been reading and put all three of the books on Papa's desk.

One by one, she picked up the chairs and the end table and carried

them across the room, out of the way. Then she fetched her cleaning supplies from the pantry and brought them into the library. She reached for
the trashcan beside Papa's desk and dragged it over to the site of the mess.
After she picked up the big pieces of lamp and lightbulb glass and threw
them away, she threw away the remnant of the lamp, too. Then she swept
the rug and the hardwood carefully. The broom disarranged so much
dust that she swept the whole floor, moving the furniture as she got to it.
Satisfied, she ran the vacuum cleaner over the rug and the wood by the
hearth and then sprayed some paper towels with cleaner and wiped the
floor to pick up any tiny shards.

She put all of her cleaning supplies away, emptied the trash can, and
replaced the furniture where it was supposed to be. Then she noticed the
fireplace. She shoveled out the old embers and swept the whole cement
square carefully with the cast-iron-handled tools. Afterwards, she laid
wood and kindling ready for Papa to light when he came home. She
fetched the Washington books and put them on the end table for him
to read. She paused over the Bible as she considered putting it back in
its place on the shelf. Then a determined look crossed her face, and she
snatched it up and put it into her purse in the hallway.

When she came back into the room, she paused at the door. The room
seemed cozy and pleasant, a tangible reassurance that Papa was coming
home to use it again. Suddenly, she missed him. Any other midmorning,
she would have come home to find him in this room, absorbed in some
book or other. She longed to feel some connection to him that sitting
beside his still, pale body would not give her.

Curiously, she walked across the room to the hearth and picked
up the book Papa had read to her last night, the book of Washington's
papers. She flipped through it until she found the Inaugural Address. She
sat down in Papa's armchair and determined to read it through.

The dateline said that it was given in New York City on April 30,
1789.[6] *That's strange; I thought that all inaugurations were in Washington
and in January. I wonder when that changed.*

"Fellow-Citizens of the Senate and of the House of Representatives,"
she read. She paused. The President's first two words, "Fellow-Citizens,"
had caught her attention. The president had reminded everyone present
that they were all equals as citizens of the new nation. She, too, was a

citizen—an equal. She felt a glow of fondness for Washington, who was so humble and generous on a day when he rightfully could have been proud.

He reminded her of her Papa, who continually stepped aside to give her the spotlight. When she was in college, he had exclaimed over her grades, never saying a word about the tuition he paid so that she could earn them. When she was a small girl, he used to exclaim in the same way over every little fish she caught, never mentioning that he was the one who taught her how to cast a line and set a hook.

She returned her attention to the address, noting places where her grandfather had written in the margins. In the margin of the first paragraph of the address, Papa had written: "Washington humbly and publicly questions his fitness for the job as the first president of the United States."

Spitz's highlighting and underlining of nearly every word of the second paragraph caught Aspen's attention next, and she read it in full, imagining how the phrases Washington used would have sounded to her Papa. To Washington, God was "that Almighty Being who rules over the universe, who presides in the councils of nations, and whose providential aids can supply every human defect." He was "the Great Author of every public and private good." Aspen saw the section Papa had read her last night about the invisible hand and about the "return of pious gratitude" we owe it.

She winced as she read. She could tell how those words had angered her Papa. *They are true, though,* she mused. *Why else is anyone good? And if God is not almighty, who is?*

She looked at the next note her Papa had written to the side. "Washington knew without doubt that God had orchestrated the affairs of America, using His invisible hand to birth this unique self-governing nation. Washington felt compelled to proclaim his belief as truth." Circled in the margin was another handwritten note: "But how did he come to this conclusion? What events had 'forced themselves too strongly on [Washington's] mind to be suppressed?'"

Aspen continued reading the next paragraph. She focused on a part of the last sentence which her Papa had underlined. "The propitious smiles of Heaven can never be expected on a nation that disregards the eternal rules of order and right which Heaven itself has ordained ... the preservation of the sacred fire of liberty and the destiny of the republican model of government are justly considered, perhaps, as deeply, as finally, staked on the experiment intrusted to the hands of the American people."

Aspen smiled. Washington sounded just like Papa used to sound. At first he talked about God setting down rules for people to obey and expecting them to obey, and then he talked about the success of America depending on its people. Evidently, Washington saw responsibility as really important, too.

Aspen scanned down the page, skipping the next paragraph and focusing instead on the last, where Washington said that "the benign Parent of the Human Race...has been pleased to favor the American people." Papa had underlined those phrases. *Of course they upset you, Papa. Here he says again that God is good and that He chose to favor America. I know that's not what you want to hear. But if someone you respect so much said so, why won't you take him at his word? Why do you have to parse every phrase and take offense?*

Aspen turned the page and saw a note in Papa's handwriting: "See page 54-55." She turned a few pages as her Papa had instructed and found the Senate's written reply[7] to the president's Inaugural Address. Aspen read it all the way through, paying special attention to the places Papa had underlined and starred.

"When we contemplate the coincidence of circumstances and wonderful combination of causes which gradually prepared the people of this country for independence; when we contemplate the rise, progress, and termination of the late war, which gave them a name among the nations of the earth, we are with you unavoidably led to acknowledge and adore the Great Arbiter of the Universe, by whom empires rise and fall. A review of the many signal instances of divine interposition in favor of this country claims our most pious gratitude; and permit us, sir, to observe that among the great events which have led to the formation and establishment of a Federal Government we esteem your acceptance of the office of President as one of the most propitious and important."

Papa had written in the margin of the paper: "Just like Washington, Congress had no doubt that God orchestrated everything, including Washington's selection and acceptance as first president. To them, God's invisible hand was the powerful cause of it all. But why were so many so sure?"

Papa had underlined just one more phrase, and he had followed it with an angry line of exclamation points. "We commend you, sir, to the protection of Almighty God, earnestly beseeching Him long to preserve a life so valuable and dear to the people of the United States." Papa didn't need to comment or explain about this part. Aspen could hear his bitter voice stating exactly how valuable that protection was and how badly it had failed.

Aspen turned the page and read a similar reply to the president by the House of Representatives.[8] Spitz had highlighted only a portion of one sentence in the middle of the body of the text. "We feel with you the strongest obligations to adore the Invisible Hand which has led the American people through so many difficulties."

Aspen was growing tired. Yes, reading these papers and seeing her Papa's notes on them felt a little like having a conversation with him. But this jaded commentary was not the side of her Papa that she missed and wanted back. She wanted the Papa who talked to her at dinner, the Papa who took her fishing, the Papa who every once in a while suggested a potential suitor for her with all of the subtlety of a flashing neon sign.

With a sigh that turned into a shuddering yawn, she looked sternly at the book of Washington's writings. *I'll sit with you for one more document in this dusty old book, Papa, but then I'm going to sleep.* She leafed through a few more pages until she found the Thanksgiving Proclamation.[9] She remembered having read it in school long ago. Papa had underlined phrases in the first and the third paragraphs.

"Whereas it is a duty of all nations to acknowledge the providence of Almighty God, to obey His will, to be grateful for His benefits, and humbly to implore His protection and favor ... I do recommend and assign Thursday, the 26th day of November next, to be devoted by the people of these States to the service of that great and glorious Being who is the beneficent author of all the good that was, that is, or that will be; that we may then all unite in rendering unto Him our sincere and humble thanks for His kind care and protection of the people of this country previous to their becoming a nation; for the signal and manifold mercies and the favorable interpositions of His providence in the course and conclusion of the late war ... for all the great and various favors which He has been pleased to confer upon us."

Aspen saw a note her Papa had written, which he connected by an arrow to the place where he had underlined the phrase "the signal and manifold mercies and the favorable interpositions of His providence." He had written, "Signal = unusual, like a sign; manifold = many, various; interposition = the act of putting something between one thing and another. So God showed a whole lot of noticeable and unusual mercy to the patriots, and He put His providence between them and Great Britain. Why didn't He do the same thing for Steve and Nevaeh?"

Seeing her parents' names written there in accusation was too much for Aspen after the night she had spent in grief and fear. She closed the book and laid it gently down on top of Washington's biography. She looked outside the window at the brilliant leaves falling in showers as the breeze moved them. This time of year, the memories of her parents were always closer as the anniversaries of their deaths and funeral approached and passed. She supposed it must be the same way for Papa.

*I wonder if either of us will be able to live through another October without thinking of their funeral. I don't suppose so.* She sighed. *I don't have any answers for your questions, Papa, and I don't have the energy or the anger to ask them with you. But I hope you find answers you'll accept. And I hope they bring you peace.*

She walked out of the library, turned off the lights, and gently shut the door, leaving the room ready for her Papa to resume his case as soon as he came home.

# Chapter Three

Something felt warm on Spitz's face and chest and hands. He tried to
open his eyes to see what it was, but his eyelids wouldn't respond.
Bit by bit, he checked other parts of his body: fingers, toes, head. Nothing
obeyed him. He felt as if he was tied up in a big sack with no way of escaping. It was dark, quiet, and mysterious. He moved in his mind, yet his body
refused to respond. He knew that he was alive because he could think,
reason, and perceive the heat above him. He gradually became aware of
sound, of beeps and footsteps and distant voices. Somehow he was still
aware of light. Like a heavy fog lifting with the morning sun, his warming
body seemed to lift the veil over his eyes and disperse the plugs in his ears.

Someone in soft shoes walked into the room rolling a tray, and then
Spitz realized that he could smell, too. He smelled chicken and apple and
bread, and they smelled good. But strangely, he wasn't hungry. His mind
drifted along, waiting for a clue to explain all the details he'd been able
to sense.

"Are you warm enough, yet, Spitz? You were so cold before I got you
this heat lamp. Let me check your hands and your face." A smooth, strong
hand lay gentle for a moment on his cheeks and his hands. "Perfect," the
woman said. He could tell from the sound of her voice both that she was
a woman and that she was smiling as she spoke. "So we can take this
away now."

The intense light and warmth disappeared. Then he became aware
of colder, dimmer lights farther away. He heard the soft footsteps again

walking a little way away and coming back. "Let's get your checkup out of the way before your guest arrives, all right?" the woman said. He felt her poking and prodding and heard her humming low and quiet. He heard the scratch of a pen against paper.

Quick, light footsteps sounded in the hall and entered his room, the footsteps of a woman wearing heels. "Hi, Angela," Aspen's voice said.

*Aspen!* Spitz wanted to call. *I'm in here; I can hear you!*

"Hello, Aspen," Angela said. Spitz heard the clank of something light being put away.

"How is Papa doing?" Aspen asked. Spitz could hear the worry in her voice, and with a pang he pictured the frown on her face.

"He's just the same today as yesterday; he's stable. Remember, that's good news right now," Angela told her. Spitz sensed compassion from Angela, and he felt grateful that someone so nice was encouraging Aspen.

Aspen sighed. "I'd had this wild thought that maybe he would be sitting up waiting for me today. I'd hoped I could talk to him."

"You can talk to him," the nurse encouraged. "You probably even know him well enough to know what he'd say back."

Aspen paused and laughed hollowly. "I guess it won't be that different after all. Usually when we talk at the end of the day, he just lets me talk while he nods and says 'uh huh,' 'okay,' 'really,' or 'yep.' Unless he's found something in his case," Aspen amended.

"Is he a lawyer?" Angela asked.

"No, no," Aspen said slowly, "that's what he calls all the research he does on the ways God has messed up in history."

Angela was very still, and then she asked, "Why does he research something like that?"

Aspen sighed. "My parents died in a plane crash when I was nine, and my dad was Papa's only child. Papa has never forgiven God for taking Daddy."

"That must have been terrible for both of you," Angela said compassionately. "I'm so sorry."

"Thank you," Aspen replied. It was her standard answer, Spitz knew, followed by a change in subject. Aspen did not disappoint him. "So what's for lunch? I came straight over."

"Chicken noodle soup, a roll, and some apple crumble," Angela said, removing the lid. "I've heard all of the jokes about hospital food, but our cafeteria here is really pretty good. Go ahead—try it."

Spitz heard spoons scraping against bowls, and then Aspen said, "You're right; it's good." He wondered if it really was, or if Aspen was only being polite. It did smell good. As if she'd read his mind, Aspen said, "I wish Papa could eat with us. It feels weird eating in front of him when he can't have anything."

"It's the best thing for him to have as much stimulation as he can handle. Smelling food may trigger a memory or a thought. You never know what will help him come back to us," Angela said. "Maybe it will be hearing your voice, hearing something you say."

"And I should really just talk to him, just like I do at home?" Aspen said.

"Just like that," Angela agreed. "Why don't you tell him about what you did today?"

Spitz heard ceramic set down against something hard. Aspen cleared her throat. "The house is so quiet, Papa. I woke up in the morning and had to make the coffee, and I didn't hear the news on the radio coming from your room. I listened to it in the car on the way to work because I missed it—I missed you. And I cleaned the library yesterday, too; so it's all ready for you to come back to it. I read some of your books and what you wrote in the margins. It's not the same as having you read them to me."

Aspen was quiet a moment. Spitz heard the familiar paper-on-cardboard sound of a tissue coming from a Kleenex box, and he knew then that Aspen was crying. *I'm sorry, honey,* he thought. *I miss you, too.*

"It's all right, sugar. I know you miss him," Angela said.

"I do," Aspen said quietly. "I wish you could talk to me, Papa, partly because it's been a hard day at work so far. You always know what to say to me when I've had a hard day. There's a new analyst in the office, a commodities analyst just like me. Bernie brought him in because he says that there's too much work for me. But I just can't shake the thought that this guy's coming to replace me. I'm showing him the ropes, and then he's going to say, 'Thanks a lot; there's the door.'" Aspen laughed sarcastically as she spoke, and Spitz hurt for her.

"This new analyst at your office—what's he like?" Angela asked.

"Oh he's perfectly nice—a real gentleman. That's what makes it worse. He insisted I take my desk back, and he's sitting in a horrible little folding chair beside me, just watching and asking questions. I feel like I'm back in junior high school taking a test," Aspen fumed. "And while I'm just nervous as anything about why he's really there, he's being polite, asking if I need anything and if he can get me coffee from the kitchen. Then I feel even worse for thinking he's going to take my job because he's so nice!"

Spitz wanted to tell Aspen to keep her chin up and be confident. He wanted to assure her that she was valuable and talented and had nothing to worry about. Angela didn't say those things, though.

"Aspen, honey, how old is this man?" Angela asked. Spitz couldn't quite place her tone, but he thought she sounded amused.

"I don't know—my age, I guess," Aspen answered absently.

"Is he married?" Angela prodded.

"No—at least I didn't see a ring," Aspen said, catching on.

"And is he a good-looking man?" Angela definitely sounded amused now.

Aspen laughed, a soft but genuine laugh this time, and she said, "I guess he's not that ugly," she joked. Then she sighed. "You're right; that's probably part of it. Guys don't usually get under my skin like this, though, even if they're—particularly not ugly, like the opposite of ugly. I don't know why Bill makes me so nervous."

"How is your boss acting around you?" Angela asked.

"Just the same," Aspen said. "But Bernie's a little bit of a joker; so you never know when he's setting you up."

"It sounds to me like you've got too many problems clamoring for attention right now, between missing your Papa and wondering about your job and training this new analyst and having to sort out what you feel about him. Can you take just one of those things and look it in the eye and get it to stop bothering you?"

Aspen was quiet for a moment, and Spitz listened hungrily for her answer. The way Angela talked to Aspen wasn't anything like the way he usually did, and he grieved again that Aspen did not have a mother to hear her confidences. She needed an older woman to listen to her.

Aspen picked up his hand. Spitz would have given just about anything to be able to squeeze her fingers back and give her some reassurance, but his body remained rebellious. "If I could pick one, I'd wave a magic wand and make Papa good as new. But that's out of my hands. I don't want to do anything about Bill, especially while he's practically a stranger. So that leaves Bernie. I could have a talk with Bernie. If he saw I was serious, he'd shoot straight with me. I could do something about that."

"Well, then, I think you have something to do this afternoon," Angela said lightly. Spitz could still hear the warm smile in her voice.

"Thank you," Aspen said, relieved. "I know it's not your job, sorting out my problems."

"Listen, honey, this job is not just a job to me," Angela interrupted gently. "I care about your Papa and about you. I want both of you to be all right. God says for us to 'weep with those that weep, and rejoice with those that rejoice.' I'm weeping with you now, and I'll rejoice with you when it's time to rejoice."

"I'd forgotten that part," Aspen confessed.

"Here's another part I'll bet you've forgotten, from Ecclesiastes: "Rejoice, O young man, in the days of your youth.'" Spitz heard the sound of one hand patting another. "You are a young woman, and there is nothing wrong with you rejoicing over being young and feeling interested in a handsome young man—even if your Papa is sick. Do you think your Papa wants you to feel sad all the time he's lying here? Do you think that would make him happy?" Spitz felt a gentle tap on his hand. "What about it, Spitz? Do you want Aspen to put on mourning clothes for you and tell this nice young man to mind his own business?"

Spitz heard a soft, amused laugh from Aspen and knew that she understood what he would say if he could. *I want you to enjoy life. I want you to be happy.* Aspen sighed and said, "I know that's not what Papa wants."

"God doesn't want that for you, either, sugar," Angela reminded her.

Spitz heard a rustling sound and wondered what was making it. Then he felt something solid and heavy being nestled between his arm and his side. "Speaking of God, I almost forgot," Aspen said. "I wanted him to have this with him."

"His Bible?" Angela asked. "I thought he was working on a case against God."

"This one was my father's. It was in the crash. I want Papa to have it with him," Aspen said, a steely note entering her voice.

To her credit, Angela didn't question Aspen's motives or pry into the complicated history. "I'll make sure it stays with him. I'll leave a note at the nurse's station when I go home."

A knock sounded at the door. A high-pitched, very Southern man's voice said, "Hi, I'm Ed Campbell, the hospital chaplain. Would it be all right if I prayed with the patient?"

*Aspen, that Bible went far enough. This is a bridge too far,* Spitz thought.

"Yes," Aspen answered decisively. "I have to go now if I'm going to get back to work on time, but you're welcome to pray with my grandfather. His name is Spitz."

"I see he even has his Bible with him," Campbell noticed. "How about I read it to him?"

"Thank you," Aspen said. "I'm sure it will do him good."

*You and I are going to have a talk about this when I'm up and around again, young lady,* Spitz thought.

"Wonderful," Campbell answered.

"I'll be back to check on you in a while, Spitz," Angela promised, and her footsteps receded beside Aspen's. Spitz heard them planning for lunch tomorrow.

Spitz heard vinyl creaking as the chaplain settled into a chair beside him. "Oh, how nice," he observed, "the sun came out good and strong this afternoon. I thought it was going to be cloudy all day."

Spitz felt the Bible removed from his side, and he heard the sound of pages rustling. "My, my, my," Campbell remarked, "this is an old copy. I haven't had to read Roman numerals in years, and all the chapters are marked in them. I don't know if I could find a particular address without some help. Let's see, did you underline anything? Did you place a bookmark?" More pages rustled. "I'll just start in the Psalms and look." After a few more pages, Campbell stopped. "There's a note here. Did you put it here on purpose?" The man was silent, scanning words. "I recognize this one—Psalm 78. It's a bit of an unusual Psalm to read to a patient, but God seems to be pointing it out. Here we are."

Spitz braced himself. He couldn't stop the man from reading.

"Give ear, O my people, *to* my law: incline your ears to the words of my mouth. I will open my mouth in a parable: I will utter dark sayings from of old: Which we have heard and known, and our fathers have told us. We will not hide *them* from their children, shewing to the generation to come the praises of the Lord, and his strength, and his wonderful works that he hath done.

"For he established a testimony in Jacob, and appointed a law in Israel, which he commanded our fathers, that they should make them known to their children:

"That the generation to come might know *them*, even the children which should be born; *who* should arise and declare *them* to their children: That they might set their hope in God, and not forget the works of God, but keep his commandments:

"And might not be as their fathers, a stubborn and rebellious generation, a generation *that* set not their heart aright, and whose spirit was not steadfast with God."

*Ouch*, Spitz thought, *that was a little too close for comfort*. He seemed to hear Rawlins' voice again, accusing him of mocking God and George Washington both. He remembered Rawlins talking about the things God had done for the colonists and about how Washington feared that coming generations would not remember them and give God His due.

He stopped short. *Did that really happen? It couldn't have. It must have been a dream.* He couldn't really have visited Mount Vernon on the day of Washington's death.

The chaplain was praying, and Spitz realized that he hadn't been paying attention. He listened now.

"God, none of us is steadfast all of the time, and all of us are stubborn by nature. I don't know this man in front of me, Lord, but You do. If he's been like that generation that didn't praise You, forgive him for it, and turn him back to You. Nothing is too hard for You, Father. Not one of us is beyond the reach of Your hand. Heal this man's body, Lord. I've forgotten his name, but You know him. You know him better than he knows himself. Bring him a new day and a new body to see it in - in the name of the Father and the Son and the Holy Spirit, amen."

The vinyl creaked again, whooshing as air re-inflated the cushion. Spitz felt the Bible being nestled back into his side. He felt a gentle tap on his nose. "Sorry about that," Ed Campbell said. "My cross fell out of my collar and hit your nose when I was leaning over. I'll see you tomorrow."

Spitz saw a flash of light behind his closed eyelids as he heard Campbell's voice say, "Would you look at that? It might as well be August, the way the sun's streaming into this room," and then he felt as if he were floating and whirling like a leaf on an October breeze.

★ ★ ★

When Spitz knew anything again, he was sitting in front of a fireplace balancing a large bowl of stew on one knee. He examined his knees and then his chest. He looked like Davy Crockett. Stout leather boots lined with fur and fastened with brushed brass buckles reached to his knees. He wore leather breeches over scratchy woolen long johns, and he could feel the comfortable padding of layers of shirts ending in a stiff leather coat lined with fleece. Leather gloves lay on one knee, and his hands holding the bowl of stew rested on the other.

His hands—Spitz held one up and looked at it in awe. It was the hand he'd seen fifty years ago—muscled and smooth and brown with sun, not an age spot or a wrinkle or a white hair in sight. He lifted it curiously to feel his face. It, too, was smooth and firm, as it had not been in years. Shaving this face would not be a delicate job; it would be a quick and positive pleasure.

He turned his attention back to the bowl of stew in his hands: meat and sausage and beans and onions and cabbage and carrots together in a thick broth, just right for cold weather. He ate it hungrily, and as he did, he looked around.

He was in a small, dim log cabin, chinked with mud and heated by a single stone fireplace raised from the packed earth floor in a stone hearth. Around him sat between fifteen and twenty other men, and just two women. One looked as if she were in her forties. She was round and red-faced and bundled in what looked like several dresses on top of each other, ending in a roughly-made fur coat. The other looked like her daughter. The teenaged girl dressed like her mother with her hair in a plait down her back tied with a tattered ribbon. The mother stirred the stew in the pot and ladled some into a bowl that she handed to a man sitting opposite Spitz at the fire. The daughter worked over a table nearby kneading bread in a long trough.

The men sitting around the fire were talking. Their ages varied from about sixteen to sixty, and they all wore clothes similar to the ones Spitz was wearing. They also wore similar expressions of anger mingled with disgust.

One man set down a tankard with an almighty thump and declared, "I'd like to get my hands round some Frenchie neck for that. I've seen battle, but seein' families laid out murdered with the top of their heads gone—it gives me the shivers. And them Frenchies is the ones settin' the Ottoway Injuns to it, you mark my words."

"Not so, Pete," a tall lantern-jawed man at another table said, shaking his head sagely and taking a long clay pipe from his mouth. "They're just like that, them Injuns. They'd put a knife in yeh as soon as look at yeh. They need no Frenchies setting them to anything."

"Maybe not, but the Frenchies are cunnin' that way, you see," Pete answered him, sitting eagerly forward to expound what was evidently a favorite theory. "Makin' up to the big chiefs and givin' them rum and guns and pointin' them in our direction—don't you see? They clear us off the king's land without liftin' a lily-white finger. Then we send word to the governor, and he sends word to King George. And our ministers jaw with them Frenchie ministers, and them Frenchie ministers just shrug and point to the Injuns! We'll be pushed out of here, too, and soon, or murdered in our beds. Them Frenchies is wicked as Satan, but they're smart." He tapped the side of his head to emphasize his point.

The tall man shook his head. "This land'll not be safe for white men, French or English, till we clear every last Injun off it. No such thing as a friendly Injun, Pete—I've said so before, haven't I, John," the man said, gesturing toward the apparent proprietor of the lodge.

"The twenty Delaware braves camped near the creek seem approachable enough, at least for now," John said in an obvious attempt to keep peace. "I trade with them, but I dare not show my back to them unless I'm moving fast!"

"I have met friendly Indians," one man said in the corner. Spitz leaned around the ample woman by the stove to see the calm, middle-aged face of the speaker, which was topped by a curiously shaped black felt hat.

"And who are you, takin' up for them savages?" Pete demanded.

"I am William Smith of Pennsylvania, and I have lived with the Indians for years of my life. I have learned several of their languages so that I may teach them the gospel of Jesus Christ. They are naturally gentle people, some of whom have come to know the Lord under my influence," the man declared.

The tall man spat. "Fancy Quaker, are yeh? Sure they'll listen while you're handing out presents, but yeh just keep your powder dry."

"I carry no weapon other than the Word of God, and it has served me well, friend," Smith answered boldly.

The tall man stood, nostrils flaring. "I'm no friend of yours if you'll see butchery and stand by the butchers. Yeh buried no babies with their mothers yesterday. Yeh've not lived out here on the edge of the world listening to that heathen screaming and drumming at night and wondering if yeh're next. So yeh've no right to speak in this place!" the tall man retorted angrily.

Smith shook his head and lifted his hands. "I want no quarrel with any man here. I am sorry to the bottom of my heart for thy loss."

"You go makin' up to these Injuns out here, Quaker, and we'll see the bottom of your heart right enough," Pete quipped. The men around him erupted into laughter. One called for another bowl of stew.

John lifted a piece of kindling and pointed it at Spitz. "You there, lad—have you finished breaking your fast?"

*Breakfast—it's so shut up and dark in here with only the fire for light that I thought I was eating supper,* he thought. But he cleared his throat and said, "Yes sir."

"You've sat closest to the fire; so you stand guard next. Straightaway you see anything, fire a shot, dash back here, and rouse the house. Have you a gun?" the man asked.

Spitz looked at his feet. Leaning open beside the fireplace was a leather messenger bag in which he could see his son's charred Bible and the neat calfskin journal Rawlins had handed him at Mount Vernon. The bag rested against a sizeable pack of supplies and a long rifle. Spitz assumed that all three belonged to him. "I have," he answered, standing.

"And have yeh any foolish Quaker scruples against shooting an Injun coming to bury a knife in my chest?" the tall man asked angrily, looking with defiance in Smith's general direction.

Spitz breathed deep and thought. He had eaten here and felt the fire warm him and heard the solid thumps of the girl's kneading. This place was real, completely real. He wondered what would happen if he died in the past. He wondered what he would do if he saw a human being taking aim to kill him. Could he stand there and take an arrow to the chest or a hatchet to the head without defending himself? "No," Spitz answered slowly. "I could shoot, if I had to do it." He put on the gloves that had been lying on his knee and wound a woolen scarf from the bench around his neck and ears.

The tall man snorted derisively. "I suppose yeh'll do."

"Hold your peace, Joseph. I give the orders at my post," John reminded the tall man. He turned back to Spitz. "Fetch your gun and walk half a mile out to the tree line. Send Roberts in to get warm."

"And keep yer eyes skinned for Injuns," the tall man blurted, unwilling to be silenced by the proprietor.

Spitz grasped the walnut stock of the rifle and set it against his shoulder. He opened the heavy door onto a world of white, and he shut it as quickly as he could. He turned around and began to walk to some trees he could see in the distance.

He saw that he was in a circle of upended logs joined with stout pegs and lashed together with pliable young branches and vines that had dried and hardened in summer heat months ago. The tops of the logs were pointed. Spitz could see the axe-strokes that had sharpened them. He could also see a building that was considerably larger than the one he had just left, which he now saw had another room beside it. The larger building steamed slightly in the bitter cold, and Spitz heard the nickering and stamping of horses inside.

Once he was out of the rough stockade surrounding the cabin and the stable, he noticed a sign that said "Frazier's Trading Post—Virginia." *So it was a trading post,* Spitz thought, *and Pete and that tall man with the long face must be friends of John Frazier.* He looked around him. He saw hills and trees and a river winding far in the distance, but he saw no other men, no houses anywhere. No smoke rose from any other fire than the one he had just left.

*It's the frontier,* Spitz thought. *It's the outer edge of everything.* Suddenly, the thought thrilled him. Here he was miraculously in this young, strong body, probably close to imminent peril, depending on no one but himself. Adrenaline pumped through him, and he found himself running, flying through the snow just because he could. It felt good. His knees and ankles hadn't moved like this in years without popping and complaining.

"Who goes there?" a deep, rough voice demanded.

Spitz whirled around and saw a frontiersman aiming a long rifle at him. Spitz looked at the rifle in his hand and dropped it to the ground, raising his hands as he had seen suspects on cop shows do. He was breathing hard from his romp and smiling despite himself. "Are you Roberts?" he asked.

"What if I am?' the man growled.

"I'm standing watch now." Spitz jerked a thumb behind him towards the cabin. "John Frazier told me to send you back to get warm."

The man eyed Spitz suspiciously. "Why were you runnin'?"

Spitz grinned. "It felt good. I just wanted to run."

The man lowered his gun, muttering about Spitz's youth and judgment and probable mental capacity, and growled, "Pick up yer blasted gun and keep yer powder dry," on his way inside.

Spitz obeyed him, resting his gun on his shoulder as he had when he left the trading post. He trudged the line of trees for a while, but then he could not restrain the impulse to run through all that untouched new snow again. Holding his gun beside him, parallel to the ground, he ran until he was winded and then stopped and looked around him. He saw no one. He ran back, following the footsteps he'd left before, and he paused at the place where he saw Roberts had been standing still until Spitz relieved him. He saw that Roberts' footprints pointed west. He stood behind them and looked the same way.

Two small figures appeared at the top of the hill opposite, probably a mile away. Spitz was genuinely shocked and pleased that he could clearly see so far away. Then he considered. Was this the moment to fire a warning shot and race back to the cabin to rouse the house?

*No*, Spitz decided. *I don't know who they are. What if they're friendly Indians, just out hunting or on their way to meet someone? I don't want Pete and the tall man shooting first and asking questions later. And they may be traders on their way to the post. I'll watch them a while.*

Spitz watched the men descend the hill and enter the valley below. As they drew nearer, he saw that one figure seemed to support the other, and that both wore woolen clothes and English boots. Spitz grew curious. Then one figure stumbled in the snow and fell to his knees. Without thinking, Spitz tore down the hill to meet them, holding his gun down low in one hand.

The men saw him coming, and the standing figure helped the other one to his feet. As Spitz got closer, he waved to them and called, "Hello! Do you need help?"

They were too far away for him to hear their answer clearly, but they waved back at him, walking at the same steady pace across the valley floor. Spitz noticed more about them as he ran closer. Underneath his woolen cloak, the younger one wore bright clothes with brass buttons, military clothes. They were both strong men, the younger in his early twenties and the older one in his mid to upper forties, he guessed. The military one had reddish hair underneath his hat, and the other had brown hair. Ice and snow covered their clothes as thoroughly as it covered the trees around him. The men's lips and noses were blue with cold.

"Hello!" he called again as he approached them. "I saw you fall; do you need help?"

"We do; my friend is frozen through with cold," the man with brown hair answered.

"Not much more than you are, Gist," the younger man with the reddish hair answered, teeth chattering. He was the man who had stumbled.

"What is the smoke ahead?" Gist asked. "We saw it from the last hill."

"It's Frazier's trading post," Spitz answered, glad he had looked at the sign. "It's warm inside; let me help you there."

"Thank you," the man with reddish hair answered. He smiled gratefully at Spitz and threw an arm around his shoulders as Spitz placed one strong arm around the man's back to support him as he walked.

"Were you standing guard when you saw us?" Gist asked.

"I was. They told me to 'keep my eyes skinned for Injuns.' There was a raid nearby not long ago with people murdered—families," Spitz said.

"How long ago?" the man Spitz supported asked him.

Spitz shook his head. "I don't know. I just got here a few hours ago myself."

"I wonder if we saw the murderers, Gist," the red-haired man said.

"We must have done," Gist answered. "Thank heaven they passed us by."

"You saw the Indians up close? How do you know they were the bad ones?" Spitz asked.

Gist looked at him oddly. "Scalps hung from their belts, some fresher than others."

"Oh," Spitz said awkwardly, feeling too innocent around men who had seen such things. "I've never seen a frontier Indian. They've been talking about them at the post."

Gist and his friend exchanged looks. "I daresay they have cause," Gist said. "But France is not the only nation with native allies. We have passed among other native peoples who have welcomed us. These Ottawa Indians with the scalps, however, we did not desire to approach. We had only two on our side, an insufficient number for making either peace or war with any success."

"And we thought our former guide might have called them," the man beside Spitz said.

"Yes," Gist said grimly, "the helpful fellow."

"What happened?" Spitz asked, intrigued. Here he had been reveling in the sense of adventure standing guard had offered him while these two men had been having a real adventure.

"At Murthering Town, we hired an Indian guide to lead us east from the cut trail, straight across country to the Allegheny River. The murderous name of the town should have been a warning to us," Gist said coldly. "At any rate, half a day's journey into the wilderness, the guide turned around and fired at Major Washington from so short a range that he should not have missed. I do not know how my friend escaped the bullet."

"My mother's prayers," Major Washington answered.

Spitz looked at him in awe. Major Washington was George Washington, and Spitz had one arm around his back. "I'm glad you're safe," he breathed earnestly.

"As am I," Washington said, humor glowing in his blue eyes, "none more so."

"What happened to the Indian guide?" Spitz asked.

"We overpowered and disarmed him and sent him away. We could not take him prisoner with us, considering his former treachery, and we did not like to kill an unarmed man."

They had reached the tree line where Spitz had been supposed to stand guard. "It's just half a mile from here," he told them, pointing forward.

"We will need to hire horses after we have rested and eaten," Gist told Spitz.

"I saw a stable; I'm sure you can get some," Spitz assured them.

"Excellent," Gist answered, smiling for the first time. "I have been from home on this journey above two months now, and I am heartily ready to return as swiftly as may be."

"We are indebted to you, sir," Washington said. "What is your name?"

"Spitzen—Stephen Spitzen, but everybody just calls me Spitz," he said, ducking his head modestly in half a bow.

"Spitz—I will remember," Washington promised, still shivering and speaking with difficulty. "I own Ferry's Landing on Chesapeake Bay, northeast of Richmond. If ever I can do you a good turn, I will, with all my heart."

"Thank you, sir," Spitz said gratefully. He led the two men through the stockade gate and left Washington with Gist to run ahead and announce them. He opened the door and looked for John Frazier. Finding him, he said quickly, "Two men are coming—one is a militia officer."

"And yeh just left watch to lead them in by the hand?" the tall, lantern-jawed man said incredulously, crossing the small room as he spoke and cuffing Spitz on the side of the head.

Spitz staggered and made to duck back outside, but Frazier only shook his head. "Get back inside." Frazier turned around and pointed at the man opposite Spitz's former place at the fire. "Porter, go stand watch," he called.

The man edged out past Frazier as Washington and Gist approached, and he stood aside to let them in. Frazier showed Washington and Gist to a place right in front of the fire and set his wife and daughter to fetching warm blankets for their backs and warm water for their feet and warm stew for their stomachs. It seemed evident to Spitz that Frazier was somewhat acquainted with the men.

Spitz edged closer to the fire while Frazier was busy and found his pack, and he set his rifle down in front of his messenger bag and his pack. He saw the calfskin journal. *I already have something to write, and more is sure to come,* he thought. He took it out and found a pot of ink, a quill, and a blotter. Determined to listen well, he sat at a table near the back of the room and set up a place to write.

While Washington and Gist ate, Spitz began writing. He looked at the clean, new page in front of him without a blot on it, like so much new fallen snow. He thought for a moment and then remembered the book he had been reading the night he fell. Boldly he loaded his quill and wrote at the top: *Signs, Mercies, and Interpositions of the Invisible Hand.*

He looked at it. He had intended the title ironically, but immediately he thought of the men he had led here and the conversation he'd had with them. He began to write, continuing when Washington and Gist finished their bowls of stew and began to speak again.

"More stew, sirs?" Frazier offered solicitously.

"No, I thank you," Gist answered. "But we are grateful for it, I assure you."

"How came you so frozen, Major?" Frazier asked, lighting a pipe and settling back in anticipation of the story.

"I suppose I have my own foolishness to thank for my dousing and my frozen clothes," Washington answered, speaking more easily now that he was warm, "but I have been headstrong since my boyhood. God willing, He will shape me into a more temperate man."

"Major Washington is too strict in his expectations," Gist disagreed, looking at Frazier. "I do not see how we could have avoided our uncomfortable night without the advantage of seeing the obstacles we would face in advance."

"Perhaps you are right," Washington told him, and then he turned to Frazier. "Several days past, we parted from a larger company, which was moving slowly through the 'scarcely supportable'[10] weather. The horses suffered abominably, and the other men rightfully insisted that they be rested and sheltered. But I felt it incumbent upon me to press forward in fulfillment of my duty. Gist bravely agreed to accompany me into the teeth of the storm."

"It was treacherous weather, hurling sharp snow and pellets of ice at us, and we suffered in it. But Major Washington was determined to cross the Allegheny as shortly as possible; so we walked east steadily." Gist shared a look with Washington, and Spitz saw that they had determined not to tell the story of the Indian guide just yet. "When we came to the Allegheny, we discovered that it was not frozen through, as we had expected. We knew then that we could return to our party by travelling south and waiting for them at the end of the trail they would follow, or we could find some means to sail across."

"And of course I insisted we sail across. So then I turned shipwright," Washington said, eyes twinkling. "I have lived on the water all my life, man and boy, and Gist is no novice to river-craft, either. Though we had but one hatchet between us, we felled a number of trees and shaped them into quite a passable raft and a long pole."

"We spent a whole day on the project and finished building it by moonlight," Gist said, "and set off for the opposite shore immediately. But in the middle of the river, we ran into a blockade of ice that threatened to sink us."

"And in my valiant endeavors to free us, I both lost us the pole and fell overboard," Washington confessed. "I swallowed quite a bit of the Allegheny and thought I should be lost in it. I struck out in the dark a number of times and just missed the side of the raft. Then I struck it and heaved myself aboard, with Gist's help."

"To see you on board again was a relief and a comfort," Gist said seriously.

Washington nodded to his friend. "You are good not to mention that, though I saved myself, I lost our means of reaching either the shore we had left or the shore in our sights. We were adrift and helpless until you spotted the island and suggested we abandon ship."

"An island," Frazier interrupted. "I should wager you mean Half-Mile Spit!"

"I suppose that we must," Gist agreed. "We made shift to camp there overnight, as we had saved our packs from the ill-fated raft, but we could not foresee how we would reach the eastern shore in the morning. Though the air was cold enough to freeze our clothes stiff, the river flowed as swift and free as at midsummer."

"Did you swim it at daybreak?" Pete asked, perched on the edge of his seat to listen. "It's a good ways out in the middle."

"No," Washington answered, eyes alight with wonder. "When we woke, the span of the river between us and the eastern shore was frozen solid. God made us a bridge, and we walked across it."

Spitz jerked his head up from the journal at those words, so clear a statement of faith: "God made us a bridge." There's the invisible hand at work, Spitz thought. At least he's sure it is.

"Major Washington," Pete began, "seein' as you both were so far west when that storm hit you, I was wonderin' if you could tell us about them Frenchies out to Ohio. I've been tellin' whomsoever might listen that them Frenchies is settin' the Injuns on to us."

A general murmur of agreement and anger rumbled through the men at the other tables. Washington found Spitz's eyes in the crowd and pursed his lips, remembering his comment. "You have half the matter straight," Washington told him. "The French are indeed allying with certain tribes to harry English settlers." The rumble grew more intense as Pete shot a look of triumph at tall lantern-jawed man. "We passed a band of hostile Ottawa as we pressed in such haste to the river. We saw fresh scalps at their belts and thus fear that the culprits of the recent nearby murders escaped into the western wilderness."

"Filthy savages," the tall man spat. "We should shoot 'em all, every last one."

"I strongly object both to the tone and to the proposition," Washington said, standing to his feet to command attention. "Certain native tribes who have allied with the English crown thereby deserve both our friendship and our protection. I have eaten and spoken with their leaders and engaged with them in negotiations for our common benefit. If France does not cease its aggression towards these colonies and the king's loyal subjects in them, then the militias here will rise and fight, and these good native people will rise and fight with us."

"We can't trust 'em," someone in the crowd shouted.

"We can, and we shall," Washington declared, and Spitz saw the steel of the future general and president in him. "In the infancy of our own race, our ancestors donned paint and animal skins and worshipped heathen gods. If we have learned better now, then our duty becomes to teach those who are willing to learn from us of the source from which our civilization flows, not to murder them in cold blood." Spitz saw that Washington looked at Pete and the tall lantern-jawed man as he spoke the last part, and Spitz was glad that someone had stood up to the men.

Washington looked at the crowd around him, holding their gaze. "I have befriended a particular chief who seems to me a good and decent man, and I have told him, 'You do well to wish to learn our arts and ways of life, and above all, the religion of Jesus Christ. These will make you a greater and happier people than you are.'[11] But do not mistake, they are now a great people in their way, valiant and loyal to those who treat them well."

"But some of them is with the Frenchies," Pete insisted.

Washington inclined his head. "I have said so. If you wish to fight them, then join the militia that Governor Dinwiddie will raise this spring. Band together with your fellow subjects to push the French and their allies from the king's land in fair combat, but do not become the kind of men who massacre families wholesale, no matter their birth or condition."

Spitz drew in a breath. He did not doubt that Washington had purposely equated the men's venomous hatred of the Indians with the massacre the Ottawa had just committed. He looked at the tall man, who had paled, and wondered what he would do.

Stubbornly, the tall man held his ground. "I still say that the whole heathen pack of 'em isn't worth one white man. They're Satan's own menace."

Gist rose to his feet beside Washington. "The French commander agrees with you. Chief Half-King sent a message to him, asking him diplomatically as one leader to another to remove his soldiers from Indian land and from the Ohio River. But the request was also a test to see who would win their alliance. The French commander told him, 'I am not afraid of flies or mosquitos, for Indians are such as those; I tell you down that river I will go, and will build upon it according to my command: If the river was ever so blocked up, I have forces sufficient to burst it open, and tread under my feet all that stand in opposition, together with their alliances; for my force is as the sand upon the seashore... Child, you talk foolish; you say this land belongs to you... I saw that land sooner than you did ... [La Salle] was the man that went down, and took possession of that river; it is my land, and I will have it, let who will stand-up for, or say against it."[12]

The crowd grew silent, listening in awe to the fantastic arrogance of the French general.

Washington spoke quietly to the crowd. "Because of that proud reply, King George now has the loyal allegiance of a number of tribes. I have seen the French try to sway the constancy of our Indian allies, who will no longer be swayed by any number of gifts. But if we treat them insolently, as the French commander has done, we will undo the work of good and brave men who have won that trust and place ourselves at greater peril than we need endure. The time for courage at arms is at hand. Know the true face of your enemy and the proper arena where you may show your loyalty to your king, and do not be swayed yourselves by demagogues who lead you toward acts you may repent."

Washington held the men's gaze for another moment, and no one answered him back. Then he sat and called Frazier over to him. Spitz heard Washington and Gist arranging to hire horses to take them back home. He wrote a few more sentences and then absently brushed his cheek with the feather end of the quill as he thought.

It seemed to him that Washington had gained incredible benefits from the diplomatic mission he described, and not just the evidence of God's intervention that Spitz was supposed to note. In this one trip, Washington had learned the character of Chief Half-King and his people, and he now understood how to negotiate with Indians. He'd learned about his enemy, the French, and how they operated. He'd thoroughly scouted the western frontier and escaped death several times along the way. When he returned, he'd be a valuable officer, one people high in government could respect, despite his youth.

*And he saw God at work*, Spitz admitted. *He saw God protect him from Indians, from drowning, and from freezing. He knew he could rely on God.* Spitz blinked and looked down at what he had written in the calfskin journal.

## Signs, Mercies, and Favorable Interpositions of the Invisible Hand

**Mercy 1**—A failed assassination (the Indian's rifle shot missed).

**Mercy 2**—Spared from encountering a band of hostile Indians.

**Mercy 3**—Kept from drowning and kept from dying of hypothermia (able to find the raft in the dark and pull himself to safety).

**Mercy 4**—Survived the freezing night while sleeping in frozen clothes.

**Favorable Interposition 1**—Invisible hand miraculously froze the river between the island and the river bank that they needed to reach; providing a safe walkway across what had been a turbulent river only a few hours earlier.

**Sign 1**—Governor Dinwiddie chose Washington to represent him on a dangerous diplomatic mission that made Washington a name.

*It's all true. I've seen it with my own eyes, just like Rawlins said I would. God protected Washington.* Spitz carefully blotted the wet ink and closed the book, wiping his quill dry and firmly stoppering the bottle of ink. Again, bitterness rose in Spitz. *It's a shame my son didn't enjoy the same protection.*

Then an image rose in Spitz of the utter joy he'd felt racing out in the snow, the freedom of using strong, young legs and lungs. He remembered his son Steve as a young man, about the age Spitz appeared to be now, playing football, fishing with Spitz, and riding his motorcycle. He remembered the joy on his son's face as he left for the mission trip to Indonesia. Flying on a puddle-jumper and riding through undeveloped country where cannibals still lived seemed like a grand adventure to Steve. He couldn't wait to go. And before the accident, Spitz had understood. It had seemed the most natural thing in the world that his brave, strong son should use his sense of adventure to serve the God he loved.

*He knew the risk, and he took it gladly,* something inside him seemed to say. *I really love that about him.*

Jarred by the thought, Spitz put his writing supplies back into the leather messenger bag and picked it up to take it back to the fire so that he could talk to Washington again. But in his hurry, he picked up the wrong side of the bag and tipped out the contents.

Steve's Bible fell out and opened to the Psalms. Light from the fireplace illuminated the Roman numerals LXXVIII (seventy-eight). Spitz looked up, and the trading post dissolved into a tunnel of stars around him.

# Chapter Four

*"We were under great pressure, far beyond our ability
to endure, so that we despaired of life itself. Indeed, we felt
we had received the sentence of death. But this happened
that we might not rely on ourselves but on God,
who raises the dead."—2 Corinthians 1:8b-9*

Aspen watched Bernie come into work in the morning, joking with the people he passed along the way, sipping his ever-present cup of coffee. She hadn't talked to him yesterday afternoon about the security of her job. As soon as she'd walked inside the door of the office suite, Bill had run into her and begun asking her questions about the different clients the firm represented. The determination she'd felt when she left Angela had fizzled as she spoke to Bill, trying not to make too much eye contact with him, and by the end of the day, she just didn't have enough energy to face trying to get Bernie to have such a serious conversation.

So she had purposely arrived early today, so early that she'd been the one to flip on the lights for the suite. Bill had not yet arrived, and now was the perfect opportunity for her to talk to Bernie alone, without any awkward questions or evasions in front of her handsome coworker. She wound through the maze of desks and knocked on the steel-framed glass door that Bernie had just closed behind him.

He looked up and waved her in. "Hey, what's up, kiddo? How's your Pops?"

Aspen shook her head. "He's about the same. They don't know when he'll wake up."

"Gee, I'm sorry, kiddo. Are you doing all right? How's the new partner? Have you used the *Cast Away* thing yet? I was going to spring that one on him today," Bernie grinned.

"I won't touch *Cast Away*, Bernie—that one's all yours," Aspen promised. "Besides, he asked me to call him Bill. I don't think it'll come up naturally in conversation now, anyway."

"Perfect, perfect," Bernie chuckled, sitting in his rolling chair. "So what brings you to my humble abode? Here, take a seat; don't break a heel standing there."

"Thanks, Bernie," Aspen smiled, sitting in the Danish modern chair he offered her. "Actually, I wanted to talk to you about Bill."

"Whoa, kiddo—has the volleyball been hitting on you? Because I specifically told him that you were out of bounds. 'Aspen doesn't date,' I said. 'She's shot down every guy in this office; so don't even try.' I'm looking out for you, kiddo," Bernie said emphatically.

Aspen winced. "You really didn't have to do that, Bernie."

"Aw, it's no trouble at all, not for you, kiddo," Bernie said affectionately.

Aspen took a deep breath. "Actually, I wanted to talk to you about Bill as he relates to the kind of future I've still got with the firm."

Bernie eyed her sternly. "What's that supposed to mean? You don't want to work here now? The new desk set is coming today, Aspen. Am I going to have to send it back?"

Aspen put out a hand, palm out. "No, no, Bernie—that's not it." Aspen took another deep breath and let it out. "I'm really worried that you brought Bill here because I'm not doing a good enough job. I'm worried that he's here as my replacement because I haven't been doing enough for the new clients."

Bernie leaned back in his rolling chair and sighed as he laced his fingers across his stomach. "I don't know how to tell you this, Aspen, but you're right. You haven't been doing enough for the new clients. I tried to talk to you about it, but you just didn't seem open to hearing me."

Aspen felt the breath catch in her throat. "I—I'm so sorry, Bernie. I know I was behind before Papa got sick, and that day off really hurt me. But I still think I'm valuable to the team here. I still think I have a good skill set. I can catch up…" Aspen trailed off. Bernie was grinning.

They were both silent a moment, and then Bernie pointed at her and said enthusiastically, "You have to admit; you walked right into that one, kiddo. I mean, can you blame me?" He let out a tremendous guffaw.

Aspen tried to laugh with him, but then the corners of her mouth quivered and turned down, and she began to cry. Tears ran thick down her cheeks, and she tried unsuccessfully to wipe them away with her fingers.

"Oh, hey, kiddo—I didn't mean anything. Look, it's going to be okay with the job and everything. I really was just joking with you. Why don't I keep any Kleenex in this office? My mother always said I was going to make somebody cry." Bernie stood and walked to the door, opening it and sticking out his head. "Hey, Wilson—get in here. I want to talk to you."

"No, no, Bernie," Aspen gasped. "Please don't."

"Let's just get all of this straightened out now, kiddo. It's best that way, trust me," Bernie said, patting her shoulder clumsily.

Aspen sank in her chair as Bill entered the office, tall and handsome in his tailored gray suit with his wavy light brown hair and clear green eyes. Bill took one look at her and immediately pulled the white silk handkerchief from his breast pocket and handed it to her, sitting in the other Danish modern chair in front of Bernie's desk.

Aspen put out a hand to push the handkerchief away. "I can't use that; I'll ruin it," she sobbed.

"Handkerchiefs are made to be used. I've got more," Bill assured her. "Please take it."

Aspen did, wiping her eyes and cheeks carefully, breathing in the smell of Bill's cologne on his handkerchief. She knew she must be a mess, mascara everywhere like some kind of a hysterical drowned raccoon. She leaned forward, hoping that her hair would hide most of the damage. "I'll wash this," she offered timidly, holding up the black-streaked silk as Bernie closed the door and sat back down behind his desk.

"I don't need it; you can keep it," Bill said, concern on his face. "What's the matter?"

"It's just a lot of things; it's a bad time. I lost it for a minute," Aspen hedged, sitting up a little straighter and trying to look more together.

"Don't be shy, Aspen," Bernie chided. "That's not helping anything. Look," he said, addressing Bill, "once you're here longer you'll know that I kid a lot. It's just me; it's who I am. Aspen came to me worried that you were here as her replacement, and I led her along for a while. It's my fault she's a wreck. Boy, what bad timing, with her Grandpop in the hospital and all," Bernie sighed in frustration. "But I thought that the three of us should talk, all kidding aside, about who's doing what and who still has a job."

Bill looked at Bernie as if he could not believe what he was hearing, and then he turned to Aspen. "I sincerely apologize if I made you think that you were losing your job by anything I said or did. Trust me; no one has ever suggested to me that you were not competent or that you needed to be replaced. Everyone speaks of you very respectfully. We all know that you're good at what you do." Bill looked honestly and sympathetically into Aspen's eyes as he spoke.

Aspen felt a flood of relief and realized that she trusted Bill. "Thank you," she told him.

Bernie leaned forward, folding his hands on his desk. "Give Aspen an idea of your background, Bill, so that we're all on the same page here about skill sets and responsibilities."

Bill opened his jacket and settled back in the chair, crossing his ankle over the opposite knee. "I'm from here in Virginia originally. My folks are from a place called Hampton, on the bay. Our family has lived there for as long as anyone can remember. But I went to college in North Carolina and stayed there for work. I went up to New York for a few years, but I didn't like the lifestyle—too frenetic." He grinned at Bernie and said, "Sorry, boss—no offense."

Bernie raised his hands chest high, palms out. "None taken," he said.

"So my background is in Appalachia and the Adirondacks—coal country, steel country. I've been looking over your client list, and I've had an idea about sharing the workload," Bill began.

"I'd like to hear it," Aspen said, grateful that her voice finally sounded calm and normal.

"Most of your standing accounts seem to be with soft commodities, oil, and precious metals, and the new client load seems to be mostly coal, iron ore, and industrial metals like copper, lead, and zinc. I'd like to propose a division of labor that leaves you with the majority of your standing accounts and pushes the newer accounts to me, as they're in my area of expertise, anyway," Bill suggested, looking between Bernie and Aspen.

Bernie leaned back in his chair and threw his hands wide. "That sounds great to me. Aspen, kiddo, what do you think? Can you handle a little less work?"

"Of course," Aspen said. She turned to Bill. "It's a good solution, and it takes a lot of pressure off me. We can go over the client list this morning and divide it if you like."

"That sounds like a plan," Bill smiled. He hesitated. "I know you usually eat lunch alone, but I'd like to take you out so that we can get to know each other better. I think we could have avoided this whole misunderstanding if you knew my background. You probably would have suggested the solution yourself."

"Hey, Wilson - didn't I tell you 'hands off'?" Bernie joked. "No dating on office hours."

Bill's ears turned red, and he looked like he wished Bernie would learn some discretion. Aspen felt sorry for him.

"Lunch actually sounds nice, Bill, but I've been going to the hospital at lunch this week to see my grandfather. I eat something from the cafeteria in his room and talk to him. Maybe we can go somewhere later."

"Great," Bill said, looking relieved. "Well, let's get to work."

"That's what I like to hear from my analysts!" Bernie said, rubbing his hands together like a cartoon miser. "Go make us some money!"

Aspen left Bernie's office, and Bill closed the door behind them both. As they walked back to their shared desk, Bill said, "I'm sorry to hear about your grandfather. He must mean a great deal to you for you to see him so often."

"He does," Aspen agreed. "He raised me, and I still live with him—or I did before his stroke. The house is so empty now. I really miss him."

"Do you mind my asking what happened to your parents? Don't answer if it's uncomfortable," Bill said, sitting in the squeaky folding chair Aspen hated.

"It's fine. They died in a plane crash when I was nine. I've lived with Papa ever since."

Bill shook his head. "I'm so sorry. I can't imagine how awful that must have been. And here your grandfather is sick now, too. You must be very strong to handle so much."

"Thank you," Aspen said, flashing him a brief, tight smile. "So we should probably begin going over those client lists," she suggested.

"Before we do, I wanted to float another idea past you," Bill interrupted.

"Sure, go ahead," Aspen said, opening her computer and typing in her password.

Bill straightened up in his chair. His seat was several inches lower than hers. "Well, it seems like the firm is overdue for a boots-on-the-ground visit to several of the mining operations that produce commodities in both our areas of concern," Bill began. "I think that you and I should organize a trip to tour the plants and the mines. Most of them are in the developing world; so it won't be a luxury vacation by any stretch of the imagination."

"I'm okay with harsh conditions," she told him. "I've been on these kinds of trips before. Besides, I was raised by an old man who thinks camping and hunting and fishing is the most fun a girl can have," Aspen joked. "Living off the land is second nature to me now."

Bill laughed. "I think your grandfather would really like my dad; he's the same way," he said. "So if you agree that the firm could do with a firsthand report of some plant conditions," Bill began, gauging Aspen's reaction.

"I do," she said.

"Then I think that the operations which could most use a site visit are primarily in Southeast Asia and Latin America. For the sake of our travel budget, we should probably choose one region or the other. Which countries sound best to you: Chile and Peru or Australia and Indonesia?

"Indonesia," Aspen decided suddenly. Then she looked down at her keyboard, embarrassed that she had broached this particular subject with Bill. "But that's just my opinion."

"I'm curious," Bill said, looking at her seriously, "why the intense reaction to Indonesia? Have you been there before?"

"No." She sighed. "That's where my parents' plane crashed. They were on a short-term mission project to deliver those shoeboxes to poor children that a lot of churches send. I've just always wanted to see the place the plane went down. Does that sound morbid?"

"No," Bill said compassionately, "that sounds very natural. And it sounds very doable. Why shouldn't we do both at once? We could plan the trip that way, maybe using the final weekend to look for the crash site. But Indonesia is a large country with over 17,000 islands and 50,000 miles of coastline. Where did the plane crash?" He got out his iPhone and started tapping.

Aspen sighed. It had never occurred to her that it might be near impossible to find the crash site. What were the prospects with such a large area? "I don't know the exact place, but Papa retrieved the bodies from a village called Timika on the island of New Guinea in the Indonesian province of Irian Jaya. I can find some more details later in Papa's files," Aspen answered. She leaned over to see the map on his phone, and he turned it towards her.

"I know the area well," Bill said. "The province of Irian Jaya is now called Papua. When your grandfather was there, Timika was probably just a small village. Today, it's a sprawling town supporting the ever-expanding mining activities in the area. The mountains of New Guinea hold large deposits of copper, gold, and silver. We can fly to Timika via Cairns, Australia. In fact, Cairns or maybe even Timika would make a perfect hub for our client tour," Bill said, eyes alight with the possibility of adventure. "What do you say?"

"I say yes," Aspen said impulsively. "Let's get to work on the client list, and then we'll see what Bernie says about the trip."

"Great," Bill grinned. Aspen noticed that he had lovely teeth, and then she blushed and looked back at her computer. Bill settled back in his chair. "So you're coming to Indonesia with me, but not to lunch. Can I talk you into a dinner instead?"

"Sure," Aspen told him, typing furiously. "Dinner sounds nice."

★ ★ ★

Spitz lay in his hospital bed, his eyes closed, feeling someone poke and prod at him and hearing a pen scratch on a sheet. But the hand that poked at him felt thin and claw-like and rough, not firm and gentle. And no one spoke to him. He listened for Aspen's voice and didn't hear it.

"Hello, Irene—are you finished with Mr. Spitzen?" a familiar voice asked. Spitz searched his memory for the name—Angela.

"Just about," Irene answered tonelessly. She had a smoker's voice—low and harsh.

"How is he doing today?" Angela asked, coming into the room. "His granddaughter is coming to see him in just a little while."

"Don't see why she bothers; there's nobody home," Irene remarked.

Spitz was stung. He imagined how he looked to this nurse, a white and wrinkled shell underneath a flimsy gown—unhearing, unseeing, and unresponsive. The picture was not at all attractive.

"Oh, but there is," Angela disagreed warmly. "He's alive, and his soul is right there inside. We never know how much he understands or when he'll wake again."

"I've worked in this ward a lot longer than you have," Irene argued. "And some of them never come back. They're sinkholes. Then the family stops coming. It makes no difference to them."

"Most of the patients do come back, though," Angela said quietly.

"Or they die. If they do come back, they come impaired. I wonder if they'd show up if they knew what was waiting—can't talk straight, can't walk, drooling like a baby." She barked a coarse laugh. "I wouldn't come back." Spitz felt icy dread at her words.

"Where is his Bible?" Angela asked. "Here it is on the counter. Did you move it?"

"Had to," Irene answered. "What, is he gonna read it?"

"His granddaughter wants him to have it," Angela explained, and Spitz felt the solid weight at his side. Oddly, it comforted him as he never thought it would. It meant that someone cared; someone was looking out for him.

"I'm off to the next one," Irene said. Spitz barely heard her light footsteps leaving the room.

"Don't you listen to her, Spitz," Angela told him, patting his arm. "I know you can hear me. You have a lot to live for. Aspen misses you. You have your studies. The world outside is beautiful now, too, with all of those bright leaves on the trees coming down everywhere. It's a sight to see. I had to push them off my windshield this morning like a fall of snow. And the air smells sharp and good, like cider does. Do you like cider? I love it, especially hot with spices and orange zest. That's how my mother used to make it. You should see the world outside, Spitz. You should at least get to smell it. I tell you what; I'm going to talk to your doctor about taking you outside these last few warm days. I think it would do you good."

Spitz felt another pat on his arm, and then he heard Angela running her hands over the Bible beside him, ruffling the pages. "This Bible has been through a lot; you can see it from the cover. But it still speaks as clearly as ever once you open it up. Most things are like that. Don't you think so, Spitz? Most things that look all used up on the outside have the best stories to tell." Angela's hand lifted. Her footsteps moved away from the bed. "You think about that for a while, Spitz, before Aspen comes. She'll be really glad to hear you're holding your own."

Spitz heard Angela leave, and he thought over the conversation between the nurses. Of course Angela would try to encourage him. He'd heard her with Aspen; Angela was just a natural encourager. Was the other nurse, Irene, closer to the truth? Was Aspen going to be shackled to him as long as he lived, wiping his mouth and pushing him around in a wheelchair?

Dread of that kind of helplessness and disability filled Spitz. He felt the despair of overwhelming odds stacked against him. He couldn't make it. There was no way out, no escape from this damaged body except through a coffin. If he could have shed a tear, he would have been sobbing. He sank down into the blackness of lost hope.

★ ★ ★

And then that blackness filled with bright stars, which shaped the spinning tunnel he was coming to expect. He shut his eyes against the dizzying whirl of light, and when he opened them again, he was walking through deep, dim woods. It was barely dawn. Spitz saw a timid rim of coral hovering over the fold of a hill, brighter in one spot where the sun would emerge when it got around to rising. The trees in front of that coral were coal black against it, and the trees right in front of him didn't have much more color. He looked up at the moon, a pale, waning sickle in the sky amid the distant stars.

He saw that he had on a pair of leather pants, soft and worked like suede. On his feet he wore moccasins, beaded and fringed and comfortable as a dream. His shirt was dark blue cotton, and even in the dim light he could see that the seams and buttons were hand-sewn. A heavy pack hung from straps across his shoulders, and the thinner straps of a leather messenger bag, a powder horn, and a canteen crisscrossed his chest. He held a long rifle in one hand. With the other, he felt inside the messenger bag for the familiar shapes of the two books inside. They were there.

Spitz looked ahead and saw another light besides the pale dawn and the paler moon. A fire burned in a large clearing through the trees ahead. He supposed he was on his way to it, and to whoever had set it.

Then Spitz heard the unmistakable click of a trigger cocking. He whirled around, eyes scrabbling for purchase in the dark wood.

A man dressed very like him stepped into dim dawn light from the shadow of a tree, pointing his rifle straight at Spitz's chest. "Who are you, and on what business are you so near this camp?" the man demanded.

Spitz sighed in relief at the sound of the man's voice and the outline of his profile. "Gist, it's me, Spitz. I led you into Frazier's trading post after you crossed the Allegheny half frozen with Major Washington."

"Come nearer," Gist ordered, and he peered into Spitz's face. The sun finally popped over the hill in the distance, and the woods grew noticeably lighter. "I do recognize you," he said, and he lowered his rifle. "You come from the west. I had to ensure that you were not a French spy come to scout Washington's position and report it. He is in enough danger at present without any sudden additions. What brings you here now?"

"Major Washington," Spitz answered without thinking. Then he scrambled quickly and added, "I heard the militia was up this way, and I hoped to meet him again."

Gist smiled kindly. "He is rather an inspiring figure, I admit, though he is no longer Major Washington. He is now Lieutenant Colonel Washington, second in command of the Virginia colonial army beneath only Colonel James Fry. You may thank providence for leading you so near Washington. He is in the middle of that meadow, and if you mean to serve him, as I gather you do, you will have ample opportunity." Gist resumed his brisk hike through the woods, and Spitz hurriedly wove through the trees abreast of him, filled with excitement at the prospect of seeing Washington again. But that prospect wasn't all that excited him.

He was strong and active again, here in the past, free of any fears about hunching and drooling. And the air here smelled redolent with life. He breathed in the scent of wet earth and new leaves and wood smoke, and he smiled. It was good to be alive, right here, at this moment.

Soon he and Gist broke through the ring of trees to the meadow in the middle. A sentry challenged them, and Gist answered for both of them and led Spitz through. A line of heavy wagons encircled the camp, the horses that drew them picketed inside to one side and a small force of irregularly uniformed men camped on the other; Spitz thought that there was probably a hundred fifty men in the circle. The men were rolling up their sleeping blankets and preparing food at a number of small fires.

Gist stopped at a fire near the center of the camp, and Spitz immediately recognized the reddish hair, blue eyes, and distinct profile of Washington. Washington looked up at the sound of their footsteps and sprang to his feet, concerned, his hand outstretched to his friend. "Gist, you have come. I looked for you last night."

Gist frowned. "You will thank Providence I have come at all when you hear what detained me. Through the woods northwest of you creeps a small but deadly force, among them the organizer of the French army: the French commissary, La Force."

"How many do they number?" Washington asked, thinking.

"I counted fifty armed men and two scouts with only a handful of the officers mounted," Gist answered quickly. "I passed them in the afternoon and followed them until they made camp last night, when I observed them from quite near. I heard La Force named by one of his officers."

"They must trespass no farther. I shall brook no French usurpation of the roads and bridges I have built these last weeks," he said, looking around at the men breaking fast and preparing to leave. "These poor fellows are worn to a raveling felling trees and uprooting stumps to clear a path west for British wagons. Those wagons shall not carry French bread and guns east."

"This advance force means as well that I may look soon for an attack upon my settlement not far from Red Stone Creek," Gist said. "Join your force to mine, and let us stand there together as far west as we may. We have only to elude these prancing princes of officers, and your Virginians can slip by them like deer."

"And withdraw my hand from plucking so ripe a plum hanging so near?" Washington smiled. "No, Christopher—I mean to take them."

"You wish to attack La Force?" Gist frowned. "I have just taken pains over your safety this morning, surprising what I thought was another

French spy, and here I find you plotting to announce your position to the entire French army with an attack on its commissary."

Washington noticed Spitz for the first time and clapped him on the shoulder. "I know your face, sir, but I do not remember your name. You aided me out of the snow after my midnight swim in the Allegheny. The name is something German, I remember," Washington said, peering into Spitz's eyes.

"Stephen Spitzen, sir, but everyone calls me Spitz," he answered, pleased to be remembered.

"Just so," Washington answered. "Have you come to enlist, Spitz? I may offer you fifteen pounds of tobacco per day and a share in a two-thousand-acre tract of land if you will take up your gun for Virginia and your king."

"He has not come for the glory of Virginia or the British crown but for you, George; the man told me he had come on purpose to serve you," Gist explained.

"I am honored," Washington said, inclining his head to Spitz.

"I am, too, sir; I'm eager to do whatever I can to help you," Spitz volunteered.

Washington considered him. "I saw you writing at the trading post; have you a fair hand?"

Spitz nodded. "I do."

"I shall take you as an aide-de-camp, then," Washington decided. "Do you know the duties I shall require of you?"

"I'm your assistant in camp; I carry your messages to your officers and take dictation when you send a letter," Spitz said, remembering the research he'd done in his comfortable library.

Washington nodded and added, "You will not be merely my clerk, though, Spitz. You will fight as well, and you will clear wilderness and build roads and bridges right along with these soldiers. I need not only a clear hand but also a strong back and a stout heart."

"Yes," Spitz agreed, "I'll work hard for you, sir, whatever you ask me to do."

"Excellent," Washington smiled, and he turned to a thin, dark-haired young man who was cooking porridge in a pot by the fire. "James, come here and meet my new aide-de-camp, Spitz. Spitz, here is our company's excellent physician, James Craik, who shares my fire and my tent and tries to make me into a Scotsman at breakfast with his interminable offerings of porridge."

Craik rose and shook Spitz's hand, chuckling. "You are well met, Spitz. Having at first only expected to bleed some men and stanch the wounds of others, I have been a desultory aide-de-camp till now, and I leave those duties to you gladly."

Spitz controlled his reaction with difficulty. Last time he'd seen Craik, the doctor had been a portly, red-faced old man with gray hair, and now he was a young man with a dark queue and a farmer's tan below his rolled sleeves. "Good to meet you, Doctor Craik," he said.

Washington turned to Gist. "Christopher, come with me. I must lay plans with Stephens and Hog and Van Braam and introduce them to Spitz, and I want you by me."

Washington speedily gathered his other officers. In the space of a few short minutes, he had ordered Captain Peter Hog with Gist as his guide along with seventy five soldiers to search for La Force's party. Washington detailed the rest of his force to press steadily west, forging the trail down which later wagons full of weapons and supplies would travel.

Sooner than Spitz thought likely, he saw Captain Hog, Gist, and the armed search party leaving camp in pursuit of La Force. Of the remaining half of Washington's men, about forty of them had dressed in light shirts and put their gear into the heavy wagons; they carried axes and shovels or harnessed horses to sledges for hauling logs. The other forty wore their coats and packs and carried their guns, already loaded with a first charge. Evidently, the first group would continue constructing the road, while the armed men would serve as their protectors.

Spitz had been assigned among the protectors during his first day on duty. Craik had petitioned on his behalf that the volunteer should perform no hard labor on his first day. "Besides," Craik had pled, "I could use Spitz's help, too." Washington had agreed. Spitz realized that he had caught a break standing guard duty instead of felling trees or joining a war party chasing French spies.

He thought so until that noon, when Washington had gathered his officers to discuss their progress and plan for the next day. While the men spoke around Washington's fire, a sentry approached leading an Indian, who had arrived in camp with news that his chief, Half King, was nearby.

Spitz hadn't expected to see any Indians up close. This man behind the sentry looked tall, fierce, deeply muscled, and tanned. He wore skin breeches and moccasins very like Spitz's own, although his belt was woven red cloth instead of leather buckled with brass, and his chest was bare. He had shaved his head to a circle at the crown, where he had wound the long, dark hair at the top with long feathers, and his upper face from the bridge of his nose to the edge of feathered hair he had painted with two bands, red above and black below.

While the Indian spoke with Washington and his officers, Spitz noticed the hatchet at his belt, swinging beside a club that looked as if it were made of bone. Hanging from the end of the handle of both weapons were what appeared to be patches of leather wound with feathers and hair; Spitz couldn't place what they were.

Craik saw him staring at the belt and leaned close. "Scalps," the doctor whispered quietly, "old ones."

Spitz's eyes widened in shock, and then looked down to the thick meadow grass at his feet. *It's a different world altogether,* he told himself. *What do you know about it? Even if you'd been a soldier before, I think it might throw you. Think of them as Washington does. They're human beings. They're allies. You don't have to like everything they do to respect them.*

Spitz raised his eyes and looked into the Indian's face. The man finished speaking with Washington and stood back, listening to the talk of the officers. If he noticed Spitz's eyes on him, he made no sign of it.

Spitz felt a tug on the fabric of his shirt and saw Craik still near him, gesturing to him to come. When they were a little space away, Craik said quietly, "If we are to leave immediately to join Half King, we must prepare. I must gather my own things, and you must pack the Lieutenant Colonel's possessions and ready his horse. I will help you to strike the tent."

As they worked, Spitz desperately recalled the early chapters in the biography of Washington he'd read and reread. This place was in Pennsylvania, near where the Ohio River met the Monongahela. Even before Washington had returned from the diplomatic mission where Spitz had met him for the first time, the Ohio Company, anxious to maintain control of its shipping and trading routes, had coincidentally sent a group of men led by William Trent to build a stockade not far from the fork where the rivers met.

When Governor Dinwiddie heard about the expedition and then received Washington's report that the French absolutely refused to withdraw, he'd made Trent a captain with orders to reposition the stockade at the fork of the rivers. Washington and Gist had identified the most strategic building site during their previous diplomatic mission, and Dinwiddie sent Christopher Gist to Trent as a guide. This assignment likely suited Gist well, as his newly established settlement near Red Stone Creek was close by, too.

Then when Trent was away on a supply run, the French had come in force, over a thousand of them with cannons and horses to draw them, and demanded surrender. Trent's force, consisting of mostly woodsmen and hunters numbering close to forty, had surrendered. With such lopsided odds, what else could they do?

When Washington reached Willis Creek, where Trent was supposed to have positioned pack horses so that Washington could transfer his supplies out of the heavy, awkward wagons that could not navigate winding forest trails, Washington found out about the surrender. He also discovered that Trent hadn't furnished the promised pack horses and that the partially constructed fort where Washington was supposed to garrison his men was now in French hands.

Washington and his men were the first wave of Governor Dinwiddie's newly established army. Its leader, Colonel James Fry, would send reinforcements as he enlisted them, along with more guns and supplies. But there was no road suitable for wagons between Washington with his company of soldiers and Gist's settlement near Red Stone Creek, let alone the captured fort at the Forks. So Washington and his men were building one. And now it looked like La Force was going to try to take it from them and use it to bring more French soldiers east into settled British territory.

Half King could be the godsend Washington needed. If they allied together, Washington could delay the French until Fry's reinforcements arrived. Then they would join their forces and push the French all the way back to Canada.

Thankful that his Gramps had taught him to handle horses on the farm when he was a boy, Spitz attended to the horse Craik told him belonged to Washington, saddling it and strapping the rolled tent and gear onto it. Then he led it to Washington and held the reins while Washington mounted it.

Spitz spent the rest of the morning walking behind that horse with the rest of the forty men carrying guns, leaving the forty men who had pulled road-building duty still felling trees. Captain Stephens rode at Washington's right hand, and Craik rode on his left. The Mingo Indian who had delivered the message walked ahead of all of them. Spitz envied those men their view. His perspective on war was changing as he saw firsthand how much of it relied on good roads and supplies. *And strong legs,* Spitz thought ruefully. *There's a reason young men have so much energy—they need it.* The men did not pause until nightfall. They ate what they carried as they walked, and those who needed to relieve themselves disappeared into the trees and then caught up again with the rest. Spitz didn't know he could walk so far or be so tired and keep moving.

Just before the sun set, Washington and his men arrived at Half-King's encampment. Spitz was glad he'd seen the messenger earlier so that the sight of the group of tall, painted men didn't turn his knees to water. He stood with Craik behind Washington and Stephens as they spoke with Half King and heard with chagrin their plans to join forces with this band of twelve Indians, which included two boys, track the French through the night, and attack in the morning. *I wonder if we'll find Captain Hog before the attack or if he's wandering around looking for the French with no idea where we are.*

Spitz heard Half King call Washington a name he didn't recognize and whispered to Craik, "What did he call Washington just now?"

"Caunotaucarius,"[13] Craik whispered back. "It means Town Taker - Half King gave George that name the first time they met."

Spitz nodded his thanks. *No wonder the chief is ready to attack fifty armed French soldiers,* he thought glumly. *He's got an awful lot of confidence in George Washington.*

Despite his reservations, Spitz walked manfully in the company of soldiers through the night, quietly following a score of yards behind a pair of Indian scouts. The air grew cool around him, and he heard the rustling of steps in the trees beyond their force. *Raccoons,* he told himself sternly. *Don't think about bears. Or Frenchmen doubling around us— don't think about that.*

Deep into the wee hours of the morning, one of the Indian scouts circled back to Half King and Washington, who called a halt. Spitz sat gratefully behind the officers and Half King and took the pack off his back. As he listened to them, he absently pulled grass and held it up for Washington's horse.

"One hundred fifty long paces," said the scout, as he pointed in a northwest direction to indicate the French camp. When Washington asked about the guards of the French camp, the scout replied, "Two men watch the ends of the trail. The rest sleep."

The scout continued to describe the place the French had camped, which was a small clearing around a bend in the trail. Where the trail bent, on the left of the camp, and on two other sides, trees surrounded the French. Only the right was exposed and dangerous where the trail widened and fewer trees grew.

"Then I shall lead men to the right as we surround the camp," Washington volunteered. "Stephens, take half your men to the left, and spread the remainder among Tanacharison's warriors."

Spitz puzzled for a moment over who Washington meant until he realized he had used Half King's Indian name rather than the title the English had bestowed upon him. Their plans laid, Washington encouraged his men to rest for a few hours until time for the assault, and Spitz dropped straight to sleep where he sat, leaning on his pack.

He jerked awake, adrenaline coursing through him, when he felt a hand on his shoulder, and he turned to find Craik standing over him, a finger laid to his lips. Spitz nodded, and Craik moved to the next man near. The imminence of the attack lay heavy on Spitz's soul, and he looked up into the stars. A day had passed here in 1754; had a day passed in the twenty-first century? Would that day be his last on earth?

Spitz laid the pack under a tree with his messenger bag on top of it so that he carried only his powder horn, bullet pouch, and patch box on straps across his chest and only his rifle in his hands. Gripping the walnut stock, he searched for Washington. The Lieutenant Colonel, like Craik, moved among the men, waking them and enjoining them to silence.

Dawn lightened the night sky in the east, though no color stained the part Spitz could see between the trees. With about twenty men, Washington was moving to the right, low to the ground. Spitz saw Captain Stephens across from them with the remainder of Washington's forty-man detachment moving carefully to the left, a few Mingo warriors crouched down with them. Leading the other Mingos, Half King followed Washington right and then moved past him. All the men were calm, grim, and silent in the dark woods, moving with the padded stealth of animals.

Washington placed his men and then crouched with them low to the ground, waiting. A rim of orange showed just above the land to the east, though the disk of the sun had not emerged. A bird called, and Spitz jumped, tense. In front of him, Washington knelt unmoving, one hand still and steady on his pistol handle while the other rested curled around the hilt of his sword.

Then the great man stood, drawing his sword and holding it forward, and he bellowed "Charge!" so loudly in that dim and silent wood that the sound echoed in Spitz's ears through the tumult that followed. Spitz ran in Washington's wake, seeing from the corner of his eye that one man spun and fell and another crumpled, clutching a ruined knee. Still Washington dashed forward, unloading his pistol into the French sentry on his side and dispatching with a swift motion of his sword a soldier who had risen to his knees to fire at him.

Spitz moved to the side and fired blindly into the seething circle of bodies. Then he fumbled with the patch and ball and powder he carried, stuffing them down the muzzle of his rifle with the ramrod attached to the barrel. He looked up and saw Washington striding through the fight, whirling with sword in hand, moving like a panther after prey, untouched and unafraid.

Spitz, too shaken and unsure of himself to aim, fired again uselessly. He heard bullets whistle and whine around him, and he heard the shouts of men attacking and the screams of those who were wounded. He stepped forward in Washington's direction, and his foot slipped beneath him on blood-soaked earth, sending him to the ground.

He scrambled up and lifted his rifle, pulling the trigger ineffectually before he remembered that he had not reloaded after his last shot. He poured powder down the barrel, spilling a good bit on the ground, and he dropped two bullets from his shaking hands before he managed to fit the third into the muzzle with a patch and ram it home. He lifted it again to his shoulder, blinking cold sweat from his eyes, and then a cheer rose from the center of the crowd.

"Huzzah for Washington! Huzzah!" one man shouted, and the men who still stood echoed and re-echoed the cry. The rest of the men either lay still forever, or writhed and screamed in pain, or knelt in submission, hands in the air. Craik dashed among the British wounded, seeing whom he could save. As Craik sought to lend aid, Washington and Stephens struggled to bring their still-raging Indian allies under control.

Before they could succeed, Half King, waving his tomahawk wildly, approached the wounded French commander, Joseph Coulon de Villiers de Jumonville. Yelling something about his father, Half King buried his tomahawk deep into the man's skull, ceremonially washed his hands from the flow of the man's blood, and completed the ritual slaying by scalping him. The dramatic scene brought the whole affair to a sober conclusion. Half King was satisfied. He had revenged the death of his father, whom he claimed the French had cruelly killed and eaten.

Once the ordeal was over, Spitz closed his eyes and sank against a tree, feeling weak and ill. Those scalps hanging from Indian tomahawks took on a grim, new reality for him, and he didn't think he'd ever see another one without revisiting the horror he'd just seen. But he didn't have the luxury of indulging his queasiness. He had duties to perform.

Spitz retrieved writing supplies from the pack behind Washington's horse and then sat on a log by Washington and Stephens as they interrogated the French officers and soldiers. Spitz recorded all of their names, ending with that of a thin, sour-looking man who spat his name at Spitz: La Force.

His expedition a success, Washington returned to camp with the majority of his soldiers. He met Captain Hog on the return journey and sent him and some of his men to convey the French prisoners to Williamsburg. Washington had taken twenty-two prisoners, including La Force.

★ ★ ★

Back at camp, Spitz again thought what a slow, grimy, back-breaking business war was, for Washington kept him busy with the rest of the men felling trees and uprooting the stumps in the places where the forest trails were too narrow to admit the wagons on their relentless westward way. At night, Washington dictated letters to Spitz, one of which went to John Augustine Washington, the Lieutenant Colonel's brother.

"I can with truth assure you," Washington said, "I heard bullets whistle and believe me there was something charming in the sound."[14] Spitz marveled over Washington's words as he penned them. Who could find anything charming in the sound of bullets? He raised his eyebrows wordlessly and kept writing.

"Among the dead Frenchmen was their commander, Joseph Coulon, the Sieur de Jumonville, whom Half King claimed to have killed. Among the French officers captured was second in command, Druillon along with two cadets. But the prize catch of the fight was French Commissary, La Force."[15]

When he wrote the name of La Force, Spitz knew that this one man made the raid and all of the trouble and blood it had cost worthwhile. Not only had Washington checked his enemy's advance, he had also disrupted the flow of supplies south from Canada to the disputed territory and so weakened the fort he meant to attack as soon as he had built a road to it.

During the following days, while Spitz built the westward road and penned letters for Washington and wondered when he would disappear back to his hospital bed, the camp swelled with new additions. Half King joined Washington with eighty Indians, some of whom were women and children. A new company arrived with cannons and a meager shipment of food.

Then Captain Hog returned from Williamsburg with additional men and supplies and an important letter. Colonel Fry had died in a chance horse accident, leaving Washington in sole command of the Virginia Army. He was now Colonel Washington, one of the most powerful men in the colony. But the letter contained other news as well. That night as Spitz lay at the mouth of the tent on a bedroll with his rifle beside him, he heard Washington discussing it with Craik.

"Whether I command the Virginia army matters not. These British army officers outrank us all, so that I may be overruled in battle by a mere captain," Washington fumed. "This rule is an insult, both to me personally and to every man who was born in these colonies. It says that King George has taken our measure and found us wanting."

Craik smoked his pipe meditatively. "Has he taken our measure, though?"

"Explain, James," Washington demanded shortly.

"Well, the war here has barely started. He's given colonial subjects no time to prove their quality. Issuing such an order looks not like the action of a ruler whom his subjects have disappointed, but like the prejudice of a king who values one man over another because of his birth," Craik reasoned.

"He does value men so," Washington agreed. "Does he not master an empire because of his own birth? Of course he sees a duke or an earl or a squire as a man of more value than his stable boy. But look you: I am a landed gentleman, and I have proved my worth in arms besides. No British officer, be he from what family he may, need feel shame in naming a rank equal to mine because I am Virginia born. No British officer need feel shame in obeying my orders because the Westmoreland County of my birth borders Chesapeake Bay rather than Lancashire. But my king assumes he will and soothes his pride beforehand, never mind mine."

"Are you careful of your pride, George?" Craik asked slowly. "Do you take offense because he has insulted you—only for that?"

Washington paused. "No—I am not a proud man. But I know my worth. I know that I am fit to command. I rankle at the injustice merely."

"When does the new Supreme Commander-" Craik began facetiously.

"Colonel James Innes, Commander in Chief," Washington corrected.

"Yes, him," Craik said indifferently, "when does he send a proper London-born officer to us here?"

Spitz heard the crinkle of paper unfolding as Washington looked again at the letter. "Immediately," Washington said. "We must look for him at every hour. I only hope for the sake of the men that he brings supplies with him sufficient for us all."

"We reached the end of the flour a week ago, and the men now cannot get enough by hunting so short a time as they do. They grow weak, and sickness comes not far behind weakness," Craik said.

"Dour Scot," Washington said sharply, "I cannot give them more leave to hunt, or my forward progress will halt entirely. I must prosecute a war, not organize a camping expedition. And so they must build the road. If you pity them, pray for manna."

Those words rattled around inside Spitz as he lay back, eyes closed, preparing to sleep. *Pray for manna.* He pondered the old story of the Hebrew nation trudging through the wilderness, moaning to exchange their new freedom for leeks and cucumbers. Back when he'd given such things his attention on a regular basis, he had seen their ingratitude and had shaken his head over it. But now that he was in a wilderness himself, trudging west with an axe in his hand and no food in his stomach, he felt a bit more sympathy. *Pray for manna—no, thank you.*

The next day, Spitz swung his axe at a young birch, sending chips flying from a wedge of raw wood in the white trunk. The summer woods shimmered with heat only partially blocked by the canopy of leaves above. Especially where Spitz worked at the edge of the cleared road, the sun beat down in a brilliant stripe on his bare back, and flies and mosquitoes hummed and whined by the runnels of sweat that trickled down him.

He'd shared a small pot of porridge with Craik and Washington this morning, a pot the size one serving had been when he'd first arrived three weeks ago. When he finished work this evening, he'd take his rifle a few miles into the woods and hope to shoot something. If he failed, he hoped Craik or Washington would succeed so that the three of them would have something to share. Thinking of his evening hunting trip, he stepped aside and let the slender tree fall.

Unbidden, the image of a Sonic cheeseburger with onion rings and a Dr. Pepper appeared to Spitz. He could almost taste them and smell them. Angrily, he set his axe in the birch stump and sighed. *Would it be too much to ask for You to send me back now? I've already seen Washington in battle with La Force. I've even written about it in the journal. Now I'm just hungry and exhausted. Why can't I go back to the hospital and lie down on clean sheets and not think about food? And if I have to stay here, why can't You send me a lousy cheeseburger?*

"Spitz!" a voice shouted in the distance. Angrily, Spitz turned around and saw James Craik, belt cinched tight around his too-small waist, waving for him to come back to camp. Men nearer Craik were walking back along the stretch of cleared road as if a magnet drew them, axes and shovels hanging heavy from their starved limbs. Then Spitz heard something and froze. Something had mooed.

With an almighty wrench, Spitz took his axe from the birch stump and picked up his gun from the ground beside it. He jogged through the loose crowd of men heading for camp, edging sideways or taking the shoulder until he reached Craik at the top of an incline. Craik grinned and pointed down the road at dust rising from the sharp, plodding hooves of sixty beef cattle. "They brought flour as well, and cannon and horses. Cheer up, Spitz lad—you'll get a good dinner tonight, bread and beef, and tomorrow you'll have cavalry horses to haul the trees you cut. The captain's a Scot, too, by the name of MacKay; so I have high hopes of him."

Spitz walked the rest of the way back to camp with a lighter heart, troubled with only a little guilt at the edges. Wasn't this close to a cheeseburger—this steak on the hoof and these bags of flour? And shouldn't he say thank you for the obvious, tangible answer to his ungrateful mutter? The words wouldn't come, though. There was too big a stone in his soul for him to move it over the answer to a mutter.

That night, as he savored a tender, hand-cut, grilled steak that had been munching grass by the side of the road a few hours before, Spitz eyed Colonel Washington and Captain James MacKay. Despite Craik's optimism about having a fellow Scotsman in charge, Spitz could see that the new British officer shared none of Craik's compassion or humor or common kindness. He was barely polite, despite Washington's determined efforts to welcome him and treat him as a gentleman should. Spitz shook his head as Washington made yet another attempt.

"Your men come in good time, captain. My own soldiers grow weak and weary from the work of building a road for resupply wagons. They will welcome the aid of men who have ridden in fresh from South Carolina, especially such strong, able men as yours seem to be," Washington said.

MacKay narrowed his eyes and drew himself up. "My men are trained soldiers, not provincial farmers and trappers. I require them to drill. The project of this road is entirely yours, Washington, and your men may carry it out."

Spitz closed his eyes in annoyance. How dare MacKay separate himself and his men that way? And how dare he address Washington by his surname alone without his rank, as if he were a butler or a tradesman? Spitz didn't know how Washington stood it.

"Surely you see the need of the road, Captain MacKay," Washington prompted. "The French are too far from Great Meadows for us to send sorties to attack them. If we wish to engage them in combat, we must move nearer, and in order to move nearer, we must have a tenable road for reinforcement and resupply."

"I do not see the need of the road, sir, just as I do not see the need to beat my way to the French," MacKay said insolently. "Let them come here. Let them have the burden of the journey. My men and I will trounce them soundly and then march unhindered to occupy their fort without dragging cannon through the forest first to beat them."

"I have sworn to Gist at the western encampment that we make our way in haste to his position," Washington said, carefully calm. "I cannot abandon him to stand alone at Red Stone Creek against a superior force."

MacKay smiled disdainfully. "You will do as you like with your colonial followers, of course, but let us understand one another perfectly. Not one of my men will touch a foot of that road. Not one of their chargers will suffer abuse as a pack animal to build it. You would do well to imitate me and train your men so that they know what to do when the enemy arrives, not busy them with questionable feats of engineering."

Washington bowed. "I give you good evening, captain."

Captain MacKay merely waved his hand without speaking and rejoined his men.

Washington sighed and sat down by Spitz. He nodded at the nearly empty plate. "The beef is excellent fare, but it is dressed with very bitter sauce."

"He sure is proud," Spitz agreed, looking at MacKay's retreating back. "And he's a real pain in the rear, too."

Washington laughed, and then he shook his head and sighed. "Did you hear that his family is quite well to do, and that some of them are admitted at court? I fear that MacKay merely speaks what he hears. You see in him the royal opinion of all the colonies and all the men in them."

"That's a pretty low opinion," Spitz said carefully. This moment was one in which he had to hold his tongue. He couldn't speak like an American before America existed.

"I have heard that the king fancies himself a father to his people. To be seen as a benevolent, loving sovereign is an issue of pride with him," Washington began.

"I've heard so," Spitz agreed. He'd read about King George III, curious about the king so roundly denounced in Thomas Paine's *Common Sense* and in the Declaration of Independence.

Washington frowned. "His daughters pine away in lonely opulence, kept from marrying. His sons idle away their time in no real responsibility, hunting and gambling and dancing. God save us from such a father who would make such children of us."

Spitz said, "Amen," before he realized it. He stood. "If you'll excuse me, Colonel Washington, I'd like another steak. I see Doctor Craik by the men cooking; do you want me to send him to you?"

Washington smiled ruefully and rose as well. "No, thank you, Spitz, for I badly need to walk and to think. I will not suffer my men to hear such abuse from Captain MacKay or his men. I must study what best to do for them."

Spitz watched Washington walk away, fighting his desire to tell Washington what the history books already said. It was maddening, knowing what was going to happen and having to stand by his word of honor not to do anything about it. He remembered his promise to Rawlins not to interfere, not to stand up and act the prophet.

What was especially maddening was that proud Captain James MacKay, with his arrogant sneer and his insulting lack of manners, was actually right. Washington was going to have to stand against the French here, at Great Meadows. And every day he spent on the road to Gist's camp near Red Stone Creek was a day he wasn't spending to build a proper stockade and fortify the trenches that already existed in the meadow.

★ ★ ★

The next morning, Washington announced that his forces would depart immediately for Red Stone Creek, leaving half of them along the way to work on the road. He left MacKay in sole possession of Great Meadows, where Spitz knew that the insolent Scot would drill and ride without building or preparing a thing. Spitz just sighed and packed

Washington's things and marched behind his horse all the way to Red Stone Creek.

And two weeks later, Spitz sighed again when Washington called MacKay and Half King to meet him to fight the overwhelming numbers of allied French and Indian forces on the way to attack him. Spitz waited mute and helpless behind Washington while Half King demanded that the English and their allies retreat to Great Meadows. MacKay agreed with the Indian chief and then refused to help with the retreat at all. Spitz spent a weary morning loading cavalry horses with supplies as if they were traders' mules while the furious dragoons stood by seething to see their fine horses so used, and then he marched by those horses every defeated step of the way right back to Great Meadows.

As he walked, he considered. What would have happened if he'd told Washington what would happen and what he should do to avoid it? Would Washington have listened? He might have, out of politeness and respect, but he would want reasons. He'd want to know how Spitz knew what would happen and why he was so sure. And what could Spitz tell him? What could he offer by way of proof?

He had his crazy-sounding story. *Actually, Colonel, I'm not really here. I'm in a hospital bed in the twenty-first century, unconscious in a coma. And I'm not sure that whatever I do here will make any difference anyway, because it might be an alternate history timeline. But just in case, you should really listen to me and change your entire plan of attack.*

He felt a jolt as something else jarred his memory: his son's Bible. Wouldn't it have a printer's mark from the nineteenth century, when it was printed? He grabbed it and opened it, flipping through the front pages before the text began. He saw no date, not even one in Roman numerals. He checked again—nothing. It had been wiped clean. He stuffed it back into the messenger bag, fuming.

Why did he have to accompany Washington during this ill-fated battle? And why was Spitz so powerless to say anything about what he knew? Then a thought struck him, a new and uncomfortable thought. *God knew that Steve and Nevaeh would die, and He knew how and when. He didn't say anything. Why?*

Spitz considered. How would God have told him? How could He have sent a warning that Steve and Spitz would believe? Spitz considered things like an anonymous letter, an angel, and a voice from the sky, but he would have dismissed anything supernatural as coming from Satan, citing the scripture passage that warned about Satan appearing as an angel of light. He would have thought Satan was discouraging Steve from doing God's work.

*He could have stopped Steve, though,* a stubborn voice inside whispered. *He could have made him sick or broken his leg or done any of a hundred different things to keep my son from getting on that plane in the first place.* He winced at the thought of wishing his son ill or hurt, but he clung mulishly to the thought that it would be for his own good, to keep him alive.

Another voice rose in him, a gentle one. *King George wants to keep his children safe as well,* the voice reminded him. *He wants to spare his daughters the pain of loveless marriage to opportunistic men who only want a connection to the king. He wants to spare them the dangers of childbed. He wants to spare his sons the finality of death in battle, even the exhaustion and risk of truly hard work. His heart is good. He has the power and the means to follow it. Yet you condemn him for confining and coddling his children, keeping them from what they desire, even if it is dangerous. Would you imitate him? Should God imitate him?*

The point hit home, and Spitz could not see a way around it. But he hardened his heart and squared his shoulders against it. *It doesn't matter if I can't reason my way around it; I'm not God. I didn't want to keep Steve from risk and adventure and joy. I just wanted to keep him alive. God should have wanted that, too.*

Spitz lifted his chin and marched ahead the rest of the way to Great Meadows, anger at this celestial trick building in him. Men were going to die, and he was going to have to watch the battle and record it just so that he could prove that God was right to spare Washington.

When he reached the stockade, Spitz looked at the too-small ring of wood planks half begun and the men already scurrying to complete it and shook his head. With McKay's men, Washington's force numbered four hundred. They could not all fit inside, let alone their horses and dogs and beef cattle and munitions. Most of them would remain outside at the mercy of French guns.

Captain Hog saw Spitz looking balefully at the stockade and paused beside him. "Colonel Washington has named the place Fort Necessity. If there is a more apt name, I do not know it."

"It's a necessity all right," Spitz sighed, "but we sure do need a whole lot more than that."

"Come with me; we shall throw our efforts into the earthworks," Hog invited.

Spitz threw down his pack and bag beside pitiful Fort Necessity and carried his gun and shovel to a place Hog directed, where the meadow grew marshy and natural depressions marked the grass. Spitz and a crew of other men dug quickly to expand those depressions into trenches that would shield them from bullets. An Indian ally sent word to Half King and Washington that twelve hundred men were on the way, two-thirds French and one-third Indian. The four hundred British and Indian and colonials allies finished what work they could and then hunkered down to sleep where they had worked.

As they woke early in the morning, rain began to fall, a torrential downpour that turned those trenches into soupy bogs. Spitz noticed that all the Indians had left. Their desertion seemed a grim warning, a notice of their opinion on which side would surely win. The dragoons and Virginia men dug together as long as they could and then abandoned the effort, stacking shovels and picks to the east of the fort and gathering in the trenches to the west, waiting, listening for the tramp of French feet and the rolling of French wagon wheels carrying guns along a newly-built forest road.

Spitz held his gun steady beside Colonel Washington. During the engagement, he would carry orders from Washington to Van Braam and Hog and Stephens and Gist and others; he was Washington's right hand and voice. He even had a horse for the engagement. He kept his eyes steady on the tree line, listening to the roar of rain against the forest ahead of him and the pounding of rain against the stockade boards behind him.

Around eleven o'clock in the morning, the rain stopped, though the sky remained cloudy and stormy, threatening another downpour at any minute. Spitz saw movement in the trees, and suddenly, the woods were full of Frenchmen. Spitz heard orders shouted in French, as well as war whoops that chilled his blood and revealed the presence of a large contingent of Indians.

"Present the captains with my compliments, and order them to form their men in line of battle," Washington ordered Spitz.

Spitz rode off as fast as he could, breathing the orders at top speed to the captains forward near the trenches. As he hurried back to Washington, Spitz heard the barked orders of captains behind him and the stepping and shuffling of men obeying orders. At the stockade, he wheeled his horse around beside Washington and watched the French forming a line at the edge of the trees. Washington and MacKay shared a glance, and both rode forward without waiting for aides-de-camp. Spitz followed them at a canter.

The French fired, and the first volley fell short. The English side did not flinch. The enemy was out of range, as MacKay and Washington must have known when they rode forward so quickly. "Hold fire!" both commanders shouted to the colonials and British regulars. Spitz echoed them and then caught up to Washington, who with narrowed eyes and flared nostrils watched the French line advancing. The French stopped. "To the trenches!" Washington shouted.

Riding furiously, Spitz took up the call and heard it passed down the line. The line of English soldiers took a step back and hunkered into the long, soupy holes. Only their hats and guns barely showed above the coarse meadow grass. Atop his horse, Spitz envied them the protection. In comparison to the submerged English line, the mounted officers and French soldiers looked like marked targets.

The French, however, suddenly dropped to the ground, took cover behind rocks and trees, and opened fire. Instead of torrential rain, French and Indian bullets now whizzed through the air and began to shower the British. In short order, the French had killed nearly all of the British livestock, horses, and even the dogs. The fight had just begun, and the English had already lost their primary means of provision and transport, as well as their beef. Grieving in his heart for them, Spitz watched the animals fall. To slaughter them all seemed such a terrible waste. Then a shot pierced the breast of his own horse, and he scrambled free of it before it pinned him. It rolled and kicked, snorting, and Spitz lowered his rifle, shooting it through the eye. After the animal shuddered and lay still, Spitz looked murderously toward the French lines and the anonymous marksman who had forced his hand.

"Fire only at the heads you see!" Washington shouted, and Spitz ran the word down the line on foot, shouting himself hoarse. Shots rang from the English trenches, and finally Spitz saw French soldiers fall. He began to cheer. Then more heads took the places of the ones who had fallen, and Spitz saw others waiting in the woods, which seemed an inexhaustible supply of Frenchmen. No matter how many they killed, more were coming, and more behind them.

And British and colonial soldiers were falling, too. As he fired at a French head and reloaded, Spitz saw the numbers of English slumped or howling in the muddy trenches. If the fight continued longer, the larger French force would overwhelm Washington's men. *We're all going to die. How can we avoid it? I don't remember reading about this fight being such a bloodbath. How does Washington escape? How do I?*

Thunder rumbled overhead, and rain poured down again, even more fiercely than before. Spitz pulled the trigger of his rifle, and nothing happened. His powder was wet. All around him, he heard a few last shots and then a series of ineffectual clicks. Everyone's powder was wet. The French powder was evidently wet as well, for no more shots rang from the trees.

Feeling water soak his clothes and watching the light fade through the sheet of rain as evening drew near, Spitz waited anxiously through the rest of the afternoon. He wondered when the tension would break and the French and Indians would rush in force from the woods, hatchets and swords and bayonets raised aloft to extinguish the much smaller force ahead.

Then three riders emerged from the woods, one carrying a flag of truce. They stopped midway between the forces and waited. Washington and MacKay and Van Braam rode to meet them. The party of six spoke for some minutes, and then all six men rode to the British side and dismounted. The rain finally stopped. Spitz rode forward to listen and arrived in time to hear MacKay's proud voice say, "We shall both discuss the terms of the surrender."

So it was over—and only because of the rain.

Spitz listened to the officers on both sides arranging details. The British would leave the next morning, surrendering their cannon and the stockade to the French. A small detachment would guard anything the British could not carry away. Only a few of the British officers still had horses alive; the British marching home would send for their personal possessions later. A troop of them would return, escorting back to the French lines the prisoners Washington had taken during the raid on La Force and claiming the British hostages that the French were taking now in order to ensure the exchange.

The terms were more than fair; they were generous. Still, Spitz could see that the loss of this first command galled Washington, who spoke with courteous deference to the officers sent by Louis Coulon de Villiers, the commander of the French forces still waiting in the woods and the brother of Jumonville, whom Half King had killed during the raid on La Force. From the pains the officers took over the negotiations, De Villiers seemed preoccupied with the exactness of the terms of surrender, determined to show himself a gentleman who was above backwoods massacres like the one he considered Washington to have ordered.

As Spitz lay down to rest that evening after the last French officers had departed carrying the signed capitulation, he drew out his calfskin journal again. He looked at the page he had written at Frazier's trading post and then looked ahead at the blank pages left to fill. He saw the title he had written so lightly the first time he opened it: *Signs, Mercies, and Interpositions of the Invisible Hand.* He was supposed to record those signs and mercies and protections, he knew. But his heart was full of too much happening. Spitz had helped to bury men today. He had seen Washington humbled in defeat. He had been afraid for his life. Where should he begin? What should he say?

"There you are, Spitz," Washington said, appearing at Spitz's side and sitting down easily on the damp grass. "I had wondered where you were. I thought that you might have left already."

"Left you, sir? I hadn't planned to leave," Spitz answered.

Washington looked carefully at him. "The terms of your service are not official. You are not an enlisted man claiming any pay or any land. You may leave my service when you choose, and as I am soon leaving the colonial army, I release you from any attachment to me."

"I'm sorry to hear that you're leaving the army," Spitz said. "I think you make a great commander."

Washington's eyes dropped. "Your words are kindly meant, I know, but I have proved myself a poor commander this day. I have much yet to learn. I shall finish the business attendant upon this defeat, and then I shall return to Ferry's Landing and farm my land. I should not neglect my inheritance." Washington's hand strayed to Spitz's journal and tapped a blank page. "You write a journal?"

Spitz nodded. "I'm afraid it's a neglected journal. I haven't written in it very often while I've been with you."

"You must cultivate the habit," Washington encouraged him. "It will greatly aid your memory, as well as augmenting your powers of observation and reflection. I have kept a journal from my youth, as my mother taught me."

"I will, sir," Spitz promised.

Washington smiled briefly. "Then I shall leave you to write in peace. And I thank you with all my heart for your willing and effectual service. I shall be glad to advance you in any way within my power if ever you need call upon me." He rose to his feet as he spoke, and then he walked away. Spitz saw him find Craik, and the two of them wandered into the darkness, deep in conversation.

Spitz turned his attention back to the journal. He had seen and noted signs that God had advanced Washington particularly. He had seen and recorded a mercy, where God had spared Washington. And now he was sure he had seen an interposition where the invisible hand had reached down and shielded Washington in a way that seemed miraculous, every bit as miraculous as the frozen Allegheny last time he had entered the past. Spitz listed that favorable interposition after the few notes he had already made.

**Sign 2**—Through Governor Dinwiddie's favor, God placed Washington in a senior position of leadership, an unusual responsibility for a person of his age. Washington was promoted to Lieutenant Colonel, second in command of the army.

**Sign 3**—For purposes of testing and encouragement, God presented Washington with an early opportunity to prove himself and was granted a small victory over the French. For leadership and character development, Washington faced the threat of a potential engagement with an overwhelming French force. He handled the depleting supply of provisions, the death of his immediate commander, and the frustrating, unaccommodating arrogance of the British officer, Captain James MacKay.

**Mercy 5**—Starvation avoided by the arrival of sixty head of beef cattle and flour brought to Washington's camp by the Independent Company headed by MacKay.

**Favorable Interposition 2:** The heavens opened, and the invisible hand drenched the battlefield at Fort Necessity, dampening the gun powder and quieting the French and English guns. The result was a peaceful escape from insurmountable odds.

Spitz looked over what he had written, and he blotted it carefully to preserve it. The leather messenger bag had kept both books he carried dry, even in the miraculous heavy rain. He put away his writing supplies and pillowed his head on the bag containing his journal and Bible, quieting his mind and trying to send himself to sleep.

*What else do You want to show me? Washington is going home defeated. He's just dismissed me. Why am I still here?*

And then, in the space of a breath, he wasn't.

# Chapter Five

*"What if he did this to make the riches of his glory
known to the objects of his mercy, who he prepared in advance
for glory?"—Romans 9:23*

hen Fort Necessity disappeared around Spitz in the now-
familiar swirling tunnel of stars, he became aware first of the
characteristic hospital smell of strong antiseptic and stale food. Then he
realized that he was once more blind and weak and trapped: a prisoner
in his old and ailing body. *Well,* he thought ruefully, *I did ask to leave.*

But a welcome sound consoled him: the sound of Aspen's voice. He
listened to her talking without paying attention to the words until one
comment brought him up short.

"I've been coming to see Papa for a week now, and he's still only
stable. Are you sure he'll be okay?" Aspen worried. *Only a week,* Spitz
thought, incredulous. *I was with Washington from May 27 to July 3 of
1754. How did those months turn into just a week?*

"Nobody knows anything for sure, sugar," Angela said. "That's why
we need faith."

Aspen sighed wearily. "I wish I had some. I've been worrying."

"Why are you worrying? What's happened?" Angela asked gently.

"I—I went to the grocery store yesterday after work, and I saw a
cashier I recognized." She paused. "It was a store near our house. Papa
and I both go there a lot. The cashier asked about Papa, and I told her
what had happened." Aspen paused again, unwilling to say more. Spitz

could guess the cashier, a thin, talkative, middle-aged woman who collected neighborhood news like a squirrel building a winter hoard.

"Did she scare you, sugar?" Angela prompted softly.

"She said that three days is really important—after three days in a
coma, the brain probably isn't going to recover. Her aunt was in a coma
after a stroke, and she died," Aspen said.

"That's not true for everybody," Angela corrected, her voice warm
with compassion. "I've read case studies of people who woke up after
months, even years."

"I spent the rest of the evening on the Internet, looking up symptoms
and prognoses. It was so scary, all the things that could go wrong. I had
nightmares about it," Aspen confessed.

"You know," Angela began, "when I was in college, I read a spy story
about parallel universes for my English class. I don't remember all of it
now, but it put into my mind the idea of infinite possibilities. I finished
reading that story and sat at the desk in my dorm room just paralyzed by
choice. What if I go out to the student union right now and meet someone
who changes the course of my life? What if I don't go, and I miss meeting
that person? What if I go to the student union while the other person goes
to the library, and we miss each other? There were so many choices out
there and so many possible futures stretching out from each one that it
seemed like I could ruin the rest of my life just by lifting my little finger."
Spitz heard her chuckle a little. "I couldn't decide what to do."

"What did you decide?" Aspen asked.

Angela said, "I called my mother and told her about what I'd been
thinking, and she calmed me down. She was so kind, but she helped me
see how foolish I'd been. She reminded me of what Solomon says. A man
can choose his way, but the Lord directs his steps. That's what calmed me
down—knowing that whatever way I chose, the Lord would watch over
me and direct me. I can't make a mistake big enough that He can't turn it
around and use it for good."

Aspen took Spitz's hand and held it gently. "How can you be sure,
though? When such terrible things happen around you to people you love,
how can you be sure that He's directing their steps? The night Papa had the
stroke, he was really angry. He read something to me from Washington's

Inaugural Address about God's invisible hand shaping America, and he was really angry that the same hand didn't save my parents."

Spitz felt Angela rest her hand on the Bible at his side. "Do you know the passage in Hebrews eleven that people call 'The Hall of Faith'?" she asked Aspen. Aspen must have shaken her head.

"No," Aspen answered, "I haven't been to church in years."

"The pastor who wrote to this Hebrew church wanted to comfort them. The members were being tortured and murdered because they were Christians," Angela answered. "All of them had lost family and friends, and they were terrified that the authorities would come for them next. They needed comfort. And here is part of what their pastor told them: 'Now faith is the substance of things hoped for, the evidence of things not seen,'" Angela quoted.

Aspen was quiet. "It's hard to connect those words to faith—substance and evidence."

"It's hard, but it's true," Angela told her. "And after their pastor told them so, he gave them some evidence. It's all in the rest of the chapter: story after story of people who held tight to faith in the middle of war and flood and wandering. And after all of those stories, the pastor brought it right back to the people sitting in front of him. He mentioned the tortures their mothers and husbands and children had suffered in the same breath with people they had read and heard praised for years. It was his way of telling them, 'Do you see how these famous people suffered? And now you see the end of the story, the one God meant for them all along. Well, God is writing a story about you, too; so don't you give up in the middle of it. All of those folks you know are cheering you on, waiting and watching for you to finish well. Reach out your hand to God and trust that your story will be just like the ones you've always heard.'"

"He didn't promise them they wouldn't be killed, though," Aspen said. "And you're not promising me that Papa will be well, are you?"

"That's not my place, sugar," Angela said. "All I can promise you is that God is good, and what He sends us is good. I can promise you that the end of all the stories is beautiful. And I can promise you that if you reach your hand in faith to God, He will help you to bear whatever happens to you and the people you love."

Aspen was quiet. She still held Spitz's hand. "It sounds like the notes to the sides of Papa's books about the Founding Fathers. He kept asking, 'How do they know? Why are they so sure?' But that's the point, isn't it? The people who survived the war all had the same evidence. They could look at it and say, 'That was luck,' or they could say, 'That was God.' But they said whatever they said because of faith. That's how they knew. That's why they were sure."

"And it's so hard in the middle of danger or sickness to look at your trouble the way you will at the end of it," Angela said. "I know it's hard to sit here in front of your Papa and understand how to feel, because you don't know the end of the story yet. Are you standing in front of a man who's going to recover and come back to you, or not? That's so hard, sugar, and my heart goes out to you for it."

"Thank you," Aspen said, already withdrawing.

"But you can do it," Angela pressed. "And if you will leave the outcome in God's hands instead of worrying about it, you'll realize that what you do right now will be the same no matter what happens to your Papa."

"What do you mean?" Aspen asked.

"Just think with me for a minute. If you knew that today was the last time you would see your Papa, what would you do right now? What would you tell him?" Angela asked.

Aspen squeezed Spitz's hand tighter. "I would tell him I love him with all of my heart. I would tell him thank you for giving up his life and the travel he loved and the job he enjoyed to raise me. And I would tell him that I'll be okay. I would tell him not to worry about me. He always worries about me."

"Now think harder, Aspen. Suppose that I'm going to call you this afternoon and tell you that there's been a miracle and that your Papa is up walking around and asking for you. What would you tell him right now?" Angela asked.

"I would tell him to hold on; that he's going to get better. I would tell him that I can't wait to talk to him again. And I would still tell him that I love him and I'm grateful for what he did for me." Aspen paused. "It's almost the same; I see what you mean."

"You're already giving your Papa every chance to be well. You called the ambulance and got him to the hospital as soon as you could. You come to see him and talk to him every day. We're taking good care of him here. The rest is in God's hands. We won't change what happens to Spitz whether we wring our hands and cry and worry over everything on the Internet or whether we ask God for calm and reach our hands to Him in faith. And which one do you think will do you the most good?"

"I know," Aspen agreed. "I know it doesn't do him any good for me to worry."

"Don't let me hear again that you're losing sleep, Aspen. You leave all of the worrying to the only One who can do anything about it," Angela ordered.

"I'll try," Aspen promised.

"Now I'm going to leave and check on my other patients so that you can talk to your Papa alone," Angela said. "I'll see you tomorrow."

"See you," Aspen told her, and Spitz heard the door close. Aspen was still holding his hand. "I meant all of those things I said, Papa, and I wish I'd said them earlier. Did I tell you thank you sometime when you heard me? Do you know how much you mean to me?"

Spitz wanted to reassure her. He knew he was loved. He knew she was grateful.

"If I didn't, I'm telling you now. I see you look at all the things you collected. Sometimes when I come into the library to talk to you, I'll see you staring at a mask or a clay pot or a statue, and I know you're thinking about where you got it and the life you used to have. I'm really sorry that you had to give it up for me," she told him.

*Don't worry about me, hon. I had a nice, long run at business, and I knew what I was doing when I stepped away from it. The retirement wasn't your fault. You've got no call to feel a bit bad about it.*

"I guess I'll have to put up some shelves of my own when Bill and I get back from Indonesia," Aspen said. "I'm going to start collecting things now, like you and Daddy did."

Spitz panicked for a moment. What was this about Indonesia? Why would she go there, of all places?

"Bernie got final approval from the corporate office today, and Bill's been communicating with the offices overseas to plan our itinerary," Aspen told him. "I'm looking forward to the plant tours and especially the mining tours, but I'm a little nervous about all the flights. I don't think you'd blame me. Sometimes I'll be on one of those puddle jumpers, the tiny ones, or maybe even a helicopter."

Spitz's blood ran cold. *Don't take her, too,* he pled. *Don't let her go there.*

"But then I remember that you were on one, too, and you were okay. Right before the funerals, you took the same kind of plane that Daddy and Mama did, and yours didn't crash. So there's no reason to assume that mine will," Aspen reasoned.

*I beg You not to let her go,* Spitz wanted to shout. *I'll give You anything; just keep her safe.*

"I can't believe I'm finally going to the place where their plane crashed. I sure hope we can find the actual crash site. I've been thinking about it for years and wondering if it holds any answers for me. I wonder if I'll feel more like they're watching me there, like they see who I am now. And Bill will be with me, which will be very nice. I told you I had dinner with him on Saturday. He's such good company. You would really like him. He's so confident about everything that I can't believe anything bad would happen to him. And as long as he's safe, then so am I."

Spitz stopped. Aspen really liked this man. She really trusted him. He'd never heard her talk about a man this way before. And if they both went away together and didn't come back—he couldn't fathom what a loss that would be. It seemed doubly painful to think of Aspen losing her life when she had finally found someone she might begin to love. Spitz's demands and pleas seemed to curl into a little ball of hurt inside him. He could do nothing to stop his only family from putting herself in danger.

"I've got to get back to work, Papa. Bill's been really nice to cover for me so that I can take a little more time with you, but I don't want to take advantage. Here's the Bible beside you." Spitz felt Aspen move his hand to rest on it and brush a kiss on his forehead. "I would like to think that you wouldn't mind if you knew. I'll see you tomorrow!"

The door opened and closed, leaving Spitz alone with his thoughts. They weren't very good company right now.

*Why do You always have to take from people who trust You? Everyone You draw to You loses by it. Look at Your disciples, hunted and tortured and murdered one by one. Look at the early church, and every man who came before it in the Old Testament. Can You blame me for looking at You the way I do? Angela stopped before she got to the part of Hebrews that I never understood before, the part that haunts me now: "For our God is a consuming fire."*

He thought the verse like an accusation, hurled it heavenward like a javelin with all of the anger inside him. *I don't trust You, and if You take her, too, I'll set myself against You. Forget the case. I'll use every day I have left to tell people the truth about who You are and what You do. I don't need any more evidence. I had all I needed seventeen years ago.*

"Knock, knock," Ed Campbell said in his high, thin voice. Spitz heard the chart clipboard slide out of the plastic holder on the door and then back in. "Mr. Spitzen—I remember you," the hospital chaplain said amiably, "Roman numerals in the Bible. You'll be happy to know that I've brought my own today. I'll let you keep yours right where it is."

Vinyl creaked and whooshed as Campbell sat down. The man sighed. "I tell you what; it's good to take a load off my feet. This hospital isn't the biggest one in the world, but it feels that way sometimes, with all of these miseries crammed together inside four walls. I get tired of seeing the fall every which way I turn some days. If I didn't know that God had it all in hand, I'd up and quit. But you know. Any man with a Bible like that one probably knows more than I do," Campbell chuckled to himself.

*You bet I do,* Spitz thought angrily. *I know what He's really like. You'd be better off quitting now.*

"Let's see," Campbell said, and Spitz heard pages rustling. "I suppose something I need to hear will be good for you, too. I think I need to hear the very end of the book, when it's all over, what's waiting for us. Someday He's going to roll the curse right away off this planet, and I'll be out of a job, praise God. Here we are—Revelation 21."

Campbell cleared his throat. Spitz tried not to listen.

"And I saw a new heaven and a new earth: for the first heaven and the first earth were passed away; and there was no more sea. And I John saw the holy city, new Jerusalem, coming down from God out of heaven, prepared as a bride adorned for her husband. And I heard a great voice out of heaven saying, Behold, the tabernacle of God is with men, and he will dwell with them, and they shall be his people, and God himself shall be with them, and be their God. And God shall wipe away all tears from their eyes; and there shall be no more death, neither sorrow, nor crying, neither shall there be any more pain: for the former things are passed away. And he that sat upon the throne said, Behold, I make all things new. And he said unto me, Write: for these words are true and faithful."

The man's voice quavered at the end, and Spitz heard his Bible close with a soft whump. "If you don't mind, Mr. Spitzen, I'd just like to sit with that passage a minute and let it soak in." Spitz heard him lean back in the chair.

But beyond any other sounds around him, Spitz heard that command to write as if a voice, low and urgent, commanded him personally. *Write,* it told him, *for these words are true and faithful. Write—I am true and faithful. I am. You must write.*

★ ★ ★

On the breath of that command, Spitz found himself once again snatched from the four plain walls around him to hurtle through a tunnel of stars. He kept his eyes open this time to watch the spiraling brightness around. It dazzled him. When it released him and shimmered away, he found that he was walking through a wild and overgrown wood composed of thick-boled oaks and beeches and maples. A narrow, winding track led northwest, parting the most tangled shrubs and vines. The whole place looked familiar to him. He moved some outstretched tendrils and branches aside as he followed the trail. He knew from his frontier clothes and rifle that he was in the past again to meet Washington, but he didn't know where or when he was exactly. He knew from the oppressive heat that it was summer again. A few persistent rays of late afternoon sunlight shone to the left of him, a little in his eyes. He put up a hand to block them.

He heard horses on the trail ahead of him and considered hiding in the underbrush to see who would pass by. But then he heard two men speaking English, and he decided to stand where he was. If they were English, then maybe one of them would know where Washington was. They had the advantage of him, though, as the sun that blinded him also illuminated him for them.

"Spitz?" a man said.

"That's me," Spitz confirmed. He stepped forward a few paces out of the light. "Colonel Washington," he said gladly, recognizing one of the horsemen. "I'm very glad to see you again, sir." He walked to the side of Washington's horse, where Washington shook his hand.

"As am I, Spitz, though I am no longer a Colonel; I have resigned my commission," Washington told him. Spitz thought that he looked thin and gaunt. His face burned with fever, and coughing interrupted his words.

Spitz eyed the military jacket and brass-buttoned waistcoat Washington wore. "You sure don't look like a civilian. Maybe it didn't take."

Washington laughed, bringing on another spasm of coughing. "I am aide-de-camp to General Braddock on his campaign to take Fort Du Quesne. I serve him as a private person, as you served me, in hopes that I will 'attain a small degree of knowledge in the military art: and believing a more favorable opportunity cannot be wished than serving under a gentleman of his Excellency's known ability and experience.'[16] Forgive me, Lieutenant Frazier," Washington said to the other horseman. "You may remember my former aide-de-camp, Stephen Spitzen. I saw him last almost exactly a year ago quite near here, when we all quit Fort Necessity." Washington's ears burned as he named the site of his great defeat, but he spoke with no other sign of embarrassment. "Spitz, the man beside me has been promoted and is now Lieutenant John Frazier. He owns land nearby, and he, too, serves General Braddock as part of his military family, though in an official capacity."

"I'm glad to see you again, Lieutenant Frazier," Spitz nodded, his heart sinking. He was headed straight into the teeth of another defeat, a bad one this time in which most of the casualties wouldn't be horses.

"And I you," Frazier said. "What brings you here, sir?"

"I suppose I'm a summer soldier," Spitz said. "I'm just fortunate I've run into my old commander. Do you have room for another gun in your company?"

"I would be very pleased to add you to the party of Virginia troops serving with the regulars," Washington offered, shuddering with chills while he mopped fever sweat from his temples with a handkerchief. "I am sure you will recognize several of their faces."

Frazier began to ride ahead, and Spitz walked beside Washington's horse on his way to the camp. "Forgive me, sir," Spitz said to Washington, "but you don't look too well."

Washington frowned. "I am somewhat recovered, but I have suffered from camp fever this last week. General Braddock ordered me into a wagon for some of those days, but happily, I am able to sit a horse once again."

"I'm glad you're better, sir," Spitz told him. Privately he thought that Washington didn't look like he was well enough to be anywhere close to a battle. "I'm curious, sir; didn't farming suit you?"

"It does suit me, Spitz, as does military life. 'I have now a good opportunity, and shall not neglect it, of forming an acquaintance, which may be serviceable hereafter, if I can find it worthwhile pushing my fortune in the military way.'[17] Unhappily for me, nations wage war in the same season when farmers sow crops. I cannot do both at once," Washington told him.

"So you chose the military," Spitz added.

"For the present I have," Washington agreed, "though the choice pains my mother. To persuade her that the God who shielded me in the past would do so again was a hard task. I cannot blame her; for any mother to send her child into danger is a test of faith."

Spitz thought of Aspen, and his heart sank. He looked up and down the trail. "By the way, where's the rest of the army?"

"We ride to meet them," Washington said. "The army is encamped scarcely ten miles from the fort, on the western bank of the Monongahela; we employed the majority of the day in crossing the river."

Suddenly Spitz remembered a passage in the biography of Washington and understood why he was coming from the direction of the French fort. A delegation of Indians allied with the French had asked to meet with Braddock, who had sent Washington and Frazier in his stead. The Indians had proposed that Braddock give the vastly outnumbered French garrison time to evacuate Fort Du Quesne, leaving it in British hands with no shots fired. But Braddock had refused. He had wanted a decisive British victory that would leave the French in no doubt as to who controlled the southern trade route and the fort that guarded it.

Spitz grimaced again over the frustrating position of knowing what was going to happen and being unable to do anything about it. Washington rode beside Spitz confident that he delivered Braddock welcome news of a way to avoid war. But Braddock would refuse it, and by this time tomorrow, Washington would be one of a thin minority of officers who survived the day.

*Why did You do this to him? Why did he have to endure yet another defeat? What possible reason could You have for allowing this blood-bath?* Spitz demanded angrily. No one answered, but Spitz read the silence: *Wait and see.*

Soon Spitz and Washington and Frazier arrived back at camp, and Washington dismounted, throwing his reins to a hard-faced man with iron-grey hair who was dressed in linen breeches and shirt and waistcoat. "Thank you, Bishop," Washington said, coughing and shaking again. "Lieutenant Frazier, I shall join you directly in General Braddock's tent."

Frazier agreed and left, walking to a tent a little larger than the others, the tent toward which Bishop was leading the horse Washington had ridden. Washington gestured for Spitz to follow him.

"The Virginia men camp apart from the British regulars; sadly, there is no love lost between them," Washington said quietly. "From here, you will see a stand of three maples by the riverbank. The colonial men are by it. Present yourself to the officers, and no doubt you will find a warm welcome." Washington's eyes twinkled with a kept secret. "I must report to General Braddock, but I will come to see you and the others before I retire."

Washington walked away toward Braddock's tent, weaving a little in his weakness, and Spitz wended his way through the rows of British infantry tents between him and the Virginia encampment. Men sat in front of their tents, some mending uniforms or cleaning and oiling guns, and others playing cards or taking long, melancholy pulls from metal flasks. None spared more than a passing glance for Spitz in his obviously colonial clothing.

The stand of trees grew nearer, and finally Spitz saw a complacent sentry leaning against one of the smaller maples, smoking a pipe and whittling, his rifle leaning beside him against the tree. The man nodded at Spitz and waited for him to speak.

"I'm Stephen Spitzen. Colonel Washington sent me," Spitz said, forgetting Washington's resignation.

"Aye - he is Colonel Washington right enough, no matter what

Dinwiddie decides," the sentry said slowly. "I know you. You served him at Great Meadows."

"I did," Spitz answered, "and I've come to serve him again. I'm supposed to go to the officers."

"Straight through to the riverside," the man answered, pointing the way with his knife.

Spitz thanked him and edged through the tents of the colonials. Hands rose in greeting from nearly every campfire, and a few men he recognized from Great Meadows stopped him to pass the time of day. Finally he came to a tent by the riverbank where he saw two very familiar faces.

"Spitz!" James Craik exclaimed. "I am heartily glad to see you again."

"You, too, Doctor Craik," Spitz said happily. "And Mr. Gist - you're here, too."

"That I am," Gist answered. "Washington assured me I was necessary to the expedition."

"Does George know that you are here?" Craik asked.

Spitz nodded, setting down his pack and leaning against it by the fire. "I met him along the trail. He said I'd find a warm welcome with the Virginia officers; I'm assuming he meant you two."

"Well, then we must make you welcome," Craik said. "Have you eaten? We have the remains of a fat trout and some tea by the fire."

"Thank you, Doctor Craik," Spitz said, unearthing a pewter mug and plate from his pack. Craik served him fish and tea and chatted to him about the adventures of the expedition so far. Washington had recommended Craik to Braddock, and now the Scot was the general's personal physician.

Once Spitz had finished his meal, he left to wash his dishes in the river. When he returned to the fire, Washington was there, and Craik was speaking sternly to him.

"Just a tincture of Echinacea, licorice, thyme, and feverfew," Craik was saying. "It will relieve your discomfort measurably, George. I urge you strongly to reconsider."

"None of your philters and potions for me, James," Washington said. "I have a strong constitution, and I mend well without them." Another bout of chills shook Washington, and Craik eyed him disapprovingly.

Then Washington saw Spitz and rose to his feet. "Ah, Spitz—I see that you have found our mutual friends."

"It was a pleasant surprise to see them, sir," Spitz told him, stowing his dishes in his pack, "almost as pleasant as seeing you again."

"Thank you, Spitz," Washington said, inclining his head. "You come in good time, as before. We have only a few hours' march in the morning to the fort before we engage the French." *So,* Spitz thought ruefully, *Braddock has forced the hand of the French.* "And this time we have the advantage of superior numbers. General Braddock is well prepared to mount a siege, once Colonel Dunbar finishes the road and arrives with the larger cannon and the remainder of the men and supplies. But without them, we number fourteen hundred men. The garrison at the fort is drastically smaller."

"Never underestimate the accidents of war, George," Gist admonished him. "We do not know what troops may be arriving by boat even now to swell their numbers. And the Ottawa and Ojibwa allied to them are especially fierce fighters. They spoil your odds."

"I have studied the thing, Christopher, and I cannot see how Braddock can escape victory," Washington declared. "It is certain. The general has been a good and wise teacher for me; the battle tomorrow will be merely another lesson."

"Have you asked General Braddock about the advance column? Shall we move ahead and scout for you?" Gist asked.

"He has declined, preferring that we preserve our strength together so near the fort." Washington rose again, mopping his forehead with his handkerchief. "I must attend Braddock, friends. I will look for you in the morning."

They all bade him good night and then settled down to sleep for the evening. Out of habit, Spitz checked the messenger bag for his journal and Bible. Craik saw the books and looked sharply at Spitz. "You carry a Bible with you? They are so rare and precious. I did not look to see one in the hands of a frontiersman who must wade through rivers and climb mountains and suffer all manner of weather in the open. Why is it not in a library or a church, where it will be safe?"

Spitz looked down at it and decided to tell as much of the truth as he could. "My child put it into my hand before I left her and asked me to keep it. I couldn't refuse her. The leather bag is pretty well waterproof; it survived the rain at Fort Necessity."

"As long as it is here and not in a library, read it to us, Spitz. We may as well all profit by your child's gift," Gist suggested.

Spitz took it out of the bag and held it in his hands. He had not opened it to read it, or any other Bible, since Steve's death. He looked up at Craik and Gist, who watched him expectantly. He quickly found the book of John and began to read.

Men at the nearer campfires heard his voice and recognized the words he spoke, and they quietly moved closer. Word spread, and more men gathered at the fire. After the first chapter, Spitz looked up and saw dozens of men in every direction, all silent, all listening. One at the back of the crowd called, "Lift your voice, man!" Nods rippled through the crowd.

Spitz looked at the men and realized that many of them would not live another day. To grant them this one request on their last night in the world felt like the smallest easing he could provide, the least comfort in his power to offer. He began the second chapter.

He read the miracles and the parables and the betrayal of Peter and the passion and crucifixion of Jesus. He read the resurrection and the restoration of Peter, right through to the end of the book: "And there are also many other things which Jesus did, the which, if they should be written every one, I suppose that even the world itself could not contain the books that should be written. Amen."

Spitz closed the book and put it away in his bag. Then the men who had gathered to hear him dispersed to their own fires, calm and gratitude on their faces. Spitz lay down with the leather bag under his head and closed his eyes. Those faces, so comforted by Scripture, accused him with their quiet faith. In the morning, those men would step into eternity on the strength of that faith. He could no longer say with any peace that he would do the same. He did not sleep well.

Early in the morning, Spitz woke and shared a pot of porridge with Gist and Craik. Then the men cleaned their dishes, packed their gear, and put out their fire. The other Virginians did the same. The whole company of Virginia soldiers assembled into a loose line to follow the British regulars. Craik clapped a hand to Spitz's shoulder. "I must go ahead to join the general's family of followers with George. Will you join me there, or would you rather fight with Gist?"

"I'm coming with you, doctor. I'd like to be of some use to Colonel Washington, if I can," Spitz said. He wrung Gist's hand as he left and wished him good luck. Spitz couldn't remember from his research whether Gist had survived the day or not.

Three miles—the figure ran through Spitz's mind like a hunted rabbit dashing for a hole, zigzagging crazily through his thoughts. Braddock's army had camped ten miles from Fort Du Quesne, and the history books reported that the ambush happened seven miles from it. Three miles— that's all some men had left.

One mile from the riverside camp, the woods had enclosed the army completely. The men walked four abreast on the wider sections of the trail, but keeping any kind of regular ranks was difficult with underbrush and low-hanging branches crowding the track and snatching at clothes.

Spitz braced himself. Surely they had walked two miles by now. He looked up at Washington in front of him, riding straight and strong behind Braddock. Spitz walked and walked, jumpy as a cat, ears straining for any odd sounds. And now it must be nearly three miles. Surely they had walked three miles by now. Where was it? Where was the ambush?

A terrifying chorus of whoops sounded from the woods on both flanks of the line, and then gunshots fired, hitting men who spun and sprawled or crumpled and fell. Spitz brought his rifle up and fired a shot, and then he looked for Washington. Washington raced his horse through the press of men to the front of the line, while the Virginia troops took to the trees to fight like the French and their Indian allies.

In horror, Spitz watched an English captain form his troops into a line and shoot blindly into the trees. Some of the shots hit men whom Spitz knew were colonial soldiers, and some of them may have hit Washington's horse, which soon fell to its side, screaming and kicking. Washington jumped free of the wounded animal just as another shot reached the side of its head. It lay still.

Spitz ran toward Washington, though he could no longer see him clearly in the melee. He ran into the trees like the other colonials, using the butt of his unloaded rifle to push away the bodies in front of him. Then he saw Washington swinging into the saddle of another horse; the officer who had been riding it lay dead on the ground. Washington raised his sword and called, "Hold your ground, my brave fellows, and draw your sights for the honor of old Virginia!" He shouted something Spitz could not hear to another officer, a major, and then he wheeled his horse around and dashed to the rear of the lines again.

Spitz retraced his steps, following him. Washington shouted back and forth with Braddock, who waved his hand emphatically towards the front of the lines. Washington nodded and spurred his horse in the direction Braddock had indicated. Winded and sure that he would never catch Washington's horse, Spitz let him go and continued running toward Braddock.

"Spitz!" a man called, and Spitz searched until he saw Craik waving an arm at him. Spitz ran to him. As soon as he was near, Craik shouted, "The wounded—get them back here, as many as you can!"

Spitz ran forward again and grabbed the first man he saw lying on the ground, straining to heave him over his shoulder in a fireman's lift. Another man hit him on the arm and shouted, "Leave the dead!" Spitz looked into the empty eyes and let the body go. He ran only a few steps more before he saw a man in a red coat rolling on the ground clutching a bloody leg with bullet holes in it. Spitz seized the man around the middle and got his shoulder under the man's arm, which he lifted, heaving the man upright on his good leg. Tottering under the weight, Spitz helped the man hobble back to the lines where Craik was.

Craik glanced up at him and shouted, "Get another!"

Spitz looked hopelessly down the forest trail, which seemed carpeted with the red jackets or buckskin leggings of fallen men. His heart sank. How could he possibly rescue so many? He put his head down and ran forward, looking only down, sorting in seconds those beyond hope from those he could help. He found another man with a bullet in his side and pulled him up, supporting him as he gasped and clutched his side and walked as fast as he could.

Spitz hauled wounded bodies and stepped over dead ones until his arms hung heavy and burning beside him and his lungs screamed for air untainted by smoke and the stench of wounds. Washington appeared only in glimpses. Still weakened by his illness, he tried valiantly to remain tall and straight in his saddle. Part way through the battle, Spitz saw

Washington commandeering yet another horse—two had been shot out from under him. Spitz shook his head in disbelief and reached for yet another hand upraised in a plea for rescue.

He took the man back and laid him in the line waiting for the army surgeons. Then he heard a piercing cry—"General!" He whirled around to see Braddock fall off the side of his horse onto his back. Two men, one of them the faithful Bishop, supported him to the rear of the line, where Spitz saw Craik kneeling over him. *It cannot be long now,* he thought. *Surely the French will leave soon. Braddock has fallen wounded. This is all supposed to end.*

Spitz looked for Washington again and saw him bellowing orders at the red-coated men who still stood. Eyes blazing with anger, he gathered them into a semblance of order and led them back. Once he reached Braddock, he knelt by the general and spoke with him, and then he began issuing the orders attendant on a retreat. Men wheeled cannon into place and aimed them down the track. Grapeshot exploded in the distance.

Spitz looked back at the forest trail, dim even in the daylight, and the same disgust and anger that Washington evidently felt rose in him. Indians wielding hatchets knelt over prostrate men. Soldiers in French uniforms ransacked baggage and bodies. *It's a waste, a terrible waste.* He turned his back on that waste and marched southeast, back to the Monongahela and beyond, toward Dunbar's trailing column.

As he marched, he remembered the faces of the men who had listened to him reading the night before, peaceful in the firelight. He remembered a story he had read to them—the story of Lazarus sealed in his tomb and Jesus weeping. One pastor who had preached that story years ago had said that Jesus wept in anger at death. Spitz thought of the look on Washington's face as he'd led the British survivors off the forest trail. People who had seen Jesus beside his friend's tomb said, "He can do miracles; why didn't he save his friend?" Spitz thought that was a valid question. Jesus had said he'd allowed the death so that all the people around the grave could see the power of God.

Spitz disagreed. *Wouldn't it be better if there weren't any death in the first place? Couldn't those people have seen the same power if You'd spoken a word where You were and healed him from far away, like the centurion's servant?*

*No,* a voice whispered, *they wouldn't have seen power over death. They would have seen chance, circumstantial and deniable. They needed to see power over death.*

*You don't care about people's deaths,* Spitz accused. *Never mind the tears.*

That insistent voice inside said, *I raised him. I brought him back.*

Stubborn and angry, Spitz thought: *What about all those men lying in the trail back there, then? Are You planning to raise them, too?*

Quiet and sure, the voice answered: *I already have.*

★ ★ ★

Spitz stayed with the army until it reached Fort Cumberland, setting up camp each night with Craik and Gist and Washington, who had rejoined his friends once Braddock had died of his wounds. Because Washington was not an army officer, he had no responsibilities toward the British soldiers.

As they travelled together, Spitz saw genuine affection and respect between Washington and his fellow Virginians. Of the three companies that had fought, totaling one-hundred fifty men, less than thirty men survived. General Braddock's personal servant, Thomas Bishop, the hard-faced man with the iron-grey hair, had joined the Virginians, too, attaching himself to Washington. Spitz was relieved to see someone insisting on caring for the still weak and sick Washington.

On July 18, over a week after the sound defeat, the body of the army arrived at Fort Cumberland. Here Washington planned to part from the army. Dunbar was intent to march them to winter quarters in Philadelphia, while Washington planned to return home. One colonial officer stationed at the fort ran straight to Washington as soon as he saw him.

"Colonel Washington—you live! I had been sadly assured you had died," the man said.

"I am as you see me," Washington replied. "From whom did you hear such a tale?"

"From a wagoner with you all who saw the battle begin; he swore he had seen your body and heard your dying words. We heard his tale and encouraged him to send an official report to Colonel Innes, so that he could inform your family," the officer said. "I rejoice that he was mistaken."

Washington grimaced. "My poor family - I must write them to ease their worry." His weary glance fell on Spitz, walking by his stirrup. "What say you, aide-de-camp? Will you write for me, as you once did?"

"Yes, sir, Colonel," Spitz agreed readily. He helped Bishop unpack Washington's writing supplies from his horse, and then he followed Washington to the quarters prepared for him, leaving Bishop to stable and feed the animal. Washington sank heavily onto the rough bed, exhausted from days of marching and fighting through illness. Spitz sat at a table beside the bed, quill and inkpot and blotter at the ready.

The first letter Washington wrote was to his younger brother John Augustine. "He has agreed to care for Mount Vernon and Ferry's Landing in my absence. I must inform him that the charge is not permanent."

"As I have heard since my arrival at this place, a circumstantial account of my death and dying speech, I take this early opportunity of contradicting both, and of assuring you that I now exist and appear in the land of the living by the miraculous care of Providence, that protected me beyond all human expectation; I had 4 bullets through my coat and two horses shot under me, and yet escaped unhurt. We have been most scandalously beaten by a trifling body of men; but fatigue and want of time prevents me from giving any of the details till I have the happiness of seeing you at home."[18]

As Spitz finished writing the letter Washington dictated, Thomas Bishop entered the room with a Virginia soldier, both carrying Washington's personal baggage and weapons. "Thank you Bishop, Gibbs. Do you stay long at the fort, Gibbs?" Washington asked the Virginian.

The man shook his head sadly. "I'm headin' for Turkey Knob as soon as may be. Neighbors of mine are widows and orphans now, and it falls to me to tell 'em. God help me."

Washington soberly sent his condolences by the man, who left imme-diately. He looked sadly between Spitz and Bishop and then passed a hand over his face. "To know that so many brave men have departed this life because of the rank incompetence and cowardice of others is scarcely to be borne. Their deaths weigh heavy upon me." Spitz waited patiently, watching Bishop arranging his new master's shaving kit by the pitcher and wash basin provided in the room.

Finally Washington composed himself. He next wrote his mother, assuring her of his safety. Spitz remembered Washington's words the evening before the battle about Mary Washington's worry for her son. Of course he wished to set her mind at rest as soon as he could.

"As I doubt not but you have heard of our defeat, and perhaps have it represented in a worse light (if possible) than it deserves; I have taken this earliest opportunity to give you some account of the Engagement, as it happened within 7 miles of the French Fort, on Wednesday the 9th...In short the dastardly behavior of those they call regular's exposed all others that were inclined to do their duty to almost certain death; and at last, in despite of all the efforts of the officer's to the contrary, they broke and run as sheep pursued by dogs; and it was impossible to rally them.

"The General was wounded; of which he died 3 days after; Sir Peter Halket was killed in the field where died many other brave officer's; I luckily escaped without a wound, though I had four bullets through my coat, and two horses shot under me; Captains Orme and Morris two of the Generals Aids de Camp, were wounded early in the engagement, which rendered the duty hard upon me, as I was the only person then left to distribute the General's orders, which I was scarcely able to do, as I was not half recovered from a violent illness, that confined me to my bed, and a wagon, for about 10 days; I am still in a weak and feeble condition; which induces me to halt here, 2 or 3 days in hopes of recovering a little Strength, to enable me to proceed homewards."[19]

Once he had finished and addressed the letter to Mary Washington, Spitz hesitantly asked Washington, "I saw the horses shot myself, at least one of them, but I don't remember your coat and hat. I suppose I was so angry about the ambush that I didn't notice details that day. Would you mind if I saw your coat and hat?"

"Bishop," Washington called, "the coat and hat which I wore the day of the battle and retreat are in the larger of my trunks. Fetch them here to me, if you please."

Bishop opened the larger trunk which the Virginian Gibbs had carried into the room from one of the wagons. "I could scarce believe my eye when

I saw them, sir. Six bullets clean gone through the fabric, with nary a stain of blood by a one of them. It is God's own hand, sir, as has shielded you."

As the servant laid the coat and hat on the bed, Spitz looked quickly at him. He had used those same words, God's hand, to describe the protection of Washington. Spitz ran his hand over the holes, even putting a finger through one in the breast. "Incredible," he breathed, imagining the coat flying open in the breeze made by the horse's running and a bullet whistling so near the beating heart of the man next to him, who was wholly unwounded.

"I mean to mend them for you, sir, but I am afraid that the work will show," Bishop said.

"No, Bishop," Washington said quietly. "I wish to leave them as they are for a testimonial to the dangers through which I have passed and the watch care of Providence in the midst of them. I am well aware that I have been protected 'beyond all human expectation.'[20] I wish to remember that protection materially. Lay them in the trunk again if you will."

Bishop obeyed, and then he took Washington's boots from the foot of the bed and began to polish them. The noise of the brush and cloth against the leather made a pleasant, homey backdrop to the sound of Washington's voice as he dictated the next letter, this one to Governor Dinwiddie.

"We continued our March from Fort Cumberland to Frazier's (which is within 7 Miles of Duquesne) without meeting with any extraordinary event, having only a straggler or two picked up by the French Indians. When we came to this place, we were attacked (very unexpectedly I must own) by about 300 French and Indians; our numbers consisted of about 1300 well armed men, chiefly regulars, who were immediately struck with such a deadly panic, that nothing but confusion and disobedience of order's prevailed amongst them: The officers in general behaved with incomparable bravery, for which they greatly suffered, there being near 60 killed and wounded. A large proportion, out of the number we had!

"The Virginian companies behaved like men and died like soldiers; for I believe out of the 3 companies that were there that day, scarce 30 were left alive: Captain La Peyroney and all his officer's, down to a corporal, were killed; Captain Polson shared almost as hard a fate, for only one of his escaped.

"In short the dastardly behavior of the English soldiers exposed all those who were inclined to do their duty to almost certain death; and at length, in despite of every effort to the contrary, broke and run as sheep before the hounds, leaving the artillery, ammunition, provisions, and, every individual thing we had with us a prey to the enemy; and when we endeavored to rally them in hopes of regaining our invaluable loss, it was with as much success as if we had attempted to have stopped the wild bears of the mountains.

"The General was wounded behind in the shoulder, and into the breast, of which he died three days after; his two Aids de Camp were both wounded, but are in a fair way of recovery; Col. Burton and Sir Jno. St. Clair are also wounded, and I hope will get over it; Sir Peter Halket, with many other brave officers were killed in the field. I luckily escaped without a wound though I had four bullets through my coat and two horses shot under me.

"It is supposed that we left 300 or more dead in the field; about that number we brought of wounded; and it is imagined (I believe with great justice too) that two thirds of both received their shot from our own cowardly English soldiers who gathered themselves into a body contrary to orders 10 or 12 deep, would then level, fire and shoot down the men before them.

"I tremble at the consequences that this defeat may have upon our back settlers, who I suppose will all leave their habitations unless there are proper measures taken for their security. Col. Dunbar, who commands at present, intends so soon as his men are recruited at this place, to continue his march to Philadelphia into winter quarters: so that there will be no men left here unless it is the poor remains of the Virginia troops, who survive and will be too small to guard our frontiers."[21]

When Washington had finished dictating, Spitz said, "I saw you gathering the regulars and leading the retreat, Colonel; I saw how angry you were at the bloodshed. It really did seem like Braddock had every reason to win, didn't he? And it was just like you said: panic and cowardice everywhere among the regulars. How could God have let so many men die like that?"

Washington looked thoughtfully at Spitz before he answered. "I have been considering the work of Providence in the ambush and retreat since the day it occurred. What can I say of my own condition, alive and unhurt when even my uniform declares that I should be shot and scalped and left for dead? 'It's true, we have been beaten, most shamefully beaten, by a handful of men! Who only intended to molest and disturb our march; Victory was their smallest expectation, but see the wondrous works of Providence! The uncertainty of human things! They only expected to annoy us. Yet, contrary to all expectation and human probability, and even to the common course of things, we were totally defeated, sustained the loss of everything; which they have got, are enriched and strengthened by it.'"[22]

"Pardon me, Colonel, but I have a hard time seeing that defeat as the hand of God," Spitz said bitterly.

"Come now, Spitz," Washington corrected him, "this mulishness ill suits you. Whose hand should it be but His to spare one and strike down another when reason cannot find an explanation? Do you not see Him in the pages of Scripture standing on the side of those who are overwhelmed? Consider Abraham, when his nephew was taken from him by the kings of the plain. Did he not take only three hundred eighteen men to rescue Lot from the hand of those kings and win? Think you such a victory came from his arm alone? Or remember Gideon with his three hundred men against the whole army of Midian. Could only three hundred prevail against thousands without the aid of God? Think of David, who stood alone against the giant Goliath. He did not boast, as the giant had. He said, 'This day the Lord will deliver you into my hand.' Was not the victory he won the work of God? Did not these men stand and say, 'God has fought for me?' The hand of God, swift and strong and sure, moves where He wills it and does as He pleases. Who are we to question Him?"

"You trust Him, then, even when He fights for the other side?" Spitz asked.

"Whom else shall I trust?" Washington asked in return. "If I am confirmed in any belief by this misadventure, it is in the might and wisdom and mercy of Providence. We may not judge Him by our own lights, for we are sure to judge amiss."

Spitz fell silent. He put the address Washington had given him on the letter to Governor Dinwiddie and then waited for Washington's instructions.

"This defeat has proved a lesson indeed, though not the one I thought to learn," Washington mused after a while. "I will never again look alone on the numbers balanced in an engagement to predict the victor. Three hundred upon one side and fourteen hundred upon another—these numbers described the forces at both Fort Necessity and outside Fort Du Quesne. I have been on the side of the lesser numbers and the greater, and I tell you that God alone chooses whom to honor."

"Will you write another letter, sir?" Spitz asked.

"No, Spitz," Washington answered. "Now that I lie down with four stout walls about me, I find that I can rest. But you have not told me what you will do now that the battle on the frontier is halted."

"I'm afraid I'll have to be going soon," Spitz answered. He had a lot to write in his journal, and then he had a feeling he would be back in the hospital.

"Bishop accompanies me to Mount Vernon on the orders of his former employer," Washington said, smiling sadly at his servant, who paused in his polishing.

"As I am very glad to do," Bishop said warmly. "General Braddock was ever a solicitous man. On the eve of battle, he drew me aside and pointed to Colonel Washington and told me: 'This young man is determined to go into action today, although he is really too much weakened by illness for any such purpose. Have an eye to him, and render him any assistance that may be necessary.'"

"I shall be grateful always for the General's kind care of me," Washington said. "And you obeyed him well. You found another steed for me when the first had been shot."

"I was very happy to do it, sir," Bishop said. "And I obey him still. As he lay dying, Braddock grasped my hand and said, 'Bishop, you are getting too old for war; I advise you to remain in America and go into the service of Colonel Washington. Be but as faithful to him as you have been to me, and rely upon it the remainder of your days will be prosperous and happy.'[23] I have done so, and I trust the old general has provided well for me."

"Can I persuade you to accompany me to Mount Vernon, as Bishop does? I have need of more than one overseer at present. I can readily find employment for a man as keen and able-bodied as you are," Washington offered.

With a wrench, Spitz declined. "It's kind of you, sir, but I'm … not my own master at present. I have some obligations to fulfill before I can enter anyone's service."

"I take my leave of you, then, with a welcome for you at any time you are at liberty to accept it," Washington said.

"I thank you, sir," Spitz told him warmly. "And I hope to see you again soon."

Spitz gathered his pack and rifle and messenger bag and left Washington to Bishop's care. He walked out of the front gates of Fort Cumberland troubled and weary. The memory of the near massacre still haunted him. And so did Washington's faith. Spitz didn't know when God planned to send him back to the hospital or what he would hear when he got there. But to listen to Washington declare so certainly that God was firmly in control even in a defeat had bothered him.

*Is that what You expect of me? If I hear that Aspen's plane went down in Indonesia while I was in 1755, do You expect me to thank You for it and say that You knew best all along? Do You expect me to bring up Abraham and David to prove how right You are? I'm not going to do it. I can't.*

Spitz walked through the intense summer heat, seeking the shelter of the woods nearby. At their edge, he sat down and opened his messenger bag, taking out the calfskin journal and writing supplies. He set the ink-pot carefully in the grass and trimmed his quill with the knife at his belt. He placed the blotter ready on his knee. Then he looked over what he had written before.

*Even in defeat, You do him good,* Spitz thought. *It's a shame You don't do the same for everybody who trusts You.*

Then he began to write.

**Sign 4**—God intervened in Washington's training and growth through a new sponsor and mentor, General Braddock, the British North American Commander-in-Chief. Providentially, the close

association with Braddock provided Washington with the chance to learn how to function as a commander-in-chief.

**Mercy 6**—God spared Washington's life during the near massacre of Braddock's column by the French and Indians. As Washington said, "I now exist and appear in the land of the living by the miraculous care of Providence that protected me beyond all human expectation."[24]

There was **ample evidence** to prove Washington's assertion: 1) the eye witness reports by people like Doctor Craik and Thomas Bishop, 2) the physical evidence of six bullet holes in his two souvenirs from the battle, his bullet pierced coat and hat.

Spitz carefully blotted the words and closed the book. Then he stoppered his ink bottle and wiped his quill on the grass. He put everything carefully into the messenger bag with the Bible.

That Bible—it had been open every time he left the past. It had been with him every time he left the present. Would it work for him if he just opened it?

He drew it out and opened it a crack at random, holding it at arm's length and wincing. Nothing happened. He let out his breath and looked at it. He opened it all the way and lifted his face to the sun, thinking as hard as he could: *I'm ready to go back—send me now.*

He was still standing at the edge of a wood a few miles from Fort Cumberland in 1755. He sat down again. What should he do? Was he supposed to go back to the fort and ask to go home with Washington?

He didn't think so. He sat back down against the tree, fuming, the Bible still open on his lap. *All right, I give up. I'll just stay here, I guess,* he groused. Late afternoon sun fell on the page and opened a way through the pages to the swirling tunnel of stars that carried him away.

# Chapter Six

*"Listen to my words: 'When there is a prophet among you, I, the LORD, reveal myself to them in visions, I speak to them in dreams.'"—Numbers 12:6 NIV*

"So tell me your greatest concern during this site visit," Bill asked Aspen, putting his phone down on his new desk and leaning back in his new chair. "We've listed several goals, but I think that we ought to have one overarching purpose that ties them all together."

Aspen considered the trip itinerary Bill had emailed her earlier. "Honestly, beyond any concerns about efficiency or modernization and growth, my primary concerns are worker safety and the environment. I want to make sure that our clients understand how important mine safety and plant safety and the protection of the environment are to investors. I don't want to leave the impression that high profits are the bottom line, no matter the cost."

"I'm behind you there one hundred percent," Bill said. "It would be so easy to come off as a pair of insensitive Americans demanding more and more. So worker safety and the environment—that'll be our underlying theme to every conversation. It should fit nicely under the umbrella of sustainability."

"Of course," Aspen said, her mind wandering again. Planning this trip had felt in some ways like an echo of that long-ago trip from which her parents had not returned. She wondered now what her parents had said to each other about the welfare of the various indigenous groups which populated the large island of New Guinea they were going to visit.

"Are you thinking about the crash site?" Bill asked kindly.

Aspen marshaled her attention and smiled at him sheepishly. "No, not this time—I'm sorry I've been so distracted lately."

"I can understand why," Bill told her. "I'd be distracted, too. What were you thinking just then? You were frowning."

"I was thinking about the native population," Aspen answered seriously. "We're concerned about working conditions, and my parents were concerned about souls. I was wondering what they thought about the people they visited. I was wondering what they said to each other about the living conditions and how people in the States could help improve them."

"I'm pretty sure I know exactly what they said to each other," Bill said confidently.

"How could you possibly know that?" Aspen asked warily, assuming that she was being set up for a joke.

"Because I see you, and what concerns you," Bill answered seriously. "People tend to look like their parents, as much as they might fight against the idea. Even though you only knew them for part of their life, I'm sure they left their mark on you. In fact, you probably look more like your parents than most people because you never had a chance to rebel against them."

"Huh—I wonder," Aspen said. "I wonder how much of them rubbed off on me."

"I'm actually amazed at your attitude, Aspen," Bill said, shaking his head. "Do you know how many people in your situation would harbor ill-feelings toward the natives the missionary team visited and project those feelings of loss and abandonment on to the Pribumi? And here you are worried about them and wanting them to be safe. That's rare."

"The Pribumi," Aspen echoed. "What does that word mean?"

"It means 'sons of the soil' and refers to groups of people within Indonesia which share a common heritage and culture," Bill explained. "It's a respectful way to address the natives of the country."

"I'm not anything special," Aspen said, blushing. "It never occurred to me to blame the natives for the crash; even as a kid I never thought my parents' death was their fault. Papa never blamed them, and if my parents could talk to me, I know they wouldn't blame those people for what happened to them. I wish I knew what else they would tell me, though."

"I can tell you that they would be glad you care about the welfare of the people they left home to serve. You're probably a lot like them," Bill said.

"I wonder about them a lot, especially my mother. Sometimes I think I'd give anything to be able to talk to her again. She's missed so much of my life already. I wonder what she would think of me now, of who I've become," Aspen mused. "I know it's silly, but I've hoped for some kind of a message from the crash site—a last letter or something."

"I hope you find it," Bill said, "or at least some kind of a connection. Do you think that anyone there would remember your parents?"

"I doubt it," Aspen answered sadly. "They were only there for a week seventeen years ago. I don't know why anyone would remember them."

"You never know," Bill said. "Sometimes a person makes an impression on you that you can't explain. Did your grandfather meet anyone who remembered them when he went to Timika?"

Aspen shook her head. "I'm sure that Papa was in no frame of mind to question people in the hills about the details of the crash site. He did tell me that he saw a few native people in town, though. He said that they reminded him of Native Americans."

"I can see how they would," Bill answered. "I've seen pictures online."

"You know, before Daddy died, I begged and begged for him to join this YMCA group with me; it was called Indian Princesses. It was supposed to help fathers and daughters understand each other and communicate. Our motto was 'friends always.'" Aspen smiled ruefully. "You know, I only wanted him to join because some friends from school were joining with their fathers. I never felt like Daddy didn't understand me or needed any help talking to me."

"I'll bet you're glad now, though, that you joined that group with him. Those must be some special memories," Bill said compassionately.

"They are," Aspen agreed. "We had to choose a clan animal, and Daddy chose eagles because of a Bible verse he liked."

"They that wait upon the Lord shall renew their strength; they shall mount up with wings as eagles; they shall run, and not be weary; they shall walk, and not faint," Bill quoted. He grinned at the surprise on Aspen's face. "My mother loves that verse, too. It's framed on her living room wall."

"That's the one," Aspen said, touched. "That's the verse Daddy liked."

"So he chose an eagle for your clan name?" Bill prompted.

"Yes," Aspen said, "and then he named me Singing Eagle because I was always running around singing back then. He used to tease me that my life was an opera."

"What was his name?" Bill asked.

"It was Running Eagle, and if you had known my dad, you'd know how well that fit him," Aspen said thoughtfully. "He didn't do marathons or anything; it's just the way he was. He had this unlimited supply of energy. He was always busy with something, and he was always up for an adventure. I think he made the Princesses group more fun for a lot of the dads, because he was always excited about the hikes and the trust exercises and the relay races. Whatever the leaders suggested, he thought it was the best thing ever."

"He sounds like a great guy," Bill said. "It's a shame you didn't get to grow up with him."

"I miss him," Aspen said quietly. Then she managed a small smile and said, "But at least I had Papa. Papa even joined the Indian Princesses for me."

Bill laughed. "I'll bet that wasn't a huge sacrifice for him, the way he likes to hunt and fish and camp. If you'd asked him to join a Disney Princess club, you might have gotten another reaction."

Aspen laughed with him. "You're right—Papa would have drawn the line at a tiara."

"So what was Papa's Indian name?" Bill asked, still smiling.

Aspen grew serious. "It was Soaring Eagle, because of his job. Before Daddy and Mama died, Papa was a corporate executive in a multinational company. He used to fly all over the world for his work. You should see his library sometime; he has souvenirs from every place you can imagine. And right along with all of those pieces of art, he still has his Indian headdress from our YMCA campouts."

"I'll bet you have yours, too," Bill said gently.

"I only ever had a feather for my ponytail, but I wore a cute leather vest," Aspen remembered. "At the campouts, we'd all dress up like Indians and compete one tribe against another at all kinds of games, like obstacle races. The winners earned rabbit furs as trophies. But the best part of each campout was the grand council. We would parade to the council site beating our tribal drums. Each tribe was made up of about six to ten pairs of fathers and daughters. Because Papa was older than the rest of the fathers, they all elected him chief. Once all the tribes were assembled, about a hundred people, I suppose, the camp leaders would invite the Great Spirit to join the grand council, and they'd light a huge bonfire. Then the chief of the nation, Papa, would tell the Princesses and their fathers a sacred story that taught a lesson at the end. Papa told the best stories."

"Speaking of your Papa," Bill said, looking at the time on his iPhone, "it's nearly lunch time. Why don't you knock off a few minutes early so you can spend a little longer with him?"

"That's really kind of you, Bill; I think I will go now. Maybe when I come back, I'll be able to concentrate a little better," Aspen smiled.

"Man, I hope not," Bill teased. "How am I going to learn all of the family stories if you've got your mind on your work?"

"I like talking to you, but I know I shouldn't be taking time at the office to revisit old memories," Aspen said. "When I come back, I've got to make some phone calls."

"You know what that means," Bill said mischievously. "If we're not going to talk at work, I'm going to have to take you out to dinner again."

As Aspen gathered her coat and purse, she blushed and smiled. *Papa, I wish I could tell you about this. You'd be so happy for me.* She looked up at Bill, still smiling. "I wouldn't say no to another dinner."

★ ★ ★

Spitz was moving, and he was upright. His eyes were still closed, but he didn't feel as blind as he had been. He suffered a confused moment in which he didn't know where or when he was, and then he heard an elevator ding. He moved forward again; something bumped him. *Wheelchair,* his mind supplied. *I'm in a wheelchair going into an elevator, and the bump was the gap at the threshold.*

A sick swoop in his stomach told him that he was going down. Another ding sounded, followed by the scraping whoosh of elevator doors opening. He moved, jolting over the threshold again before the rubber-tired wheels found the smooth, slick tile of the hall and whispered the rest of the way along it.

Someone was pushing him, someone who wasn't speaking to him. *So it's not Aspen or Angela,* Spitz thought. *I hope it's not Irene. I'd really rather not hear all about how terrible my life as a vegetable is going to be.*

He felt sunlight on his face, regular sunlight interrupted by bars of shade—windows. *I'm out of my room; I'm in a hallway with windows,* he thought exultantly. After so long lying still in a bed in the same room, being in a hallway seemed like a luxury. And the windows: what would they show him? If he could manage to open his eyes, what could he see?

He concentrated all of his willpower on his eyelids. *Open,* he commanded them. How many years had they worked flawlessly, and he hadn't appreciated the miracle of commanding them? He wouldn't make that mistake ever again. *Open,* he thought again, even more forcefully.

They obeyed.

Spitz drank in the color and movement and shapes around him. He was headed into a cafeteria filled with people colored marvelously, gorgeously varied shades of brown and cream. He loved them all instantly, because they fed his starving eyes that had seen nothing for weeks. *You're beautiful, every single one of you,* he thought. He felt as if he could weep. Even the loose scrubs of the nurses and the garish paint on the walls and the out-of-fashion clothes of the visitors were miraculous to him. They were there. He could see them.

His eyes felt dry; so he closed them again. And then he panicked in case he couldn't get them open again. But they opened and closed at his command again. Some synapse had begun firing that hadn't worked before. He could blink. If someone had told him a month ago that he'd be thrilled that he could blink, he'd never have believed it.

"Hey, Angela," a deep voice said. The speaker sounded as if he had sinus problems; his voice was thick. He was behind Spitz, pushing him; so Spitz couldn't see him.

"Hey, Michael—thank you for bringing Mr. Spitzen down," Angela said.

Spitz saw her for the first time. She was tall for a woman, and strong-looking. If she wore any makeup on her brown skin, Spitz couldn't tell. She was wearing rose-colored scrubs, and her hair was pulled into a twist at the back of her head. Her face reflected the compassion and encouragement and intelligence Spitz had heard in her voice. Right now, Spitz didn't think he had ever seen anyone as lovely.

"No problem, Angela—it's one of the new wheelchairs; so you shouldn't have any problems wheeling him back," Michael said.

"I'm sure he'll appreciate being out of that hospital room; won't you, Spitz?" Angela said, finally looking down. She paused and fell to her knees, looking intently into his eyes. "Michael! His eyes are open! When did his eyes open?" Angela asked, excited.

"I don't know," Michael said, coming around to the front of Spitz's chair to see. Michael was a short, stocky man with light brown hair in a buzz cut and an unfortunate goatee. "They were closed when I put him in the chair."

"He blinked! He blinked while you were talking!" Angela rejoiced. "Oh, Spitz—Aspen is going to be beside herself! You can blink!"

Spitz felt proud of himself, despite the smallness of the achievement. *That's right,* he thought. *I blinked. I did it.*

"Can you blink when I tell you to?" Angela asked.

Spitz concentrated and deliberately closed his eyes.

Angela clapped her hands quickly and then clasped them. "Okay, Spitz—try this one. Blink twice in a row. Let me see you."

Spitz tried, but closing them twice in a row was hard. Doing anything fast was hard. He tried again, and he tried again, several more times. Finally, he got it. He could blink twice.

"Oh, Spitz, that's wonderful; that's just wonderful!" Angela praised him. "I'm so proud of you, and I'm so happy for you, too!"

"Do you want me to take him back to his room and call a doctor?" Michael asked. "Maybe he should get checked out."

Spitz blinked wildly, panicked. He didn't want to go back to his room when he'd just gotten out of it. He didn't want to miss seeing his granddaughter. He didn't want to start the battery of tests that would no doubt begin as soon as he returned to his room.

"I see you, Spitz," Angela said, putting a gentle hand on his arm. "I'm going to assume that all that blinking means that you don't want to go back. Blink just once for yes if I'm right."

Spitz calmed himself and blinked once, purposefully.

"Once for yes—good," Angela encouraged him. "Now let's work on no. Do you want Michael to take you back to your room? Blink twice for no."

Spitz focused on making his eyelids obey him: two blinks.

"Wonderful!" Angela said, patting his forearm happily. "Michael, he'll be ready for tests in about an hour. You can let someone know. But I want him to have lunch with his granddaughter first; he deserves a reward for all of that hard work."

Spitz beamed gratitude at her from his barely working eyelids and motionless face.

"Angela!" Aspen's voice called from a few feet away, "what are you so excited about?"

"Aspen, you'll be so happy!" Angela called back. "Your Papa just blinked at me!"

Spitz heard running, and then Aspen appeared, crashing to her knees in front of him. "You can blink, Papa? You can really blink?"

Slowly and carefully, Spitz lowered his eyelids and raised them once.

Aspen clapped her hands, laughing gleefully. "You did it, Papa—you blinked!"

"That's yes—that one blink," Angela said, beaming at her. "Now watch this. Spitz, say no."

Spitz blinked twice.

Aspen and Angela, both kneeling on the floor, laughed and cried and hugged each other, and then Aspen stood up and hugged Spitz. "You're getting better, Papa! You are! You're going to be okay! I just knew it!" She wiped happy tears from her face.

"He can talk to you now, you know," Angela said. "He blinks once for yes and twice for no. Go ahead—you can ask him anything with a yes or no answer, and he can tell you what he thinks."

Aspen thought. "Papa, while you've been unconscious, have you heard what we've been saying? Do you know what's been happening?"

Spitz first blinked once, and then twice, and then once again. He knew some, but he had been wandering in time for long stretches. He hadn't heard everything she'd said to him.

"I think that's too big a question, Aspen," Angela said. "Try again, something simple with a yes or no answer."

Aspen began to smile. "Do you remember the YMCA group, Papa? Do you remember the Indian Princesses?"

Spitz wondered what had brought that up, but he blinked once, slowly, for yes.

Aspen beamed at him. "I was just thinking about that group today, Papa, and remembering how much fun we had together. I was telling Bill about it." She stopped. "Do you know who Bill is? Have you heard me talk about Bill?"

Spitz blinked once: yes.

Aspen picked up his hand and held it, her eyes shining. "That means that you did hear me, at least some of the time." She looked at Angela. "He heard me. You were right. He was listening when I talked to him. Thank you so much—I don't know how to thank you."

"Keep talking to your Papa," Angela smiled. "That's all the thanks I want."

Aspen sighed happily. "Papa, I have so much to tell you that I don't know where to start. I'm just so happy that you're here and that you can respond to me. I've been so scared, and now I can talk to you and know you hear me. It's more than I ever thought I'd have again."

Spitz blinked once to agree with her.

Aspen's eyes popped open wide. "Indonesia—have you heard me talking about Indonesia?"

One blink said yes.

"Are you upset with me for going?" Aspen asked, worried.

Spitz blinked twice.

Aspen squeezed his hand. "I know you're worried, though."

Spitz blinked once.

"I'm worried, too, you know. I'm scared about how small the planes over there might be. And I've never ridden in a helicopter; that scares me, too," Aspen confessed.

Spitz blinked once.

"I feel like I have to go, though. I don't know if I can explain it well, but I feel like there's a missing piece deep inside me that I'll only find again over there. I have to see the wreckage, what's left of it, anyway, and I have to try to make sense of things. Does that make any sense?" Aspen asked, frowning.

Spitz blinked once. *But there aren't any answers over there, hon. I know what you want to find, and it doesn't exist. I wish it did, though. I wish it did for you.*

"Bill's coming with me. I'll be really glad to have his company." Aspen blushed. "We're going out to dinner again this weekend. I know you haven't met him yet. Do you mind that I've been going out to dinner with him?"

Spitz blinked twice. Then he blinked twice more. He kept blinking.

"That's clear enough," Angela said dryly.

Aspen laughed.

Spitz enjoyed that lunch with his granddaughter like he hadn't enjoyed anything in a while, even though he was still motionless and propped in a wheelchair. He drank in the sight of Aspen, safe and smiling, chatting happily to him about the good changes in her office. She wasn't staying as late anymore. She wasn't bringing work home at all. She wasn't worried over any more nebulous chats with Bernie about her work load.

And Spitz noticed something else, too, now that he could not speak. He remembered the tone and drift of dinner table conversations between the two of them before his stroke. When Aspen had talked to him like this before, laughing and telling him stories about her day, he had only half listened. While she had worked all day at her office, he had been studying all day in the library, and he brought the gloom and resentment of his case with him wherever he went. It stopped his ears against her cheerful anecdotes and shortened his replies.

But now that he could not read and could not speak, he thought only of Aspen while she spoke. He brought no thorny academic questions to this table, only gratitude that he could see and that the person he most wanted to see in the world was right in front of him. The glow of that thankfulness warmed and relaxed him so much that he wished he could smile.

After Aspen had to leave, promising to come over again after work, that thankful glow carried Spitz through the round of examinations with his doctor, a thin, Asian man who radiated calm and assurance. Through blinking, Spitz correctly answered that he remembered his name and address and the year and the President of the United States. He only got one question wrong: the month was November now, not October.

He listened to Angela arranging with the doctor to take him outside in the afternoons, and he was glad. For the past weeks, he'd relied on hearing and smell to tell him where he was and what was happening to him. He was more than ready to smell something besides hospital air and hear something besides beeps and intercoms—especially now that he could see again, too.

After the examination, Michael accompanied Angela back to Spitz's room, and the two of them together lifted Spitz into his bed again. Spitz's eyes followed Angela until he caught her eye as she leaned over to tuck the Bible beside his arm. Carefully, he blinked twice.

Angela frowned and leaned her head to the side. "You don't want the Bible?"

Spitz blinked twice and then once.

"I'm sorry—that was confusing. Do you want the Bible with you like Aspen asked?"

Spitz blinked once.

Angela tucked it beside him. "Okay. So why are you telling me no? You don't like being back in your bed?"

Spitz blinked once.

Angela patted his shoulder compassionately. "I know; I understand. You've been lying in this bed so long that it's the last place you want to be. But you won't be here forever. You believe that?"

Spitz blinked once.

"Good," Angela nodded firmly. "So you get some rest for a little while. Sleep will help you heal. I'll bet your momma told you so when you were little."

Spitz blinked once again.

Angela chuckled. "And I'll bet you didn't like hearing it any better from her." Her face grew more serious. "Look, Spitz, I know this part is going to be hard for you—the recovery. I hear Aspen talk about you, and I can guess what kind of person you are. You need to know that you're going to be starting over in a lot of ways now, just as if you were new born. You'll have to learn to talk and swallow and walk again. You'll have to learn to hold things straight, like a book or a pen. All of that learning is going to be frustrating for you, because you're going to remember doing those things easily, with no trouble."

Spitz blinked once to show that he understood.

"You have to think of your recovery like climbing a mountain. You can't just wish yourself to the top. You're going to have to earn every step along the way there. You can't give up."

Spitz blinked once again.

Angela chuckled again. "I'm going to hold you to that blink, Spitz, when the physical therapist makes you so mad you'd throw something at her if you could aim straight."

Spitz blinked once more.

"Now the first thing you should do to help your body recover is go to sleep if you can. Don't be afraid you won't wake up. You will." Angela gave him one last reassuring pat and left the room.

Spitz closed his eyes and tried to sleep. *It's like climbing a mountain,* he reminded himself. *This is just one step along the way. Just take a nap; it's not that hard.*

But it was hard. To relax his mind into sleeping required an act of surrender akin to sidling up to a cliff edge and diving over. A rigid knot of consciousness inside him refused to untangle, insisting that it was the only thing anchoring him to working eyelids and the acknowledgement of his caregivers, the only thing saving him from a mute and silent existence and the careless disregard of the Irenes around him.

He gave up and opened his working eyelids. He rolled his eyes to the window, to the early afternoon brightness outside. Storm clouds piled up in the east, dark and swift, and sunbeams shone on them from the west, lighting the last straggling leaves on the trees in the parking lot outside. Aspen had mentioned that daylight savings time had begun while he had been ill; so this light would disappear sooner than he was ready for it to go. He decided to watch it as long as he could. He couldn't sleep, and he had nothing else to do.

The door opened a crack, and Ed Campbell knocked on it softly. Spitz's eyes swiveled to the sound. The hospital chaplain swung the door open wide, beaming at him.

"Well, sir, they told me you might be asleep, but I figure you've had enough sleeping for a while. I know if I was you, I'd keep my eyes open as long as I could." Campbell stood by the bed, rocking back on his heels and smiling. He was a tall man who was thin in a permanent sort of way, with prominent bones and teeth. Looking at him, Spitz could imagine exactly how he'd looked all the way back to childhood.

Campbell folded himself into the vinyl chair beside Spitz's bed and opened his Bible. "I'll pray for you here in just a minute, but while you're awake, I thought you might like to hear some Psalms. Nobody puts celebration to words like King David, and you sure do have something to celebrate. Welcome back," Campbell grinned.

*Thanks,* Spitz thought drily.

"Say, since I'm reading the end of the Psalms, I can just go ahead and use your Bible; I'll count backward five chapters from the end. I bet you'd like to hear your own Bible read," Campbell suggested.

Spitz blinked his eyes twice.

Campbell didn't get the message. He reached a long, bony arm up to the bed and retrieved the old, burned Bible. Pages flipped, but Spitz was too far away to see them. He turned his eyes back to the window outside, watching the sunbeams backlighting the storm clouds.

"Lots of writing in here," Campbell remarked, "that must be one reason why this Bible's so special. Let's see here; I'll count back five. Here we are, extolling the Lord."

Campbell began to read the exhortations of the psalmist to praise the Lord, and Spitz heard him with the beginnings of his old resentments rising again. Here he was, happy to be awake and communicating again, and God had to come right back into the picture and demand credit. Spitz's happy glow of gratitude wasn't enough; he had to be grateful to God specifically and tell Him so.

The words of the Psalms in Campbell's high, soft voice washed over Spitz as he watched the yellow maple outside bending in the breeze, its bright leaves glowing yellow in the sun. The leaves were a hundred hands, clapping for joy. He could almost hear the roar of the forest applause now. He shut his eyes. Those bright leaves shone with an independent light and tossed and swayed in a dizzying whirl, like a cyclone of leaves, a cyclone that pulled him along a path only it knew. There were hundreds of trees with tens of thousands of leaves above him, around him. He could smell them. He could feel leaf mold beneath him, dusty and springy. He sneezed.

★ ★ ★

The sneeze lifted the brim of a felt hat off his head and moved it off his face. Bright sunlight fell on his face, and he lifted a hand to shield his eyes.

He was in an autumn forest—late autumn, for most of the trees had lost their leaves. Thin, white clouds scudded across a blue sky webbed by bare branches stretched high above him. The trees around him were old and towering. He sat up and immediately jumped back, startled.

George Washington leaned against the tree opposite Spitz's feet, sitting with his booted feet outstretched while he contentedly munched an apple and waited for Spitz to wake. He looked somewhat older, with pronounced crow's feet at the corners of his eyes and a few strands of gray in his hair, but he was still a young man. He swallowed and grinned.

"This time I have the advantage, sir, for I knew you by your luggage," Washington said. "I have seen that bag serve as your pillow far too often to mistake it now."

"Colonel Washington," Spitz said gladly. "I didn't expect to see you."

"Nor I you," Washington answered. "I have not seen you since 1755 after that terrible business with Braddock. Fifteen years is a long while for an acquaintance to languish. I thought to see you at Mount Vernon some years back."

*It's 1770,* Spitz calculated. He scanned his memory for the pertinent details of Washington's life. The former officer was now landed gentry as well as a representative at the Virginia Assembly. He was also married to Martha and stepfather to her two children: Jacky and Patsy.

"I spent a great part of my young adulthood traveling as a merchant," Spitz explained. "I've seen a good bit of the world."

"Have you indeed?" said Washington, keenly interested. "May I ask where you have travelled?"

"I've been to Europe a few times, but my business mainly takes me to Asia and Africa and South America," Spitz told him. "I've seen India and the Pacific Islands and the Sahara and the jungles at the source of the Nile."

Washington looked at Spitz curiously. "You say you are a merchant; in which goods do you deal?"

"I import foodstuffs and household goods like cloth and furniture," Spitz answered.

Washington nodded. "Considering the destinations to which you travel, I had feared that you dealt in slaves. I am relieved to learn that you do not."

Now it was Spitz's turn to look at Washington strangely. "Don't you own slaves, sir? Why would you dislike my dealing in them?"

Washington sighed. "In a better world, I would not own them, but their fate is not a question I may decide alone, apart from my neighbors. For now, the slaves on my properties are families who have served mine for generations. If I did not care for them, how would they provide for themselves? How would they fare apart from my concerns, my properties? No," Washington said. "And I would fare poorly without them. We do each other well, as far as we see to do it, and we leave the world to God to change."

Spitz decided to let the issue drop. He remembered the weeping slave at Mount Vernon who had fetched him by the river—that man had loved Washington. And Spitz remembered as well that on his deathbed, Washington freed all of his slaves. In the end, he did what he could.

Spitz stood and extended a hand to help Washington up. "Surely you're not traveling alone, sir," Spitz said.

Washington took the extended hand and stood up, brushing the leaves off his clothes. "No, I travel with an expedition. You see me today engaged in my first profession: that of a surveyor. Do you remember, Spitz, the offer I extended you to enlist in the army, the one you declined in order to do me the honor of becoming my aide-de-camp at Great Meadows?"

"You offered me some pounds of tobacco daily and a share in a tract of land," Spitz recalled.

"Yes," Washington nodded, "and now I have the honor of measuring and dividing that land for the men who enlisted."

"Where is the rest of the expedition, Colonel?" Spitz asked.

"They wait below in the valley with some flags and some other instruments of my work. I walked ahead with the rest of my equipment to take measurements from the top of this hill because I preferred to be solitary with my thoughts," Washington explained.

"I'm sorry I interrupted you, sir," Spitz apologized.

"But you are mistaken," Washington chuckled, "for I interrupted you. God has crossed our paths again, and for my part, I am glad of it. Will you walk with me up the hill and then join our expedition for a time? We may at least offer you a hot meal. Several of our fellows have been hunting this morning."

"I'm glad to join you, sir, especially when there's slim chance of an ambush," Spitz joked. He put his pack on his back and hung the straps of his messenger bag and reloading supplies across his chest. He also picked up the rifle which had been leaning against the tree.

Washington had slung his rifle across his back by a strap, and he carried an instrument that looked like an oversized camera tripod as well as a small wooden chest like a large tackle box with a leather handle in the lid. As he looked around him, Spitz saw that the forest around him did slope upwards, ending in a clear space at the top. He walked upwards beside Washington.

"Is this expedition the farthest west you've ever been, sir?" Spitz asked Washington.

"It is," Washington answered. "I am farther west at this moment than I ever was during the last war. You may not be so moved as I am because of your own wider travels, but the sight of that vast westward horizon thrills me. Each time I climb a hill, I see land lying fallow and rich as far as the eye can look. The sheer expanse of it is a marvel."

"The sight does move me, sir," Spitz agreed. "It's a great country."

"And the land so varies in its abundance!" Washington exclaimed. "The hills and plains here differ vastly from my coastal plantations in the east, and in the south, the forest and farmland transform into tropic paradise and lovely islands. Then to the north you may see ancient forests and lakes like seas stretch beyond the horizon. In my youth I wished to join the navy, and when I see such rolls and swells of land beneath me as we will see at the end of this climb, something like that desire stirs yet. Some sense of wild adventure lures men in such a place."

"I can't see you as a sailor, sir," Spitz said, shaking his head.

"Nor could my mother," Washington smiled, "or at least she would not see me so. I cannot blame her. The sea is full of dangers, and she had just lost my father. I was thoughtless to raise the prospect to her then."

A thought crossed Spitz's mind. *He lost his father, too—like Aspen.* "You must have suffered growing up without a father," he said soberly.

"I did feel his loss keenly when I was a boy. He was a good and kind man while he lived. He was a surveyor, too," Washington acknowledged, half smiling and nodding to the equipment he carried. "But I did not want for guidance. My mother attended faithfully to my education, seeing that I mastered the skill of horsemanship, gained the knowledge of plantation management, and became proficient in mathematics, reading, writing, and the social graces so that I could find success at whatever pursuit I chose. To the degree that I am a moral man and an informed one, I owe that attainment to her."

"You've always spoken of her very respectfully," Spitz noted.

"As is no more than her due," Washington agreed. "But she did not have the care of me alone. My brother Lawrence, who was fourteen years my senior, bought and sold land. From the time I was very young, I thought him a great man. And shortly after my father's death, he made a good match."

"Who was the lady?" Spitz asked. He remembered from his reading that the marriage had advanced not just Lawrence but his little brother George as well.

"Anne Fairfax, the daughter of Colonel William Fairfax, cousin of the powerful Lord Fairfax, who has become my own benefactor," Washington answered. "She added nearly four thousand acres to Lawrence's holdings, but the land was nothing to the greatness of her family. Her father, Colonel Fairfax, was a former member of the Royal Navy and served as Lord Fairfax's agent responsible for issuing land grants. He also held the influential political positions of Justice and Burgess.[25] You may see by those duties how his influence benefitted a man so concerned with building a great estate as Lawrence was."

"Sounds like Lawrence was lucky to get her," Spitz said.

"They were well matched," Washington disagreed. "Lawrence had been schooled in England, was a veteran of war, and held the military position of Adjutant of the Colony of Virginia. He, too, served in the House of Burgesses. Both Lawrence and Colonel Fairfax were esteemed gentlemen of the upper classes possessing large land holdings. Lawrence had no need to fear holding up his head before his wife's family."

"Then it sounds like you were lucky to have a brother like Lawrence," Spitz amended.

"He was the best of brothers and the architect of any success I have enjoyed," Washington said. "When my mother and uncle discouraged me from going to sea, I took up my father's rifle, axe, and surveying instruments.[26] I studied the craft diligently, and once I bid fair to master it, Lawrence arranged for me to practice it on land Lord Fairfax had just won in a boundary dispute with five Indian nations. The survey trip afforded me the opportunity to study with James Genn, the experienced official surveyor of Prince William County."[27]

"You chose your career well, considering all of this territory west of here. It doesn't look like you'd run out of work in a lifetime of charting and measuring," Spitz observed.

Washington paused and readjusted the tripod instrument in his hand. It looked heavy. "The career was a good one, but I did not mean to pursue it exclusively. I saved my earnings and bought land to add to the holdings my father had left to me. I was bent upon being a great gentleman, like Lawrence and Colonel Fairfax, and those great gentlemen had all set their sights west, to Ohio. My craft was a tool in my hand to aid them and then to join them."

"It looks like that plan worked out pretty well for you," Spitz said drily.

Washington looked up to the crown of the hill, which was much nearer now. The afternoon sun was behind it so that Spitz and Washington walked in shadow. Washington looked over at Spitz and nodded. "I am sensible of my good fortune and the ways in which great men have advanced me, yet I am not yet so great a man as I mean to be."

Spitz asked, "What else is left for you? What do you really want to do?"

Washington smiled fondly at him and nodded upwards. "I shall tell you at the crown of the hill, where the view may match the ambition."

"I look forward to it," Spitz said. "So what happened after the surveying trip?"

Washington shrugged the rifle into a more comfortable position as he walked. "The trip proved an education indeed, in more ways than I had anticipated. I grew competent in the art of surveying under the guidance of James Genn, but I also proved hardy in rough living and inclement weather. I learned as well to understand the Indian nations who lived along the Ohio. Without that early foundation of respect and mutual effort, I may not have proved as able as I did to negotiate their support on the diplomatic mission I undertook for Governor Dinwiddie."

"Where I met you first," Spitz added.

"Exactly," Washington smiled. "And you have done me one good turn after another each time I have met you, while I have yet to repay you for any of them."

"You've offered," Spitz hedged. "If I'd been free to accept, I expect I'd be doing pretty well by now. But tell me more about Lawrence. Was he the one who got you the diplomatic mission, too?"

Washington looked soberly into the sky above the crest of the hill. "I suppose he did, after a fashion. You see, Lawrence grew ill after a time, and his doctors advised him that a change of air would do him good. He took me with him for the cure to Barbados." Washington smiled ruefully at Spitz. "That island was the farthest from home I had been, and it was like a lovely dream. You have been to the tropics; I need not describe to you the particular beauties of the place. But it was nearly the death of me."

"Was your ship attacked?" Spitz asked.

Washington shook his head. "I contracted smallpox immediately I set foot on the island, and my recovery was a very near thing. The doctors there hovered between Lawrence and me for a time with equally grave faces. But I grew strong again." Washington fell silent.

"Lawrence didn't?" Spitz guessed.

Washington sighed. "He sent me home when I had recovered, but the cure did him no good. He came home the next summer, still grievously ill, to set his affairs in order. I grieve for him still, as does everyone who knew him. He was an extraordinary man."

Spitz pursed his lips. "It doesn't seem fair, losing your father and your brother when you were so young. It doesn't seem right."

Washington looked curiously at Spitz. "You have a particular aversion to death, Spitz," Washington noted. "You repined at the deaths in the ambush fifteen years ago as well."

"Death is such a waste, especially when good people die," Spitz said bitterly, "and more so when they die young."

"Each man owes God a death," Washington said calmly, "and though those who remain may grieve for our losses, we grieve in hope, as Paul says. We do not part forever from those we love."

"As you say, sir," Spitz said. He walked in silence beside Washington for a space, lost in his thoughts as the trees thinned and blue sky opened past them. *It's not the same,* he thought. *It's different losing a father and a brother than losing a son. If he lost a child, he wouldn't take it like that. He wouldn't quote Scripture at me then.*

"We have achieved our goal, Spitz," Washington said, placing a hand on his companion's shoulder, "and now here is our reward." He strode with strong, even steps across the level space at the top of the hill, breathing deeply. He set his surveying equipment down in the center and then opened his arms exultantly to the spread of land unfolding to the horizon before him.

Spitz joined him, looking westward as far as he could. In his travels, Spitz had been to nearly every western state, from Arizona to California to Nevada to Oregon to Washington, the state named for the man standing beside him. Spitz knew the wonders waiting where neither man could see them now: the primeval redwoods and volcanic heights and stomach-dropping canyons. But even with all of his knowledge of what lay beyond, Spitz knew that he came nowhere near matching Washington's awe and gratitude and joy in the view before them both.

He wondered what secret ambition Washington harbored that this view was supposed to match. He wondered whether it had come true. But he waited for Washington to speak.

Finally Washington turned to Spitz, his heart evidently full. "My dear friend - I promised to tell you how great a man I mean to be, and I hope that the grandeur below will temper my words so that you may see them in the tenor of service, not pride."

"I have the highest opinion of you, sir," Spitz said. "I'll give your words the most generous meaning I can and trust that's what you meant."

Washington inclined his head. "You honor me with such confidence. Here, then, is the honor I wish to be granted to me: I wish to heal a breach of nations."

Spitz let the words sink in: a breach of nations, plural, more than one sovereign nation.

"You have no doubt watched with me the breach as it has grown: first, the utter abandonment of these colonies to the depredations of enemies by our mother country, and then the late and haphazard efforts to secure them. And since then, the breach has deepened in unjust demands for monies and loyalty beyond what is natural or desirable and the denial of right and responsibility to match. So the colonies have arisen in dignity to push away the hands that grasp and stifle. What may any man see here but the well-grown man assuming what is due him at his majority? Does not the law of nature show us the adult leaving the parent when he no longer needs provision or defense?"

Spitz looked at Washington awestruck. "It does, sir."

"You see then the necessary progression of relationship from subordinate and superior to equals?" Washington demanded.

"I do; that's exactly what needs to happen," Spitz agreed.

"See then the part I know I must play," Washington said, pacing. "I have pondered the preservation of Providence through the whole of my life. At sundry times I ought to have died, and no man can reason why I still breathe except for the good grace of God. Smallpox, bullets, drowning, and freezing—I have passed through them all as untouched as Daniel in the lion's den, and not because of any especial virtue I possess."

Spitz nodded. He had recorded those dangers in the journal in his bag. He had seen Washington survive miraculously.

"A time ago, after my escape from the ambush near Fort DuQuesne, Reverend Samuel Davies penned a sermon entitled 'Religion and Patriotism the Constituents of a Good Soldier.' Though I abhor undue praise, I noted what the good man said, for he did not praise me. He wrote, 'As a remarkable instance of this, I may point out to the public that heroic youth, Colonel Washington, whom I cannot but hope Providence has hitherto preserved in so signal a manner for some important service to his country.'"[28]

"I've read his words," Spitz said. He'd read them in a biography of Washington.

Washington nodded, unsurprised. "Davies circulated that sermon widely. When I read it, I felt a great destiny settle upon me, and it humbled me. God has spared me to serve Him. 'For unto whomsoever much is given, of him shall be much required: and to whom men have committed much, of him they will ask the more.' Who am I but a debtor to Providence? And how shall I refuse to pay what I owe?"

Spitz hesitantly said, "Colonel, I've seen God spare you, and I know something great is waiting for you. But you said 'heal a breach.' For the colonies to be equal to England, doesn't that mean war?"

Washington stopped and looked into the afternoon sunlight. "I pray not. The chasm gapes before us now, and only God knows whether blood may be required to seal it. But if we remain humble and implore Providence to grant us peace, we may escape war. To be the agent of Providence who may stretch a hand forth in peace and help the mother see that she must send her grown child forth with a blessing instead of a curse—this is the honor I mean to attain."

"And what will you do if it comes to war?" Spitz asked quietly.

"God grant I may do my duty, whatever it may be," Washington said firmly, "but for the present He has pleased to make of me an assemblyman, not a Colonel." He breathed the cold, thin air deeply, and then he smiled and clapped Spitz's arm fondly. "Come—we have maps to chart, Spitz."

Washington directed Spitz in how to set up the surveyor's equipment and assist him in taking measurements. Men in the valley raised bright flags as Washington peered through a metal assembly atop the tripod and noted figures in a neat, sure hand in a blank book. As they worked, the sun sank lower toward the horizon. By the time they finished and packed Washington's equipment, the lower clouds glowed pink against the brilliant blue sky. They began to descend the hill.

Washington smiled at Spitz. "You know my history nearly as well as anyone by now, but I do not know yours. You must relate it to me as we descend."

Hesitating at first on how to translate his twentieth-century life into eighteenth-century terms, Spitz soon found comfort in talking about Gramps and his parents and the farm where he'd spent a good deal of his boyhood. He talked about the droughts and lean years and the feeling of wanting to go anywhere in the world to escape the heartbreak of land that wouldn't yield and never-ending days and nights of labor. He talked about the places he'd seen and the men he'd met in the far corners of the world. But he said not a word of Mia or Steve or Nevaeh or Aspen. The time didn't feel right.

When they reached level ground, Spitz was delighted to see Craik waiting with the lower survey team who had worked in the valley. Washington walked ahead with some other men and left the two old friends to talk. Craik shook Spitz's hand with enthusiasm and told Spitz about his work and his life since Braddock's defeat. He lived in Maryland and practiced medicine there. He had married and begun producing children with great regularity and enthusiasm.

"And you have heard of course that George is married as well," Craik assumed.

"I'd heard so," Spitz said, "and he has children, too?"

"Not his own," Craik said quietly, "the smallpox closed that door to him. But God was good to send him a wife with children. They do him good, and he is very fond of them. Their own father died when they were so young that George is the only father they remember."

The party arrived in camp to find a feast nearly prepared. Washington and the men with the valley survey team put their equipment into their tents, and Washington sat quietly on an upturned section of log outside his tent, calculating the figures he'd recorded. Spitz tagged along with Craik, meeting the other men travelling with them. Many of them, like Spitz, still thought of Washington as Colonel Washington, and sitting around a crackling campfire, they traded stories about the French and Indian war.

His work completed, Washington joined the other men to wait for dinner. The atmosphere around the fire was relaxed and friendly, like the feeling inside a good neighborhood restaurant or at a ballpark half an hour before the game. Then it tensed.

A small party of frontiersmen and hunters, some of them in fine gentlemen's clothing, appeared at the edge of the wood and crossed rapidly to the campfire. "We saw the smoke and smelled the meat," one of them said, "and so we hurried along. We can add some of the day's takings to the meat as it cooks, but best save the bulk for the morrow."

Spitz relaxed. By the cheerful welcome, it was obvious the men belonged in camp. The hunters had been out gathering provisions for all of them. The men around the campfire agreed with the hunters, and several men left for the cooking fires, their game bags groaning with fresh meat.

Observing one man missing from the joining party, Washington asked, "Is Joseph Nicholson far behind?"

"He dropped back to relieve himself, sir. I suspect he'll hustle, though, seeing how it's gotten dark and all. He's easily spooked, you know," one of the men chuckled in a friendly way.

The new arrivals warmed their chilly hands at the flames and described where they'd shot which kind of animals. In return, the survey team described the lay of the land to the west.

Then another party arrived. All the men around the campfire stood, either reaching surreptitiously for weapons or calculating silently how fast they could get to them.

The latest arrivals emerged from the forest slowly and cautiously, pausing at the edge both to see and to be seen. A wide-eyed frontiersman led a small party of Indians, who advanced slowly behind him, toward the campfire.

"Nicholson, it seems you weren't as alone in them woods as you thought," said the man who had laughed at his expense moments before.

Nicholson, offering no smile in return, said, "Ye know I hunt, trap, and trade along the Ohio, and fortunate for me, I know several Indian languages. They say they come a long way looking for the one called George Washington!"

Washington stepped forward, looking at the Indians as he spoke and placing a hand on the breast of his coat to make his meaning plain. "I am he."

The Indians studied Washington carefully, taking a long, full measure of the man who had just stepped forward.

"Nicholson, you had best translate for us," Washington said, realizing that the Indians were gazing at him in wonder.

Nicholson gestured as he spoke to one of the Indians, an old man withered like an apple in February. A collation of feathers adorned his thin, cotton-white hair, and a significant number of scalps adorned the weapons hanging from his intricately beaded belt.

"He is most welcome to my fire," Washington said respectfully, looking into the old chief's eyes. "I will hear whatever he has come to say. Please tell him so."

Nicholson turned and spoke in a language that was guttural and sibilant by turns. Spitz could hear the trader's backwoods accent marring the beauty of it. The men who had been sitting by the campfire sat down again and widened the circle, making room for the Indians who now joined it.

Once Nicholson had translated his words, Washington walked to the old chief and attempted to shake his hand. But the chief would not touch Washington. He shook his head and raised his hands as if to say that he dared not.

Perplexed, Washington signaled for Craik to hand him a flask of brandy. Washington took a pull and then attempted to hand the flask to the chief, who once again refused. Washington tried two more peace offerings, one a lit pipe of tobacco and the other a plate of roast meat straight from the spit. Both times, the chief again refused, raising his hands chest high, palms out.

Craik leaned over to Spitz. "George has nothing left to offer the old sachem. By all rights, the chief should either have scalped him or partaken in the peace offerings by this time. I have never seen an Indian behave so; it is most uncanny."

One Indian beside the chief stood and began to speak to Washington in the Indian language, paying no more attention to Nicholson than to the trees surrounding the clearing. Nicholson translated.

"The old chief is 'a very great man among the northwestern tribes and the same who commanded the Indians on the fall of Braddock, sixteen years before.' He heard 'of the visit of Colonel Washington to the western country'; so he 'set out on a mission, the object of which himself will make known.'"[29]

The Indian who had been speaking sat down. He waited for the old chief to speak, respectfully silent. His courteous attention spread to the rest of the men, who all fixed eyes on the chief. An eerie hush prevailed, like the space of soundless calm after cannon fire or between breaking waves—only this hush stretched to minutes. A chill ran down Spitz's spine, and he shivered.

Finally, the old chief stood and turned toward Washington. He lifted his hands and eyes to the heavens. Spitz heard the majesty of his speech beneath the translation Nicholson offered.

"I am a chief, and the ruler over many tribes. My influence extends to the waters of the great lakes, and to the far blue mountains. I have traveled a long and weary path, that I might see the young warrior of the great battle. It was on the day, when the white man's blood, mixed with the streams of our forest that I first beheld this chief: I called to my young men and said, mark yon tall and daring warrior? He is not of the red-coat tribe—he hath an Indian's wisdom, and his warriors fight as we do—himself is alone exposed. Quick, let your aim be certain, and he dies. Our rifles were leveled, rifles which, but for him, knew not how to miss—'twas all in vain, a power mightier far than we, shielded him from harm. He can not die in battle. I am old, and soon shall be gathered to the great council-fire of my fathers, in the land of shades, but ere I go, there is something, bids me speak, in the voice of prophecy. Listen! The Great Spirit protects that man, and guides his destinies—he will become the chief of nations, and a people yet unborn, will hail him as the founder of a mighty empire!" [30]

Having spoken, the Indian chief remained in an attitude of communion with the stars above for several long minutes. Then he quietly walked away and disappeared into the dark forest. Obediently, unspeaking, the Indian warriors who had accompanied him followed him there. Not a one of them had taken a bite of food or a sip of drink. Only Nicholson remained with the hunters and surveyors.

That eerie hush, broken only by soft, wondering conversation and the sounds of eating, prevailed into the night, when the men camped in tents arranged around the fire. The hunters and Nicholson and Spitz spread bedrolls on the bare ground close to the glowing embers. Spitz was glad of his thick buckskin clothes and well-made boots, as well as the felted wool blanket he'd carried tied to his pack.

But before he went to sleep, he opened the leather messenger bag and set his writing materials ready to hand. He paused over the next blank page, remembering the conversation with Washington on the way up the hill and the eerie prophecy he had seen delivered just a short time ago. The thought struck him that, as different as they were, both Reverend Samuel Davies and the old Indian chief agreed on one thing: God had preserved George Washington to fulfill some great destiny.

**Sign 5—God provided for Washington's needs:** 1) a sizeable inheritance and a legacy to uphold, 2) a dependable caregiver in his mother Mary, 3) well-meaning and capable mentors in Lawrence Washington and Colonel William Fairfax, 3) quality instructors in County Surveyor James Genn and experienced guide Christopher Gist.

**Sign 6—God provided for Washington's diverse education and growth:** 1) life on the plantation (a basic education and learning about enterprise, horsemanship and social graces), 2) frontier life (33 days of intense survey training), 3) island life (the study of shipping and fortifications), and 4) diplomatic mission (a two and a half month study of statesmanship and military affairs).

**Sign 7—Reverend Samuel Davies' prophesy** regarding the important purpose of the divine protection of Washington. Davis proclaimed that, "Providence has hitherto preserved [George Washington] in so signal a manner for some important service to his country." [31] The affecting story was publicized in newspapers and widely circulated.

**Sign 8—A** mystical servant appeared, suggesting he was directed to come and deliver to Washington a prophecy. "There is something, bids me to speak, in the voice of prophecy," [32] the Indian Chief said.

**The Indian Prophecy:** "He cannot die in battle... Listen! The Great Spirit protects that man [referring to Washington], and guides his destinies—he will become the chief of nations, and a people yet unborn, will hail him as the founder of a mighty empire!" [33]

**The Confirming Evidence:** Washington's coat and hat were pierced by bullets, fired from leveled rifles which rarely missed, and his horses were shot from underneath him, but, miraculously his life was spared.

Satisfied, Spitz blotted the book and put the journal and writing utensils away. He looked at the spine of the Bible inside his messenger bag, but
then he closed the flap to seal the bag and pillowed his head on it.

What had he just seen? The old Indian chief traveling for who knows
how long from who knows how far away just to prophesy over George
Washington—it was like something out of the Old Testament. Spitz
mused over the prophets, those strange characters so moved by the Spirit
of God that they would lie in the middle of roads for months on end,
marry whores, or literally air their dirty laundry in public just to create
vivid pictures of what God wanted to say.

Samuel had been a prophet, one whom God had marked for His own
even as a boy. How many times had Spitz read the story of Someone
calling to Samuel from the darkness of the temple without feeling the
otherworldly power of that disembodied voice? How many times had
Spitz read about the anointing of David without understanding the aura
of mystery and power that streamed from the old man as he poured holy
oil over a nobody, a youngest son, the least valued member of the family used to do the most dangerous and unappealing job? How had that
Cinderella story never sent chills down his spine before?

Now that Spitz had seen a real anointing from a real prophet, all of
those old stories of prophets crackled to life, glowing with a real and
inexplicable power that surged through his memory of the old words.
What kind of God was this that used men to breathe life into the dead, to
call down fire from the sky, to cast drought on a nation, or to tell a queen
to her face that dogs would devour her in the street? What kind of God
was this who reversed fatal diseases and crippling disabilities and death
itself at a word when He came in person?

Awe and dread of that kind of power built up in Spitz until he shook
where he lay. And then he realized something else. The Indian's prophecy
had come true.

Spitz himself had walked in the shadow of that prophecy his entire
life. He was one of the people yet unborn who honored Washington as the
founder of a mighty empire. He had read book after book puzzling over
Washington's unnaturally good luck in battle.

Washington hadn't died in battle. He'd never even been wounded.
Some force guided every bullet from its intended path, turned the edge

of every sword, and blew each arrow off course. Some hand placed itself between that man and anything that could harm him. If you wanted to see it, it was plain and inescapable. More than that—it was present and insistent.

Spitz closed his eyes, hair standing up on the back of his neck. Flames danced red behind his closed lids. Another dimension of reality seemed to open to his consciousness like the door of an airplane, terrifying him with its height and enormity and the irresistible force of its being, and he quivered in the wafts of its essence like a gnat at Niagara. It was too much to behold.

It withdrew gradually into a tunnel of lights, through which he passed like a feather in a windstorm. And then it was gone, as if that door had shut with a whisper, and Spitz lay in stillness and silence and fear, red still glowing behind his eyelids. Panicked, he opened them. Late afternoon sunlight streamed through his hospital windows. It was mere moments from disappearing. Storm clouds, nearer now, still roiled and blackened in the east.

Campbell was gone, and Spitz was by himself. Footsteps passed in the hall outside his room, but none slowed or entered. He was lonely and still half-frightened. The utter helplessness of his paralyzed body oppressed him. Feeling as he did now, he wanted to run away, fast and far. He wanted to hide from that presence among crowds of people eating and drinking and living with no consciousness of that awful, awesome Being just behind the veil of the world. He wanted another human creature near to ground him to this existence and quiet the rush of power still ringing in his ears.

# Chapter Seven

"Papa, you're awake!" Aspen cheered as she walked into the room. "I saw Angela on the way in, and she told me you slept through most of the afternoon. I stopped by after work on the off chance that I might be able to talk to you. And I can! Did you sleep well?" Aspen sat down in the vinyl chair and looked at him expectantly.

Spitz could feel himself calming near Aspen and her pleasant personality. He blinked once.

"Good!" She took his hand and held it. "I had a good afternoon, too. Bill and I finished planning the Indonesia trip, right down to the visit to the crash site. A few days ago, Bill talked to a travel agent in Timika who knows a local guide; the agent was supposed to get in touch with the guide and ask him if he remembered the crash site. Well guess what? Bill called the agent today, and the guide remembered the crash and knew right where to find the wreckage! So I put down a deposit right then to rent a helicopter to take us there. Can you believe it? I'm going to ride in a helicopter over New Guinea. Bill said it will be like flying over Jurassic Park."

Inside his motionless body, Spitz cringed at the idea, for he knew from experience that the journey could be treacherous, especially in bad weather.

"At first I wanted to rent a Land Rover, but the travel agent said that there are only a few roads beyond the Timika area and that the ones that do exist are restricted for official use. So it would be next to impossible to get to the crash site using a road, even if we were to backpack in from the closest trailhead. He said it could take more than a week one way and would be really dangerous because of the wildly dangerous terrain and extreme climate changes. We would have to cross dozens of deep ravines without the benefit of a bridge, and because of the steep grades, a sudden surge of pounding water could easily sweep us away if it rained, which I'm told it'll almost certainly do. The crash site is on the side of a mountain, Papa," Aspen said somberly.

She shook her head to clear the dangers away. "But the whole trip won't be so dangerous. Some of it will be really nice. We'll stay at the Rimba Papua Hotel in Timika, the same hotel where you stayed when you were there, only then it was a Sheraton. I was surprised to learn that it was such a high quality hotel. I've seen pictures online, and it looks wonderful. The agent said that it was originally built by a mining company for executive use and that the Sheraton group had managed it on their behalf. Anyway, the day of our arrival in Timika, we'll check into the hotel and then go to the airport to make necessary arrangements for the trip to the crash site."

Aspen laughed, embarrassed. "I'll have to be weighed. The agent said that it's important to know how much weight the copter will be carrying, due to the altitude and flying conditions. He promised that if we have good weather, we should have time to fly to the crash site, spend two or three hours on the ground, and then return to the Timika airport the same day."

Aspen was quiet a moment. "Of course, the company is paying for our hotel and ground transportation, the expenses we would have incurred anyway, whether we toured the crash site or not. Bill offered to help pay for the guided helicopter tour, but I told him no. This is something I want to do for myself."

Spitz saw the stubborn lift in her chin. He felt a little sorry for Bill.

Slipping off her heels, Aspen drew her knees up to her chin and laced her hands around them, the way she always had when she was talking to Spitz. "I had no idea when I chose this destination for a business trip how much it would bring up everything with Mama and Daddy. Honestly, I thought I would probably be sad once I got there, and a little relieved, too, but I didn't expect to think about the place night and day like I've been doing. I even dream about it now." She smiled sheepishly. "In my dream last night, I was nine years old again, all skinny and freckled. I flew on a plane with you to New Guinea and found out that it was all a mistake. Mama and Daddy were alive and safe, and we got to take them home with us."

Spitz blinked twice.

Aspen's face fell. "I know it's not true. I know I won't find them over there. Honestly, I don't know what I'm hoping to find. I just feel like something is waiting for me at the crash site, something I'll know when I see it."

Spitz blinked twice, and then once.

Aspen squeezed his hand. "Let me take a stab at that one. You don't think that anything is waiting for me, but you hope I feel better once I find that out for myself?"

Spitz blinked once.

"I know, Papa," Aspen said kindly. "It's just one more of those areas where we'll have to agree to disagree. Like this Bible here—I know you've always hated the sight of it, but I love it. It's something that ties us to them. That's why I wanted it here with you. But now that you're awake again, I can ask you. Do you want me to take it away?"

Spitz hesitated and then blinked twice.

Aspen grinned. "Good - I feel better knowing it's with you here."

Thunder boomed out the window, near enough to rattle the glass, and Spitz and Aspen both looked outside. The storm clouds had rolled nearer, and lightning hidden in cloud pulsed bright for an instant. Aspen sighed. "It looks like I'd better try to beat that home," she said.

Spitz blinked once.

Aspen hesitated. "You know, before you woke up, I told you something I want to tell you again now that you're awake. I love you, and I'm so grateful that you raised me. You gave up so much for me. I appreciate you; I want you to know that. You gave me a wonderful childhood, Soaring Eagle."

Spitz blinked once. Thunder crashed loudly outside, and the room dimmed noticeably as the last of the sunlight disappeared into the storm.

"All right—I'm headed home," Aspen said, squeezing Spitz's hand one last time and leaning over to kiss his cheek. "I'll be back tomorrow."

The first fat raindrops hit the window in a sheet as Aspen left the room. *Singing Eagle, you were worth every minute of my time for the last seventeen years—worth it and more. I don't regret being earthbound for you. But I'm not the only one with clipped wings. When was the last time you sang? Did being around me rob you of your music?* Spitz closed his eyes, regretful. *I hope some time really soon you find it again.*

After Aspen left, the weather worsened. The night grew black outside, and Spitz could hear the wind buffeting the hospital. Thunder followed right on the heels of lightning with little pause. And within the hour, the temperature inside his room dropped. Spitz could feel cold rolling from the windows, pressing through invisible cracks and thin glass where it could not pass through brick and drywall and insulation.

Spitz remembered his old life woefully. Part of the reason he'd appropriated the library for his own use was that he liked the wood fire. He kept cords of wood stacked between two trees at the side of the house, and he made sure he carried enough split logs inside each day to keep a fire going whenever he wanted one in cold weather. That wingback armchair right by the hearth was one of his favorite places to curl up like a cat and absorb warmth.

*What I wouldn't give to be there now,* Spitz thought mournfully. *On second thought, what wouldn't I give to get up and get myself a blanket, even one of these thin hospital numbers? I can't ask someone for a blanket. I can't even ring a bell to let anyone know something is wrong.*

So Spitz lay still and shivered and thought about powerlessness. He thought about his most recent trip to the past and Washington's frustration with the British government. In his research before the stroke, Spitz had wondered how Britain expected its colonies to take the kind of insulting legislation it had passed.

Though the British parliament knew that levying taxes on citizens who weren't allowed to vote was an offense any Englishman would call robbery, it passed a raft of petty taxes only applicable to American Englishmen who had no representatives in Parliament. Then it used some of the money to pay British-born governors and judges whose loyalty was to the British crown alone. The whole system was both wasteful and insulting, and it left American colonists powerless to sway either local government or Parliament.

*And if I never really empathized with them before, I do now. Feeling helpless is maddening. If I could get free by signing a declaration or dumping tea into a harbor or forming a militia, I'd do it in a heartbeat.*

Spitz felt the icy cold creeping into his room, and he heard the thunder crash and watched bolt after bolt of lightning split the sky. He was so cold. He didn't think he'd be able to stand it another minute. Lightning flashed again suddenly, very close to his window, startling him.

The hospital room disappeared in a whirling flash of light that tugged him forward, but the bitter cold and the dark only strengthened. The lights let him go behind a tree at dawn in a heavy fall of snow. His layers of flannel and buckskin and his stout leather boots held the cold at bay, but he still felt it, keen and cutting, on his face and neck. He looked to the sky. The sun would not rise in this mess; it would only lighten the gloom of the storm.

He looked in front of him, to a small building that stood a little ways out from the town. Finished barrels lined the outside wall, and Spitz saw wood stacked in the back, ready to be made into more barrels. Men stood outside that building with guns at the ready, looking west. Spitz looked past the building to the town. More men waited there, alert, expectant. All of them wore blue jackets with curious, gold-fronted, cone-shaped hats.

The sound of a gunshot pierced through the deafening winter wind. A man in a blue uniform jacket wearing the same cone-shaped hat as the rest of the soldiers suddenly ran from the west toward the barrel shop, holding his shoulder. *"Ich sah sie und feuerte auf sie! Sie kommen!"* he yelled as he ran.

Spitz crouched small behind the tree. *I don't know what he said, but that wasn't English.* Where had he come this time? Washington wasn't overseas, was he?

As the running soldier neared the building, the blast of another shot chased him down, hitting him in the back. Spitz saw him arch backwards and fall to his knees. He looked in the direction from which the man had run. A loose line of men, some in buckskin and others in buff and blue, ran as well as they could through the snow towards the building. The men inside it emerged and formed a line, firing at the men who were running towards them. The rag-tag group halted and brought their rifles up to fire. Most of the shots went wild in the buffeting wind. The group by the building advanced meticulously and fired another round. Troops from the town, who had been advancing quickly, joined the line and fired at the same time. The small group of colonials fired one more shot and then fell back into a disorderly retreat.

As they ran, Spitz looked down at his own clothes and out to the soldiers still massed in formation. If they found him, they'd surely think he was with the men they'd just beat. But all of them were still outside, waiting and watching, and he was near enough for them to catch and imprison. He decided to wait where he was.

The orderly troops closer to town waited a few minutes more, and then they marched back to the loud accompaniment of a military band. The soldiers stationed at the barrel shop cast envious glances backwards at the men returning to warmth and shelter.

After perhaps a quarter of an hour, most of the men at the barrel shop went back inside. Spitz heard them stamping feeling back into their feet and clapping their hands together, laughing in a comradely way and making jokes Spitz couldn't understand. Through a window glowing with firelight, Spitz saw the sentinels passing bottles around, celebrating their victory. One of the men began to sing a hymn that Spitz recognized from Christmas services: "Lo, How a Rose ere Blooming." Only these men sang, *"Es Ist ein Ros Entsprungen."*

It was Christmas, and Spitz could tell now that these men spoke German. These were Hessian soldiers of the same clan, according to the history books, that Washington would overwhelm at Trenton after crossing the ice-jammed Delaware River. Spitz looked around him dubiously. *Is this Trenton? If so, where's Washington? He couldn't have been with that haphazard bunch of colonials taking potshots, could he?*

Two Hessian sentries remained outside, calling remarks back and forth to each other. They didn't make much of an effort to patrol the area, or he'd have been sunk. Instead, they stamped their feet and huddled inside their uniforms and glanced again and again at the warmth and merriment behind them, inside the barrel shop.

The sky lightened; dawn had given way to early morning. With a clatter like gravel on the rooftop and a sharp stinging that hurt Spitz's exposed face, hail descended from the sky. The sentries lifted their hands to ward it off, exposing their bodies to the driving wind. Snow whirled with even more violence in the hailstorm. Finally one of them shouted to the other, and both men dashed inside.

Sensing his opportunity, Spitz hurried away from the tree by the barrel shop, trusting to fate and the storm to hide him from view until he was out of firing range. But the sprinting he intended foundered and slowed in the deep snow that had been falling all night. Desperate, he waded and kicked through it as fast as he was able. His pack and rifle and messenger bag slowed him, too, but he knew better than to discard any of them.

He didn't catch up with the colonials, though he did gain much ground. He got within a half mile back from the last of them, making sure to keep them in sight so that he didn't end up wandering alone in the snow with no idea where anything was. The snow seemed to be coming down harder, mixed with more sharp hail than before. Spitz tugged his woolen scarf over his mouth and nose and tipped his hat down to shield his eyes.

He walked for what seemed like hours, barely keeping the group of colonials in sight. He was glad of the exercise, for it helped to keep him warm. As he walked, he shifted his rifle from one hand to the other, alternately raising a free hand to blow on it and warm it. His fine-knit gloves seemed to admit the wind at every crevice.

The countryside around him was beautiful, like a Christmas post-card. The farmer bred in him appreciated the neat fields and hedgerows and stands of woods arranged with regularity. It was good ground that promised good crops in peace time, whenever that would be.

The men ahead of him stopped. A gust cleared the view, and Spitz saw a regular troop of colonials with officers on horseback marching bravely through the snow. An officer questioned the leader of the rag-tag group. Spitz kept walking closer as quickly as he could.

Another officer on horseback joined the first, and Spitz recognized him: George Washington. Spitz had only seen Washington this angry once before, after Braddock's defeat. Though he couldn't exactly hear what Washington was saying, he was heartily glad he wasn't on the receiving end of it.

Both officers wheeled their horses around, and the rag-tag group fell into formation beside the colonial troops marching in good order. Before Washington could move too far away and become lost to sight in the swirl of snow, Spitz lowered his scarf and hailed him. "Washington! General Washington—halloo," he yelled.

Washington pulled his horse's reins and looked in Spitz's direction. He showed no sign of recognition, but he halted and waited for Spitz to jog up to him.

"It's Steven Spitzen, sir. I'm sorry to hold you up, but I didn't want to lose you in this weather," Spitz shouted above the howling wind.

"Spitz?" Washington frowned. "Had you any hand in this tomfoolery just past?"

"No, sir; but I saw it," Spitz volunteered. "I saw everything. The Hessian soldiers in town were on the ready, just waiting for those boys as if they'd been forewarned. It only took a few minutes to rout them."

"They were waiting, alerted, you say?" Washington demanded.

Spitz nodded, stamping his numb feet in the snow. "It looked like they expected the attack. Somehow they had been tipped off. They're not expecting anything now, though, and especially not in this storm. There's merriment in the town. Since they've sent the colonials packing, the men at the sentry post are drinking, singing Christmas carols, and celebrating."

Washington eyed Spitz thoughtfully. "Come with me, Spitz; I ride with General Greene. I have sent General Sullivan by another road. We shall between us afford the Hessians no escape but the creek beyond, which, I have been assured, is icy, deep, and swift."

"The weather's much worse now than at dawn, too—much more hail, sir."

"I have noted the change," Washington said, distracted. "Doubtless the men on foot have noticed it as well. Let us pray that the change works to our advantage." He rode in silence a while, thinking. Finally he turned to Spitz and said, "I had counted on the element of surprise this morning.

The entire plan of attack depends upon it. Yet you say the Hessians yonder in Trenton expected Stephens' men?"

"They did, sir; they had guns ready before the first colonial appeared," Spitz confirmed.

Washington continued quiet and thoughtful. He rode a space apart from the line of troops, and he kept his eyes on them and on General Greene. "You find me at the end of my plans and my resources, Spitz," Washington finally said, lifting his voice against the storm. "I have retreated across New Jersey, harried by the British ever farther away from New York. I would doubtless have lost my command by now if General Lee had not been captured a fortnight past."

Spitz nodded, "I heard about General Lee's arrest, sir." It had been an embarrassment to the colonies. Lee was habitually unkempt and careless. Spitz had read how British troops had literally walked into his quarters and picked him up, unwashed and unshaven, on his way to breakfast.

Washington gestured to the column of men marching beside him. "We turn today like a bear cornered in its den. Most of my men will finish their enlistments within a month. They have not been paid and have scarcely been fed. We have won nothing of note. I must have a victory at Trenton this morning, or our situation will become even direr than it now appears."

Spitz again wrestled with what to say, as he had so often in the past. He knew Washington would win, but he had no way to say what he knew. Finally he said, "I am sure you have a victory coming, sir." It was the kind of bland encouragement anyone could offer.

"Thank you, Spitz," Washington said, smiling briefly. "As ever, you remain a faithful friend. When the day is done, you must tell me what brings you to these parts in such conditions." Washington's horse halted at the top of a small rise, and he looked before him. "We should be one mile from the town by now, just half a mile from the sentries, yet I see no town."

"It's there," Spitz said lamely. "I just came from there. I don't understand."

Washington pulled out a pocket watch and consulted it, and then he gestured for a uniformed rider to join him. "My compliments to General Greene, and he may take the sentry post immediately."

"Yes sir," the rider shouted, saluting. He galloped forward, to where Greene rode at the head of his troops.

Washington held his horse still, and Spitz stood beside him. "Now we shall see whether all is indeed lost or whether Providence will rescue us from spoiled plans with storms of hail," Washington said, straining to see and hear above the keening wind.

Spitz barely heard the shots fired ahead, and he looked eagerly to see what had happened. He saw the small group of sentries raising hands in surrender, and he cheered the colonials who had won the first small skirmish. But he looked anxiously at the main streets of the town, where the disciplined groups of Hessian soldiers had tactically formed before his eyes early this morning in support of the sentries. No one was there.

The column of soldiers beside Washington advanced, and the rider who had delivered orders to Greene returned. Suddenly the column surged forward into the streets of the town, finally meeting some scattered and unprepared resistance. Hessians wheeled cannon into the street, but the colonials captured the artillery. Possession of the cannon changed hands between the two armies several times as the alarm spread and more Hessians poured, half-dressed and some half-drunk, from the doorways of nearby houses.

A band began to play a bombastic marching tune, and the sound of the instruments and the sound of the storm together deafened Spitz. He didn't see how anyone could hear orders in such a racket. According to plan, Colonial soldiers moved steadily up the main streets of the town, driving the Hessians before them. Spitz heard more artillery from his right, and he turned to see another column of colonial soldiers marching into Trenton, pushing the enemy in from the opposite side. *General Sullivan's column*, Spitz remembered.

Suddenly Spitz saw colonial soldiers shouldering rifles and holding a line. He peered beyond them to where he could barely see some Hessian officers talking with the colonial officers, Greene among them. Greene called a rider to him and spoke, and then the rider galloped back to Washington.

"They have surrendered the town, sir!" the rider shouted as soon as he was in earshot. He checked himself and began, "Excuse me, General Washington. I mean to present General Greene's compliments to General

Washington and to inform you that the town is ours. General Greene is negotiating terms of surrender."

Washington's face relaxed. "Thank you, Lieutenant Baylor. Inform General Greene that I shall join him straightaway."

"Yes, sir," the rider grinned, and he spurred his horse back to the officers.

"You see I am well provided with aides-de-camp at present," Washington told Spitz, "and we are more than enough men to take the prisoners in hand. So I have special orders for you, Spitz, if you are willing to fill them."

"I'm willing, sir," Spitz said.

"My most pressing needs at the moment are shelter, food, and a fire. I have kept a poor Christmas and should like to remedy the deficit, especially in light of my new cause for thanksgiving. Find me a hearth and some cheer, if you will," Washington said.

"I've never heard an order I'd rather obey, General," Spitz chuckled, "one fire, with cheer, coming right up."

Spitz was still at the outskirts of town, where the houses looked poor and drafty. He decided to find a place further toward the center of town, where he could see Greene and the other officers negotiating with the Hessian officers, while the Hessian foot soldiers stacked their guns at the side of a road under the direction of some colonial soldiers.

Spitz pressed past them all to the center of town. He saw a tall, plank-sided house with regular windows at the heights of first and second stories. The place looked cheerful and sturdy and large enough for Washington and the most senior officers. And he saw smoke rising from the chimney. He walked boldly to the front door and knocked on it.

A rather fat man with a red face and flyaway gray hair answered the door, opening it just a crack. "May I help you?" he asked.

"Yes, you may," Spitz answered, pleased that the way should be paved for him with an offer. "I serve General George Washington, the man who's just accepted the surrender of the Hessians garrisoned here."

"Has he really?" the man said, grinning broadly. "That's welcome news, sir."

"General Washington needs a place to rest for a while; I can't say how long," Spitz said. "And he'll need some food. His officers will probably be with him, too. Can they stay here?"

"My home is not large. I fear I cannot house a number of officers indefinitely," the man hedged, opening the door further and allowing Spitz to see that the whole place was one large, barnlike room on the ground floor. "However, I can offer the General some refreshment and a place to rest for the afternoon. Washington is most welcome. You all are most welcome." The man beamed at Spitz. Spitz guessed that either he hadn't been thrilled with the occupying force, or even if he was a Tory, he was excited to host a patriot as esteemed as General Washington.

"I'll let him know. You'll get some food together for them while I'm gone?" Spitz asked.

"I will," the man agreed. He patted his stomach. "I keep a good table, as you can see."

Spitz laughed and thanked him and then marched back to the place he'd left Washington. He noted landmark churches and other buildings along the way so that he wouldn't get lost. When he found Washington, he told him about the arrangements and then led him back, together with General Greene and General Sullivan and their aides-de-camp and several colonels.

The large man welcomed the generals and the men with them, ushering them to a large table before a cheerful fire in the one room of the house. Spitz saw only one servant, a thin and timid girl who kept to a corner as much as she was able; so he guessed that the man had no family. He proved gregarious, though, and seemed to enjoy his guests.

From a corner opposite the maid's, Spitz let the warmth of the fire soak into his bones. He sat at a small desk and accepted a generous plate of meat and fish and pastry and stewed fruit from the little maid and finished it quickly. Then he took his messenger bag from the floor, where he'd put it beside his rifle and pack when he sat down.

The warmth felt so pleasant after his long chill. He supposed he'd stood or trudged for close to six hours in the snow this morning, fending off hail and angry winds. Before he had stepped into this house, he had felt as if he'd never be warm again. Now he felt so full and comfortable that he thought he'd like to go to sleep. But he didn't know how long he would remain with Washington, and he didn't want to miss recording the miracles of the battle.

He opened the calfskin journal and read over the signs, mercies, and interpositions he had recorded inside. The last entry had been about the Indian prophecy. Spitz looked at Washington, ever the gentleman, who was complimenting his host on the meal. *What would that man say if he knew he'd just entertained the first president of the United States?* Spitz mused. He smiled and returned his attention to the book, dipping his quill and pausing over the page. He remembered a quote he'd read about Trenton and decided to include it.

Spitz remembered the unplanned skirmish and the hailstorm before the battle, and how Washington had been so angry at the commander who had spoiled the surprise and so grimly resigned to the hail. But now, after victory, they both seemed like the best possible preparation. The mighty hand had orchestrated an unthinkable battle plan: a diversionary attack followed by the shock and awe of hail stones. Washington got his surprise attack, but not by his doing.

Washington had no way of knowing that a spy in his camp had warned the Hessians to expect an attack the morning after Christmas Day. Fortunately, the Hessian officers had taken the small, easily routed group of colonials who attacked at dawn to be the only attack planned for that day. After they defeated the small, disorderly group, they relaxed their guard. Who knows how Washington's attack would have fared had the Hessians still expected him or if their posted sentries had properly alerted them?

But the storm of hail and snow had been Washington's greatest ally. The sentries left their posts to take cover from the hail, and the white whirl blinded them to the approach of the colonials until it was too late to rouse the town. Then, the howling wind had deafened the Hessians to their officers' orders. The favorable interposition of stinging hail and freezing snow had driven the Hessians inside, away from the sight and sound of the advancing army.

This victory would cement Washington's place as leader of the American armies. Even the arrest of Lee two weeks before had benefitted Washington and the new country, removing a most serious rival for the position of commander-in-chief. And the victory here would rekindle hope in the suffering, losing colonial army that they might actually win.

**Sign 9**—The British capture General Lee; so the faction support-ing him can't replace Washington with him.

**Favorable Interposition 3 (Godsend at Trenton - interses-sion of the elements)**—a perfectly timed winter hail storm drove the Hessian sentries from their garrison posts, allowing Washington's surprise attack to overtake them. Washington's men had just daringly crossed the Delaware River at night in freez-ing conditions. The victory recharged the American cause, which was in desperate need of a win. As Henry Knox said, "Providence seemed to have smiled upon every part of this enterprise."[34]

When Spitz looked at the entry he'd just written, he thought that God couldn't have done more for the colonial army's chances of victory if He'd sent the Hessians a plague. The invisible hand was plain to see again.

Spitz closed his calfskin journal and replaced it in the bag along with his writing materials. His hand paused over the Bible. He heard Aspen's voice asking him whether he minded having the Bible beside him. He'd answered no. The answer had surprised him just as much as it had her. But it was true. After carrying it around for months at a time in the eighteenth century and after using it to comfort the Virginians who were about to die during Braddock's expedition, it had come to feel different for him. He had connected his own memories to it, not just the painful ones associated with his son.

Spitz yawned hugely. The plate of food the maid had given him had been large, and the fire in front of him was warm. He took the Bible from the messenger bag. *May as well pass the time until Washington is ready to leave,* he reasoned. He looked over at the table at all the men conversing together, the generals with the aides-de-camp and their host. The little maid was pouring drinks from a steaming clay pitcher. No one was paying a bit of attention to him. Spitz opened the Bible. Outside, the storm eased and quieted, and clouds parted to let pale rays of winter sun shine through the clean, regular windows of the comfortable house where Spitz sat. Unnoticed by anyone else, that pale sun exploded into a spinning cloud of stars that enveloped Spitz and took him away.

★ ★ ★

Outside the windows of Aspen's comfortable home theater room, the storm raged and tore at the house and the trees around it. She was watching NCIS, which the station continually kept interrupting throughout the evening in order to issue severe thunderstorm warnings. The last one had showed yellow on the part of the map where Aspen lived, with a line of red approaching.

Her cell phone buzzed beside her, and she muted the television before she picked it up. Bill's face smiled at her from the screen, a candid shot she'd taken of him when they had exchanged numbers at work. She sighed in relief.

"Hi, Bill—I'm glad it's you. I thought the hospital might be calling," Aspen said.

"No, I just wanted to check in with you. Was your grandfather any better when you saw him after work?" Bill asked.

Aspen pulled a pillow close and folded her arms over it. "No, he was the same, which is a whole lot better than he was yesterday. You can't imagine what a relief it was to see him awake. We talked some more, or I guess I should say that I talked some more and he blinked."

Bill chuckled. "That's a good sign, though, that he can respond to you. It was great to see you coming back from lunch so happy. I've never seen you look like that."

"You met me during one of the worst times of my life," Aspen said. "I'm usually a lot more cheerful, a lot more upbeat."

"Your situation would stress anybody out," Bill encouraged her. "I think you've handled things incredibly well. And things are only going to get better for you from here."

"Thanks, Bill," Aspen said. "I really think that they are. How are you doing?"

"I'm great," he said. "I'm just watching NCIS, when the station will let me."

"Me, too," Aspen said excitedly. "I didn't know you liked that show."

"I've watched it since college. The storm warning breaks are getting annoying, though. I'm new in town; so tell me: is the weather as serious as they're saying?"

"It depends on which square mile the storm decides to hit," Aspen answered. "I wouldn't worry about it unless you're living in a trailer park, though."

"No, no cause to worry there," Bill answered. She could hear him smiling. "And you're hunkered down in that old farmhouse; so I guess I don't need to worry about you."

"Nope—I'm far from the first Spitzen to weather a storm in this old place," Aspen said. "Although it is different without Papa here—it was just reassuring to know that he was here, too. I can't wait until he comes home and things are back to normal."

"You think he'll be back to his old self, then?" Bill asked her.

Aspen smiled to herself. "I actually think he might be better than his old self."

"What do you mean?" Bill asked. "You sound hopeful. Did the doctors say something?"

"No, nothing like that," Aspen said. "It's just that he's been so angry for so long about what happened to my parents, and he seems like he might be letting go of that a bit. We have a Bible that Papa brought home from the crash site; it's all burned on the outside from the accident. Granny used to carry it around with her before she died—never reading it, just holding it. Well, Papa has always hated the sight of it. But I've thought for a while that it might help him. And when he had the stroke, I brought it to him and asked the nurses to keep it by him."

"He must have been upset to find it there when he woke up," Bill guessed.

"I was sure he would be," Aspen confessed, "but I asked him tonight whether he wanted me to take it away. He said no. When he said that, it just made me hope that he's changing, that he's letting go of his old grudge against God."

"I hope so; I really do," Bill told her. "I've always thought that things happen for a reason. Maybe this stroke is just what your grandfather needed to help him slow down and think differently. It's probably been hard on him having you grown up and gone so much of the time. He poured all of his energy into you until you didn't need him to do that. He's probably dealing with things now that he's put off for a while."

"I think you're right," Aspen told him. "I asked him about some things I said before he woke up, and he knew about them. He's been able to think the whole time; he just couldn't respond. If he needed time to think, he's had it. Oh, look—they put NCIS back on. I'll let you go."

"It was good to talk to you. I'm glad you're safe," Bill said.

Aspen said goodbye to him and hung up. Only then did it register with her that Bill had been worried about her. He'd seen the storm coming on television, and his first impulse had been to make sure that she was all right. *But I don't need anyone to take care of me. I can take care of myself,* she thought, irritated. She pressed the button to turn the sound back on. *All the same, it was sweet of him,* she admitted. And even though the show continued uninterrupted to the end, she had a hard time paying attention to it.

# Chapter Eight

*"Yet give attention to your servant's prayer and his plea for mercy, Lord my God. Hear the cry and the prayer that your servant is praying in your presence this day."*—*1 Kings 8:28*

ngela pushed Spitz through the sunlit halls of the hospital, pausing occasionally to turn the chair toward a window with a low casement so that Spitz could see outside. The storm last night had made a mess of the grounds. Trash cans had upended and spilled their contents, which the wind had seized and tossed all over the grass. Branches had broken from the large, old trees, some of them sizeable and dangerous. At one place, a huge branch had smashed a wooden bench by a duck pond. At another, a smaller branch had gone through a windshield.

"Would you look at that?" Angela said, pointing over Spitz's head to the shattered windshield. "That must have been some wind last night tearing around here."

Spitz thought of the buffeting winds at Trenton that had driven stinging hail into his face. He pitied anyone who'd had to be out in the winds that had blown through Virginia last night. And he thought of Aspen, driving home through the leading edge of the storm. *I hope she got home okay,* Spitz fretted silently. *Surely they'd tell me if anything happened to her.*

Angela pulled the chair away from the window and kept pushing it along the hall. "You know, you were just freezing cold when I checked on you this morning," Angela told him. "The temperature dropped twenty degrees in an hour. I felt so bad for you. I got the sun lamp on you as soon as I could and got you a couple of blankets. You didn't wake up until you were warm through. That's a mercy. I hate to think of you lying there cold."

*But I was,* Spitz thought. *I was colder than I've ever been before.* He paused a moment. *Wait a minute. I was cold before I went to sleep, but it was only bitter cold when I got to Trenton. What's happening to me? Am I dreaming when I go back in time to Washington, or is it really happening?*

He thought of the past. He had been hungry there, and tired and sore after working a full day hauling wood. The first time he had felt bitter cold at the trading post, it had still been mild and warm in the present. He had seen men die in front of him in ways he'd never imagined. He'd never actually seen a scalp being taken before, and the reality was much more gruesome than any movie he had ever watched. Surely he wasn't imagining things.

Spitz saw other patients along the hall, and Angela commented on them occasionally. One woman grimaced in pain, holding her stomach with one hand and the flat metal rail on the wall with the other as she walked step by shuffling step toward Spitz and Angela.

"You're doing great! Keep up the good work," Angela told her when they reached her.

"Thanks," she breathed, rounding a corner away from them.

"We were close to the maternity ward. She's obviously just had a C-section, and she needs to walk to heal the right way. She's only got a little farther to go before she can put up her feet and rest and see her baby again," Angela explained.

Down other hallways, Spitz saw people in wheelchairs with bandaged limbs or no hair and deep circles under their eyes. Some people walked pushing IV poles ahead of them. Some people he only saw in glimpses as he approached their doors, as he still could not turn his head. Those people lay prone under sheets, some conscious and others not.

The totality of the suffering weighed on Spitz. Everywhere he looked, he saw pain and disability and sadness. *You could do something about this, You know,* Spitz thought with a trace of his old bitterness. *I've never doubted that You're powerful. But that just makes it worse when I see people sick and wounded like this. Where are You? Why do You let things like this happen? Why don't You do anything about it?*

That quiet, insistent voice he had heard before said, *I am.*

*So what are You doing about it?* Spitz demanded.

As if in answer, Spitz remembered Rawlins talking to him in the library at Mount Vernon. "You forget on whose orders you travel. All times are now to Him," Rawlins had said.

*All times,* Spitz thought, really examining the phrase for the first time. A thought hit him.

The plucked fruit, the Roman cross, the rolled stone, Steve's birth, the plane crash, this moment now, the moment when the world would gasp to an end, and the next when it would rise reborn—all times were now to Him; He comprehended them all in an instant. Spitz's head swam.

*I have done. I am doing. I will do. I have been. I will be. I am. I am that I am. I always am, world without end, amen.*

Angela turned a corner into the hospital cafeteria. Spitz saw Aspen waiting for him, waving from a table by the window. She seemed a little subdued, though she smiled readily enough.

Angela pushed him to the table just as if he were about to eat a tray of food himself. Aspen got up and gave him a hug and a kiss on the cheek. He breathed an internal sigh of relief to see her safe and unharmed after the storm-brought destruction he had viewed outside.

"Don't worry; the house is still standing," she said lightly as soon as she sat back down. "We had a big limb fall from the huge elm way down the drive, and the rest of the yard is littered with branches. I told Bill about it, and he offered to come out this weekend to fire up your chainsaw and to restock your woodpile."

Angela frowned. "You don't seem too happy about that," she said.

Aspen sighed and put both hands over her face for a minute, and then she put them in her lap, where she twisted her napkin. "I think I blew it with Bill."

"I don't think you did if he wants to clean up your yard," Angela disagreed.

Aspen shook her head. "I told him no thanks on the yard this morning. And when I was leaving for lunch, to come here, he asked if he could come along. I told him no, and," she winced, "I wasn't very nice about it."

"Why do you think you weren't nice?" Angela asked.

Aspen sighed. "I don't know. It felt like a knee-jerk reaction. I'm so used to pushing people away that I didn't think before I spoke."

Angela leaned her head on an upraised palm. "You've seemed very nice to me. You haven't pushed me away."

"Men," Aspen clarified, "I'm used to pushing men away."

"Ah," Angela said delicately, "that's different."

"And he's so nice," Aspen worried, "he called last night during the storm just to make sure I was all right. And now I've gone and bitten his head off. I didn't mean to do that."

"You know, you don't have to wait until New Year's to make a fresh start. Every minute you draw breath is another chance," Angela told her, looking at her intently. Then she smiled gently and patted Aspen's hand. "Listen, why don't you talk to your Papa about what's happening? Ask him for some advice. I'll be back in half an hour to take him back to his room."

"Thanks, Angela," Aspen smiled. She looked back at Spitz. "She's right, I know. I need to apologize. It's just so embarrassing to tell somebody you were wrong, especially somebody you really like." She told Spitz about the conversation the night before. Spitz heard with surprise Bill's assessment of what was happening. He had never considered the way he had felt when Aspen had left for college and then for work. He had never connected his increased obsession over his case with his increased loneliness, but he had to admit that Bill had a point. Had Aspen sensed that point before someone told her about it?

He had always told her she didn't need to take care of him. He'd even tried his hand at matchmaking, setting Aspen up with promising young men. But despite his words and his efforts, did she somehow feel that she wasn't free to pursue anyone? Did she somehow sense his deep loneliness and seek to fill it herself?

She shouldn't. He didn't want that kind of sacrifice from her. But he could see now as he never had before that Aspen wouldn't listen to any assurances from him. She had to see for herself that he was all right. And that meant that Spitz had to be all right.

He had always thought of his loneliness as his problem. He assumed that he wasn't bothering anyone else. But he was. He was bothering the one person he would never want to hurt, just by being unhappy.

Aspen finished telling him about her talks with Bill the evening before on the phone and this morning at work. "I wish I knew how to relax around him, Papa," she said. "I keep acting so confident and put together, almost like I'm shouting at the people around me that I'm fine and don't need their help."

Spitz blinked once, to show he understood.

"Do you feel like that, too, Papa?"

Spitz blinked once. He did feel like that. He hadn't been honest with Aspen about how lonely he was without his wife and son.

"Have you been acting that way around me?"

Spitz blinked once again, realizing how wrong he had been. He hadn't recovered from his loneliness because he'd never acknowledged that it was there. Burying this hurt so deeply and shielding Aspen from it had only robbed her of the chance to learn how to be lonely and recover from it.

"I'm sorry I made you feel that way, Papa," Aspen told him.

Spitz blinked twice: no. He waited and blinked twice again.

"I know what you're saying, Papa, but I feel like it's my fault."

Spitz blinked twice again. This problem was his to solve. She had shouldered enough of what he hadn't bothered to fix. She wasn't going to shoulder the blame for his mistakes, too.

"Thank you, Papa," Aspen said, holding his hand. "And I want you to know that it's not your fault that I haven't dated. It's not your fault I've acted the way I have."

Spitz blinked twice again. How could she say that, after what he'd just realized?

"No, no—listen to me. You can apologize for your part in how messed up we are, but I have a part, too. I'm not a little girl anymore. If I've ruined chances I've had before because I was feeling sorry for you, it's my own doing. I'm stubborn. Any time I wanted to do it, I could have told you that feeling sorry for ourselves and holding grudges wasn't doing either of us any good. I could have said that. I could have let myself be happy and hoped you would be happy with me. But I didn't. I didn't say anything. That's my part."

Spitz blinked once. She was an adult. She was talking to him like an equal for the first time in their relationship. He was so proud of her.

"I want us to be happy, Papa—both of us," she said. "I think you have a really good chance now to start over. I do, too. I'm really glad for that chance."

Spitz blinked once. Aspen leaned over and kissed his cheek. Spitz saw love and admiration in her eyes. Touched, he realized: *She's proud of me, too.* Then she sat back and finished her lunch, between bites telling him a funny story about Bernie. If he could have laughed, he would have.

All too soon, Angela arrived to wheel him back to his room. Aspen said goodbye to him and left from the cafeteria. Angela backed Spitz's chair away from the table and pushed him back along the halls.

Once again, Angela provided a running commentary on the people they passed: a woman getting chemotherapy for cancer, a man who'd broken several bones in a fall, and a woman with a large bandage over her head, covering a gunshot wound. Spitz began to fret over the other patients again. The suffering around him seemed overwhelming.

"You know, Spitz," Angela began, "when I walk up and down these halls and see all of the patients inside, I just feel so grateful that we can help them."

The comment brought Spitz up short. He hadn't thought of things that way.

"You know, there are so many people in the world right now suffering because there's no one around to take care of them. One of the doctors here volunteers in Kenya every summer for a month, doing surgeries for free for as many people as he can see while he's there. When he's not around, there's no one else to perform the surgeries. It just breaks my heart. So when I see these people with bandages and IV bags and casts, I'm grateful they're healing. I'm grateful we can help them."

Angela chuckled and looked down at Spitz. "Just look at you, with your eyes open now. Pretty soon you'll remember how to talk or move your hands. You're getting better by the minute. I'm so happy when I see how far you've come."

Spitz was touched. Angela didn't have to care what happened to him one way or another, but she did. When she looked around, she saw healing taking place, not just suffering. Her perspective amazed him.

At the nurse's station, Angela got an orderly to help her put Spitz back in bed, and she smoothed a sheet and two blankets over him. Then she picked up his Bible from the counter and tucked it securely beside him. "I'll be back in a while to take your temperature and make sure that you're warm enough," she promised.

When she left, Spitz closed his eyes, grateful for the warmth and weight of the extra blanket. He was also grateful for Aspen: for the solid fact of her safety as well as for the way she had grown up and learned to see him and herself more objectively. Bill had something to do with that change, and while he was feeling grateful, Spitz went ahead and decided to be grateful for Bill as well. Adrift in gratitude and warmth, Spitz felt himself sliding into sleep, images from coming dreams flickering across his mind like scenes on a television with bad reception. One of them caught and stayed.

Then that image began to spin and to break into separate points of light, pulling him forward to another place and time. Spitz opened his eyes and gasped at the sudden cold. He was in the snow again, but it wasn't falling. It was drifted and banked over what looked like a village of tool sheds built of logs. He was on a hill above the poor village, shaking in the cold and watching smoke from the hearths stream away in the wicked wind.

He had read enough books and studied enough paintings and examined enough maps to need no further clue as to where and when he was. He was entirely sure that he was standing above Valley Forge, Pennsylvania, in the winter of 1777 through 1778. Below him in the valley, George Washington was staying in the house of Isaac Potts.

Spitz climbed down the hill a little stiffly. His body in the past had aged as Washington's had. In the present, he was seventy-six, born in 1937. In the past, he looked to be in his forties, like Washington, who would turn forty-six in February of 1778. But this middle-aged body was still much more active and capable than the one that had suffered the stroke. Even though he didn't feel the surge of joyful strength he'd experienced at the trading post, he had power enough and more for the descent to the valley and the journey across it.

As he neared the first cabin, he heard the sounds of wracking coughs inside, from not just one man but several. The sound repeated from every cabin he passed, a symphony of sickness, counterpart to the wind moaning around the cabins and shrieking through the trees and the river rushing past only partially frozen on his left. He knew from his reading about the sickness devastating the camp, a sickness compounded by starvation and freezing. Reading about it was one thing. Feeling the cold penetrating his bones, hearing the coughs, smelling the putrid air of illness, and knowing that the men inside languished with little food was another.

"Halt where ye stand," a voice called. A sentry appeared in the twilit winter gloom, leveling his rifle, bayonet fixed, to Spitz's chest. The poor fellow's cheekbones stood out in sharp relief, and his eyes sunk deep into his face. He coughed as he spoke and swayed against the wind. The bayonet point bobbled and wove with him, tracing a crazy pattern in front of Spitz's chest.

Spitz inched back and raised his hands. "I'm here to see General Washington," he explained. "Can you tell me where to find him?"

The man looked at him as if he'd spoken a different language. "General Washington? Do ye want me to take ye to King George and the Apostle Paul after, too? No, man, I take ye to Lieutenant Monroe, and there I leave ye."

Spitz grinned despite himself—he'd read about the Monroe at Valley Forge. Lieutenant Monroe was James Monroe, future president of the United States. "I'll be pleased to go with you to the lieutenant."

"Pleased or no, ye walk before," the man said, gesturing feebly with his rifle.

Pitying the weak man behind him, Spitz walked ahead of the sentry, who followed him with the rifle. Spitz was sure he could knock him over with little effort if he tried.

The sentry led him to a fire of logs burning in a pit dug in the ground. A group of men, most wearing officer insignia, warmed their hands and stamped their feet around it. A somewhat short, thin, very young man saw him coming with the sentry and walked forward. "Who have we here, Private Gray?" he asked briskly.

"Some man to see General Washington," Gray shrugged. "I know him not."

"I have him in hand, private. You may return to your post," Monroe said firmly.

Gray saluted rather casually, Spitz thought, and trudged back through the snow.

Monroe eyed Spitz seriously. "Who are you, sir, and on what business have you come here?"

"My name is Stephen Spitzen, and I'm an old friend of General Washington's," Spitz said. "I heard he was encamped here and wanted to see him."

Monroe nodded to another man, who loped off through the snow to Spitz's right. "I shall pass your name along to the general and inquire whether he will see you." Monroe stretched his hands out to the fire.

"Thank you," Spitz said. He took a tentative step forward, hands still up, and stretched them slowly to the fire. Monroe made no objection. Spitz rubbed his hands together vigorously over the flames. "I'm sorry to hear you men have had such a rough time out here," he offered.

Monroe nodded to him, not willing to complain to a stranger. "Though the conditions are far from adequate, our knowledge that we suffer hardship for a worthy cause both comforts and betters us."

"I'm sure it does," Spitz agreed. "And I agree with you that the cause is worthy."

Monroe eyed him skeptically, evidently reserving judgment until word arrived from General Washington. "You say that you are an old friend of the general's. May I ask how you know him?"

Spitz readily answered, "I met him the first time in January of 1754, when he was on a diplomatic mission for Governor Dinwiddie, and that summer I served as his aide-de-camp at Fort Necessity. Since then, we've run into each other a few times. The last time was at Trenton."

Monroe raised his eyebrows. "You were at Trenton, sir?"

"Just before," Spitz said. "I was near the town and ended up getting caught in the battle."

Monroe nodded. "I was wounded at Trenton. It was a great victory."

"It was," Spitz agreed. "I hope your wound is healed."

Monroe bowed slightly. Footsteps sounded off to Spitz's right, and the runner returned. "He's to come to the general straightaway, Lieutenant," the runner panted, his breath steaming like the plume of a freight engine.

"Thank you, Sergeant," Monroe said. "You may take him."

Still in disbelief that he'd had a conversation with another future president, Spitz said goodbye to Monroe. As he followed the sergeant through the maze of cabins, he wondered why God had allowed him such significant meetings. The sergeant led Spitz across a snowy meadow to a snug, stone, two-story farmhouse. At the door, the sergeant leading him handed him to a servant and instructed him to leave his belongings outside.

As Spitz stacked his pack and rifle by the front door, keeping only his messenger bag, he looked closely at the servant. He'd seen this man before, at Mount Vernon, then older and shedding tears for his dying master. He was sure it was the same man. Spitz looked from the man to the staircase and the front room. Several low-ranking soldiers slept in awkward positions on the stairs and the floor and the plain wooden chairs. No matter how uncomfortable they looked, Spitz knew that they were much warmer and more comfortable here than in the small cabins he had passed. His heart glowed to think of General Washington opening his quarters to house some of the men.

The servant quietly opened a door off the hall and ushered Spitz inside a dining room. He saw a long farmhouse table, covered in a white cloth and good china to make the best of the short rations. Spitz saw a steaming tureen of soup, a plate of bread, and a plate of pickles: meager fare for so many. Ten chairs stood around the table, and at each one an officer or a lady sat. Several officers sat in other chairs around the room.

When Spitz entered, Washington rose and extended a hand to him. "Mr. Spitzen, I bid you welcome. Have you dined? Please do join us."

Spitz raised a hand to decline. "General, you're very kind, but I ate a short time ago."

The servant returned through the door Spitz had just entered. Spitz hadn't even noticed him going. He carried a chair, which he placed beside one of the officers at the edge of the room. He extended a hand, motioning for Spitz to sit down. Spitz did, nodding at the man and flashing him a brief smile. What did you say to a man who had done you a courtesy when he was not free to refuse it? How could you say anything to him that did not smack of capitulation to his condition?

"Thank you, Billy," Washington said. The servant half bowed and walked to the general, where he stood behind Washington's chair, gazing over the heads of the company and looking supremely unconcerned with anything they said.

Martha Washington smiled at Spitz and said, "Mr. Washington was telling us all before you joined us, Mr. Spitzen, about your kind assistance to him when he was nearly freezing to death from a splash in an icy river."

Eyes turned to Spitz, who ducked his head, a little embarrassed, and said, "I'm only glad I was nearby when he needed some help."

"You are too modest, Spitz," Washington said, shaking his head.

"Mr. Spitzen was on sentry duty for a trading post during the aggression by France and her Indian allies preceding the Seven Years' War. There had been a terrible massacre at a settlement the day before, and the post filled with men enraged by the deed and maddened to avenge it." Washington paused and looked at Spitz for confirmation

"They were pretty worked up," Spitz agreed.

"The man who owned the post instructed Mr. Spitzen to view any new arrivals with a presumption of hostility. Now you must picture that Mr. Gist, who acted as my guide through that rough land, wore skin clothes very like Indian winter raiment, and the poor, draggled rags that clothed me after my sojourn in the Allegheny were scarcely recognizable as the uniform of an official person, especially from so far away as Mr. Spitzen stood. Would you call that hill by the post a mile distant from the valley, Mr. Spitzen?" Washington asked.

"About that, sir," Spitz nodded.

"Gist had valiantly assisted me through the snow for seven miles from the river. However, we both suffered abominably from the cold, and I stumbled to my knees. By all rights, Mr. Spitzen could have fired a warning shot and roused the rabble within to begin shooting at the intruders. But compassion ruled him instantly, and he flew to our side. That moment of empathy showed me what manner of person he was, and further acquaintance has established that judgment." Washington raised a glass to him. "I drink to your health, sir," he said.

"To your health," the other officers repeated, each one drinking to Spitz, whose ears would have turned red with embarrassment if they had not already been so with cold.

"Thank you, General Washington," Spitz told him, happy that his hero thought so highly of him. "But I have to say I owe as much to you. If you hadn't fired grapeshot on the French soldiers and Indians who attacked Braddock in '55 and stopped their pursuit, we wouldn't have been able to retreat. Every one of us still alive owes you thanks for that day."

General Washington inclined his head, accepting the thanks. "All of us owe our thanks to a kind Providence who has watched over us and protected us so far. I know that for me, 'Providence has a… claim to my humble and grateful thanks, for its protection and direction of me.'[39]"

A murmur of assent ran through the room, taking Spitz off guard. He had imagined Washington's faith as isolated to him, the strong man who singlehandedly pulled his army through Valley Forge on the strength of his titanic generalship and fervent prayers. But the officers around this table shared that faith. Evidently they called on God, too. The revelation didn't diminish Washington, though; it only showed a little more plainly the invisible hand that Washington trusted.

"You have known Mr. Washington for quite a lengthy span of years then, Mr. Spitzen," Mrs. Washington said kindly. "I wonder that we have not seen you at Mount Vernon."

"That lapse has not been for want of asking, my dear," Washington told her, blue eyes twinkling. "Mr. Spitzen travels the world as a merchant, and he is most diligent to his business. Perhaps if we arrange to host Mr. Spitzen on board a ship in the middle of the Indian Ocean, he may accept the invitation."

Laughs went round the table, and Spitz joined them. When they quieted, he said, "I've managed to see you often enough without an invitation, sir. I don't want to wear out my welcome."

General Washington smiled. "You are most welcome, whenever you choose to come. I have been most fortunate in the character of new arrivals to camp this late winter. A week ago, my dear wife and Baron von Steuben arrived within a day of one another, and now I may count an old friend among the number. Tomorrow, the month of March arrives, and I trust that it will bring an abatement of the poor gifts of sickness and poverty January and February had in hand."

"Hear, hear," an officer said. "We are all cheered by the presence of Mrs. Washington and encouraged by the appearance of the baron, who demonstrates to us that our cause does find friends among other nations."

Baron von Steuben stood and bowed formally to the officer who had made the remark. "I trust that my own contributions may materially benefit your new nation," he said formally in heavily accented English. "And I rejoice with you that you may now count France as an ally." The baron sat down again. Spitz could see in his every gesture the mark of military service and rigid discipline.

"Vive la France!" another officer called, and some officers echoed him cheerfully while others laughed.

"You know that Mr. Franklin has been working assiduously on our behalf in France," Washington told Spitz. "Baron von Steuben met the French Minister of War, who in turn introduced him to Franklin. Von Steuben has served among the ranks of the general staff of Frederick the Great, the King of Prussia. He retired from his king's military service and has timely presented himself to serve America, for which offer we are all most truly grateful."

The baron nodded vigorously at Washington. "Yes, I have nearly completed my observations of the army at drill. I trust that the recommendations for training I will soon offer will unite these men of different colonies into the army of one nation."

The officers murmured fervent assent again, and Spitz was struck this time with the love these men felt for their nascent country. Their devotion to creating America warmed him.

He sat back through the rest of the dinner, content to listen to the conversation around him and recognize the occasional profile from a history book. Among them, very near Washington, Spitz recognized the distinguished features of the Marquis de Lafayette as well as the imposing girth and ringing voice of the artillery chief, Henry Knox. The fact that a baron and a marquis could sit at table and share poor rations with common-born descendants of English immigrants made Spitz proud of his country, where all men were created equal.

Then he looked above Washington's head to the immobile face of his servant, Billy, and his heart sank. *Not quite all men,* he thought. *It will be a stain across the founding of this country forever that men who were so moral and upstanding didn't recognize and correct the one glaring evil in their society. They did well, but they could have done much better.*

After dinner, the officers and their wives rose to go to their own quarters. After shaking a few hands and talking to a few men and kissing Martha Washington's hand, General Washington came over to Spitz and clasped his hand firmly. "The sight of you puts me in good heart, Spitz," Washington said. "If men of your caliber have come to join the cause, forsaking all their material concerns, how can we but win? Walk with me while we search out a space for you."

"Yes, sir," Spitz said, not knowing how to correct Washington's assumption that he had come to stay and not knowing how long he would actually stay in the past. How long would pass until he saw what he was supposed to see and wrote what he was supposed to write and disappeared from view without a word?

At the door, Washington paused while Billy hung a cloak over his shoulders and handed him his hat. Spitz was already in all the clothes he possessed, and he knew from the looks of the sentry who had halted him that he was better dressed than most of the other men here. He retrieved his pack and rifle and followed Washington through the bitter cold to the cabins for common soldiers. Their boots squeaked in the clean, powdery snow.

But Washington did not stop at the cabins. He passed right through them and walked over a narrow footbridge across the Schuylkill River. On the other side, past a grove of trees and a rise of ground, Spitz saw row after row of dead men being loaded into carts and wagons. *They're enough to people a small cemetery back home*, he thought.

Washington halted. "Here you see the casualties of an internecine war," he said hollowly. "I have already lost more than a thousand men in this valley, and I fear more will fall. These men need not have died. Had we proper channels in government to look to the supply of these brave soldiers who lay their lives in our very hands, I would command so many more men. I regret their loss; I regret it most deeply. Now I must have the fallen carted far away from their comrades in order to sustain morale. Such a dramatic daily picture of the vastness of the toll paid here would be too much for any of us to bear."

Spitz looked over at Washington and saw tears standing in the general's eyes. He looked away quickly, not wishing to embarrass the great man. "I'm sure that you've done all you can to help them."

"I have written again and again and stated the gravity of the deprivations the men suffer as clearly as I can. But we languished for months until Congress deigned to send a committee to examine the truth of my reports, and now we have languished another month with no material relief. I have even sacrificed my most trusted man, General Nathaniel Greene, to supply the deficit in leadership along the chain of supply. And still the men decline day by day," Washington lamented.

"I didn't realize how serious things were when I came," Spitz said. It was true. The descriptions in the books he had read could not possibly do justice to the sights and smells and sounds of sickness and starvation in this place.

"Unless some great and capital change suddenly takes place … this Army must inevitably be reduced to one or other of these three things. Starve, dissolve or disperse, in order to obtain subsistence in the best manner they can."[35] Washington sighed, his eyes fixed on the men loading another wagon not far from him. "We have been on the point of dissolution, and I know not whether the melancholy event may not take place."[36]

"Surely the men wouldn't just desert," Spitz said. "They can't—the whole country is depending on them!"

"Would you blame them for wanting, as every creature does, to hold body and soul together at any cost? 'The skeleton of an Army presents itself to our eyes in a naked, starving condition, out of health, out of spirits.'[37] I do not blame any man so reduced for desiring to keep his life. What maddens me is how easily Congress could relieve this suffering with the few strokes of a pen. Yet we wait in want while brave and loyal men continue to die needlessly!"

The general turned away from the death wagons and began walking back toward the bridge and the cabins beyond. Spitz followed him. "I have a devoted guard of men, Spitz, who fight near my person in every engagement, though they perform other duties as well. I trust each man with my life, as I also trust you. If you are willing, I would have you join their number. I can think of no more fitting place for you to serve." Though Washington had just conferred a tremendous honor on Spitz, the general smiled humbly at Spitz, the way Spitz thought he might smile if he had to apologize to Aspen for a substandard Christmas present.

"I'm willing, sir," Spitz said.

Washington's smile broadened. "You do realize, sir, that having given me your word, you have at last placed yourself in a condition guaranteeing that I shall know when and where to expect you. Apart from those few months at Great Meadows when you served as my aide-de-camp, such an expectation has not characterized our acquaintance."

"I know it, sir," Spitz admitted. "Our meetings have been a bit—irregular."

Washington chuckled. "I have a cat in the stables at Mount Vernon who reminds me of you. He calls no man master, for he appears and leaves as he pleases. Yet he is a valiant fighter and a terror to the mice amongst the grain. I wonder whether he would submit to the character of a pet if I asked him. I suspect not."

Spitz chuckled, too. "At least I'm one up on the cat," he quipped.

Washington grinned, and he clapped Spitz on the shoulder. The two of them wended their way through the cabins to a section Washington evidently knew well; it was the closest to his own quarters at the farmhouse owned by Israel Potts, the Quaker blacksmith.

Washington knocked on the door of the cabin and introduced Spitz to the men inside. One of them was Caleb Gibbs, the commander of the Life Guards. Gibbs welcomed Spitz and promised to take him under his wing. From the lean, grizzled look of Gibbs, who reminded Spitz of the typical gunnery sergeant in a World War II film, Spitz was pretty sure that taking him under his wing meant assigning him extra drills.

He wasn't far wrong. The guards drilled longer than the other units, practicing maneuvers and marksmanship and running and hiking through the hills for physical conditioning. They also had set up a regular rotation to guard General Washington personally. Several of them followed him wherever he went in Valley Forge and stood guard outside his quarters whenever he went inside. Before long, Spitz joined this rotation, too.

He lived with fifteen of the other guards in one of the tiny cabins. The place was barely large enough for all of the men to lie down in it, and the drafty chimney blew the smoke from their fire into the room. Spitz marveled at how the cracks in the log walls managed to keep the smoke from escaping while letting the cold wind in at the same time. There was no window; so the only light came from the cracks in the walls and around the casement of the door or the fire at the hearth and the daylight mingled with it that found its way down the chimney, not that the guards spent much time in the cabin during the daylight.

And Spitz lived on army rations, too—the meager dole of salt fish and coarse flour that all the men got. Spitz soon learned that anything tastes good if you're hungry enough—even the flour and water gruel the men often made at breakfast. Occasionally, he got to eat bread. He hadn't missed bread so much since the time Aspen had persuaded him to try a low-carb diet.

Gibbs regularly frowned at Spitz's frontier clothes. "As soon as

General Greene sorts out the supplies, you must get a proper uniform. A guard cannot attend Washington dressed like an Indian trader."

Spitz agreed. Next to the other men in the guard, he definitely looked shabby. *On the other hand, I'm definitely a lot more comfortable,* he thought. He especially liked his stoutly-made leather boots. He wanted to get some just like them when he was up and walking around back in the twenty-first century.

One day, about a week after he'd arrived in camp, Spitz left duty outside the general's headquarters with nine other guards. The dawn was foggy and cold, though the afternoons had been warm enough lately to allow most of the snow to melt. The men marched in formation back to their cabins, ready for a few hours' sleep after their night of standing watch over Washington. Spitz's stomach growled. He looked forward almost happily to his morning flour and water gruel.

The fog parted in a freshening wind, and Spitz saw movement on the water at about the same time as several other men. Abandoning the formation, the men ran to the seething river, which churned like a boiling pot. "Fish!" a man beside Spitz called, dropping to his knees. He thrust a sure hand into the icy river and pulled up a wriggling shad. "Fish!" he yelled again, running toward the cabins with his prize in his hand.

Word spread swiftly, and dragoons leapt barebacked to their horses and raced them to the river. The shad were spawning upstream, battling the fierce spring current just like salmon, and unless something stopped them, they would escape to the creeks and tributaries of the Schuylkill out of the valley. The horses scared them and turned them back downstream, where they roiled and clashed with thousands of other fish just as determined to go the other way.

Men came running and shouting with nets, with poles, with baskets, with branches hastily stripped from trees, and with their bare fists. They stood on the bank or waded in to their knees or their chests, scooping fish from the water and tossing them to the bank. Men filled wagon beds and hastily emptied and refilled chests and trunks and baskets with fish and fish and more fish.

Soon an appetizing aroma wafted to Spitz's nostrils. He handed the tree branch in his hands to a man on shore and climbed out of the river, wet to his waist. His buckskin clothing was sodden and dripping, but he didn't care. Someone somewhere was roasting fish over an open fire, and he wanted some. He joined a line of men around a huge bonfire, all of them wet through and freezing in the early March morning. And after too long a wait, he accepted with gratitude a portion of roasted fish, gutted and cleaned and spit on a stick. It was marvelous. And though it wasn't near enough, he finished it and went back to catching more in the Schuylkill.

Over the next days, as long as the run lasted, the men abandoned every other occupation but catching and cleaning and gutting and preserving the miraculous, mobile chain of supply that had just arrived at their collective front door. As Spitz worked, phrases and stories kept recurring to his mind, things he didn't intend to recall but couldn't quite suppress.

*"Cast your nets to the other side;" a widow with a never-ending supply of oil and flour; a man waiting for ravens to bring him bread and meat; thousands and thousands of women on their hands and knees in the desert, gathering grain that had rained in the night; a single widow, following the threshers, finding more than she ever expected; hundreds of people passing bread and fish from hand to hand—bread and fish that never grew smaller, no matter how many hands broke them—miracle after miracle after miracle, all of them saying in different times and places, "I am. I am more than enough. I am the God who supplies your need. This is My body; this is My blood. Take and eat."*

The next week, when the first supply wagons arrived from General Greene, Spitz had another cause for rejoicing, though it was one he acknowledged was more than a little vain.

He had his Life Guard uniform.

The buff-colored accents of his blue coat matched his breeches. The facings on the front of the coat were white, as was the pair of shirts issued to him. The cast pewter buttons adorning the coat bore the insignia USA. A blue pleated turban encircled the sides of his brimmed black leather helmet and fastened with a silver chain. The left side boasted a white cockade and an impressive white feather plume tipped in royal blue. Over the top center, fashioned from front to back like a Mohawk, was a large strip of genuine black bearskin-fur. The ensemble together looked impressive.

Now that he dressed like a soldier and ate more like one, Spitz found that he could drill more like a soldier, too. He carried himself more surely in that magnificent uniform, and Gibbs no longer looked at him with quite as much disappointment. The trusty rifle that had appeared for him everywhere from Frazier's trading post to Great Meadows to Trenton got a thorough workout.

In the evenings, Spitz was tired from his unaccustomed exercise. He ate and talked and traded stories with the other guards, keeping the leather messenger bag tucked in a corner of the cabin behind his pack. Spring warmed and breathed around him, quickening the grass and trees and birds and squirrels as surely as it did the men.

One mild evening as he sat at the door of his cabin and gazed over the Schuylkill, the leather messenger bag seemed to press on his mind with inexplicable urgency. He got up, moved his pack aside, and picked it up. Somehow, he knew where he wanted to go to write.

He walked slowly to the footbridge over the river and passed through the grove of trees on the other side. *Praise God*, he thought before catching himself. The death wagons were now far fewer in number and much less active than was the case when he first cast eyes on them after his arrival in camp. He thought of Washington's anguish, and he remembered something he had heard Washington say to Lafayette while he had been standing guard only a few days before, "Thanks to heaven the tables are turned."[40] Seeing the decrease in the number of death wagons finally brought that change home to Spitz as nothing else had.

He lay on his stomach at the edge of the fresh meadow overlooking the few mostly idled wagons, pondering what to write. But this time, as he wrote, he took his Bible out and laid it on top of the messenger bag, its burned cover crumbling, sending leather dust to mingle with the dust and ashes beyond.

**Sign 10 (Godsend at Valley Forge)**—The February 6, 1778 decision of France to ally with the United Colonies and its promise to send significant numbers of troops along with a powerful naval

fleet seemed to answer Patrick Henry's March 23, 1775 prophecy that "there is a just God who presides over the destinies of
nations; and He will raise up friends to fight our battles for us."[38]

**Sign 11 (Godsend at Valley Forge)**—Baron von Steuben mysteriously and unexpectedly arrived at Valley Forge; Steuben became
Inspector General of the army, trained trainers, and developed the
first military training manual of the United States. Miraculously,
he molded a dysfunctional force of twelve thousand militiamen
into a disciplined and synchronized fighting army, just in time for
the early summer campaign. He was the direct answer to specific
prayer for leadership in the area of military training.

**Sign 12 (at Valley Forge)**—George Washington actually per-
ceived he was being directed by God: 'Providence has a... claim
to my humble and grateful thanks, for its protection and direction of me...'[39] 'Thanks to heaven the tables are turned,'[40]– George
Washington.

**Favorable Interposition 4 (Godsend at Valley Forge)**—A miraculous early run of shad arrived at the Valley Forge encampment,
ending the starvation of the men. Their prayer for provision was
answered in an unexpected way and in biblical proportions.


Spitz looked at the record in his handwriting. Then he set the calfskin
journal very carefully beside the Bible. *I can keep writing,* he said. *It's
all true. You've saved Washington's life over and over again. You've provided for the people around him. You've advanced his career. But look
at that Bible. That's true, too. And so far, knowing what good care You
took of Washington doesn't make me feel any better about You falling
down on the job with Steve. I just don't know what else You could have
to say about that. And why did You pick Washington? What's so special
about him that nothing ever touches him? Why doesn't he have to suffer?*
"Spitz," Washington said gently. "Have you come to pray for
them, too?"
Tears streaming down his face, Spitz looked up to Washington. He

hastily wiped his face on the sleeve of his uniform, but Washington had seen.

"You are distressed, Spitz. What can I do to aid you?" Washington asked, concerned. He sank to one knee and fixed Spitz with a look of compassion.

"Nothing," Spitz coughed, scrubbing his face more roughly, though his tears continued to fall. "No one can do anything."

"Surely the case is not as hopeless as you think it now," Washington encouraged him. "Confide in me, friend, and allow me to repay a small part of the debt I owe you. Whatever is in my power to give is yours."

A dam in Spitz's soul seemed to break, a dam that had been holding back his resentment and jealousy, and he saw Washington not as the Founding Father, the noble patriot, or the friend at whose side he'd fought, but as a pampered, wealthy favorite of God who was kept from all real harm. Washington lived some charmed life while men around him starved and suffered wounds and lost loved ones. Rage at the inequity filled Spitz.

"Can you raise the dead?" he demanded. "Can you give me my son back? Is that in your power to give? No one can help me, no one—especially not you, the man nothing can touch," Spitz nearly shouted. Then, ashamed of his outburst, he covered his eyes with one hand and turned away.

Silence stifled the air in the clearing, seeming to mute all sound but his heaving breaths and Washington's calm ones. Miserable in his own grief and decades-old bitterness, Spitz waited for Washington to get up and call the guard who was doubtless a few steps away to clap him in irons and lead him away for disrespecting a commanding officer and conduct unbecoming. *Control yourself, Spitz.* Silently, he admonished himself, guiltily hoping for mercy from the man he'd just accused.

A strong hand fell on his shoulder. "I am sorry for your grief," Washington said, voice trembling. "I am sorry for it most because I do know it. You say that nothing touches me, but you have not heard, perhaps, that my daughter Patsy is lost to me. She was seventeen, lovely in youth and blithe spirits, all that was good and bright and fresh. I loved her, and grief at her death oppressed me for a season as well. Any parent who loved a child would feel as you do."

"I didn't know," Spitz said contritely. If the biography of Washington he'd read had mentioned Patsy at all, it was as a footnote, a trivial setback in the life of the great man.

"You had no cause to know," Washington said kindly. "But you must not think of me as a man untouched by death. I have more than a passing acquaintance with him, as you remember that he has taken my father and elder brother as well. And these deaths, too," Washington said, nodding to the path along which the wagons had traveled so busily when the snow was thick on the ground, "these deaths touch me as well, though not so near as my own family. Do you remember the words of King Henry V before Agincourt, Spitz? 'We few, we happy few, we band of brothers; / For he to-day that sheds his blood with me / Shall be my brother.'[41] Already in this war, many of my brothers have freely laid their lives on the altar of liberty and gone with death willingly. Their losses touch me as well."

"I'm sorry; I didn't mean to say what I did," Spitz winced.

"Think no more of it," Washington said kindly. "Have you just learned of your child's death?"

"No," Spitz said, embarrassed and defensive. "But it feels like it was yesterday."

"I condole with you most sincerely," Washington said warmly. "Parental feelings are too much alive in the moment of these misfortunes to admit the consolations of religion or philosophy; but I am persuaded reason will call one or both of them to your aid as soon as the keenness of your anguish is abated. He that gave you know has a right to take away, his ways are wise, they are inscrutable, and irresistible."[42]

Spitz shook his head. He laid his hand on the Bible, and his words escaped in a kind of wounded whisper. "My son and his wife died in a terrible fire. He was my only son, and he died when he was still young in a kind of pain I can't even imagine. My wife died of her grief, and all I have left in the world is my granddaughter. How can you believe that God had a right to take them? How can you say that what He did to me is wise?"

Washington placed his hand beside Spitz's on the burned cover. "This book escaped the burning?" he asked.

Spitz nodded.

"Inside its covers you may read of another Father who lost His only Son while he was yet young to a torturous death beside which any other agony pales in comparison. That Father's grief for His Son shook the world, opened graves, rent rocks, and turned the noon sky black as midnight. He knows how deep the sorrow of the bereaved is. Yet his grief abated, for His Son was not lost to Him forever. Nor is yours," Washington said softly. "You will see him again, when he welcomes you to glory."

Another tear fell from Spitz's saddened face onto the burned cover of the book. He could not find suitable words to say in return. He wanted to accept the comfort Washington offered him, but it felt cold and thin, like ice water when he wanted soup. More tears fell on the book. Spitz drew in a startled breath. Those were not his tears.

He looked over and saw Washington, one hand on Spitz's shoulder and the other on the charred Bible, shedding tears over Steve's death and Spitz's grief. His eyes were closed, and his lips moved slightly. Spitz realized that Washington was silently praying. Then Washington began to pray aloud, for him. Spitz closed his own eyes and kept quiet, warmed and heartened and humbled at the response.

After a while, Spitz felt a gentle pat on his shoulder. He sensed Washington getting up and heard him walking away silently, leaving Spitz to his thoughts. Other steps withdrew as well, and Spitz knew that his fellow guards were leaving, following Washington.

Spitz sighed, his soul in a wretched muddle. He had provoked a fight, taunting Washington with his invincibility, and instead of returning the hostility, Washington had comforted him and cried with him and prayed with him: two broken, bereaved fathers calling on a third for help.

And most of Spitz's soul wanted that help desperately. He was weary of his bitterness, weary of the toll it had taken on him and on Aspen, and weary of life alone, with no help from God. He missed the consolation of prayer and worship and the company of other believers.

But to rest from his bitterness and accept the consolations he had missed meant that he had to agree with Washington that God had a right to take Steve and Nevaeh and Mia. He had to let go of that grudge utterly; he had to withdraw his accusation. And that hard knot inside of him would not yet untie.

Part of what bound it was a voice which whispered that Washington still had a son. He didn't know the depth of Spitz's pain; so he couldn't really say anything about it. Losing a daughter was different than losing a son, and losing one of two children was not as painful as losing an only child. The cases were entirely different, that voice whispered. You couldn't really even compare them.

Spitz recognized that voice from a book of the Bible he hadn't read in years. But the voice had urged the same argument against another righteous man. He had his wealth, his children, his health, his life: of course he would worship God. The voice had dared God to take it all away and see what happened. And God had taken everything away from Job. But Job, childless and poor and ill, huddled in a heap of ashes, still blessed God.

*Is that what you wish? Do you want to see everything stripped from Washington, too? Would you take the part of the accuser against your friend?*

The voice was gentle, but the rebuke scared Spitz. *No,* he thought quickly. *I don't want to see him hurt. I don't want to see him lose anything else.*

But part of him wondered if that was really true, and if God knew secrets deep in Spitz's heart that he would never find, let alone admit. He shuddered.

A shadow fell over him, and he looked up quickly, startled. A tall man with broad shoulders and an odd, flat hat over his long, gray hair stood beside him. The man backed a step away.

"Peace, friend," the man said, "I mean thee no harm."

Spitz rose to his feet. "I didn't think anyone else was here," he said.

"No more of thy brethren," the man agreed, "but I bear no arms."

Spitz put the heavily muscled arms together with the sober clothes and the old-fashioned speech and recognized Isaac Potts, the Quaker blacksmith who owned the whole valley. "I'm sorry, Mr. Potts," Spitz apologized. "I should have expected you on your own land."

Mr. Potts nodded, accepting the apology. "I walk this grove often now on chances of meeting thy commander. He comes here often to pray. It is no wonder God blesses him. And God is sure to bless thee, too, seeing how thou dost remember Him."

Spitz shook his head guiltily. "That was General Washington praying for me. I only listened. He's a far better man than I am."

"He is a far better man than many of us," Potts agreed. "The first time I saw the general at his prayers, weeping and crying aloud for help for his poor men yonder, a holy hush settled on this whole place, like the one around the bush that Moses saw. I walked right away home and described to my wife what manner of man had camped his force in our valley, and I told her, 'If there is any one on this earth whom the Lord will listen to, it is George Washington; and I felt a pre-sentiment that under such a commander there can be no doubt of our eventually establishing our independence, and that God in his providence hath willed it so.'"[43] He fixed a confident eye on Spitz, expecting agreement.

Spitz nodded. Even a conscientious objector, committed to peace on principle, saw God's hand in Washington's command. That kind of faith from such an unlikely source shamed Spitz further, especially when he remembered that the British army had burned Potts's forge and outbuildings, leaving only his home and the homes of his relatives intact. He'd lost his living and his wealth, but he still saw God's invisible hand at work.

"I know that God has something great in store for George Washington," Spitz said.

Potts nodded and began to walk away. Then he turned and said solemnly, "If thou dost mean to fight, friend, look to thine own prayers." He lifted a hand in greeting and kept walking in the other direction.

Spitz looked down to the Bible at his feet. The sun had set while he talked to George Washington and Isaac Potts, and now bright, distant stars spangled the eastern sky as twilight dimmed in the west. He stooped and put away his journal and his writing materials, and then he carefully put the Bible back into his messenger bag.

He walked back to his cabin, lifting a hand in greeting to the men who called to him but stopping to talk to none of them. His heart was heavy, and he didn't want to think any more. He only wanted to lie down and look at the stars and go to sleep without trying to solve the unsolvable puzzle of his case that he could neither drop nor win. When he finally did lie down to sleep by the open door of the cabin, his bag acting as his pillow yet again, he gazed at those stars for comfort. And then they became a tunnel, drawing him deep into the night in a fantastic whirl of lights.

# Chapter Nine

*"His eyes are on the ways of men; he sees their every step."*
*—Job 34:21 NIV1984*

*He rescues me unharmed from the battle*
*waged against me, even though many oppose me."*
*—Psalm 55:18*

spen punched the elevator button and looked up at Bill as the doors closed. "I'm really glad you're going to meet my Papa. And listen, about this morning, I just wanted to say that I'm really sorry for snapping at you."

"Apology accepted," Bill said, smiling across at her. "I know it's been a tough time for you. I'm sure you wouldn't have snapped like that six months ago."

Aspen's cheeks turned red. "Actually, I think I might have. It's just been me and Papa for so long that I'm not good at letting anyone else in. I've been scared to leave him alone one day. He needs me."

Bill's smile faded. "Is that what Bernie meant by the warning he gave me?" he asked lightly.

Aspen grimaced. "That's what he meant, although that warning was completely embarrassing and unnecessary in your case." She turned even brighter red and cleared her throat. "Not that I'm ready to start dating anyone," she clarified, "I just want to stop pushing people away. I'm starting to realize that I don't need to be some superhero. I need other people. I need help sometimes." Aspen sighed. *Okay—let's see if we can make this anymore awkward,* she thought sarcastically. *I actually don't think that's possible.*

"That's a hard lesson to learn, especially for independent types," Bill said. "My mother is a really strong woman, too, and so is my sister. I've had practice stepping back and letting them handle what they can do alone. And they've had practice asking for help when they need it. Granted, we still step on each other's toes, but that's going to happen with family, and with friends." He held up his hands in surrender and smiled again. "From now on, your chainsaw is off limits."

"Deal," Aspen grinned. The elevator doors dinged, and Aspen looked at the numbered floor panel. "This is us," she told Bill.

They walked off the elevator and down the hall. A nurse who recognized Aspen waved, and Aspen waved back, though she didn't stop to chat. She didn't want to deal with any more embarrassment so soon after her apology, like questions from friendly nurses about her exact relationship to the tall, handsome man beside her.

Aspen stopped at Papa's door and started to knock out of habit, but then she caught herself. She saw the hospital chaplain bent forward with her father's Bible in his hand, reading to Papa. Papa's eyes were open, and he looked at the chaplain as he read. Tears of happiness pricked Aspen's eyes. She turned a glowing face to Bill and whispered, "He's listening! He's listening to the chaplain read my father's Bible!"

Bill put an arm around her shoulders and hugged her from the side, smiling kindly. "That's great!" he whispered back.

Aspen felt a little dizzy when Bill let her go. As she hadn't expected that kind of spontaneous affection, the sudden hug unsettled her. She blushed and kept watching her Papa, suddenly unsure of what to do with her hands and whether she was swallowing too loudly.

Papa looked toward the door, and Aspen knew he had seen her through the panel window above the knob. She opened the door and smiled brightly. "I didn't want to interrupt," she said, looking from her Papa to the chaplain, who stood when she came in.

"Oh, it's no trouble," Ed Campbell smiled. "We've been reading for a while now. The verses are in regular numbers, but I printed a cheat sheet to help me along with the chapters," he said, waving a piece of paper in Aspen's direction. Roman numerals into the hundreds lined one side of the page, and their Arabic equivalents lined the other. He folded the paper and put it into the center of the Bible to mark a place, and then he tucked the Bible beside Spitz.

"I didn't know the numbers were in Roman numerals," Aspen confessed. "I've never read that copy. It's a kind of family heirloom." She didn't want to explain further.

"You should read it," Campbell encouraged, "lots of writing in there."

Aspen looked at him nonplussed. Of course there was lots of writing inside. It was a Bible; it had thousands of pages. "I'm sure," she said noncommittally.

Campbell sensed that Aspen wasn't fully engaged and took the cue to head out. "It was real nice to meet you," he said, shaking hands with Aspen and then Bill. "I'm Ed Campbell; I pastor at Fourth Street Community Church. Come and visit sometime."

"Thanks for the invitation," Bill said. "I'm Bill. I'm new in town; I might take you up on the offer."

"Be glad to have you, Bill," Campbell said, waving on his way out.

Aspen took her Papa's hand and smiled. "Papa, I want you to meet Bill, the man who works with me. He's the one coming with me to Indonesia."

"Nice to meet you," Bill nodded. "Aspen talks about you all the time. I've heard about the fishing and camping trips and the Indian princesses. I come from the same kind of family: we're outdoors more often than not." Bill got another chair from a corner of the room and sat down, leaving the more comfortable vinyl chair for Aspen.

Papa blinked once.

Aspen turned to Bill. "I forgot to tell you; he blinks once for yes and twice for no. He just agreed with you. That's the kind of family he likes."

"My family is from Hampton; I don't know if you've heard of it," Bill began.

Spitz blinked once for yes.

"So you know we're right on the Chesapeake between Newport News and Norfolk. The area around Hampton is great fishing country and great beach and boating country, too. On summer weekends when I'm home, my dad will take me and my brothers out all day fishing, and we'll come home in the afternoon with dinner for my mom and my sisters to cook. There's nothing better than eating fish at night you were fighting in the morning," Bill declared.

Spitz blinked once, and then he waited and blinked again.

"Double yes," Bill grinned at Aspen. "We think the same way."

"If you keep talking about fishing, you'll get nothing but yeses," Aspen told him.

"I think I will, then," Bill said. He lapsed into a largely one-sided conversation with Papa consisting of the family fish stories. He stopped in between to ask Papa if he was getting bored yet or to ask if he'd ever caught a particular kind of fish.

On a few of the fish stories, Aspen recognized the name of the fish and remembered one of Papa's stories. She could practically see the gratitude in Papa's eyes that she'd been paying attention all these years and that she was helping him to participate in one of his favorite kinds of conversations: swapping fish tales.

After Aspen related one story of Papa catching salmon in Alaska, Bill sat back, impressed, eyes twinkling. "You sure must be a good listener."

Papa blinked once.

"See, your Papa thinks so, too," Bill said, nodding in his direction.

Aspen smiled and shook her head. "I've just had plenty of chances to hear. Papa tells that one a lot."

Bill smiled at her. "We should go fishing. It's different back here in the mountains than where I grew up, but it would be fun."

"Sure," Aspen agreed. "Let's go. We'll probably have to wait until we get back, though."

"That's right," Bill said. "That reminds me of something. Mr. Spitzen, I know you're worried about Aspen going to Indonesia."

Spitz blinked once.

"She can take care of herself, I know," Bill said with a glance and a smile in Aspen's direction, "but I'll be watching out for her, too. I'll do my best to make sure she stays safe."

Papa looked intently at Bill, and then he blinked once. He moved his eyes to Aspen, and he blinked once again.

"What did he say to you?" Bill asked her.

"I think that means I'm supposed to look out for you, too," Aspen said mischievously, squeezing Papa's hand.

He blinked twice.

"I know, Papa; I was teasing," Aspen said. She looked at Bill. "I'm supposed to let you keep me safe." She arched her eyebrows at her Papa. "So does that include throwing himself in front of headhunter spears aimed at me, Papa?"

Papa blinked once.

Aspen and Bill both laughed, looking at each other. Aspen stood up, blushing. "I think it's about time I went home. It's been a long day."

Bill stood with her. "Okay. Do you want to get some dinner?"

Aspen nervously gathered her coat and purse. "I think I'll just have something at home."

"I'll walk you to your car, then," Bill said, tossing his overcoat over his arm. "I'm glad I met you, Mr. Spitzen. I'll see you again sometime, whenever Aspen lets me come." He grinned at Aspen, teasing.

She shrugged. "That's up to Papa. It's his room."

"So can I come back, Mr. Spitzen?" Bill asked.

Papa blinked once.

Bill smiled widely. "Excellent—it's decided. I'll be in the hallway, Aspen." He walked out of the room, pulling the door closed behind him.

Aspen looked down at Papa, blushing again. "Do you like him, Papa?"

Papa blinked once.

"Are you just saying that because you see I like him and you think it's high time I liked somebody?"

Papa blinked twice.

"And you really want him to come back sometime?"

Papa blinked once.

"Okay, I'll bring him," Aspen promised. She leaned down and kissed her Papa's cheek. "I'm happy you were letting the chaplain read to you, Papa—really happy."

Papa blinked once.

Aspen patted her Papa's shoulder and left, face lighting in a smile when she saw Bill leaning against the wall, waiting for her.

★ ★ ★

Satisfied, Spitz watched his granddaughter leaving. He didn't know when he'd last seen her so happy. She was different around Bill, but it was a good different. And it had felt really nice talking with them, just the three of them in the room.

Spitz could tell that Bill was a good person from the kind of stories he told, the way he talked about his family, and the way he treated Aspen with such consideration and respect. He liked her; Spitz could see so. But he wasn't a shark. Aspen wouldn't have to worry about him taking advantage of her overseas. Spitz felt himself relaxing.

After all, he had nothing to do but wait. He didn't know what was happening in the past. Had he been gone for hours or days or weeks? Did Washington think he had deserted the Life Guards? Time obviously moved differently in the past. He'd spent months in 1778 in just the space of one afternoon. Aspen had been wearing the same clothes and jewelry at lunch today; it was the same day. When would it be when he went back? How would Washington treat him?

The conversation with Washington didn't worry Spitz half as much as his reaction to it. That small, carping, jealous voice inside him had wanted to see Washington hurt. Some part of him was like a small boy pointing a magnifying glass at an ant, waiting to see how long it took to burst into flames. Some part of him thought that given a little more pressure, Washington would break, too.

*Is that what I've become?* Spitz thought. *Has missing my boy made me into someone who can't be happy for another man to have what I can't? Am I like Satan in the throne room accusing Job?*

The thought ate at him like a cavity in a back tooth he hadn't noticed until it hurt, or like a timber eaten through with termites you never saw until your floor caved. The closeness and comfort from Washington had felt like sudden weight or pressure that his shrunken, resentful soul could no longer bear. The jealousy and ingratitude that rose up in him felt like a painful bite or a missed step. He hadn't expected it, and it worried him. He didn't want a wormy, tunneled soul. He didn't like the feeling.

*Help me,* he asked tentatively. *Help me not to be like this. Help me to control some of this spite welling up in me.*

He felt a wave of gentle sadness wash over him that was quite distinct from the panic and discomfort he'd been feeling a moment earlier. In its wake, that wave left a single thought behind: *I won't help you with some of it. You must give Me all of it.*

Spitz's inner, stubborn knot clenched again at the idea of submitting to that Being who had superintended the tragedies in his life, and a wordless, absolute refusal shouted in his soul. The gentle offer withdrew, leaving Spitz feeling sadder and more helpless than ever, and scared now of what was happening to him besides. In desperation, he thought again, *Please?*

The hospital light above him seemed to grow brighter and larger and whiter until it blazed like the sun, and then a whirling storm of suns spiraled around and around him, blotting out every sensation except for their motion.

They slowed and ceased, resolving into familiar patterns of constellations in a night sky. Spitz was lying on his bedroll, his messenger bag beneath his head, looking out the doorway of a cabin as small as a toolshed. Rows of similar cabins spread far beyond him to the rushing bank of the Schuylkill. He reached a hand into the bag and felt the crumbling, charred cover of his son's Bible. Patches of tears still moistened it. He drifted to sleep with his hand on the Bible.

Someone shook his shoulder, and Spitz opened his eyes to gray dawn light. Mist hung white and slowly swirling over the river. He rolled over to find the owner of the hand. It was a fellow guard in his cabin, a man named Hurley from New Hampshire.

"Guard duty," he said laconically.

Spitz nodded and rose. He walked quickly to the river and splashed water on his face and neck and hands. He dug a small tin of salt from his pocket and used his wet finger to put some on his teeth and scrub. He rinsed his mouth in the river and arranged his clothes as neatly as he could without a mirror. Then he hurried back to the cabin in time to share bread and fish with the other guards on this rotation. They were still eating shad they'd salted and preserved from the early March run. The guards beginning duty all finished quickly, and marching in formation, they left for the two-story farmhouse where Washington lived.

From here, he could see over the camp, which looked vastly more pleasant against new spring grass than it had against bitter winter snow. Far away at the parade ground, Henry Knox sat on an upended powder keg with a book in hand, waiting for his artillery men to gather for morning target practice. Among some of the farther huts, Lieutenant Monroe roused his men for the day's work. Smoke from morning cooking fires still rose from most huts. The scene was pleasant and busy but unhurried.

Spitz passed an uneventful rotation on guard duty, followed by the rigorous drills and conditioning exercises Gibbs demanded of all the Guards. He went to sleep that night unsure of where or when he would be in the morning. But the next day passed in much the same way, as did the next and the next, until Valley Forge felt like a kind of home for him.

He marched and drilled and guarded his way through the spring into the early summer, when he could tell that the men, who were fit and fed and confident in what they had learned from Baron von Steuben, were eager to fight again. Wherever Spitz went in Valley Forge, he heard jokes about going over the mountains to Philadelphia and paying a call on Cornwallis. And once the army broke the winter encampment and began to move, following the trail of the British army north, heading for New York, their eagerness became nearly palpable.

One day in late June, Spitz took up his post by Washington's tent, which was now pitched near the Baptist Meeting House at Hopewell, New Jersey. The Commander-in-Chief had called a war council, and the men waiting to enter Washington's quarters to take part in it comprised the cream of the American army. The most obvious addition of leadership was the esteemed General Charles Lee, Washington's former rival. He had arrived Valley Forge in late May following a prisoner exchange. Though a prisoner, Lee had been allowed to spend the winter in more comfortable gentlemen's quarters under the oversight of British officers.

Having just left their winter encampment, most of the officers expressed a spirited, comradely eagerness to meet their foe. But Lee seemed less vigorous, perhaps because he had not endured the struggles of Valley Forge or witnessed the miraculous provision of fish or seen the strength and polish Baron von Steuben's meticulous training had place on the troops. Their skill and capabilities were now foreign to Lee.

As the officers waited for Washington to call them inside, they began speaking about the campaign ahead. General Lee cautioned, "Doubtless the British are equally keen to meet. Both armies will fight like bears fresh awake in the spring, hungry for their first kill. We must not be too hasty and seek a fight we cannot win," he said.

Just then, Doctor Craik arrived. Spitz had not seen much of the doctor since his arrival, as both of them had been busy in different areas, and he hoped for a chance to greet his old friend.

Colonel John Fitzgerald, seeking to acknowledge Craik's arrival and to add a bit of humor to the conversation said, "Yes, we wouldn't want to charge foolishly into a hornet's nest and in so doing provide the good doctor with more practice than otherwise necessary."

Craik responded, "My good men, I believe it has become necessary to endure the sting of the *genus Vespa* in order to rid the country of its pestilential presence."

The officers readily agreed with the doctor, though Spitz guessed that Craik's words had sailed above everyone's heads, and they all knew it.

"Speaking of measuring our aggressiveness," said Fitzgerald, "we must keep close watch over our beloved general during the forthcoming pursuit. We all know how daring he is in the heat of battle."

A murmur of assent greeted this announcement. Captain Caleb Gibbs, leader of the Life Guards, said, "I have just impressed this need on Baron von Steuben. Fitzgerald, you were at Princeton. Tell the Baron what the general did there."

Colonel Fitzgerald continued, "Sir, you would scarce believe what danger General Washington took upon himself. Our own forces had scattered, seeing General Mercer fall and believing ourselves soundly beaten. But Washington advanced over the hill at the head of a column, and he rode backwards and forwards over that hill, calling to the fleeing men to stand fast. The British Lieutenant Colonel Mawhood 'ordered a halt, in battle line, and drew up his artillery with the intention of charging upon Moulder to capture his battery.'"[44]

"He faced the enemy guns himself, at the head of his men?" the baron echoed incredulously.

"He did that," Fitzgerald affirmed. "He reined his horse to a stop with its muzzle to those guns and sat it without flinching. The line rallied around him, but still he stood between the armies. They exchanged fire, and I gave him up for lost, bemoaning within how bravely he had died. I could scarcely believe my eyes when the smoke cleared and I saw him sitting still, unharmed, before the fleeing British and waving our men on in the chase. I rode to his side and shouted, 'Thank God! Your excellency is safe!' [Then I] wept like a child, for joy.'"

"No one could blame you," Craik said, "anyone would weep with joy to see him safe in such a case."

Fitzgerald laughed. "Evidently, I was much more moved than he, for 'Washington, ever calm amid scenes of the greatest excitement, affectionately grasped the hand of his aid and friend, and then ordered—"Away, my dear colonel, and bring up the troops—the day is our own!"'[45] He rode after the men with never a further thought for his person."

"Colonel Fitzgerald's tale of our chief's apparent disregard for his own safety reminds me of the battle of Germantown," said Major General John Sullivan. "When he rode forward there to 'rally [the] broken columns, the exposure of his person became so imminent, that his officers, after affectionately remonstrating with him in vain, seized the bridle of his horse...I saw our brave commander-in-chief, exposing himself to the hottest fire of the enemy in such a manner, that regard for my country obliged me to ride to him and beg him to retire. He, to gratify me and some others, withdrew to a small distance, but his anxiety for the fate of the day soon brought him up again, where he remained till our troops had retreated."[46]

"There is no doubt that a courageous heart leads your new nation's army," von Steuben said.

"He is indeed most valiant and noble, a very worthy general," Lafayette added.

Lieutenant Colonel Alexander Hamilton agreed. "Gentlemen, these stories of our chief's 'daring and contempt for danger at the battle of Princeton, and again at Germantown' give me little comfort when mixed with the knowledge which I, too, hold of Washington's heroism. I am all .the more 'anxious for the preservation of a life so dear to all, and so truly important to the success of the common cause.' To this serious matter I propose we resolve 'upon a memorial to the chief, praying that he would not expose his person in the approaching conflict.'"[47]

General Sullivan turned to the doctor. "Doctor Craik, you have known General Washington the longest of any of us, from his youth in the Virginia militia. If he will heed any man asking him to temper his zeal for his own safety, that man is you, sir. Will you present him a petition on our behalf, begging him to exercise more prudence in the risk to his person?"

"Oh, aye, if you gentlemen insist on drafting such a petition, I shall carry it to him and add my voice to it as well. But you must regard what manner of man you address. His native manly courage and patriotism will not allow him to bide in the rear when he sees where he may be of use," the doctor argued.

Spitz could testify to that argument. He remembered the look Colonel Washington had shared with Captain James MacKay before the battle at Great Meadows and the way both men had then galloped to the front of the lines instead of sending their aides.

"You forget as well the prophecy spoken over him, to which I was a witness. General Washington cannot fall in battle, for God's hand shields him," Craik declared.

Hamilton interrupted, "Doctor Craik, surely you put no real faith in the ramblings of an Indian chief, be he ever so mysterious and impressive. Bullets and cannon shot fly where the powder sends them. As a man of science and a man of the Kirk, surely you agree."

"As a man of science, I agree with the premise," Craik qualified. "But as a man of the Kirk, I place no bounds on what God may do if it pleases Him. And if it pleases Him to shield our commander in chief in battle as He did King David or to speak through the mouth of a heathen chief as He spoke through Balaam and his ass, who am I to question Him?"

"Was the prophecy then so very striking that you believe it absolutely?" von Steuben asked.

"It was," Craik declared firmly. "As you say, I have been bred in the Kirk of Scotland, and I hold to the catechism as fast as any man there. But had you seen the chief himself, grave and intent as he was, and had you felt the air in that woodland clearing charge with an eerie hush as if the trees and stars were listening, you would know beyond doubting that the old man spoke God's own truth—'that the enemy could not kill him, and that while he lived the glorious cause of American Independence would never die.'"[48]

Silence greeted Craik's words, and Spitz wondered how the officers had taken them. How many believed that God shielded Washington directly? How many remained skeptical and only hesitated to refute the doctor's story out of respect for him?

The tent flap opened, and Spitz saw the officers straighten their posture respectfully as Washington emerged. "Good morning, gentleman. I trust that you each have good heart in you to harry the British tomorrow." Spitz could hear the bravery and good humor in Washington's greeting, and he grinned. The officers passed between him and Hurley, the other guard at the entrance, and then the flap closed. Spitz could hear every word passing inside, though.

"We do have such a heart in us, sir," Fitzgerald began, "but before we lay our plans, we each wish to petition you solemnly on a matter of great import to us all."

"This matter touches each of you?" Washington said. Spitz imagined his piercing, grayish-blue eyes searching his officer's faces. "Very well—who among you will speak?"

Craik quietly cleared his throat. "The other officers have appealed to me, General Washington, on the basis of our long friendship and deep mutual esteem."

"What have you to say to me, Doctor Craik?" Washington asked calmly.

"Every man in this room knows you to be a man of unparalleled courage and patriotism as well as fervent devotion to his duty," Craik began. "We have this very morning recounted your heroic stands at Princeton and Germantown, when you alone stood at the head of the army to rally the men to fight. We know there is not a bone in your body that shrinks from a fight. But your officers collectively beg you to exercise greater prudence in your gallantry so that we may not lose so valiant a man whose life is so intricately bound with the fight for freedom that to extinguish one is to extinguish the other."

"Fair words fairly spoken," Washington noted. "And what have you to say for yourself, my old friend?"

Craik sighed. "I know that to ask you to remain behind where other men venture is as useless as to ask a dog not to bark or a horse not to run or a wind not to blow." Scattered soft laughter greeted the resignation of that remark. "And I know as well that God guards you where you go. For that reason alone, I shall not gainsay your own inclinations."

"Gentlemen," Washington began, "I am sensible of the honor you do me by your great devotion and your concern for my health and life.

No leader could ask for braver, truer hearts than yours to command. But as I have your love, so lend me your faith—not in my own courage but in the God who set me so great a task and who shall guide and keep me through it."

Washington paused, waiting for any man to counter him. When no one did, he resumed. "And mention of our great task leads me to discussion of tomorrow's action. Considering that the rear of the British army passes so near us here, with its baggage and supplies lightly guarded, it is incumbent upon us to relieve them of those supplies with an attack tomorrow."

"General, while I agree that the capture of those supplies is a worthy goal, I question the timing," Lee objected. "Should we not wait to attack en masse? Even now the French fleet sails to our shores. Might not the battles at sea decide the question of the war without engaging the army so soon after leaving our winter quarters?"

"France fights as an ally to America, not a proxy," Washington said firmly. "We shall win our liberty in fair combat. As to the question of engaging the army in battle, I propose to send a light force only—say four thousand men. As second in command, the honor of that engagement falls to you, General Lee."

"But only a third of our number," Lee spluttered, "when their force equals our own—it is madness. It cannot possibly succeed."

"On the contrary, General Lee, it can succeed," Lafayette interrupted. He began to outline a plan of attack on the rearguard, surprising the British and cutting the supply lines off from the rest of the army. "You see, it can be done, if the men are led properly to do it."

"If you protest the action," Washington began, evidently looking at Lee for a response.

"I question it strongly," Lee answered. Spitz could tell he was stung.

"Then the Marquis de Lafayette shall have the honor of the attack," Washington decided.

"I accept, with all my heart," Lafayette said.

Obviously pleased with Lafayette's zeal, Washington stated, "Then you will prepare at once to move forward, accompanied by Wayne's thousand men, and join forces with our advance reconnaissance column now near Cranford. Altogether, the numbers under your command should approach four thousand."

"And cannon, sir?" Lafayette inquired.

"Twelve cannon should serve you well," Washington replied.

The subject then turned to the supporting role the van of the army would play. The officers agreed that all regiments must be prepared to move at a moment's notice. Lafayette would not strike at the enemy's heel until the British passed through Monmouth Courthouse, affording the remaining troops at least a couple of days to organize and rest.

Soon Washington adjourned the war counsel, and Spitz observed the mood of the officers as they filed out of Washington's tent. Lafayette walked firmly with his head held high, while Lee stubbornly shook his head in defiance. The other officers seemed to gravitate to the side of one or the other of these two leaders.

After an hour more, Spitz and his companion guard, Private Hurley, were relieved of duty, but within a couple of days their rotation brought them back to Washington's tent in time to overhear General Lee's surprising turnaround.

Washington was engaged with his aides-de-camp, Gibbs, Doctor Craik, and a couple of other officers when General Lee entered the commander's tent.

"General Lee," Washington said enthusiastically, "I have heard from Lafayette that the army is now in position to deliver a fatal blow to the British attempt upon Sandy Hook."

"General Washington, if I may," General Lee interrupted, waving a letter of his own, "I have heard from the Marquis as well. The addition of the last thousand men and cannon does make a material difference to the stratagem he proposed. In consideration of their addition, I have corresponded with the Marquis to beg him to cede me command of the engagement, which he has done." Lee set the letter down on the table with an air of triumph. "I now claim the honor of commanding the action."

A long pause followed this announcement. Spitz could imagine the looks on the faces of Washington, Craik, and the other men.

Lee implored again, "My honor is in your hands, sir."

"Very well, General Lee, the engagement is yours. Take with you two brigades, and endeavor to attack the rear of the enemy immediately upon their departure from Monmouth Courthouse. As the marquis has already preceded you, taking lead of the advance column now numbering four thousand, with your two brigades you will have overall command of five thousand men. Additionally, I have already dispatched Morgan with six hundred marksmen to harass the enemy's right. If plans go as expected, you may expect support from Dickinson, who will soon arrive on the left with his thousand-man Jersey Militia to harass the British line. And know as well that we stand ready with the remainder of our army to support you at the center."

Spitz was disgusted. Lee obviously just didn't want to lose face before the other officers and let an important command fall to a foreigner. From the body language Spitz had read following the war council meeting, Spitz could tell that Lee's heart was not in the fight. Changing his mind like he just had was just pure politics, and Washington was too much of a gentleman to call him on it.

Washington, Lee, and the other officers and aides discussed the shape of the summer campaign and its ultimate objective: to keep the remainder of the British army from reaching British-held New York, where the massive harbor would keep them supplied with so many reinforcements and supplies that the Americans may never be able to defeat them. At the end of the brief strategy session, Washington issued one last command to be dispatched by the aides-de-camp to every officer throughout the army.

"Each man of you must study the land around us, and cause your junior officers to study it as well, to 'critically examine the position, all it's avenues, and the adjacent ground, that in case we should have occasion to make use of it, we may be prepared to avail ourselves of its advantages, and apply the best possible remedy to its defects.'"[49]

The men all agreed and left one by one. As Gibbs left, he paused by Spitz. "Spitzen, you will join the detail of guards assigned to Doctor Craik. The man asked for you personally. After the engagement, you will rejoin the main body of Guards."

"Yes, sir," Spitz said, saluting. It was the very assignment to suit him, to work alongside someone he knew so well and to stay in close proximity to Washington. Besides, being assigned to Craik meant that most of his work would consist of saving lives, not taking them, though he'd still carry a gun to protect the medics and doctors behind the lines.

Gibbs left, and Craik nodded and smiled to Spitz as he left, too. Spitz fulfilled his last two hours of guard duty until his relief came, and then he walked through the encampment to the hospital wagons. Craik was glad to see him.

"Spitzen - how happy I am to work alongside you once more," the doctor said warmly.

"I heard you asked for me," Spitz replied, shaking his hand.

"I did, Spitz, seeing that you have done the work before and seem not to be squeamish of wounds and blood," Craik answered. "Any man who can rescue the fallen during the chaos of Braddock's expedition is a man I want by me in the surgery. I hope you can forgive me for keeping you from the action your fellow Guards are seeing, though."

"What action is that?" Spitz asked.

"I have a tithe of Guards learning field hospital work so that they may attend me immediately when we enter action. I hear that the rest of them are off larking with Morgan's sharpshooters, harassing the British flank," Craik explained. "Go fetch your gear; you'll camp here. We begin early in the morning to follow Washington, and as soon as we engage, we must establish the hospital to the rear. I shall need you close by at an instant's notice."

Spitz fetched his gear from the area of the encampment near Washington's tent, where the Life Guards always stayed. He spent the rest of the afternoon with Craik and the medical officers and orderlies and the detail of Guards assigned to hospital duty. The other Guards were young, strong, handsome men, and Spitz knew from his months training in Valley Forge that serving to the rear with the hospital felt like a punishment for them. All of them would far rather have been harassing the British flank with the prospect of fighting in the front lines, but Gibbs had trained them so well that none of them offered a word or sign of complaint.

The afternoon and evening passed quickly, and in the morning Spitz woke early, just in time to see Lee's contingent marching away to engage the British rearguard. The rest of the army diligently prepared to move out in support of Lee's engagement. Knox supervised the movement of his precious artillery, while teamsters readied supply wagons and harnessed anxious horses to hospital wagons. Behind the baggage came the camp followers who had remained with the army during the long winter at Valley Forge. These wives and sisters and older daughters of the enlisted men provided laundry and sewing and cleaning services, and they also played a key role in improving camp morale. During action, the women generally stayed to the rear, though some of the more compassionate served in the hospital, while others bravely carried water to the men on the front lines.

Also gathered at the rear were a grousing group of British prisoners the Life Guards and Morgan's sharpshooters had apparently captured the day before. They were kept disarmed and under guard in preparation for being sent to prison in Reading, Pennsylvania, as soon as anyone was available to take them.

As soon as the main body of the army was prepared to move, Spitz and the other Life Guards assigned to Craik's medical team began to march beside the hospital wagons in the rearguard, following the trail Lee had taken earlier in the morning. The van of the Life Guards who had returned with the prisoners had already marched forward, a regiment in front of and behind Washington, always keeping their bodies between him and the enemy. The day grew hot, and Spitz's uniform became uncomfortably sweaty and heavy. He seriously began to question the wisdom of including bearskin on the hat. He paced himself to keep up with Craik's wagon, always staying within hearing distance of Craik's voice.

After some hours, Craik looked up and said, "The sun is nearly overhead. Surely by now Lee's men have engaged the redcoats. We must be ready and on guard when we reach Washington's field position. Today will not go well for the weak at heart." Suddenly their wagon halted, and the men scurried out, taking up their usual positions within Washington's military family.

But things were not normal. Confusion filled the air. Anxious officers of the Guard were quizzing straggling soldiers returning from Lee's advanced position: "Why are you here? What happened ahead?"

One wide-eyed young fifer panted to a stop and breathed, "General Lee ordered the retreat, sir; the redcoats are too many for us."

Spitz could not believe his ears. "Impossible," he said. For Lee to ask for the command and then order such a hasty retreat was unthinkable.

Washington, noticeably troubled, rode his charger to an elevated part of the field. His Guard immediately followed, including Spitz, Craik, and the others. As Washington peered through his field glass, reconnoitering the enemy, Spitz felt a blast and saw a fountain of earth spring up by the general's horse. A "round-shot from the British artillery struck but a little way from his horse's feet, throwing up the earth over his person, and then bounding harmlessly away."[50]

Having arrived to the scene just ahead of the cannon ball, Spitz, too, was covered in dirt from head to toe. Startled but coming to his senses, Spitz first made sure of General Washington's welfare, then looked toward Doctor Craik (who unbelievably was smiling), and then surveyed the others. "Thank God," Spitz blathered, "everyone is okay."

Baron von Steuben, obviously recalling the stories he'd heard yesterday before the war council, looked in shock at General Sullivan and said, "That was very near." [51]

But Craik shook his head and told them both, "Gentlemen... recollect what I have often told you, of the old Indian prophecy. Yes, I do believe, a Great Spirit protects that man—and that one day or other, honored and beloved, he will be the chief of our nation, as he is now our general, our father, and our friend. Never mind the enemy, they cannot kill him, and while he lives, our cause will never die."[52]

Suddenly Washington's mount broke into a full gallop. The general was charging straight toward the action. Spitz wondered what Washington had seen, and instinctively he and the others followed.

As he ran, Spitz marveled at Washington's calm. The projectile had thrown dirt in the general's face and over his clothes, yet he continued to give orders as if he had not even noticed the cannon ball had struck. A little dirt was not going to distract him. Washington was truly fearless, pushing forward like David running toward Goliath when most men would cower. Did Craik's assertion about the Indian's proclamation alone explain such courage?

As Spitz reached a hedgerow where Washington had stopped, he found General Washington interrogating every man who was fleeing towards him along the road; trying to determine what had happened to cause the disorder. Spitz gazed forward. The backs of most Americans were facing the enemy. A narrow pass was quickly choking with confused and exhausted men trying to make their way toward the rear of Washington's division.

In the midst of the confusion, Washington spotted Lee and dashed toward him. "What is the meaning of all this?" boomed the general's voice. "What have you done?"

Lee was stunned by the tone and firmness of his superior's words. Moving toward the two men, Spitz watched Lee stammering and making excuses. Finally, Lee said, "The Continental army is simply unable to stand against the British, sir! They cannot do it!"

Spitz quavered at the fire in Washington's eye as he faced Lee and shouted, "Sir, they are able and by God they shall do it!"[53] With that proclamation, Washington charged forward again all the way to the rear of the retreat.

Washington stopped another retreating soldier, who looked up in surprise at being addressed by the great man himself. "How far away is the enemy?" Washington demanded.

"Just a fifteen minute march away," he answered, pointing, "just up the road over there."

"Who knows this ground?" Washington called into a crowd of retreating Continental soldiers and junior officers.

One of them stopped and ran to Washington's horse. "A moment earlier, Lieutenant Colonel David Rhea passed by—he said that he knows the area and that it is good ground, sir."

Washington's spirits lifted. "That hedge will serve us as a natural barrier. Bring Lieutenant Colonel Rhea there directly," he commanded the officer.

When he arrived, Rhea indeed proved to be a remarkable guide. "This hedgerow here, sir, separating these two farms, is part of a line of high ground stretching northeast by southwest. It will help us hold the line. And below it is a swamp that should slow the redcoats good and proper. On their left, our soldiers will find protective protrusions, and to their rear, the woods will cover and conceal our supplies and supporting regiments."

The intelligence seemingly emboldened Washington, as if he had received a message from heaven. He called for several aides-de-camp, who rode forward, alert. "My compliments to the Marquis de Lafayette, General Wayne, and General Grayson - the army should take advantage of the high ground and make an unrelenting stand against the enemy's onslaught. The generals and the marquis must delay the British advance until the army is in place." He waited until the aides had left and then called several more. "My compliments to General Knox—emplace artillery at the crowns of the left and right flank along the hedgerows. Spread the word among the other senior officers to attend me here immediately with their troops."

There was little time to spare; preparations must be made immediately. The retreating Americans filed in safely behind the hedgerow while General Washington established strong lines of defense along the hedge as well as on his left and right flanks, where he brought forward artillery and cleverly positioned it on the crowns of their wings.

Spitz made his own preparations with Craik, falling back to establish the field hospital well to the rear with the other Life Guards detailed to medical command. They laid ready cloths and knives and pails of water, and before they finished their work, the medics dashed forward to retrieve the first wave of wounded men. Spitz followed them, ducking bullets and helping to carry bloodied, shattered men.

The British commanders Clinton and Cornwallis, who had previously reinforced their rear guard to protect their baggage and supplies, took heart from the flight of the Americans and decided to attack. Before long, both armies had fully engaged one another. First Clinton struck on the left, and then Cornwallis attacked the right of the American lines. In each case, the big guns of General Henry Knox deterred the British assault. The British brought forward their own artillery, and a loud and smoky duel commenced.

As the American artillery suffered a particularly intense assault, William Hays fell mortally wounded beside his cannon. Moving in with a medic to provide aid to the dying man, Spitz witnessed an event he had read about as a child in school. Molly Pitcher (Mary Ludwig Hays), a camp follower who had been carrying water to the troops, bravely took her husband's place at the cannon. The Hays' cannon once again began firing on the redcoats, just in time to help turn the tide in favor of the Americans. But in the interval, Hays died. Helping the medic load a nearby soldier with a wound to his legs onto a stretcher, Spitz saw Washington and von Steuben riding up and down the lines. The general persistently guided and encouraged his men, sometimes moving within ten yards of the enemy, protected from sight only by the drifting smoke of gun fire.

Failing to pierce through either of the American flanks, the British launched their next attack against the center of the hedgerow. The British had advanced to within forty yards of the hedge when the resistance of a thousand American muskets crumpled their lines. The redcoats regrouped and pressed forward, but again the Americans drove them back. Before the day ended, the British launched yet a third attack on the hedgerow. The fighting was fierce, including hand-to-hand combat. Throughout the day, the Americans counter attacked again and again, and the momentum shifted back and forth. When sunset finally ended the fighting, the exhausted Continental soldiers had proven that they could stand against the best of the British regulars.

Throughout this battle of Monmouth, Spitz caught glimpses of Washington's unrelenting courage. Throughout the heated engagement, "heedless of the remonstrance and entreaties of his officers, the commander-in-chief exposed his person to every danger."[54] Spitz remembered the worry of the officers before the war council. Seeing Washington continually in the thick of the fight, Spitz could understand it.

Well into the night, Spitz finished helping the medics carry back the last of the men who could be saved. But he was far from the last man on the field. On his last run, Spitz stopped to rest on an outcropping of boulders, and he watched some men he hadn't properly noticed before. All of them wore black, and the moonlight glinted from the white tabs of clerical collars at their throats. The one who paused by Craik had a rifle slung over his back. He stooped, holding the hand of a man dying from a large wound to the abdomen. Spitz had passed the man by earlier. A trip to the field hospital would do him no good.

Before too many more minutes had passed, the man's life faded, and the chaplain closed his eyes and laid the hand he'd held back on the man's chest. He looked up and saw Spitz watching him, and he made his way over to the boulders and sat down. His face was round and cherubic, and he wore his thinning brown hair in the customary queue. He had lost his hat sometime during the day.

"Thank God for the night and the silence of guns," the chaplain said.

Spitz gestured to the rifle across his back. "I wouldn't expect to see you carrying one of those. Are you allowed to fight?"

"I would venture to say that my captain expects me to fight. I am a private in the Tennessee militia," the man said.

"So you're not here just to pray?' Spitz asked.

"No," the man said, shaking his head. "I have fought the day long here on the left flank, where my company encamped, and since the fighting has ended, I want to extend what comfort I can to the men dying on the field. But now the groans and weeping have fallen silent, too, along with the guns."

"We saved the ones we could," Spitz said, looking up to the stars.

"I saw you with the medics. Your uniform is sadly the worse for your efforts," the chaplain noted, touching a red stain on Spitz's sleeve. He was right. The beautiful uniform was more red than buff now, and the blue was stained dark, nearly black, with other men's blood.

"So what is a chaplain doing with a gun?" Spitz asked.

"Have you not heard of the Black Regiment?" the man asked. "General Washington has thanked us for our presence and our efforts on behalf of the men. As you serve so near him, I thought you would have heard of us."

Spitz shook his head. "If I had, I'd have thought it had something to do with African-Americans—with slaves."

"No," the chaplain smiled. "In every regiment of American soldiers, you may find men like me, men of the cloth who serve with the army while they serve the army. To fight is our duty, as well as to comfort. After all, the clergy ignited the spark of the revolution."

"How do you mean? I haven't heard of any preacher patriots," Spitz said.

"Have you never heard of Dr. John Witherspoon, who has preached revival and freedom for so long, or of Reverend Jonathan Mayhew, the father of civil liberty in America? I have read his sermons. His words showed me my own call to ministry. He called for aid to Boston when it was besieged, and he organized his fellow clergy into an organ of communication to promote resistance in the colonies," the chaplain explained. "Had Mayhew not passed to glory, Samuel Adams would never have needed to form the Committees of Correspondence. He borrowed the idea wholly from Reverend Mayhew."

"Your Mayhew seems like kind of a rebel. My old preacher always said that Christians are supposed to be subject to the higher powers," Spitz said.

"Yes, but thoughtfully, sir," the chaplain qualified. "As Reverend

Mayhew said in 1750, 'It is the duty of all Christian people to inform themselves what it is which their religion teaches concerning that subjection which they owe to the higher powers.'[55] Christ does not make of us slaves to despots."

"Of course," Spitz said. "Mayhew is kind of a hero of yours, isn't he?"

"I admire his character," the man said. "He has influenced the course of my life a great deal. But he is far from the only fighting clergyman. Did you know that local churches provided the famous minute-men in the north, and that their deacons often served as regiment drill leaders? In fact, it was Deacon Parker under the shepherding of Reverend Jonas Clark whose militia first shed blood for the cause of freedom at the battle of Lexington, following Patrick Henry's famous warning that the British were coming. Parker and his men sacrificed themselves, receiving the first assault from the British regulars. The attack wounded ten patriots and opened the door to martyrdom for eight others. With divine insight, Reverend Jonas Clark boldly prophesied that 'from this day, will be dated the liberty of the world!'"[56]

"I didn't hear that those men were part of a church," Spitz said.

"The clergy consistently preaches liberty, both spiritual and temporal, and encourages enlistment in the colonial militias and the Continental army. Though I am new to their number, I am glad to count myself among them. The battlefield is the mission field where Christ has placed me," he said solemnly.

"Doesn't it upset you as a religious man, seeing so much pain and death?" Spitz asked. "I mean, doesn't it ever make you wonder sometimes how God could allow so much suffering in the world?"

The clergyman shook his head. "What you see before you is the fruit of the fall. Christ has crushed the serpent's head, and all the sorrow of the world is the violence of his death throes, which will end soon when Christ comes in glory."

"You think He's coming back soon, then?" Spitz asked, knowing that the Second Coming hadn't happened yet in his lifetime.

"I look for Him every day, and I build a better world for Him while I wait," the chaplain answered. "Do you wait for Him, too?"

Spitz studied his hands and forced himself to speak calmly. "No, I don't," he said. "Not anymore. I've got enough to do right here without thinking about that."

The chaplain clapped him on the shoulder as he rose. "I shall pray for your soul," he said. "You are a good and gallant man. You could do much for the kingdom of God if you would let Him near your heart." The chaplain squeezed Spitz's shoulder and then walked back over the battlefield to rejoin his company.

Tired and spent with the grief and work of the day, Spitz watched the chaplain picking his way carefully around fallen bodies and earth churned by horse's hooves and artillery wheels. He was plucky and optimistic and kind, but his talk had wearied Spitz even further. It brought to mind again his task of recording the times he had seen the invisible hand moving.

Slowly and stiffly, Spitz rose from the boulders and walked back to the field hospital, where he had stowed his excess gear in one of the hospital wagons. After a search in the dark, he found his pack and messenger bag. He found a quiet place under a tree beside the campfire of some other Guards, a fire far enough from the field hospital that the groans and cries of the wounded men were somewhat quieter. He remembered the chaplain from the Black Regiment offering comfort to the dying when he was so tired from a day of fighting. He wished he felt like comforting the wounded men behind him, but he didn't. He was tired, yes, but he also felt empty. He didn't have comfort inside him to give to anyone else. He hadn't had that even before the battle.

Spitz removed his jacket, soaked with sweat and blood, and sighed at the welcome coolness of the night air. Beside him, the other guards talked quietly. Spitz took his journal and writing materials from the messenger bag and thought carefully about what he would write. Then he loaded his quill with ink and began.

Mercy 7—Cannon ball narrowly misses General Washington and his military family as they reconnoiter the enemy. Doctor Craik saw the near miss as a **confirming sign** (referring to the

old Indian Prophesy) that their revolutionary cause was favorably in God's hand.

**Mercy 8**—God safeguards Washington's army from General Lee's disorderly, dangerous retreat. The pursuing British army was only fifteen minutes away when General Washington arrived on the scene.

**Sign 13 / Favorable Interposition (Godsend) 5**—Providentially, Washington had previously ordered all officers to be ever mindful of critiquing the land where they would fight, determining its advantages and defects for use in battle if necessary. Right after Washington dismissed Lee, an officer notified Washington that Lt. Col. David Rhea had just passed through declaring his knowledge of the area and asserting that it was militarily good ground. The hedgerow provided a strong natural barrier, and Lt. Col. Rhea was a remarkable guide (**a Godsend**). The intelligence emboldened Washington, who responded as if he had received a directing sign (or order from heaven) to take advantage of the high ground and make an unrelenting stand at the Battle of Monmouth.

**Mercy 9**—Molly Pitcher's courage helped turn the tide in favor of the Americans, and smoke from the guns shielded Washington from the eyes of the enemy, who were only ten yards away. Washington continually exhibited unrelenting courage, 'meeting personal dangers with the calmest unconcern,' [57] despite numerous entreaties by his officers.

**Sign 14:** The Black Regiment, clergymen - God providentially deployed His distinct representatives on the battlefield to carry the light of the sacred fire, illuminating the path to ultimate freedom. George Washington witnessed the positive results of the Black Regiment's presence among the troops.


Spitz yawned and put his journal and writing utensils away. He was past ready to fall asleep. The day had been a whirl, from the first conversation with Craik to the last conversation with the nameless clergy-man. And between talking to the man charged with the cure of bodies and the man charged with the cure of souls, Spitz had seen terror and bravery and pain on the battlefield. He felt overwhelmed and exhausted. He lay down on his bedroll, pillowed his head on his bag, and shut his eyes, curling his fingers in the clean, soft summer grass below him.

The familiar whirl of lights enveloped him, and with a jolt, Spitz realized that he was back in his hospital room. The bloody battlefield was gone, and so were his bedroll and leather messenger bag and the summer grass on which both had lain.

But his fingers still curled against the sheets as if they sought grass to touch.

Spitz opened his eyes in shock. His fingers had moved.

# Chapter Ten

*"For since the creation of the world God's invisible qualities—
his eternal power and divine nature—have been clearly seen,
being understood from what has been made, so that people
are without excuse."—Romans 1:20*

*"You will increase my honor and comfort me once more."
—Psalm 71:21*

*A*t first, Aspen didn't notice the buzzing in her purse, which she'd hung on the back of her chair. She might have been at lunch, but as it was a working lunch with clients, she had muted her phone. She had felt guilty for scheduling this meeting, because it meant missing lunch with Papa for the first time since he'd been in the hospital, but this Friday afternoon was the only time these clients could meet with her and Bill. And as the clients' plant in Australia was one of the destinations on the itinerary for the trip next week, Aspen and Bill had to meet with them today.

But Aspen toyed with the artistically arranged plate of sushi and tempura in front of her and wished that she was eating hospital cafeteria food with Papa and Angela. *Is Papa worried, not seeing me at lunch? Did Angela remember to tell him where I am?*

Bill understood how she was feeling without her saying a word. When the waiter delivered their entrees, inducing a pause in the conversation, Bill leaned over and whispered, "You could excuse yourself to the powder room and call to make sure he's okay. I can hold down the fort for a few minutes."

Aspen had smiled warmly at him and shook her head. "I'll call at the office," she had whispered back. All the same, she appreciated the gesture, and part of her wished that she'd taken him up on it.

The meeting ended on a good note, and Aspen and Bill stood to shake hands and tell the clients goodbye. Then Aspen noticed the buzzing in her purse and glanced down at it—light glowed in the front pocket where she kept her cell. She waited until the clients left and then sat down hurriedly and looked at the screen.

"It's the hospital," she told Bill, frowning in worry and touching the screen to redial. "I've missed three calls."

He sat down beside her and patted her shoulder. "Let me know what's up," he said quietly as the phone rang.

She nodded distractedly, leaning her head on her hand. The hospital operator who answered directed her to the nurse's station on Papa's floor, and a nurse there transferred her to Papa's room. Angela answered on the second ring.

"Aspen? Is that you?" Angela asked quickly.

"What's the matter, Angela—what happened?" Aspen blurted.

"It's not bad news, sugar," Angela laughed. "It's wonderful! Your Papa moved his fingers!"

"Are you serious?" Aspen asked excitedly. "Did he really move them?"

"Yes!" Angela said happily. "I checked on him before lunch, and he blinked yes at me three times in a row before I noticed his fingers wiggling. Can you believe it?"

"Oh, Angela," Aspen nearly sobbed, "that's the best news I've heard in a long time."

Angela said, "Isn't it wonderful? Now that he's moving his fingers, we can start some basic physical therapy. We'll watch him a little more closely to see if he moves his toes or some larger muscles. But this is such a good start."

Beside her, Bill nudged her arm and mouthed, "What did he move?" In answer, Aspen lifted her hand and wiggled her fingers and grinned. He grinned back and gave her the thumbs-up sign.

Aspen nodded. "Bill's here, too; can you tell Papa he said 'great job'? And tell him the same from me, too."

"You can tell him yourself, honey. I'll hold the phone up to his ear so he can hear you, and I'll call out to tell you yes or no, all right?" Angela offered.

"Thank you, Angela!" Aspen beamed. She heard Angela explaining the arrangement to Papa, and then she heard the static of the phone brushing Papa's pillowcase fabric. "Hey, Papa - I'm so proud of you for moving your fingers! That's such great news! I'm so happy for you!"

"One blink for yes," Angela's voice called in the distance.

"I'm so sorry I missed seeing you today. Did Angela tell you where I was?" Aspen asked.

"One blink for yes," Angela repeated.

"I should have known she'd tell you. We lucked out on our nurse for sure, Papa. By the way," Aspen remembered, looking up at Bill, "Bill's here beside me, and he says hi and you're doing a great job." Bill nodded at her and then signaled the waiter to bring them coffee. Obviously, he didn't want to rush her.

"One blink for yes," Angela said again. "And another yes blink. You must have said something he liked. There's another blink; I'm right," Angela chuckled.

Aspen blushed, wondering if Bill could hear Angela repeating how enthusiastic Papa was for her to be with Bill. "Papa, I'm going to stop by after work to see you."

"Another blink," Angela called.

"I'm coming to tell you goodbye," Aspen said. "I'm leaving tomorrow morning for the trip to Indonesia."

"Two blinks for no," Angela called.

"I know, Papa; I know it's going to be hard for you to know I'm over there," Aspen sighed.

"One blink for yes," Angela said.

Aspen felt Bill's hand patting her forearm, and she looked up, surprised. "Can I come with you to see him?" he mouthed. Aspen shrugged. Bill smiled. "Ask him," he said, nodding to the phone.

"Bill wants to come with me this evening. Is that all right with you, Papa?" Aspen asked.

"One blink for yes," Angela said, "and another one—that's a double yes."

Aspen, turning red again, nodded at Bill. "So we'll both see you after work, Papa. I love you so much! I'm really happy you're doing so well."

"One blink," Angela called. Aspen heard the static sound of brushing fabric again, and Angela said, "Your Papa just kept looking straight up at me like he was trying to tell me something. Are you all done talking?"

"Yes, I'm coming by to see him after work," Aspen said. "Thank you so much for calling me. It's such a relief to hear he's moving something."

"You're welcome, Aspen," Angela said warmly. "I won't be here when you come; so I'll tell you goodbye now. You take care of yourself, all right, sugar? I'll be praying for you every day while you're gone."

"Thank you, Angela," Aspen told her. The women said goodbye and hung up.

Bill sipped his coffee and nudged the tray with the sugar and cream toward Aspen. "Thanks for letting me tag along," he said. He watched her sweeten and lighten her coffee, looking thoughtful. "I know it's all right with your grandfather, but are you sure it's all right with you?"

Aspen kept looking down at her coffee. "It's all right with me," she said.

"Do you want to talk about something?" he asked, frowning in concern. "I can back out if you'd rather I didn't come."

"It's not that I don't want you there," Aspen said, still stirring. "I just wonder why you wanted to see Papa again."

"Well, this may come as something of a surprise after a few dinners out," Bill said lightly, "but I kind of like being around you. Your Papa means a lot to you, and you light up and relax around him. I like seeing you that way. So I guess I'm coming so that I can see you happy. And your Papa seemed to like hearing my fish stories. It's kind of a win-win for everyone but you."

"I'm not losing anything," Aspen said nervously.

"Look, Aspen—I'm going to lay my cards out on the table," Bill said, sitting back in his chair. "We haven't known each other long, but I feel really drawn to you. And I know this is a terrible time for you, with your grandfather being in the hospital and the stress at work shifting clients and planning for the trip, but that's the best thing. Here you are under enough pressure to make most people snap at everybody, and you still have a great sense of humor and a great smile. There it is," he said as Aspen finally looked up and smiled at him. "And as long as I'm being honest here, it doesn't hurt that you're attractive. So I just want to be around you. That's all."

"You're really kind to say so, and I like being around you, too," Aspen confessed, blushing again. "But you're new in town. You haven't had a chance to meet a lot of people. I just don't want to get attached too deeply yet, while you're still figuring things out here. And I'm not in any shape to make any big decisions now, either."

"I don't want to put any pressure on you, Aspen," Bill said gently. "I'm not going to change how things have been between us so far unless that's what you want. But you should know that I know myself pretty well, and I know what I like in people. I'm also really patient." He grinned. "I'll let you in on my game plan. I'm hoping that if you see enough of me, you'll eventually decide you like having me around." He winked and sipped his coffee again.

Aspen laughed. "So much for the element of surprise," she said, finally picking up her coffee, too. "I hope you weren't counting on it."

Bill smiled. "Actually, I don't think you like surprises. I think you like time to mull things over. If I was counting on anything, I was counting on that."

Aspen didn't know what to say; it was a little unnerving how well Bill understood her. She finished her coffee and changed the subject back to the clients they'd just met. They talked a few minutes longer, and then Aspen drove Bill back to the office. For the rest of the afternoon at work, while she cleared her desk in preparation to be absent for a week and reset her voicemail to relay that information to callers, she thought about what Bill had said.

She was flattered that such a handsome, confident, successful person found her interesting and wanted to pursue her. But she reasoned his interest away. *He's around me all the time at work; maybe he's just curious. And he'd heard from Bernie that I don't date; maybe Bill just likes a challenge. He's seen me upset about Papa; maybe he just feels sorry for me.* Whatever his reasons were for laying his cards on the table, she didn't really think that she'd heard them all. *There must be something I'm missing. He can't just like me.*

The long afternoon of work finally ended, and Aspen switched off her work laptop. Her desk was clear except for the few personal items she kept on it: one framed photo of her and her parents the summer before the crash and another of her and Papa holding up fish on lines and grinning, and a small candle in a jar that she liked to uncap and smell every once in a while. She paused. If what happened to her parents happened to her, then Bernie would pack these items in a box to return to Papa when he was well enough to receive them.

She clenched her fist in her lap for a moment, thinking of Papa grieving her loss and thinking, too, of being lost. The thought terrified her. But she pushed it away, unclenched her fingers, and took a deep breath. She pulled a pad of Post-It notes and a pen from her top drawer. On the top, she wrote her computer password. Then she replaced the notepad and the pen and stood up, gathering her purse and coat.

"Are you ready to leave?" Bill asked her.

Aspen nodded. "Let's go."

★ ★ ★

Spitz kept his eyes on the door, watching the thin, rectangular window above the knob for a glimpse of Aspen's face. His fingers tapped in a senseless semaphore of joy. Though he felt a little foolish to be so proud of such a little accomplishment, he couldn't help the glee he felt. His fingers moved. Soon his hand would move, and then his arm and his back. He was waking like a tree in the spring, bursting with life. He was going to be well. He could feel it.

All day he had waited, awake the whole time, to show first Angela and then Aspen what he could do. He had no idea what was happening with Washington in 1778; that life felt like a dream. Now that his body was beginning to respond, he was impatient to stay here and get back to normal. If he could only concentrate hard enough, he felt sure he could move something else: waggle a toe, bend an elbow, jounce a knee, or mumble a word.

He'd thought of what his first words would be. He would say them to Aspen, of course. When he could finally speak, what would he say to her after so long a silence? What would make up for the fear and worry he'd caused her? He'd thought of "I love you," and "I'm sorry," but they didn't seem big enough. They didn't seem to say enough at once.

More than once today, Spitz had regretted his failure to learn Morse code and teach it to Aspen. It would be perfect for a man who could only tap his fingers. He longed with all his being to communicate again. Before the stroke, he'd voluntarily spent so many silent nights and lonely days in the library over his books, brushing off Aspen's stories and invitations to watch a movie or play a game or take a walk. But right now, he could think of nothing he'd rather do than sit down with her over dinner and talk. He couldn't believe he'd ever taken such a sweet pleasure for granted.

*There they are!* Spitz recognized Bill's head against the glass as he opened the door for Aspen, who smiled broadly at the sight of her Papa. She rushed over and sat at the side of the bed, taking his hand as she had every day she'd visited. This time, he pressed it back.

"You did it, Papa! You can move them! Are you excited?"

Spitz blinked once. Excited didn't half cover it.

Aspen clasped her other hand on top of his. "I was thinking about you on the way over here from the office. You know, now that you're showing such definite signs of improvement, I feel a lot better about leaving on the trip. You'll be improving the whole time, and I won't have to worry about you. Who knows? Maybe by the time I come home, you'll be able to write me a note."

Spitz blinked once. If she wanted a note, he was determined to write her one.

Bill stepped closer. "Hey, Mr. Spitzen; it's good to see you again."

Spitz blinked once.

Bill smiled. "Thanks! I won't bore you with any fishing stories today. I just wanted to tell you congratulations."

Spitz blinked twice.

Aspen looked wryly up at Bill. "I think that means you can bore him with all the fishing stories you want," she said.

Bill laughed. Spitz saw how easygoing he was. He'd be nice to have around more often. "When we come back from our trip, I'll tell you all the fishing stories I know. Aspen half-promised to take me fishing out here in the mountains; so we'll have some new tales to tell you soon." He smiled at Aspen, who blushed.

"Anyway, Papa, I just wanted to tell you again not to worry about me," Aspen said.

Spitz saw the blatant attempt to change the subject. Poor Aspen—she wasn't used to letting a man pay attention to her. At least she was trying;

she'd let Bill come today. But Spitz took the bait anyway and blinked twice. No matter what she said, he was going to worry about her. He couldn't help it.

"I'm going to be fine," she said, determination in her eyes. "People go to Indonesia all the time and come back perfectly okay. I'm going to be one of them."

*She's trying to convince herself more than me,* he thought. And he really, really hoped that she was right. He blinked once.

"That's the spirit, Papa," she said, squeezing his hand. "We'll both just believe that way and keep up our hopes until we see each other again. And I'll call a couple of times to check on you if I can."

Spitz blinked once. He'd like that.

"Do you want to hear about what I'll be doing? I have our itinerary on my phone," Aspen said, taking it from her purse.

Spitz blinked once.

"Great," Aspen smiled. She found the itinerary and told him about the flights and the hotels in Australia and Indonesia and the plants and mines they would see. She told him about the helicopter that would take her to the crash site. Bill joined her and fleshed out details for Spitz. Bill had a gift for description, and he sounded really enthusiastic about the work ahead. Spitz was glad he'd be with her.

Too soon, they were ready to leave. Spitz got his last kiss from Aspen, his heart breaking as he watched her leave. He didn't know if he'd ever see her again. He closed his eyes. If he lost her, too, he couldn't bear it. *You couldn't do that to me; You wouldn't—not after all the rest of it. She has to be all right. Please—let her be all right. If one of us has to go, let it be me. Don't make me live without her. Don't leave me here alone.*

Spitz's only answer was a sense of lightness stealing over his body as the fluorescent light over his hospital bed broke into a thousand flashes against deep darkness beyond, spiraling faster and faster around him. He waited for them to leave him, shrinking into a campfire or a sunbeam or candlelight or a constellation of stars as they usually did. But they didn't leave all at once.

They seemed to surround him as he rose from his bed on the grass at Monmouth, and they stayed with him as he packed his gear and ate his breakfast and reported to Craik to prepare the field hospital to move. But then they sped up, dizzying Spitz, who felt as if he were gliding through days and weeks and months. He was dimly aware of marching and fighting and carrying more wounded bodies and talking to men around him and shivering in another winter encampment ... and another one ... and then another one. Years flew past him, aging and hardening this body he wore in the past. A few more grey streaks appeared in his hair. His skin loosened and wrinkled in three years of hot sun and short rations and tearing wind.

The lights slowed, and when they disappeared into a swirl of sparks around a fire blazing in front of a tent, Spitz looked around him in all directions, searching for a familiar face. He was standing outside a large field tent on an autumn afternoon. Fog swirled over the sunburned grass and hid the purpling sky. Cannon boomed in a desultory barrage nearby. The cold air smelled of the salt sea and city filth and sharp gunpowder and the earthy muck of river water.

The wind picked up, sweeping the fog away, and its keen edge bit into Spitz through his Life Guard uniform, which had definitely seen better days. It showed three years of wear and rough mending, as well as stains from battle and field life. It hung on him more loosely than it had in Valley Forge. Spitz recalled the blurred passage of time he had just endured and wondered at this physical evidence of it as he held his hands to the welcome, warming fire.

The wind buffeted the tent as the light sank further over the horizon, and finally a tent flap opened. A young man came out, recognized Spitz near the fire, and walked unsteadily towards him, nodding in greeting before he was in earshot. Spitz saw that he was dressed in expensive, well-cut civilian clothes marred with mud and sweat and grass. The man was also ill, with spots that looked like chicken pox against his pale skin. He mopped sweat from his forehead and neck and winced against the firelight, looking away to the east.

"Quite a storm piling up over there," the man said, turning away to cough loudly.

Spitz looked to the east, as the final, mellow rays of sunlight illuminated a lowering, gray mass of cloud. "It is, sir," Spitz said. "It's moving fast, too, with the wind."

"We had better cross the York as quickly as possible," the man said, staggering backward a step in the stiff wind. "The general expects us before nightfall, and I need my bed."

"Let's get you to it, then, sir," Spitz said, genuinely concerned. He began to walk quickly toward the river, which he now knew was the York, looking across it to the city beyond: Yorktown. The York River flowed between Gloucester and Yorktown, which Washington had started besieging in September of 1781. Cornwallis had surrendered by proxy on October 19. The woods around the French and American encampment where he had waited were mottled green and gold and orange; October had definitely arrived.

But the sick man soon fell behind, and Spitz went back for him. "Let me help you, sir," Spitz told him. "I can see you're in bad shape."

"I have only a cold; 'twill pass," the man told him impatiently.

Just then, a black servant ran to meet them, waving a hat. "Mr. Custis, you've left this behind," he said formally when he reached them, extending the hat with a slight bow.

"So I did," the man said sheepishly, "it was so warm inside. Thank you, Marcus."

As the servant returned to the tent and the sick man beside him settled the lost hat on his head, Spitz regarded him with more interest and respect. *Mr. Custis must be John Parke Custis, Washington's stepson.* Spitz vaguely remembered him mentioned in the biography he'd read, but he couldn't remember why Yorktown was important to him.

Mr. Custis, hat in place, looked sternly at Spitz. "Promise me that you will not start playing nursemaid, Spitz. Doctor Craik is bad enough without all of Poppa's old friends fretting over me. And when did you commence with calling me 'sir'? I have been Jack to you this last month, as you have been Spitz to me." Another coughing fit interrupted Jack's words, and soon he left off covering his mouth to hold his head as if he were afraid it might split open with pain.

"I'm sorry, Jack," Spitz said earnestly, "but I sure wish you'd just let me help you walk. We'd get to the river a lot faster."

Jack finally ceased coughing and looked up at the darkening sky, drawing in deep, slow breaths. Then he sighed and nodded. "You are right. The general would not want me to delay his message by standing on my pride. I thank you for the help."

Spitz could see that the admission cost Jack something to say and sought to ease his embarrassment. "No trouble at all," he said, placing Jack's arm around his shoulder and putting his own arm around Jack's waist to support him. "I'm looking out for myself as much as you. I don't want to be caught in that storm headed this way."

Jack looked east again and saw the mass in the sky drawing steadily nearer as the sun finally slipped below the horizon and cast the world into darkness. "We must beat it to the river, or the boatman will be loath to cross." With an effort, he began walking as quickly as he could, Spitz helping him every step, pulling against his weight to keep him going straight toward the York River.

In between comments on the prospective fierceness of the storm and its possible effects on troop movements, Spitz took stock of his companion. The biting wind could not hide Jack's feverish heat, and he seemed to speak with an effort, as though it was hard for him to concentrate. Spitz knew that the times he'd felt the way Jack looked, he'd taken a few days off work to sleep. But Jack seemed determined to do just the opposite.

Well before they reached the docks, the storm hit with fat raindrops yielding quickly to a steady torrent. He and Jack were soaked through before they got to their boat, where the boatman they had hired to wait for them looked at them with poorly-disguised irritation.

"Can you get us across?" Spitz shouted above the noise of the rain and wind.

"I could've done half an hour ago," the boatman spat. "Ye might as well swim now."

"You have to try," Spitz ordered him. "Mr. Custis has to get a message to General Washington tonight."

The boatman huffed and mumbled and waved them into the boat, followed by his mate, who took the rudder. Spitz helped Jack inside and sat near him. As weak as Jack looked, he could easily tumble over the side if Spitz didn't keep hold of him. The boatman cast off from the dock and set his sail to capture the driving wind.

"You know, the first time I met your Poppa, I helped him just this way," Spitz said.

Jack smiled feebly. "I know. He has told me the story."

"He's been ill and weak, too. I've seen him. He'll understand if you need to take a day or two to rest," Spitz suggested.

Jack shook his head ruefully. "The general never failed to perform his duty, no matter how sick he was, and neither shall I. Tell me, Spitz, when you helped him inside from the snow, did he rest a day at the trading post?"

Though Spitz had been carried away before he saw Washington leave, he knew the answer. "No, he rode straight back."

"And when he suffered from camp fever on Braddock's expedition, did he abstain from battle to rest?" Jack pressed.

"He fought very bravely," Spitz admitted. "But he loves you, and he'll understand."

Jack paused. "Spitz, Poppa has had to understand a great deal for my sake. I did not strive to excel as a scholar, and I married against his wishes. He has been unfailingly kind toward me in every case. I do not fear him. I only wish to serve him once without fault."

Spitz recognized that desire to please that he had felt toward his own father and grandfather, not to earn their love but to feel their recognition of his success. It was a strong drive in a young man, especially the son of a great man. With a stepfather as renowned as Washington, Jack must feel that urge doubly.

The boat, which had been rocking with the stormy waves, suddenly heeled nearly over and shipped a great deal of water, which sloshed over Spitz's already wet feet and ankles. Spitz looked to the east again, and he gasped at the sight.

Downriver from his boat were several boats full of British soldiers, halfway to the northern shore and safety in Gloucester with Tarleton. He nudged Jack, whose eyes widened at the sight. Jack immediately stood to peer around the sail, and Spitz stood with him to steady him.

"Look there," Jack shouted, pointing to the docks on the southern shore. "It's a retreat!"

The docks were a mass of red. British soldiers lined the docks and the streets behind them as far as Spitz could see through the town. Cornwallis wasn't leaving a man behind. This force in the advance boats would land and overwhelm the American patrols before they could get word to the encampment. By the time the Americans knew what was happening,

Cornwallis' entire army would be across the York, ready to overwhelm them, join with Tarleton, and retreat to New York to join Clinton.

Spitz panicked. He and Jack couldn't reach Washington in time to stop the whole retreat. Cornwallis was going to get away and leave Washington the possessor of an empty town.

The boat was bucking dangerously, and the boatman at the boom and his mate at the rudder both strained against the shearing wind. Spitz walked forward a step to call above the storm.

"We have to hurry! The British are retreating!" Spitz pointed to the boats in mid-river.

"Sit ye down before I knock ye daft!" the boatman shouted angrily. "What I have to do is not to sink!"

Spitz sat quickly and pulled Jack to his seat, too. Just then the boat heeled again, and more of the York flooded into the bottom of the boat. The boom swung out of the boatman's hands and swung across the deck very close to Spitz's head with the force of a baseball bat in the hands of a pro. He was suddenly very grateful for the boatman's warning.

The wood of the boat groaned against the force of the wind and buffeted the shortened sail. The boatman and his mate fought it for only a few minutes further. "We go back!" he shouted.

"We have to cross!" Spitz argued.

"Tell that to God!" the boatman yelled. "He makes the wind, not I!"

He and the mate adjusted the boom and tiller, and soon the driving wind pushed them back to the dock. As Spitz and Jack disembarked, Spitz grabbed the boatman's arm. "We have to cross the moment it calms. Stay nearby."

"Come to the inn," the boatman shouted, "nearest the fire and the largest tankard of ale!" He and the mate laughed and ran to a building across the street and down the harbor. Its windows glowed invitingly, promising shelter and warmth.

"Should we join them? We can't cross," Spitz said dejectedly.

"I cannot see the retreat from inside. I must count the force that passes to tell the General," Jack said stoutly.

"We'll go closer to where the British will land," Spitz told him, feeling proud of Jack's bravery. "Maybe we'll find a place to shelter where we can see."

Jack began to walk forward again, Spitz helping him as he had before. The two men braced their shoulders against the wind and walked a quarter of a mile or so before they found a kind of fishing shed that was open to the river. It didn't provide much shelter from the battering wind and rain, but it was better than open ground. They crossed their arms and leaned against the walls of the shed, peering out to the tossing, rocking boats.

Suddenly Spitz blinked. He was sure that he couldn't be seeing what he was seeing. What looked like a pillar of cloud descended to the river, just south of the boats, and swept north, across them, to the opposite shore. Everywhere that pillar touched, the waves of the river swelled and crashed into an angry melee, as if an enormous arm had reached into the river and stirred the bottom with its hand. The heightened waves capsized a few of the boats completely and drove the rest violently towards shore. Spitz saw red-coated soldiers drowning in the heaving river like the armies of Pharaoh, while the rest of the landing craft either flipped sideways into the mud or smashed to pieces against the northern bank like the Egyptian chariots.

He and Jack looked at each other, amazed. Already they could hear the shouts of the French and American patrols, who had heard the crashing boats and the cries of the wounded and drowning redcoats. Only a few unhurt men would escape to tell Tarleton what had happened. The rest would scurry back to Yorktown rather than risk spending the remainder of the war as prisoners.

Spitz put a firm hand on Jack's shoulder. "We should go to the inn. Their boats are smashed in unbelievable ruin; so there's no retreat to see here anymore. And the first duty of a soldier is to keep himself fit for action. We'll cross after the storm."

Eyes still wide in amazement, Jack nodded.

★ ★ ★

The storm abated in the wee hours of the morning, and Spitz roused the boatman and his mate to carry him and Jack across the river. From there, Spitz found a pair of horses at a camp by the river and took Jack carefully to headquarters. The soaking rain and bone-rattling cold last night had done Jack no favors, and sitting in wet clothes in a drafty inn had only worsened his fever and cough. As the two men rode, Spitz watched him surreptitiously lest he fall off his horse. When they arrived, Jack reported to his stepfather while Spitz cared for the horses and arranged for their return. When he had finished, he returned to the command tent and paced the outside, nodding to his fellow Guards on duty. Then the flap of the tent opened, and James Craik walked out.

"Spitz," he called, lifting a hand. He looked tired to death and sad as well.

Spitz walked up to his old friend. "Hello, Doctor Craik," he said. "You don't look so well."

"Physician, heal thyself," the doctor said with a wry half-smile that faltered quickly, "and I could if what ailed me required physic." He sighed.

"What does it require?" Spitz asked.

"A miracle," Craik answered glumly. "Walk a while with me, and let us talk."

Falling into step beside Craik, Spitz was glad for the chance to talk to someone he knew. The doctor walked well away from the tents, evidently brooding over the miracle he needed.

Finally he stopped at the edge of a little grove of trees and sat on a large, fallen log, its underside crumbling and spotted with lichen. He unbuttoned his coat and crossed his arms over his stomach, stretching his legs out in front of him and sighing despondently. "Spitz, he's no better, and I cannot make George see his danger."

Suddenly afraid for Jack, Spitz stood very still. "What have you said to him?"

Craik shook his head. "I have told him that Jack must lie still and rest and take the dose I give him, not ride to the French lines or take messages by boat across the York to Gloucester, but he insists that Jack knows his own state of health better than I do."

"Is Jack very sick?" Spitz asked. "Jack tells me it is only a cold, but you said he was in danger."

"Of course he is," Craik retorted. "He has camp fever, advancing rapidly. You've seen him staggering in and out of George's tent, weaving like a man deep in his cups with the pain in his head and sweating like a cold jug. Have you not noticed him?"

Spitz shook his head. "I'm sorry. I knew he was sick, but I didn't know how badly."

"I suppose I should lay the cause to my own profession. Tailors see patches and cobblers see worn heels. I see fever and plague," Craik muttered.

"Maybe it's just that Washington's so strong," Spitz suggested. "He survived smallpox when he was young. And he had camp fever before Braddock's expedition. I remember how he could barely sit his horse, but he still wouldn't let you give him any medicine. And he fought all the next day and led that forced retreat to join Dunbar. Maybe he thinks Jack can do the same."

Craik considered the point. "George does have a strong constitution himself," he conceded. "But he must understand that Jack is not the son of his body. A fever carried off Jack's own father, though Martha nursed him tenderly. Jack is likelier to follow his father than his Poppa."

"Does Jack know how sick he is?" Spitz asked, cold dread settling in his stomach even as the sun gained strength and burned away the fog.

"He will not own it," Craik answered. "He takes his doses and runs away to the command tent to find another errand. He tells me he is well, though I know he is not. Any man who cares to look may see the fatal spots upon his face. I have pled with him to go to his mother and his wife in the country, where the air is clear and he may mend, but he will have none of it."

Spitz shook his head in frustration. "Why not - what's so important that he has to stay?"

Craik looked at him oddly. "Cornwallis is all but defeated; we expect his surrender every hour. Jack may have had his failings, but he is as ardent a patriot as I have seen. He tells me he will see Cornwallis fall before he will stir a step from his Poppa's side. Surely you have heard him say so."

"I never imagined he would risk so much to see it," Spitz confessed. "I wish I'd paid more attention." This situation was the first in Washington's past he hadn't been prepared to face. In every battle, he'd known the outcome before it happened. Right now, he knew that Cornwallis would surrender, and when, and even some of the terms. But he'd never really thought about Jack. Now he didn't know whether Washington's stepson would recover or not.

*Surely You wouldn't let him die,* Spitz thought. *Washington's already lost his stepdaughter. This son of Martha's is his only child. Surely You wouldn't take Jack—not after everything Washington has done for You.* Spitz thought of Washington's sad face at Valley Forge as he confided how deeply death had touched him when it took his father and brother and stepdaughter. Washington had done faithfully and well everything God set before him, and he'd given God all the credit for doing it. If anyone should get a pass on future suffering, Washington was that person.

Craik shook his head mournfully. "Do so, Spitz—pay attention to him today, and tell me I am mistaken. If you cannot, then I beg of you as an old friend and an old fellow in arms to persuade George to send Jack home. I fear for Jack's life if you and I together cannot prevail upon George."

"I'll do my best," Spitz said, determined to do just that. Washington had stood by Spitz, saved his life, offered him work and friendship, and cried over Steve's death. If Spitz could do anything to spare his friend and hero the same pain he'd suffered, he'd do it.

"What is that?" Craik said, suddenly standing.

"What?" Spitz demanded, springing alert and tense to his feet.

"Listen!" Craik ordered, holding his breath and cocking his head in the direction of camp.

"I don't hear anything," Spitz said dumbly.

"Exactly!" Craik laughed, clapping Spitz on the shoulder. "The cannons have ceased firing! We must return at once to see if Cornwallis has finally bowed to General Buckskin!"

Spitz laughed. It served Cornwallis right for insulting Washington with that nickname; now he'd have to surrender his sword to him. Oh, how the mighty had fallen!

Spitz and Craik hurried back to the encampment behind the French-American lines, where Spitz could see the lines of artillery and the troops arrayed around the massive earthwork forts outside Yorktown. Trenches scarred the ground close to the earthwork redoubts, which guarded an inner ring of British defenses. Beyond them, Yorktown hulked dim and silent, the tops of its roofs still tipped in mist.

As the two friends reached headquarters, they saw a group of officers on horses reining to a halt outside Washington's command tent. Craik and Spitz sped up to see who they were. In their midst rode a redcoat officer, blindfolded and carrying a flag of truce. A Continental officer helped him to dismount and led him inside.

"An offer of surrender, no doubt," Craik rejoiced, "God be praised. Clinton has lost half his force, then, and no army impedes us on the way to New York. Will Clinton bide there and wait for us, I wonder, or will he withdraw to Quebec and give the colonies up for lost?"

Spitz could have told him that this field was the deathblow to the British hold on America. When British Prime Minister Lord North heard the news, he had exclaimed, "Oh, God! It is over." But Spitz decided to let Craik savor the victory on his own, as well as the pleasure of forecasting what would happen next.

"Who knows?" Spitz said, smiling up at the pale disc of the sun in the sky. "Cornwallis is done here, and that's all that matters for now."

"He is done indeed," Craik agreed happily. Then he nodded to his right, where Spitz could see several of the guards who had stood duty with him earlier gathered by their tents. "Captain Gibbs will want to see you, Spitz, as you have been absent all night," he said. "Go and tell him what you have seen and fetch him here."

Spitz agreed and walked quickly to the guard tents, where he saw Gibbs striding toward him from the direction of the French lines. Spitz started to speak, but Gibbs held up a hand. "I saw the party pass," he said. "I shall see General Washington and learn the truth for myself."

Watching Gibbs walk quickly to the command tent, Spitz thought he looked like a boy who didn't want his little brother to spoil a Christmas surprise. He chuckled at the image and continued to a Guard campfire, where Hurley was sitting with two men in buckskin trousers and hunting shirts. Spitz was sure he didn't know them.

Hurley nodded to Spitz as he sat and then pointed to the men one by one. "Hawkins and Sterling," he said by way of introduction, "from South Carolina."

Spitz introduced himself and shook hands. No sooner had he gotten settled than Hawkins, a deeply tanned, thin man with light brown hair and a scar down his chin, leaned forward and said excitedly, "Is it true that the British are surrendering the city? Cornwallis raised the white flag?"

"He must have, but I don't know much more than you do," Spitz said. "I just came from the command tent, and I saw a British officer being escorted blindfolded to Washington."

Hawkins laughed and punched Sterling lightly and playfully on the upper arm. "I told you, Peter, the whole time he chased us through the Carolinas, that as soon as he met General Washington, he would shake in his boots, and so he has!" Hawkins' eyes shone with glee as he turned back to Spitz. "Mind you, General Greene led him a merry dance all the summer long, and he has worn through his lordly pumps dancing it!"

Sterling nodded. His brown eyes were grave behind his small, wire-rimmed spectacles, and his wide mouth pressed into a thin line, grimly satisfied. "He was diminished, and that soundly."

"You were both with Greene in the southern campaign?" Spitz asked, excited. "Did you fight at King's Mountain and Cowpens and Guilford Courthouse?"

"Not at King's Mountain, though I intended to fight," Hawkins said, looking indignant. "That Patrick Ferguson ordering the folks across the way to lay down their arms or he would 'lay waste to their country with fire and sword.'[58] Well, no freeborn man could abide by that kind of a threat, especially seeing as how he led their turncoat neighbors against them. We came north as soon as we could leave, Peter and I did, but they took only men on horse for speed."

"Didn't need us anyway, Paul," Sterling remarked proudly. Spitz guessed he was about as talkative as Hurley.

"That they did not!" Hawkins chuckled. "Just nine hundred mounted militia men against fifteen hundred of the loyalist militia with Ferguson— well, you would think we would be beaten beyond hope. But Ferguson ought to have known not to threaten a man's land and family."

"That he should," agreed Sterling.

"He raised the country against him, and raised the wrath of God against him, too," Hawkins said fiercely.

"So it was the wrath of God that beat the loyalists?" Spitz asked dubiously.

"Look at the numbers, man," Hawkins chuckled. "We were

outnumbered and outgunned, and we lost less than a hundred wounded or killed. But proud Ferguson, he lost four hundred killed or wounded, and we took nearly seven hundred prisoners away with us. You cannot tell me that God was not in that trouncing."

"A real boost to the cause," Hurley agreed taciturnly. Spitz had yet to see the man excited about anything. By his tone, he could have been talking about the weather or the price of wheat.

Sterling nodded. "Truly the victory was a boost for the American cause and a crippling blow to the Tories. It has been 'the turn of the tide of success.'"[59]

"From that day, Continentals could not lose," Hawkins declared. "You heard of General Sumpter, cutting down two hundred of Tarleton's regulars in the field and losing less than ten of his own. And then there was daring William Washington, fooling the British into thinking he had artillery when 'twas naught but a pine log."[60] Hawkins slapped his knee and laughed. "I wish I had seen their faces when they saw the truth!"

"I heard about that trick," Spitz smiled, "William Washington's Quaker Gun."

Hawkins chuckled and then shook his head. "Peter and I fought with Greene right along, and we served Morgan at Cowpens. I thought we were lost sure enough at the start of that day, with redcoats lining up against us, and Tarleton, proud as Herod, prancing on his charger ready to lop off our heads. Morgan was a smart one though, using us in the militia to lure the British up over the hill and straight into the whole patriot army. We ran right over top of the whole passel of them, and Tarleton lost the van of his column to us. I only wish we had taken him, the black-hearted menace."

"Another trick, like Washington's Quaker Gun," Spitz said. "Our officers are creative thinkers."

"They have inspiration," Sterling said solemnly, "like Joshua at Jericho."

"And Lord Cornwallis," Hawkins mocked, "was properly stung by General Morgan's uncanny success against Tarleton's elite division. Cornwallis's British pride drove him straight after us, as fast as he could make men march. He badly wanted the prisoners we took. And we would have been lost for sure if not for the flood."[61]

"Our own Red Sea on the Catawba River," Sterling said. "With the British closing in on us, we crossed the river just before flood waters began to flow, splashing along the sides of the banks and raising the river to an impassable level. All of the sudden, the Redcoats were stuck on the opposite side. It was a godsend, it was; kept us out of harm's way while the British army across the way watched us catch up to General Greene and his men and merge ranks."[62]

"Lord Cornwallis crossed the Catawba as soon as ever he could, of course," Hawkins told Spitz, "and raced hotfoot after Greene and Morgan. But the same thing happened at the Yadkin River." [63]

"And the Dan," Sterling added.

"And the Dan," Hawkins echoed. "Greene took all the boats for miles either side of the crossing, and Cornwallis had to circle 'round and find a ford. Cornwallis had no luck with rivers. Every time we crossed one, it flooded behind us and stranded him. And look at him now! He still can't cross a river! You saw that uncanny storm hit the York when he tried to escape last night with his redcoats."

"It sure was uncanny," Spitz said, shivering at the recollection of that pillar of storm stirring the waters of the York.

"You see?" Hawkins crowed triumphantly. "The very moment the first load of men arrived to Tarleton's position at Gloucester on the opposite side of the river, high winds scuttled their boats, leaving the rest penned in town like a flock of sheep, waiting to be sheared."

"Or worse," said Sterling, bringing a chuckle to the group.

"But before you got to Yorktown, you fought him with General Greene," Spitz reminded him. "You fought him at Guilford Courthouse."

"Where he won," Hurley noted.

"Another such victory would ruin the British,"[64] Hawkins declared. "God shield America from such victories. Cornwallis lost a great many men, and the ground he gained did him precious little good. He left it right away to chase Greene, did he not? And the whole time, Greene led him closer and closer to General Washington and his French allies and the vast French fleet cutting off any reinforcements Cornwallis might have gotten."

"He's trapped, is what he is," Sterling said, nodding in satisfaction at Spitz, "like a cornered pawn in a game of chess."

Hawkins pointed at Spitz triumphantly. "And who is king in this game? Those redoubts Cornwallis built and the inner ring of defense, too: they are naught but the bars to his prison, and good General Washington holds the keys to his cell."

"General Greene is off at Charleston now, keeping the redcoats there from joining Cornwallis," Sterling said.

"Greene handed Cornwallis to Lafayette like a lady at a country dance," Hawkins said happily. "But praise God, we were sent to support General Washington. I wanted to serve the great hero of Trenton, and now I have. I can tell my children and my wife at home that I saw the famous Washington with my own eyes."

"With all I heard about the southern campaign, I never noticed the weather. It's strange that there were so many floods," Spitz said.

"Not just the floods and the storm last night, friend," Hawkins said. "God sent the fog these last weeks, too, the fog that shielded us as we dug trenches for the artillery to shell the redoubts. How should there be fog and then a clear moon on the very nights we needed them unless God sent them?"

Something awakened at the back of Spitz's mind. "I remember hearing something else about General Washington and the fog, but I don't remember what."

"It covered his retreat from New York across the East River," Sterling said. "My cousin Thomas was with him that night."

Sterling looked expectantly at Hurley, and Spitz and Hawkins followed suit. Hurley met their gaze for a moment before he finally said, "So I was."

Sensing that Hurley would elaborate no further, Hawkins returned to the tale. "Howe's navy would have split the boats to kindling without the wind that blew—strong winds all night that kept his men to the sails and ropes and away from their guns. Washington's retreat lasted all night into the morning, and then the fog hid it like a great hand set down between him and Howe."

*The invisible hand again—there it is,* Spitz thought. Hearing the stories of flood and fog and storms timed so perfectly to help the Americans, Spitz felt like he had hearing ghost stories around a campfire as a kid. It was eerie. That number of weather events that no one could have planned, like the hailstorm at Trenton, did seem to point to God fighting for America.

Captain Gibbs walked back to the Life Guard encampment then, and Spitz saw his chin lifted high and his lips curved in a fierce smile. Spitz excused himself from Hurley and the South Carolina militiamen and walked to meet him.

"Have you heard good news, sir?" Spitz prompted.

"I have heard the beginnings of good news," Gibbs told him. "Lord Cornwallis asks for generous terms, naturally, but he sits in no position to dictate them. General Washington looks to come off handsomely in the end. Go and find Doctor Craik, Spitzen; he asked after you at the command tent."

Spitz saluted and wended his way through the growing crowd around the command tent. The men smelled victory, and they were in a holiday mood. He spotted the doctor near the entrance to the command tent and called to him.

Craik waved to Spitz and motioned him to walk with him away from the crowd. After pushing past the milling men, Spitz reached Craik and listened to the doctor's account of Cornwallis' proposed terms. His lordship wanted mercy for loyalists and freedom for all the redcoats to sail back to England, as well as parole for himself and safe conduct for all of his personal baggage. Craik snorted at the arrogance. But as soon as they were out of earshot of the rest of the men, Craik stopped and clasped his hands behind his back.

"Just now I spoke briefly with Jack and again urged upon him the necessity of his removing to the countryside as speedily as he may," Craik said. "He wishes fervently to see Cornwallis deliver his sword to the encampment, and after he has seen it, he will go. All day tomorrow, he has promised to rest instead of delivering messages. It is well, for the poor young man can barely stand. And then I have a commission for you, if you are willing to undertake it."

"I'm willing; just tell me what to do," Spitz volunteered.

"When Jack removes to Eltham, his aunt's house, you will accompany him as a guard and as a friend and aide. You will daily ride to Yorktown to deliver news of the young man's condition. Undertaking this duty means relinquishing your place among the Life Guard, but thereby you may do George a service he would not readily entrust to many men. It is a service I would not entrust to many men, either. Jack is the only remaining child of my oldest and dearest friend, and I will use every means at my disposal to see him safe and well again."

Spitz didn't even have to think about what to do. "I'll go with him."

"Good man," Craik said, smiling sorrowfully. "I knew you would stand ready to help."

As Spitz left Craik to tell Captain Gibbs of his plans, he thought of the feeling that had haunted him at Valley Forge, the quiet, jealous insistence that Washington wasn't really faithful, that he hadn't suffered enough to prove anything. *I take it all back, even if I did think so deep down. I don't want him to suffer. Please make Jack be all right. Please don't take him away.*

The prayer brought him up short. He'd asked the same thing for Aspen. Would God listen to either request, especially considering the source? God had no reason to listen to him. If Spitz were God, he wouldn't listen to him.

That afternoon, a skeleton force manned the artillery and the lines. The rest of the men, who had been fighting and digging and firing so valiantly for the last month, came back to the encampment to rest. Spitz informed Gibbs of his decision and received his commander's brief good wishes. Then he wandered through the encampment, finding every southern soldier who was willing to talk about the feats of Greene and Morgan and Campbell and William Washington. He also overheard soldiers reminiscing about the early engagements in the north: Brooklyn and Saratoga and even Bunker Hill. He drank in the first-hand accounts, relishing the gradual addition of color and light and personality to his reading.

He ate his rations at the Life Guard encampment, where he would sleep for one last night before leaving with Jack Custis for Eltham. And then he lay on his stomach by the campfire, listening to the happy, relaxed talk of the men around him discussing what they would do in the peace that was coming—the fields and homes and shops that were waiting for them. Spitz was happy for them, but he wasn't looking to the future. He thought about what had just passed and all of the stories he'd heard today.

He took his calfskin journal and writing utensils from the messenger bag and read over the pages he had filled so far. The little book was worn and dirty now with smudges of ash and candle wax and smears of blood and dirt and stains of grass and food. It was a book that had lived where he lived and absorbed the forests and fields through which he had passed. How much longer would he write in it? How much longer would these journeys to other times continue? As he was recovering and gaining strength in the hospital, would he soon cease traveling? He had to admit; he would miss seeing Washington. The man had grown dear to him. When Spitz anchored and stayed in his own time, he would feel he had lost a true friend.

But he knew what he was going to write now. This entry would be far from short.

**Favorable Interpositions 6 and 7 (Godsends at Long Island— intersessions of the elements)**—Surrounded and greatly outnumbered, with backs penned against the East River and anticipating a barrage of naval bombardment, Washington ordered a secret overnight evacuation of Long Island. A failed retreat would bring swift closure to the fight for independence. Providentially, the powerful cannonade of Howe's navy was held back by **sustained winds** providing time for the escape. The massive undertaking began with nightfall, but takes more time than is available in one evening. Significant loss of life and supply could be expected once the British discovered the retreat was underway. Miraculously, a **dense fog** arose over the entire escape route, shielding the retreating forces from the vision of British sentries. The evacuation was not detected until every man was out of harm's way on the opposite side of the East River.

**Sign 15–** Providentially, an enraged and self-organized army of 900 Patriots, representing militia volunteers of several colonies (including Davy Crockett's father), succeeded in winning the surrender of a superior Loyalist detachment of British General

Cornwallis' army at the **Battle of Kings Mountain.** This battle marked the first link of a long chain of events which caused an attrition of Cornwallis' army, which in turn set the stage for the siege at Yorktown, which then set the stage for the favorable peace terms established in the September 3, 1783 Treaty of Paris, ending the revolutionary war. Jefferson called the Battle of Kings Mountain, 'the **turn of the tide of success.**'" [65]

**Sign 16**—The zeal of Greene's small and ill-equipped southern army triumphs over the aggressive actions of British Colonel Banastre Tarleton. First, American Brigadier General Sumpter successfully deters an attack at Black Storks on the South Carolina Tyger River. Then, Brigadier General Daniel Morgan and Lieutenant Colonel William Washington win a **decisive victory at the Battle of Cowpens** in South Carolina virtually destroying Tarleton's army—a major setback for Cornwallis and the **beginning of the end of the war.**

**Favorable Interposition 8 (Godsend at Catawba River—flooding waters)**—British General Cornwallis destroys his own baggage in order to speedily chase after Brigadier General Daniel Morgan's men and his British prisoners captured at the Battle of Cowpens. **Morgan miraculously evades Cornwallis** when an overnight rise of the North Carolina Catawba River to flood stage delays Cornwallis' advance. Morgan's men are able to rejoin Greene's army safely.

**Favorable Interposition 9 (Godsend at the Yadkin River—flooding waters)**—The Cornwallis' subsequent advance on General Greene's army is again deterred by the flooding waters of the Yadkin River in North Carolina.

**Sign 17**—**Boats are providentially arranged** for Greene's army to cross the flooded Dan River into Virginia ahead of the advancing army of Cornwallis. When Cornwallis arrives all available boats are on the opposite side of the river.

**Sign 18**—Greene's army is bested at the Battle of Guilford Court House, but the losses of Cornwallis' troop are not insignificant. Providentially, the **continued attrition of Cornwallis' army** causes him to leave a detachment in the south while he marches toward the sea seeking reinforcements. At the Battle of Eutaw Springs Greene succeeds in forcing the British detachment to withdraw to Charleston granting the Americans control of the rest of the south and providentially allowing Washington along with the aid of the French to attack Cornwallis at Yorktown unmolested.

**Favorable Interposition 10**—**Fortuitous weather.** A storm places a **veil of clouds** under a full moon shielding American trench workers from the vision of British sentries.

**Sign 19**—Under a **moonless night** at Yorktown, two British redoubts (small forts) are simultaneously taken, almost instantly, one by the French and one by the Americans.

The list was long enough for tonight. He put away his supplies and fell asleep with his head on the messenger bag, listening to the detailed list of farm equipment Hurley planned to obtain in New Hampshire. It was the most excited Spitz had ever heard him.

The next morning, Spitz reported to the command tent again. He saw Jack, who lay on a cot in the corner, looking impatient to be confined. But Spitz could see what Craik meant. Jack's skin glistened with sweat, and his coughs wracked his body. While Spitz was talking to him, he fell asleep and lay exhausted against the small cushion under his head.

Spitz took Jack's place for the day as aide-de-camp, a familiar position for him by now. He carried letters from Washington to the officers who had pinned Tarleton down in Gloucester, right across the York River from Yorktown. As Spitz crossed the York in a fishing boat conscripted to the army, he saw the extent of the earthworks around the city and the hopelessness of any escape for Cornwallis while the French ships of Count de Grasse and Admiral Barras bobbed threateningly in Chesapeake Bay just beyond the town, and especially now that the storm had wrecked the conscripted British boats. The letters Spitz carried dealt with the negotiations being conducted for Tarleton's withdrawal, considering that Tarleton had never surrendered Gloucester and was only removing his men in concert with Cornwallis.

Spitz spent most of his day on the task. By the time he received an answer to take to Washington, the sun had nearly set. He caught a boat across to the south bank and delivered the message to Washington and then ate dinner with Washington and Jack at the command tent. Jack seemed a little more alert, and the camaraderie around the campfire reminded Spitz of the months he had spent as aide-de-camp to Washington at Great Meadows.

In the morning, the camp buzzed with preparations for the surrender ceremony, which seemed incredibly formal to Spitz. And all of the preparation turned out to be an anticlimax when Cornwallis sent a proxy with his sword instead of coming in person. Spitz thought it was pretty shabby behavior for someone who was supposed to be a gentleman. But Washington handled the affair with grace, stepping aside to let Cornwallis's second in command surrender to his second in command, Benjamin Lincoln. Washington wasn't going to give Cornwallis the satisfaction of accepting such an insult.

Cornwallis's soldiers mirrored his petulant attitude, too, weeping openly and refusing to meet the Americans' eyes, some of them even throwing their weapons down in anger, like toddlers deprived of toys. Cornwallis had given them up, every one, to be prisoners of war, while Cornwallis and his officers could sail to England after giving their parole not to reenter the fight. When the proceedings of the redcoats' formal capitulation were finished, the victors, guided by Washington's example and the principle to love your enemy and practice brotherly love, began treating the British officers graciously, like they were gentlemen under distress. The public display of the contrasting behaviors of each side caused Spitz to marvel at the distinguished character of America's early military leaders. Afterwards, Spitz helped Jack's servants finish packing his luggage and strapping it onto his carriage. He harnessed two horses to the front, and then he helped Jack inside and sat across from him. Standing beside Washington, Craik frowned at Jack's condition. "I await your reports, Spitz. Add your own observations to Mrs. Washington's messages."

"I will, Doctor Craik," Spitz promised. He looked at Washington. "I'll do all I can to make sure he gets well."

Washington nodded gratefully at Spitz and handed him a small note. "Deliver this note to Mrs. Washington with my esteem and sincere wishes for her health and strength." Then he reached through the carriage window to press Jack's hand. "Mend well, son," Washington said soberly. "You have done your country and me good service, and you may be proud of your conduct. When you have rested and Doctor Craik is satisfied with your progress, perhaps you may join me again."

"I shall try to come soon, Poppa," Jack said thickly, "if Nelly will give me leave."

"Give your dear wife my fond regards," Washington said affectionately, "and remember me to your children as well." Washington smiled and pressed Jack's hand again. Then he let go and rapped the side of the carriage to signal the driver to move. As the horses started and camp receded from view, Spitz saw a group of officers close in on Washington, demanding his attention for a hundred urgent and legitimate tasks. Spitz pitied him. He had few moments to spare for himself or his family.

Jack slept all the way to Eltham. The carriage arrived there after an easy journey of less than two hours. Martha Washington and her sister Anna Maria Bassett and Jack's wife Nelly Custis all clustered around the carriage when it arrived, all of them concerned to see Jack so ill. Pain shot through Spitz when he saw the fear on their faces, especially Nelly's. A young black servant behind her in a capacious dress and colorful turban held a baby on one hip and a toddler on the other. Two older children clung to the servant's skirts; from the tears running down their faces, Spitz knew that they must be Jack and Nelly's children.

With one arm around Jack's waist and Jack's arm around his shoulder, just the way they'd walked from the encampment by Gloucester the night of the storm, Spitz helped Jack inside and up the stairs. The women undressed Jack and put him to bed, setting the household into a flurry with orders for clean cloths and basins of cool water and bowls of hot broth and bottles of wine and home-brewed herbal infusions.

The sickroom was an overwhelmingly feminine place, one where Spitz felt useless and uncomfortable. He only entered it usually once a day, greeting Jack when he was conscious and able to speak. Every morning, Spitz asked Mrs. Washington how Jack was doing, sneaking glances beyond her at the patient in the bed. Jack patiently swallowed every medicine his mother and aunt gave him and submitted to being warmed and cooled and bled and fed whatever Martha and her sister decided would strengthen him. But he most often looked at his young wife Nelly when he was awake. Though she did not order his course of treatment, she seldom left his side.

Spitz stored up those observations and the reports Martha Washington gave him and rode every morning to Yorktown. Washington had abandoned the field headquarters and moved into an impressive brick home near the river. When Spitz arrived, he told Washington and Craik whatever he had seen and whatever Martha had told him. Sometimes Martha sent her husband letters, which Spitz delivered. Often Washington saw him right away, but occasionally he had to wait in an anteroom in the brick headquarters while Washington finished speaking to a senior officer or a French ally.

When Spitz had been performing these errand services for about a week, he arrived one day to find Craik waiting in an anteroom, too, for Spitz to arrive. As Billy Lee showed Spitz in, Craik motioned for Spitz to join him.

"Count de Grasse and Admiral Barras are within, consulting with George," Craik explained. "You may have to cool your heels a while here before you may see him. How is young Mr. Custis this morning?"

"Mrs. Bassett had the overseer in to bleed him last night. Mrs. Bassett and Mrs. Washington said to tell you that they hope Jack is better. His fever is down, and he mutters less. They've given him a tincture of feverfew in strong red wine this morning. But he's very pale, and he looks weaker to me."

Craik shook his head. "The abatement of the fever is not always so hopeful a sign. Occasionally, it does presage a return to health and spirits. But more often, it attends the progress of the disease through the final stages. Have the spots faded or increased in number?"

"I think they're about the same; I know they haven't faded," Spitz reported.

Craik pursed his lips. "The hopeful signs are ruddy cheeks, the fading of spots, the return of vigor, and sensible speech. Search young Mr.

Custis for those signs, Spitz. If you cannot report them to me in another few days, I shall attend him to try what my skill may do."

"I'm sure the ladies would be glad to have you there, Doctor Craik," Spitz agreed. "They talk all the time about what to do for him next. They've brought one of the old servants in to care for him lately. She's supposed to know all about herbs. But they worry what to give him."

"His loss would be most grievous, and his illness is acute. They are right to worry."

Craik and Spitz sat in silence for a moment. Then Spitz gestured to the door behind him. "Why are the admirals here?" Spitz asked.

"They discuss the further disposition of the French fleet, now that Yorktown is won. And George is likely to take their advice, as those gentlemen ensured his success here," Craik said.

"You mean the Battle of the Capes?" Spitz clarified. That battle had sent two British ships limping home to New York for repairs and left the French navy undisputed masters of Chesapeake Bay. In addition to that battle, a sudden squall at sea had also damaged several British ships but mysteriously left the French ships undamaged.

Craik nodded. "Of course the battle was a definitive stroke, but I also refer to the timely influx of supplies and artillery and men and silver the navy carried, as well as Count de Grasse insisting that he could only sail here instead of New York. That insistence shaped every felicitous event after it."

"Do you think it would have been a success, attacking Clinton in New York like Washington wanted to do instead of attacking here?" Spitz asked. Washington had wanted New York. Ever since Howe had chased him out of Brooklyn across the East River in 1776, Washington had skirted the perimeter of the city, determined to capture that stronghold with its deep harbor and large community of Loyalists. To capture New York would be to defeat the British army at one blow. He had stayed north, guarding Clinton and strategizing to get enough men to attack, while he sent his trusted general, Nathaniel Greene, to fight in the south in his stead.

"It might have been, had Admiral de Grasse been free to come so far north to join Barras off the shores of New York, and had General Greene's army been able to come so far north unimpeded. But de Grasse must sail to Chesapeake, and Cornwallis must come to Yorktown seeking reinforcements, due to Greene's relentless bruising. So George must go where the fighting is, not where he would rather fight," Craik admitted. "Our mutual friend is wise enough to see things as they are, not as he would have them to be."

Spitz shook his head in wonder. "It seems like a stroke of luck that de Grasse got the Spanish to guard his commercial fleet, allowing him to sail here with so many gunships, soldiers, and needed funds at just the right time to meet up with Barras, who was carrying essential artillery and supplies and who got here undetected, though he sailed right through the British fleet."

"No man who weighs the evidence impartially can attribute to luck the manifold blessings of God on this war," Craik disagreed. "Luck favors no man and no cause so steadily and powerfully as our commander in chief and our new nation have been favored. Fortune's wheel turns round and round. One day she raises a man, and the next, she dashes him down. The aid of the Spanish, the alliance of the French, our gallant southern army suddenly rising from near ashes, Clinton's blindness to Washington's movements before he marched to Yorktown and his inability to refit troop ships afterwards, the fog shielding our trench diggers, the clear moon allowing for the surprise taking of key British redoubts, and the storm blocking Cornwallis's retreat north: so many favors at once are beyond chance. God has bent the branch low enough that we may pluck the fruit, and we may not attribute to any other cause His mercy to us without incurring His wrath and removing ourselves from His favor."

The door opened, and Craik and Spitz both stood respectfully as Washington walked with Admiral Barras and Count de Grasse to the door of his study. The men all bowed, and Billy Lee showed the French naval officers to the front door of the house.

When Washington saw Spitz, his brow creased in anxiety. "Spitz—come in. Tell me: how is Jack? Is he mending?"

Spitz turned to Craik, who extended a hand to usher Spitz ahead of him into the room. Spitz walked in and sat down in a chair near the one Washington chose, and Craik followed him.

"Mrs. Washington asked me to tell Doctor Craik that Jack's fever is down, and he mutters less. But to me, he looks much paler and weaker," Spitz reported.

Washington looked out the window, silent, still, and sad. Finally, he looked to Craik. "What say you, James? Is he better or no?"

"I cannot tell without conducting an examination, George," Craik hedged, "but I fear for him. If he is no better in three days' time, I shall go to him myself."

Washington nodded distractedly, looking back out the window. "Go as soon as you may. His mother cannot bear the loss," he said, not looking at Craik. "Nor can I."

Craik looked back at Spitz and nodded. "If I hear he is no better tomorrow, I will go to him. I should set the hospital affairs in order here before I leave."

Washington nodded again, and Spitz ached for him. He could only imagine the worry and turmoil of knowing your son was in terrible danger and at the same time having to carry a separate weight of responsibility for the fate of the nation. The pressure on Washington must have been nearly unendurable.

Then Washington turned to Spitz and smiled sadly. "I do hope that you are getting better cheer from Mrs. Bassett than you are from me. Are you well? Are you happy at Eltham?"

Spitz blinked back tears. "Mrs. Bassett has given me the run of the stables and the library. I have everything I could want. You are kind to be concerned for me at such a time."

Washington feebly waved away Spitz's thanks. "You do me a good turn, riding daily to tell me how Jack fares. I am grateful."

A knock sounded at the door, and Billy stepped in. "General Lincoln and the Marquis de Lafayette have arrived to speak with you, sir," he said softly in his deep, quiet voice.

"I shall see them at once," Washington said, rising and clasping Spitz's hand in farewell.

Spitz pressed his old friend's hand warmly. "I'll see you tomorrow, sir."

Spitz left and mounted his horse to ride back to Eltham. The whole of the way there, which was closer to an hour and a half without the heavy carriage, he thought of Washington's reaction to the news of Jack's health and his appeal to Craik to attend Jack soon. He also thought of Washington's kind concern for him. How could he spare a thought for a friend while he was so sad about his son and so busy conducting the war? *He must be much stronger than most men.*

But Spitz also realized that he had more to record in his journal now, since he'd talked with Craik about the French admirals. At Eltham, he gave Mrs. Washington her husband's greetings and comments, and then he went to the guest room Mrs. Basset had allotted him. He sat at the desk and took out his writing materials.

**Sign 20**—Providentially, Admiral Count de Grasse reached an agreement with a Spanish agent in Santo Domingo whereby Spain would provide security for French merchant ships during his absence. This pledge allowed the admiral to sail to Chesapeake Bay with all of his armed ships in order to provide the necessary difference to exceed the strength of the British fleet—the butterfly effect.

**Sign 21**—Besides his ships, Admiral Count de Grasse brought with him 3000 French troops and a large sum of silver to help defray the costs of the siege at Yorktown and meet the payroll of the Continental army.

**Sign 22**—A storm damaged British ships but left the French ships unharmed.

**Sign 23**—(Godsend at the Capes—Superior French Fleet)—The Battle of the Capes prevented the main contingent of British reinforcements from reaching Cornwallis.

**Favorable Interposition 11**—A timely squall prevented Cornwallis' nighttime retreat across the York River, providentially closing his window of escape.

**Sign 24**—Cornwallis' definitive capitulation at Yorktown paved the way for the end of the war and the signing of the peace treaty.

**Favorable Interposition 12**—Washington preferred to attack General Clinton in New York, but the Lord purposely ordered circumstances to support a siege of Cornwallis at Yorktown instead. The Lord's plan prevailed. "Many are the plans in a man's heart, but it is the Lord's purpose that prevails"– Proverbs 19:21.

**Sign 25**—Washington designed a series of troop movements to fool General Clinton into believing that the combined American and French armies intended to launch an attack on him in New York instead of attacking Cornwallis at Yorktown. Providentially, the stratagem worked perfectly.

**Sign 26**—French Admiral Barras' fleet containing essential siege artillery and salted provisions mysteriously sailed undetected through waters frequented by British ships to join Admiral de Grasse's fleet in the Chesapeake for the siege of Yorktown.

**Prophesy fulfilled:** Chief Half King gave George Washington the Indian name Caunotaucarius: Town Taker. The crowning moment of Town Taker's revolutionary struggle was the taking of Yorktown.

**"The Success of the Combined Arms against our Enemies at York and Gloucester, as it affects the Welfare and Independence of the United States, I viewed as a most fortunate Event... I take a particular Pleasure in acknowledging, that the interposing Hand of Heaven in the various Instances of our extensive Preparations for this Operation, has been most conspicuous and remarkable." George Washington**[66]

The next day after another report of no improvement, Craik accompanied Spitz back to Eltham and took charge of the sickroom, which became much more businesslike. He ordered a fresh letting of blood followed by a diet of rich broths and puddings to build Jack up. He dosed Jack with concoctions of herbs and medicines that he brewed and mixed personally. He took Jack's temperature and felt Jack's pulse and peered into Jack's eyes and examined his spots.

Spitz watched all of the treatments with dread mounting in him. Jack needed antibiotics, and he needed them immediately. But no antibiotics existed in the eighteenth century to give him. Spitz took to sitting in a chair outside the sickroom in easy calling distance from anyone who needed him. At night, he slept in his clothes with the door open, ready to ride for Yorktown at a moment's notice.

On the fifth of November, Craik came to the door of the sickroom, visibly upset. He motioned for Spitz to follow him to the library, and once inside, he turned around and closed the door. Stricken and spent, he leaned against it.

Tears leaked from the corners of Craik's eyes, tears he didn't bother to wipe away. He didn't sob, and his voice sounded steady but sad. "Spitz, I think you had better ride to Yorktown to fetch George. I have done everything in my power to purge this fever, but it has burned too hot too hastily. There is no hope left."

Grief weighed in Spitz's stomach like a rock. "There's nothing left? That's it? He's just going to die?"

"Unless God sends him a miracle, he will die," Craik sighed. "George must come in haste to tell him goodbye, for he will not wait long to leave. Tell him so, Spitz."

"I'll leave now," Spitz said, rising from his chair and starting towards the door.

"Interrupt him, Spitz, even if every senior officer in the French and American armies surrounds him," Craik said. "I shall return to Jack and pray for mercy. It is all that remains to me to do."

Spitz rushed out the door and ran to the stables, asking a groom for help to stable his usual horse. Spitz's hands shook in his haste so that he could not buckle a strap or tighten a girth. But once the groom had saddled the horse, he climbed quickly into the saddle and dug his heels into the horse's side, calling to him to urge him to gallop. The horse kept his pace as long as he could, and Spitz alternately cantered and galloped to let his mount rest as much as he dared. But panic urged him to Yorktown. To think of Washington losing his son was bad enough without adding

Washington not saying goodbye at the end because Spitz had not arrived soon enough.

At the general's headquarters, Spitz ran up the outer stairs and pounded on the door.

Billy Lee opened it, his face calm and composed except for one eyebrow which he had raised in wordless comment on the bad manners of whoever was knocking. He recognized Spitz, though, and he read the desperation on his face. "Is General Washington required at Eltham?" he asked quickly and intelligently.

"I have to bring him right now; Craik says there's no time to lose," Spitz gasped.

Billy said, "Wait here, please," and ushered him inside. He disappeared down the hall, and a few moments later, Washington walked quickly into the anteroom.

"Thank God you're here, sir. You must come to Eltham. Craik says that there is no hope left, and you must ride quickly to say goodbye," Spitz told him, hating the words he had to say. Before, he had heard bad news called a sad blow, and he had wondered why people had chosen those words. But now, he saw Washington step back and cave his chest as if Spitz had hit him. *A sad blow,* Spitz thought ruefully, *it fits.*

Washington recovered immediately and walked through the rear of the house toward the stables. Spitz followed him, feeling sorry for his poor horse that had run so far so fast and now would have to do it again. But when he left the back door and crossed the courtyard, he saw a groom unsaddling his horse. Billy Lee led two fresh horses to a pair of mounting blocks set near one another and held the reins while Spitz and Washington climbed onto their horses' backs. As Billy handed the reins to Washington, Spitz heard him say, "God speed you, sir." Washington leaned down and put a hand on Billy's shoulder, wordlessly thanking him.

Swerving rapidly and changing course often to avoid traffic and obstacles, Washington raced through the town as quickly as he could. Spitz had a great deal to do to keep up with him. Finally the two riders reached an open road northwest, and Washington urged his horse to a gallop.

Spitz followed Washington all the way to Eltham, sorrow for his friend seizing his mind and heart. He did not know what to say. He did not know how he would comfort Washington after Jack's death. He wanted to offer him some solace, some relief, but he had never found any for himself, let alone any he could offer to a fellow sufferer. So he just watched Washington's straight, strong back in the saddle and felt sad and angry.

*This is Your fault!* he accused. *You could have kept Jack home or kept him from getting the fever. You could have sent me some antibiotics to give him. But no—You're just going to step back and let him die and then blame Washington if he doesn't handle the loss well enough—just like what happened to me.*

The further Spitz traveled, the angrier he became. When he and Washington arrived at the house, Spitz dismounted and grabbed the reins of Washington's heaving, snorting horse. He held the reins of both animals in his hands and led them to the stables in the back of the house. A groom offered to take the horses from him, but Spitz kept the one that had carried Washington. Too agitated to stand still, he walked it around in circles to cool it, and then he followed the groom to a trough. While the horses drank, Spitz stared into the rolling hills in the distance, but his eyes kept straying to the house.

Finally he sighed and handed the reins he held to the groom. He washed his hands in the icy pump that fed the trough and then walked to the house. When he opened the front door, he heard sobbing, and he knew that the long struggle was over. Jack was dead.

Spitz slumped into a chair in the anteroom and put his hands over his face, grieving for the young man upstairs that left behind his wife and children. Spitz's heart began to ache unbearably, too, for the father who lamented over that man right now. But Spitz also wept for himself, for his own unrequited grief and pain over the loss of his own son. His long years of bitterness and resentment overflowed into a torrent of angry tears like he hadn't allowed himself since Mia's funeral. He lost track of time. He forgot where he was. He sank into his pain.

A hand clasped his shoulder, and Spitz looked up to see Washington, eyes and nose red and still wet, standing beside him. Washington dropped into the chair beside Spitz's and turned him a quivering smile.

"I should have known that you would understand, Spitz," Washington said, a remnant of his tears still running down his cheeks. "You lost your son, too. I remember."

"I'm so sorry," Spitz said shakily when he could find his voice. He shook his head. "I'm just so, so sorry." He dissolved again into hot, angry tears.

Washington's hand still clasped his shoulder, and he leaned forward, spent. "What would we do without the comfort of God?" Washington said softly. "How could we otherwise bear such sorrow? But thank God; He is near."

Spitz bowed over in half, slumped under the weight of his pain. *He is near. How could we otherwise bear such sorrow? You understand. You lost your son, too. The comfort of God—He is near. What would we do without the comfort of God?* Washington's phrases reechoed in Spitz's mind. *What would we do without the comfort of God?*

The comfort of God—Spitz longed for it like a drowning man longs for air, and hesitantly, fearfully, he reached for it. He opened his soul in a last gasp of hope and turned it toward the light. *Comfort me. Please comfort me,* Spitz earnestly pled with a pure heart for the first time.

And the light came, filling his soul with warmth and fellow-feeling and soothing rest, lifting him from the cold flood of anger and setting him somewhere sure and safe, beyond resentment and questioning. He thought of the image he had hurled at God from Hebrews: "For our God is a consuming fire."

*Yes,* a firm yet soft voice reminded him, *I am.*

The light in his soul burned brighter and hotter, turning to flame and then ash and dust his hatred and accusation and grudge-keeping, and incinerating his case beyond recall—beyond hope of recall. The years of despising God fell away from him like a nightmare when the morning dawns, and he woke to the remembrance of the love and comfort of God as if he had never lost it. His sobs gave way to quiet tears that did not suffocate him with their passion. He lifted himself and wiped his face on his sleeve.

"I don't know," he told Washington. "I don't know what we would do without the comfort of God. But we have it." He nodded, and Washington nodded back. They knew.

Washington leaned back. "I have asked too much of you, Spitz, and I fear that my grief has reopened yours. We grow old in this war, and though I cannot leave it to nurse the wounds of my soul, you may. Return to your home and your family. You have a granddaughter, you said?"

Spitz nodded. "Aspen," he added.

Washington smiled kindly at him. "Grandchildren are the balm of an old man's soul. Go home to your granddaughter. Like you, I have just now adopted my two youngest grandchildren as well, to remove a burden from their mother and to comfort their grandmother. Though I cannot remain home with mine for some years yet, you can. I will certify your discharge myself."

"Thank you," Spitz said. "I'd like nothing more than to go home to Aspen."

"It is done, my old friend," Washington told him. "Rest here for a while." Washington rose and walked outside. Through the windows, Spitz saw him ride away south with Doctor Craik.

Quietly, Spitz walked up the stairs to his room. On his way, he saw the three bereaved women in the sickroom, where Jack's body lay covered with a sheet. Martha and Anna Maria and Nelly all clung to each other, patting backs and stroking hair and exchanging assurances.

*Yes,* Spitz recognized, *that's what comfort looks like—sharing the grief, not hiding it and burying it underneath a pile of books. That's what I ought to offer Aspen.*

Then he remembered that right now, Aspen was on a plane to the place where her parents had died. He turned away from the door and went to his room. He closed the door and fell to his knees.

*What can I do?* he lamented. *She may die; I may never see her again. I'm sick with worry. Will You guarantee me that she'll come home all right? Will You promise me that I won't lose her, too?*

Spitz's desperate pleas faded into quietness, and then he heard that gentle, insistent voice again, speaking so kindly and lovingly to him.

*Do not be afraid; I am with you always, even to the end of the world. Cast your cares upon me, for I care for you. I do not withhold any good thing from those who walk uprightly. I will bless you and keep you and make My face shine upon you and be gracious to you and give you peace. When you walk through the valley of the shadow of death, I will be with you. I will feast with you and rejoice over you with singing. I have called you by your name. I have searched you and known you. I have gone to prepare a place for you, and I will come again for you. You will be mine, my own adopted child, dear to me, beloved and treasured, and I*

*will be your Father and your God. Behold, I am making all things new.*
*I am He who lives, and was dead. I am the Alpha and the Omega, the*
*beginning and the end. I am the open door. I am bread for the hungry*
*and living water for the thirsty. I am light to the darkness, freedom to the*
*oppressed, and joy to those who mourn. I am.*

The light within Spitz's soul grew and brightened and broke into a
chorus of stars that circled him in fierce joy and sped away in utter delight.

# Chapter Eleven

*"How good and pleasant it is when God's people*
*live together in unity!"—Psalm 133:1*

*"Finally, brothers and sisters, rejoice!*
*Strive for full restoration, comfort one another,*
*agree with one another, live in peace; and the*
*God of love and peace will be with you."*
*—2 Corinthians 13:11*

*T*he Sprite in Aspen's glass sloshed over her hand as the plane bounced and rocked its way across the Pacific Ocean. She glanced over at Bill, who was sound asleep, and thought of Bernie nicknaming him *Cast Away* after the volleyball in the movie. *That had better not turn out to be prophetic, Bernie, or I'll never forgive you,* she moaned internally.

Out the window, the sky was blue fading up to misty white above an enormous expanse of grey-green sea. Aspen had never imagined that the ocean could be so big. It dwarfed her imagination and seemed to gape below her in enormous indifference. The thought of being lost in it somewhere sank into the pit of her stomach and lodged, hard and cold, like a lump of ice.

*Were Mama and Daddy scared on their way over here?* she wondered. She instantly dismissed the idea of her father being scared. She remembered him laughing on his motorcycle while she squealed behind him and clung to his back, her skinny arms not quite reaching all the way around his waist. He had taken her up and down the street where they lived while her mother stood on the porch, nervously biting her nails.

Aspen suddenly realized that she was doing the same thing and snatched her hand away, balling it into a fist in her lap.

*I'm like her,* Aspen thought, looking out the window and breathing deeply, *I'm not the adventurer that Daddy was, or Papa even.* Aspen remembered the shelves of curios in Papa's library. When he'd shown them to her and told her the stories connected to each one, he'd never mentioned being scared. He talked about twenty-hour flights and helicopter rides like other people talked about taxis or commutes. Daddy and Papa had been cut from the same cloth.

She thought of her mother, so young when she died—only thirty-one. *I'm twenty-six; that's only five years' difference,* Aspen thought. But her mother's life had been full of joy and love. Her mother had married her father and had her. And her mother had God as well. When Aspen had lived with her parents, God had been a part of the daily conversation. Her parents had loved and included God. They had been excited to do something for Him in return, they had said, for all that He had done for them. They were grateful. And just as they adored God, they sincerely loved each other.

An image surfaced of her parents hugging as they talked in the kitchen. They were always hugging or holding hands together or sitting with Daddy's arm around Mama's shoulder. And they had made room for her, too. She remembered the sensation of being held and hugged and rocked, of a gentle hand stroking her cheek and gentle lips kissing her hair.

Tears filled her eyes. That kind of love was no longer part of her life. As loyal and dedicated and giving and thoughtful as Papa was, he wasn't very demonstrative. She might hold his hand or kiss his cheek, but he usually pulled away from her. He never reached out to her first. She missed having someone who liked her just hold her hand.

And she realized, too, the reason why she had nearly gasped aloud when Bill hugged her briefly at the hospital. He was impulsively affectionate, like her parents, and his hug was the first she'd felt in years. She looked over at him.

He was still suffering from the jet lag that had dogged him in Australia, where they had spent the first few days of the trip; so he slept now with his head on a flimsy airline pillow and his seat just barely reclined so that his neck was at an awkward angle. She leaned over him and tugged at the pillow to readjust it, and he nearly woke. His eyelids barely parted, though he seemed not to register her presence at all. But he straightened his neck, and she quickly tucked the pillow into a roll so that he could rest more comfortably. He half-smiled in his sleep.

Aspen breathed in the smell of his cologne, and then she quickly sat back in her own seat and shifted away from him. She raised the glass of Sprite and drank it, tasting the clean lemon and letting it erase the other scent. Then she stopped and put the glass down slowly on the fold-down tray in front of her.

This stifling and erasing was her customary impulse when any-thing moved her. When someone offered her sympathy, she changed the subject. When a man asked her out, she thought of an excuse not to go. When a woman invited her to go for coffee and talk, she agreed that coffee sounded wonderful and then neglected to follow up on the invitation.

So now her life looked very different from her parents' lives. She worked and came home to Papa, who stayed in his library. She had no close friendships. She had no romantic love. She had no comfortable rela-tionship to God. Sadness filled her over the life she had chosen to live. Being vibrant and cheerful and shallowly liked and admired by dozens of people who didn't really know her was not nearly enough. It was laugh-ably, pitiably, most definitely inadequate.

She closed her eyes. *I don't even know how to talk to You anymore. Have I waited too long?* she thought silently.

She instantly felt a kind of wordless welcome and reassurance. She grasped it eagerly.

*I'm afraid. I'm afraid of dying on this plane or on a tinier one later. I'm afraid of living alone,* she confessed. *I know that Papa never intended for me to curtail my life like I have, but it's done now. What do I do? How do I change?*

Again, though she heard no words, she felt an impulse to look beside her.

She glanced at Bill, who had so honestly confessed his interest in her. What did she really feel about him? *I don't know. I haven't let myself think that far, have I? I've been too busy inventing reasons why he didn't mean what he said.*

She thought of what she knew about him, how he was so relaxed and outgoing and likable and smart and naturally happy. She liked being his business partner. As soon as the two of them walked into a room, Bill put everyone at ease and smoothed the way for her to speak. He respected her and listened to her and led the way for the other men in the room to do the same. In situations where she'd always felt defensive, amped up to demand attention, she now felt welcomed and valued. Bill had done that. She appreciated him for the way he treated her.

But he'd also asked about her Papa and her past. He had listened to her childhood memories and remembered them and then shared his own. He'd covered for her at work so that she could spend time at the hospital. He'd come with her to the hospital and quickly figured out how to talk to Papa and treated him like a regular person, not ignored him like a vegetable or talked down to him like a half-wit. He had called her during the storm to make sure that she was all right. He was thoughtful and giving and genuinely kind. He was definitely a good friend.

But she still wasn't being completely honest. She really did like the scent of his cologne and his wavy light brown hair and his soft green eyes, usually crinkled at the edges in a smile. She really liked that smile. And she'd really liked that hug, too. So why was she holding back? What was so hard about just telling him, "I changed my mind - let's make the next dinner a date"? From what he'd told her, she didn't need to be afraid of rejection.

*It's not rejection I have to fear,* she realized. *I'm afraid of being attached. I'm afraid of loving him and losing him to a car crash or to cancer or to a mugger. I'm afraid of fate.*

But being afraid of fate meant that she would always be alone. And that lonely life was starting to frighten her more than fate.

A quiet voice whispered at the back of her mind. *If you can't trust fate, can you trust Me?*

She looked over at Bill again, and hope took root inside her. *I want to trust You. I want to believe it's not too late for me to change.* She made up her mind and lifted her chin. *I can tell him. When I find the right time, I will. I won't be afraid anymore.*

★ ★ ★

Spitz saw the tunnel of lights receding from him into the fluorescent light over his hospital bed. He felt spent, as if he'd just run a long distance or carried something heavy or climbed a steep hill. He lay still and appreciated the rest that this body afforded him. He couldn't do any hard work in this body if he tried.

But he could move his fingers. He stretched and wiggled them to make sure that they still worked. And then, without quite intending to do it, he bent his wrist, lifting his hand.

Shock jolted through him. He straightened the wrist, and then, very carefully and deliberately, he bent it again. Excitement filled him at the small accomplishment. He strained his eyes looking down his body at something on the hospital bed he could reach, but he couldn't see much over the mound of his ribcage. He placed his hand flat against his son's Bible, and then he lifted his wrist and extended a finger. Although he couldn't see them from where he lay, he could feel buttons on the inside of the bed frame. Perfect.

A finger extended as far as it could go, helped by the bent wrist, and a button depressed. The bed lowered slightly. He removed his finger and slid it along to the next button in the row, expecting it to raise the bed. Instead, static sounded, and a woman's voice said, "Yes? What do you need?"

Spitz was shocked. He'd pressed the call button, not that he could do anything about it now. The static lingered for just another moment, and then it ceased. The lingering silence of the room afterwards pressed into his ears. He pressed the button again.

"This is the nurse's station. Do you need something?" a woman's voice said.

The woman wasn't Angela. Spitz really wanted Angela. Angela would understand. Angela would notice what he'd done.

The static ceased. Spitz rolled his eyes to the window. The light outside glowed; it didn't shine through his blinds. So it was still morning. Angela should be here.

Purposefully, hopefully, and carefully, Spitz pressed the button again. He heard the static, but no one asked him a question. The static stopped.

Footsteps sounded outside in the hallway, and Spitz's door opened. He couldn't move. A heavyset nurse with wavy, bright red hair pulled into a loose twist pushed the door open and looked around. She saw Spitz unmoving in the bed and shrugged. The door fell closed behind her.

Irritated, Spitz immediately pushed the button again.

"Hello—can I help you?" Angela's voice answered.

Spitz relaxed. He heard a sharp intake of breath, and the static stopped again. But this time, the footsteps that approached his door hurried. A moment later, the door burst open, and Angela rushed to the side of his bed. She searched his eyes.

"Are you pressing the call button, Spitz?" she demanded excitedly.

He blinked once.

She clapped her hands and bounced up and down. "Press it again; show me."

Spitz bent his wrist and extended a finger, pressing the button. Static sounded. An impatient, short-of-breath voice said, "Yes? What do you need?"

"It's Angela, Debra," Angela called. "The patient in 503 regained mobility in his wrist! He can push the call button now!"

"Lucky me," Debra scoffed. "Tell him to stop."

Angela laughed. "You can bend your wrist, Spitz! It's coming back!"

Spitz blinked once. He felt like laughing. He wished he could laugh with her. Shoot, he wished he could get up out of this bed and go home. His spirits fell. He blinked twice. He waited a moment and blinked twice again.

"Hey, now, that's no way to be," Angela scolded him happily. "Look at you! You can move your wrist! You need to be happy about that. You need to celebrate."

Spitz blinked twice. Gloom overshadowed him. That bent wrist suddenly seemed like precious little progress, and his hospital bed felt more confining than ever.

"I understand," Angela said kindly. She sat down in the visitor's chair beside him. "Do you remember what I said to you when you first woke up?"

Spitz remembered. The recovery was a mountain climb, one hard step upward after another. It wouldn't happen all at once. He blinked once.

"I know that you're an ambitious man, and you're determined to get well. I know you want to be able to stand right up this minute and walk out of here under your own steam," Angela told him.

Spitz blinked once. She understood.

Angela patted his hand sympathetically. "It's going to take courage for you to celebrate each of these little milestones, but sometimes a little perspective helps. Can you remember the time before you woke up?"

Spitz blinked once. He remembered lying helplessly on the bed, able to hear and smell, but unable to see or communicate.

"And think of how different things are now than they were then. You can open your eyes. You can let us know what you're thinking. You're even starting to move. Can you see how far you've come?" she asked.

Spitz blinked once. He could see it. The perspective helped. But he was still frustrated. He blinked no.

Angela chuckled. "That ambition is just going to have to be your cross to bear, then." She looked thoughtful. "You know, God could help you with all of that frustration if you asked Him. You've got plenty of time for a good, long talk with the Almighty while you're lying here. Do you want me to find Pastor Campbell and send him in here after a while?"

Spitz thought of the lanky, comfortable preacher with his high, thin voice and uncanny knack for selecting scriptures to read. Despite the miraculous healing of Spitz's old grudge at Eltham, he hadn't prayed in a while, and he felt that he would like some help. He blinked once.

"He'll be here after lunch; I'll find him then," Angela said, standing up. "You know, when you're up and walking around again, you might want to try Pastor Campbell's church. He's a good, caring man, and the other people there are just like him. I go there, and they care about me. They've cared about me through some hard times. Just think about it. I'll go to the nurse's station and leave a message for Aspen about the wrist. She'll want to know."

Spitz blinked once, and Angela smiled broadly at him as she left. Spitz wondered what hard times she meant. If seeing the life of George Washington had taught him anything, it was that no one escaped sorrow. Everyone had a sad story in the past; even cheerful, caring Angela did. He respected her even more for her patience now that he knew her life hadn't been perfect.

He closed his eyes and sent his attention outward, beyond him. *I'm* *getting better now; thanks for that. And while I'm at it, thanks for the trips to see Washington. I'm glad I met him. And I'm glad I was there to see him on his darkest day.* I can't imagine suffering like that during such an important time and being able to react like he did. It was amazing to see. If anyone was going to show me the way out of my own dark days, it was him, and You knew it. I can't believe You were kind enough to give me such an amazing life with him while I was still so mad at You.*

Spitz felt wordless love and peace envelop him in an acceptance so strong that it brought tears to his eyes. Those tears led to other ones.

*I still miss Steve, God. I miss him every day. And I miss Mia and Nevaeh, too. I miss our family the way it used to be when we were all together. That still hurts. I wonder if it will ever stop hurting.*

Suddenly Spitz remembered the realization that all times are now, and he coupled that realization with what Washington had said at Valley Forge about God grieving for His lost Son.

*A part of You sees that grief all of the time. You feel it every second, if all times are now to You.* The enormity of that cosmic pain awed Spitz. *You understand. You are there with us.*

The voice inside him said: *I am with you always. I will never leave you or forsake you. I will turn your mourning into dancing.*

Spitz resisted the voice at first. But then his imagination showed him Aspen, dressed in white and smiling, holding out her arms to dance with him at her wedding. And he was dancing.

*I guess I've got some work ahead of me if I'm going to learn to dance,* he thought wryly.

The picture shifted. He was still at a wedding, but every woman there wore beautiful bridal clothes and dresses, all of them different colors and styles and all of them suiting that particular woman exactly. He saw bright silk pantsuits and elegant muslin gowns and sunset-colored saris and calico sundresses and satin confections with magnificent hoop skirts. And the men looked every bit as fine in everything from tuxedos to jeans to graceful morning suits.

An unimaginably long banquet table stretched further than Spitz would have thought possible along two sides of the room, and people at the edge of the dancers hugged each other and talked, laughing together, and introduced each other to people who had just finished dancing or who had just gotten a plate from the banquet table.

As he whirled Aspen around the floor, he saw another couple dancing near them, beaming at them: Steven and Nevaeh. A hand tapped his shoulder, and he saw his wife Mia the way she had looked on their wedding day, young and vibrant, wearing a soft, bright green dress that suited her much better than her bridal whites had. He embraced her tightly, sweeping her off the ground in his joy and laughing; she was laughing, too. It had been so long since he had heard her laugh.

He turned around to show Aspen the miraculous change in Mia and saw her dancing with a man he didn't recognize, a man with straight, dark hair like hers and startling, sea-green eyes that seemed somehow familiar. She met his gaze and smiled and said, "All times are now, Papa. We are all together now." She winked at him and nodded to the young man dancing with her, saying, "Aston's been waiting to take you fishing. Let's all go after the party." Bill, whom Spitz readily recognized, then appeared beside Aspen and put an arm around her while he waved good-naturedly toward Spitz. Spitz wondered about the young man named Aston while more and more faces he knew and had known and didn't yet know crowded into his vision, all of them delighted to see him and each other.

Confused but happy, Spitz held that picture in his mind while he saw and felt the tunnel of lights that transported him to the past encircling him again, taking him by surprise. He had surrendered his resentment. He assumed that his visits with Washington had ended. Though he longed to stay in his dream of that amazing party, joy surged through him at the thought that he would see his old friend again.

When the lights stopped spinning, they resolved into a pattern of diamond sparkles on the surface of a river. Late morning sunbeams filtered softly through colorful leaves that swayed in a gentle breeze. He recognized the familiar sound of a cascading stream, and then he noticed that he was standing six inches deep in its waters. *By now,* he thought, *I should be used to landing some place I don't recognize, but every time has been unique.*

He stood still in the flowing water and gazed around at the beautiful scenery. Rolling meadows began at the steep river banks and ended in the tree line of a quiet forest. Birds sang in the air overhead, and insects buzzed contentedly around him. Spitz could smell the baking-bread scent of wild grass in high summer sun. Spitz half wondered if he had been transported to heaven. He was holding in his left hand a primitive fishing pole, and the line was dangling downstream. He wore breeches made of fine black linen and a well-cut white cotton shirt, and back on the bank beside his familiar pack and leather messenger bag, he saw fine knit socks and expensive-looking leather buckled shoes. *I sure am dressed well for a fishing trip,* he thought.

Soaking in the moment as the current splashed against his legs, Spitz studied the fishing pole and the hand that held it. He recalled how just this morning he had lifted his hand, bent his wrist, and waved his index finger: three useful movements for casting. He would make a full recovery soon, he hoped. *Maybe things will be back to normal before too long. To celebrate, I should take Aspen fishing,* he thought. It had been a very long time since they had been fishing together. And his face brightened further at the thought of including Bill, who liked fishing and liked him and most importantly, liked Aspen.

Spitz always enjoyed fishing, especially with his granddaughter. A mounted largemouth bass alongside an eight-by-ten photograph of the two of them catching it hung proudly in his library. During his childhood and corporate career, he had been blessed with many unique opportunities to go fishing. He had caught northern pike and walleye in Canadian lakes, salmon in Alaskan and Norwegian rivers, red fish in the Louisiana Gulf, crappie in Oklahoma reservoirs, and largemouth bass in alligator-infested pits (remnants of phosphate mining) in central Florida. He had fished in the deep sea near offshore drilling platforms and in the blue waters of Hawaii. He had even fished among Australian coastal reefs. But he had rarely fished for trout in a stream. *Have You sent me here to learn patience?* he joked during his first few lousy casts. Then he began to study the best method of casting using the primitive equipment he held. In short order, he had the hang of it and was fishing like a semipro.

The pleasures of the morning outing enchanted Spitz. Though he had not yet felt the tug of a fish on the end of his line, the peaceful sounds of nature and the pleasant aroma of the fields and woods were reward enough. The cares of the world were drifting far from his mind when a voice interrupted the serenity.

"Sir, I do believe your luck will improve should you decide to cast beyond the rocks by the fallen tree."

Startled by the sudden voice on the bank behind him; Spitz took a step and nearly slipped below his waist into swirling water.

Picking his way down the bank, the man who had spoken before said, "I am very sorry to have surprised you. I should have announced my presence more directly. I have spent a pleasant morning fishing a bit further upstream, caught two, and decided to walk this way. Have you had a good morning?"

For a brief moment Spitz considered the alternative; being confined to the boring hospital bed with only his hands and eyelids moving. "It's been a glorious morning," Spitz replied.

He considered his fishing companion. The man, who was dressed in clothes similar to the ones Spitz wore, was a large man, but not fat. He was tall, with a large nose, a wide mouth, and wide-set eyes that seemed to fit with his broad shoulders and capable hands to broadcast boldness and merriment to everyone who looked at him. Added to that jovial large-ness, the wooden peg that replaced his lower left leg made him look like a merry pirate. He sat down, removed his right shoe and sock, and began to talk to Spitz while he tied his hook and baited it and waded out into the water.

"Do you live hereabouts, or are you on holiday?" the man asked.

"I'm on holiday," Spitz answered. Taking a cue from the apparent age of his hands, he added, "It's a permanent holiday; I'm retired from business."

"What sort of business?" the man asked carefully, a little reserved.

"Trade—I've traveled the world supplying merchants in the colonies. Of course, I took a little holiday from my work for a few years to fight in the revolution," Spitz answered.

The answer seemed to delight his companion and banish all reserva-tion from his manner. He waded into the water barefoot beside Spitz and reached out to shake hands. "I am Gouverneur Morris," he said warmly, "and I am beyond pleased to make your acquaintance."

"Stephen Spitzen," Spitz replied. He didn't add the nickname. He didn't think Morris was the type to appreciate it.

"My dear Mr. Spitzen!" Morris exclaimed. "Most men of our station and our years served quietly by advancing personal loans or battling in Congress, as I had the honor and pleasure of doing, but you, sir! To take up the fight in person must have been thrilling!"

Spitz pursed his lips. "I don't know that I would call it thrilling. It was hard work and bloody. Any thrill I found in it came from being near General Washington."

"You know our illustrious commander-in-chief in person!" Morris exclaimed. "Then fate has led you here, man, for Washington himself is in the valley on this very day! He and I have traveled from Philadelphia in my phaeton for a brief respite from the brawling cattle market that purports to be a Constitutional Convention. Washington is having his phaeton relined and repainted on my advice, of course. I have told him that he is back among gentleman, not chasing harum-scarum after Clinton anymore; so of course, he must look the part."

"Of course," Spitz said. For all his exuberance, Morris seemed to be something of a snob, though Spitz tempered his judgment out of respect for the man himself. Though he was an über-Federalist who didn't believe that the poor should vote, Morris had lost his family home to the British and opposed the Loyalist half of his family publicly at a time when it seemed that all he'd get for his trouble would be a hanging. He was the man who physically wrote the Constitution and spoke at length of what it should contain. An independently wealthy man of the world, he was destined to be the American ambassador to France during its revolution. Now Spitz understood why his clothing looked so fine. Morris would never have approached a commoner so familiarly or spoken to him so respectfully.

"At any rate, we are staying with Mrs. Jane Moore nearby, and if you know Washington personally, you simply must come to dine with us," Morris said.

"I'd love to come to dinner. Are we catching it?" Spitz asked.

Morris laughed. "I did promise the lady that I would endeavor to supplement her table, and with two of us fishing, we should all feast on the catch. But tell me, when did you see Washington last?"

"It must have been nearly six years ago," Spitz said, calculating quickly. "The last time I saw him was at Eltham, the day his son Jack died. I had left my services in the Life Guard for the honor of carrying messages between Eltham, where Jack was, and Doctor Craik and Washington while they remained in Yorktown."

"Then you are a dear connection, and he will be pleased that I have stumbled upon you," Morris said warmly.

"You compared the convention to a cattle market," Spitz said. "Is it going that badly?"

"My dear sir—such thundering ultimatums! Such standings on principle and refusals to negotiate! Such passion and hot language! But really, I do not see how I could have tempered my speech in consideration of what the other side proposed," Morris said, winking.

Spitz smiled. Morris was an entertaining character, and he was growing on him. "But hasn't Dr. Franklin been able to make any headway?"

Morris grew serious. "Ah, sir, Dr. Franklin is wisdom personified and the soul of brotherhood and encouragement. He did present a most affecting speech urging us to seek almighty God in our dealings. I have moderated my language somewhat in consideration of it, and the whole convention at once accepted his proposal to include prayer in its negotiations. I have a bit of the speech by heart; would you like to hear it?" The boyish gleam of excitement reentered Morris's eye.

Spitz nodded. "I'd like that very much."

So Gouverneur Morris, barefoot in the stream with fishing pole in hand, began to declaim.

"In this situation of this Assembly, groping as it were in the dark to find political truth, and scarce able to distinguish it when presented to us, how has it happened, Sir, that we have not hitherto once thought of humbly applying to the Father of lights to illuminate our understandings?

"In the beginning of the contest with Britain, when we were sensible of danger, we had daily prayers in this room for Divine protection. Our prayers, Sir, were heard and they were graciously answered. All of us who were engaged in the struggle must have observed frequent instances of a superintending Providence in our favor.

"Have we now forgotten this powerful Friend? Or do we imagine we no longer need His assistance? I have lived, Sir, a long time, and the longer I live, the more convincing proofs I see of this truth: that God governs in the affairs of man. And if a sparrow cannot fall to the ground without his notice, is it probable that an empire can rise without His aid?

"We have been assured, Sir, in the Sacred Writings that 'except the Lord build the house, they labor in vain that build it' (Psalm 12:1). I firmly believe this, and I also believe that without His concurring aid we shall succeed in this political building no better that the builders of Babel. We shall be divided by our little partial local interests; our projects will be confounded and we ourselves shall become a reproach and bye word down to future ages.

"I therefore beg leave to move that, henceforth, prayers imploring the assistance of Heaven and its blessing on our deliberation be held in this assembly every morning… and that one or more of the clergy of this city be requested to officiate in that service." [67]

Spitz nodded in acknowledgement. "It's a very moving speech, and a wise one, too."

"Yes, it is," Morris said mournfully. "It nearly convinces me afresh to embrace the southern delegates, but alas, the task is too hard."

"What's wrong with the southern delegates?" Spitz asked, stung. As a native Virginian, he took the insult personally. "Washington's a Virginian, and you seem to like him well enough."

Morris smiled genuinely. "May I surmise from your evident offence that you, too, are southern? I offer my apologies; truly I do. Rest assured that I find nothing objectionable in the person or address of my southern neighbors. I have entertained Washington as a guest in my home in Philadelphia during the length of the convention. Surely I would not live with a Virginian if I found the whole tribe of them intolerable."

Somewhat mollified, Spitz pressed the question. "Then what's so hard about agreeing with them? Is it just the whole question of representation with big states versus small states?"

"That question is a serious one, and a matter of extensive debate," Morris conceded. "The Articles of Confederation stipulated an equal number of votes per colony, a practice I think wise. I confess myself opposed to the assignation of votes based on area of land; such a distribution places unfair power in the hands of a few men with extensive land holdings. An aristocracy may need to exist for the good of the poor, but if it assumes all power to itself, we shall end in crowning another king. And no matter that I love Washington as a brother, I will not see him king. But do not fear: because I know the man, I shall not fear the outcome."

"But you don't agree that every man should vote," Spitz said.

"How shall we place such a burden upon the poor, who cannot even care for themselves?" Morris asked. "People in desperate straits would surely sell their votes to the rich, who would aggregate undue power through the purchase of votes. We want no plutocracies here, sir. The vote must fairly reflect the population."

"Well, then what's the main problem?" Spitz prodded. "Why can't you agree with the southern states?"

"The problem is slavery!" Morris exploded. "Dear God, what a pestilential institution it is, from first to last! 'Upon what principle is it that the slaves shall be computed in the representation? Are they men? Then make them citizens, and let them vote. Are they property? Why, then, is no other property included? The Houses in this city," Morris said, waving his hand back in the direction of Philadelphia, "are worth more than all the wretched slaves which cover the rice swamps of South Carolina. The admission of slaves into the Representation when fairly explained comes to this: that the inhabitant of Georgia and South Carolina who goes to the Coast of Africa, and in defiance of the most sacred laws of humanity tears away his fellow creatures from their dearest connections and damns them to the most cruel bondages, shall have more votes in a Government instituted for protection of the rights of mankind, than the Citizen of Pennsylvania or New Jersey who views with a laudable horror, so nefarious a practice.'"[68]

Spitz was thunderstruck. He hadn't realized that someone as foppish and snobbish as Morris would be such an ardent abolitionist. He also hadn't realized that anyone had spoken so strongly for enslaved African Americans at the founding of America, and he was glad to find that someone had.

"I agree with you. Slavery is a sin, and allowing it is a stain on the nation. It does no one good, and it does a whole race of human beings a lot of evil," Spitz said hotly. He thought of Angela, who had been so selflessly kind to him and Aspen. To think of her in chains or mistreated horrified and sobered him. He had never thought of slavery so personally.

Morris looked shocked. "You are the first gentleman from a southern state I have met who does not swear to defend the institution with his heart's blood. How come you by such a view? How do you farm your lands? And how do your neighbors treat you for it?"

Spitz shook his head. "I have only a small family farm, and I lease it to tenant farmers, respectable, free men who do the work of farming themselves and pay rent to me from their profits. Most of my wealth is portable, money I've earned from trading and shipping most of my life. I'm afraid I don't have the problems Washington would if he freed his slaves right now."

"Problems be damned!" Morris shouted. "Shall we brook kidnap and murder and assault of the basest kind because we will not suffer a few problems? No, we cannot hold such a plague to our hearts and not suffer the infection. No part of a free nation can excuse slavery."

"You're right; I wish the convention could figure out a way to outlaw it right now," Spitz told him.

Morris shook his head impatiently. "Herein is the great frustration of our purpose. If we do outlaw slavery by fiat, our cause is lost, for unless we stand as a single nation, strong and undivided, we cannot stand against the princes of Europe who would carve us to bits and undo all the work we have done these last years. And if we make their livelihood illegal, the southern states will leave us and form not another strong nation but five small and vulnerable nations, squabbling among themselves: a confederacy, not a republic. They leave us no choice but either to condone their abominable practice or to plunge afresh into another war to uproot it."

"You see that now?" Spitz asked surprised. "You see another war coming?"

"I am not the only one who does," Morris told him. "Washington himself says, 'It is too probable that no plan we propose will be adopted. Perhaps another dreadful conflict is to be sustained. If, to please the people, we offer what we ourselves disapproved, how can we afterwards defend our work? Let us raise a standard to which the wise and the honest can repair. The event is in the hand of God.'"[69]

Spitz paused. "Washington believes very strongly in the hand of God." *The invisible hand—he saw it in these deliberations, too, not just in the war.* Another thought struck him. "Washington trusts the future generations, too. He knows that what's happening now is imperfect and that his grandchildren and their grandchildren will have to fix the mistakes that are happening now. That's amazing."

"If our children are no wiser than we are, then this American experiment will not last," Morris agreed. "But we hope and pray that they will learn from us and then supersede us."

"Well, aside from the big disagreements about representation and slavery, what progress have you made so far?" Spitz asked.

"We have settled on three branches of government, finally led by an executive," Morris said exultantly. "You bore the brunt of the faults in the Articles of Confederation, under which I served in congress. When all parties are equal, none carries the day. Government needs a head to guide it. Had we one when you fought in the war, you might have eaten and dressed and stanched the wounds of your fellows with more comfort and regularity than you did."

"That would have been nice." Spitz winced at the memories of flour-and-water gruel and men beside him who marched with rags bound around their bare feet.

"I am heartily ashamed of the deprivations our army suffered at Valley Forge and before. I cannot revisit that ground with any peace in my heart. You see why today I have chosen to fish rather than accompany Washington on his rambles in that place." Morris shuddered.

"That will never happen again," Spitz said confidently. "Our soldiers in future wars won't suffer that way ever again." He stopped suddenly, remembering his promise to Rawlins not to act the prophet.

"I pray they will not," Morris nodded. "And we have formed a legislative arm to make sound law and a judicial arm to review it, both arms working in concert with the executive head. We have set in place certain checks and balances to be applied between the branches, devised a method of electing the executive, and planned for the admission of new states. And most importantly to my mind, we have ensured that the nation takes precedence over the individual states. The structure is sound, and I am pleased with it."

"It's a good structure; I'm sure it'll work," Spitz assured him. "But if we're going to take our hostess any fish, we'd better concentrate on casting."

"You are right, Mr. Spitzen," Morris agreed. "We will converse further with the happy addition of our mutual friend at dinner. I see a promising spot farther upstream. I shall try my luck there and leave you to fish here."

After Spitz watched him go, surprised at how nimbly Morris moved along the stony stream bed with his peg leg, he turned his attention to the trout near the hole Morris had showed him and enjoyed the peaceful rhythm of casting and playing the line. He caught four fat trout before Morris returned to fetch him, and by that time, he didn't know if he could wait for Mrs. Moore's cook to prepare them.

He searched his pack and found some bread and cheese and sausage, which he shared with his new companion, and then the two of them walked a little more than an hour to Jane Moore's house. As they drew closer, Spitz began to recognize the lay of the land where he had encamped with the Life Guard during the cruel winter of 1778. He could only imagine Washington's thoughts as he rode through the valley.

Mrs. Moore turned out to be a gracious hostess who greeted Spitz warmly when Morris introduced him. She politely offered Spitz a place to stay in the loft, as all her guest rooms were taken. "How could I fail to welcome a guest who brings supper with him?" she laughed, holding up the strings of fish Morris and Spitz presented her. "Sit down on the porch to catch the breeze while I take these fine trout to Lizzie, and I shall have Dolly bring you some blackberry tarts to take the edge off your hunger and some raspberry shrub to cool you."

Morris and Spitz thanked her and washed their hands at the pump by the horse trough before walking the garden path around the house and sitting on the Shaker rocking chairs lining the front porch. Soon a blonde girl who looked fourteen or fifteen, her hair done up in braids and a linen apron tied over her sprigged cotton dress, brought them a plate of succulent tarts and tall glasses of pink drink so cold that it beaded the outside of the glasses.

"Fresh from the spring house, no doubt!" Morris said appreciatively as he took his glass.

"Yes, sir," the girl said softly, dipping a curtsey and fleeing back to the kitchen before anyone required her to say anything else.

"What a great house," Spitz sighed happily as he rested in his rocking chair, watching the roses in front of the porch catch the breeze and sway.

The raspberry shrub was delicious, better than lemonade, and the tarts were delicate and juicy. He felt spoiled.

And then he saw George Washington riding a chestnut horse up the front path. Washington waved to the men on the porch and let a groom take his horse as he climbed energetically up the steps, his hand already out to Spitz. Spitz rose and shook hands with him.

"I'm delighted to see you again, sir," Spitz said.

Washington beamed at him. "After spending the day revisiting old memories, I welcome the sight of an old friend, which seems a fitting end. What brings you here, Spitz?"

Spitz shook his head. "Call it providence, if you like. I was fishing at Trout Stream with no idea you were here, and Morris found me and insisted I come for dinner."

"Well done, Gouverneur!" Washington smiled, sitting down and gesturing to the other men to resume their rocking chairs as well. "Have you any idea whom you have brought to me?" Washington briefly summarized their encounters, ending with the sad parting at Eltham. "I sent him home to his granddaughter, though I do not see her by you. Where is the girl?"

"Aspen took over the family business, and she's on a long trip now to the East Indies," Spitz explained, not sure that Washington and Morris would recognize the names of Australia and Indonesia.

"What a brave girl she is!" Morris exclaimed. "I do love to see a young woman possessed of courage and an independent spirit."

"But surely she does not travel alone," Washington said, worried. "She has proper guards and chaperones to ensure her safety, of course."

Spitz thought about his many prayers for Aspen's safety. "She does," Spitz reassured him. "She also has a partner in the business, Wilson Rawlins. I think that he wants to marry her someday. So he'll be extra-careful of her while they're over there. He promised me to look after her. Honestly, all that scares me about allowing her to go is the journey over and back. Her father died on one of these trips, during the journey home."

Washington nodded soberly. "It is a fearful thing to leave a person so dear to you in the hands of Providence, but then, it is a more fearful thing to take him out of those hands. All we may do when we fear for them is to say like Peter, 'Lord, to whom else shall we go? Thou hast the words of eternal life,' and like the supplicant father, 'Lord, I believe; help thou mine unbelief.'"

Spitz nodded. "That's exactly how I feel right now."

"Then be cheered, for Christ saved Peter and healed the child," Washington smiled. "You stand in good company."

"Thank you," Spitz said sincerely. "And how have you been since I last saw you? How are your grandchildren?"

"They thrive beyond reckoning, as becomes young creatures. Wash, who was a babe in arms when you last saw him at Eltham, is now an energetic young sprig full of life and passion. He is very like Jack was as a young boy, never happier than in the stables and kennels. He shall ride to hunt soon; I have promised him. And Nelly is a little beauty and a constant companion to Martha, who is much cheered by her for those other losses which still grieve her," Washington reported.

"They still grieve you, too, sir?" Spitz asked.

Washington nodded soberly. "I miss Jack. I had hoped that he would become a fellow servant with me to guide this new nation we all have founded. With the gifts of his handsome person and sizable estate, as well as his native empathy and intelligence, though he never cared for books, he might have done much good and relieved me of much care in my old age. But God knows best, and He has given me Wash. I must not repine at the acts of Providence."

"The nation still needs you, sir," Morris said warmly. "I doubt not that Mr. Custis would have been a valuable addition to our work, but he could not replace you. No one could ask it of him."

"And so disappear my hopes of a quiet retirement," Washington smiled at him. "I have been a public man from my youth, and I have served in every capacity God has allowed me. In a man of my age, his 'Morning and Evening hours, and every moment (unoccupied by business), pants for retirement; and for those domestic and rural enjoyments which in my estimation far surpasses the highest pageantry of this world.'[70] But alas, it is not to be."

"You will forgive us, perhaps, for assuming that our present need surpasses your own? For you know, this nation is still in its infancy, and such is the nature of an infant: to wail and demand with no care for the exertions of the parent," Morris teased.

Spitz laughed, and Washington smiled at him. "It may be a petulant infant who survived a violent birth, but the nation as a full-grown youth will be fine and splendid, indeed. 'Our region is extensive, our plains are productive, and if they are cultivated with liberality and good sense, we may be happy ourselves, and diffuse happiness to all who wish to participate.'"[71]

"You sound like you did on the survey trip to Ohio, at the top of the mountain," Spitz remembered. "You were in love with this country even then. All you wanted was its freedom."

"I do remember that day and that thrilling view westward," Washington said. "The Citizens of America, placed in the most enviable condition, as the sole Lords and Proprietors of a vast Tract of Continent, comprehending all the various soils and climates of the World, and abounding with all the necessaries and conveniences of life, are now by the late satisfactory pacification, acknowledged to be possessed of absolute freedom and Independency; They are, from this period, to be considered as the Actors on a most conspicuous Theatre, which seems to be peculiarly designated by Providence for the display of human greatness and felicity; Here, they are not only surrounded with everything which can contribute to the completion of private and domestic enjoyment, but Heaven has crowned all its other blessings, by giving a fairer opportunity for political happiness, than any other Nation has ever been favored with."[72]

"May we use it well," Morris said, raising his glass of raspberry shrub in salute. "And may the generations to come use it better than we have."

"Hear, hear," Spitz said, raising his own glass. Washington joined them, and the three of them drank to the welfare of America.

But Spitz was troubled. He knew, because of the time where he belonged, that future generations had taken far too long to eradicate the evil of slavery and for a long time afterwards had tolerated the evil of racial hatred. America now no longer acknowledged Providence publically except at election time, and did not ask for providential guidance about its mounting debt and foreign wars. These men didn't know what America had become. He felt an overpowering urge to warn them.

"But what if they don't use it well?" Spitz said hesitantly. "What if they ruin it?"

Morris and Washington both looked at him in concern and then at each other. Then Morris laughed, shaking his head. "Who is this timid milksop suddenly among us?" he asked. "Why should a soldier of the revolution and a venerable elder suddenly talk of qualms and queasy queries like an old maiden aunt with a cold in her head? No, man, we bravely seize the work before us and trust our heirs to do the same."

Washington nodded along with Morris. "The warmest friends and the best supporters the Constitution has, do not contend that it is free from imperfections; but they found them unavoidable and are sensible, if evil is likely to arise therefrom, the remedy must come hereafter; for in the present moment, it is not to be obtained; and, as there is a Constitutional door open for it, I think the People (for it is with them to Judge) can as they will have the advantage of experience on their Side, decide with as much propriety on the alterations and amendments which are necessary [as] ourselves. I do not think we are more inspired, have more wisdom, or possess more virtue, than those who will come after us."[73]

Morris looked ruefully at his empty glass and looked over at Spitz. "What was that young girl's name—the one with the braids? Daisy? Molly? Dolly!" he remembered. "Dolly? Dolly!" he called loudly.

The girl appeared moments later, evidently having run from the kitchen to judge by her flushed cheeks and flour-smudged apron. "Yes, sir?" she said timidly.

Morris held up his empty glass. "May we have another, pretty lass? Do say yes, and leave the jug." He winked at her and grinned.

The girl turned bright red and disappeared.

Washington raised his eyebrows at his friend. "You are asking only after the shrub, Gouverneur, and not the young blossom?" Spitz knew that Morris had been a notorious rake who kept company with dozens of women during his life and only married at fifty-seven. Evidently his reputation was well-known.

Morris laughed loudly. "I charm against my will, General Washington; I cannot change my nature."

Washington frowned. "She reminds me of my granddaughters; she has only a few more years than Betsy or Patsy. I should dislike seeing her corrupted, even in tone or in jest."

Morris sobered and reddened, smiling honestly. "She is safe from me, sir; I assure you."

When Dolly reappeared, Washington took the brimming jug from her hands and said, "You need not pour out for us, Dolly. Go, and help your mistress."

"Mrs. Moore said that dinner needs a half an hour yet and do you want another plate of tarts?" Dolly breathed quickly.

"We await dinner with prodigious patience and profess ourselves perfectly sated with tarts," Washington smiled kindly. Dolly didn't move. "Half an hour is quite all right, Dolly, and we need no more tarts."

Dolly nodded with her eyes cast down and whisked herself away.

Morris chuckled in his chair. "I think that you may have scared her quite as thoroughly as I did," he told Washington.

"She was more likely just awestruck meeting the great general in person," Spitz disagreed.

"Either way, we have seen the last of her for the present," Morris shrugged. "And it strikes me that I have not asked you about your time at Valley Forge this morning. How fared you at the scene of your former trials?"

Washington rocked a moment in silence in his chair, watching the bees in the roses beside the porch before he spoke. "I was much moved by my journey today. 'To have viewed the several fields... over which [I] passed, could not, among other sensations, have failed to excite this thought, here have fallen thousands of gallant spirits to satisfy the ambition of, or to support their sovereign... For what wise purposes does Providence permit this? Is it as a scourge for mankind, or is it to prevent them from becoming too populous?'"[74]

"Perhaps they suffered to prevent us from holding our liberty too lightly," Morris mused. "A God who would sacrifice His own Son for our sake in such an extravagant display of generosity and love knows our nature. Perhaps He knew that we, too, required a costly sacrifice to endear our nation to us."

"Or to refine us and to endear us to each other," Spitz said. "Wasn't the horrible winter at Valley Forge one reason why the army finally united into an American army instead of a lot of state militias?"

"I cannot help but think that you are both right," Washington said thoughtfully. "For who has before seen a disciplined Army formed at once from such raw materials? Who, that was not a witness, could imagine that the most violent local prejudices would cease so soon, and that Men who came from the different parts of the Continent, strongly disposed, by the habits of education, to despise and quarrel with each other, would instantly become but one patriotic band of Brothers?"[75]

"And that lesson lasted us the rest of the war," Spitz added. "I served with men from New Hampshire and Pennsylvania and Georgia, and they were all just Americans who were willing to give everything to found the nation. No matter what they suffered, they never gave up."

"The disadvantageous circumstances on our part, under which this war was undertaken, can never be forgotten. The singular interpositions of Providence in our feeble condition were such, as could scarcely escape the attention of the most unobserving; while the unparalleled perseverance of the Armies of the United States, through almost every possible suffering and discouragement for the space of eight long years, was little short of a standing miracle,"[76] Washington agreed.

"And their teamwork with our allies, especially at Yorktown, was a miracle, too," Spitz added, remembering Washington's willing cooperation with the French admirals and the camaraderie he saw among the French and American troops.

"As you say, Spitz," Washington nodded, "'the singular Spirit of emulation, which animated the whole Army from the first commencement of our operation... filled my mind with the highest pleasure and satisfaction, and... gave me the happiest presages of success.'[77]

"Unity, not only among the army but also among the people and their government, is the chief gift of the struggle for independence," Morris added. "And that struggle started not on the battlefield but at the kitchen tables where ladies refused to serve tea and at the harbor where men dumped it into the water. It started at the pulpits where the Black Regiment fought their first battles for the souls of Americans to embrace freedom and at the printing presses where patriots urged one another to take up arms for the cause. Long before Concord, God was shaping Himself a country."

"He shapes it still," Washington declared.

"He shapes it despite us," Morris teased, "for I never saw a body of men so compounded together to thwart Him as the Constitutional Convention."

"Morris, you recall too forcibly the bitter beginnings in the spring," Washington chided him. "Have you not seen a remarkable change in recent days?"

"You are right; I admit to a great degree my own stubborn nature," Morris conceded. "It is impossible to conceive the degree of concord which ultimately prevailed, as less than a miracle."[78]

"And we owe that miracle largely to Franklin's wise admonishments for every man to seek God's counsel," added Washington.

"Over the years, certain miracles in the founding of the country have impressed me," Spitz said, "but I never thought to count the unity of the colonies as a miracle."

"You must, though, because it is the grandest miracle of them all," Washington told him. "It will be so much beyond anything we had a right to imagine or expect eighteen months ago, that it will demonstrate as visibly the finger of Providence, as any possible event in the course of human affairs can ever designate it. It is impracticable for you or anyone who has not been on the spot, to realize the change in men's minds and the progress towards rectitude in thinking and acting which will then have been made."[79]

"The present unity really is astonishing," Morris told Spitz. "You cannot imagine the former strife among the delegates. 'The various and opposite interests which were to be conciliated; the local prejudices which were to be subdued, the diversity of opinions and sentiments which were to be reconciled; and in fine, the sacrifices which were necessary to be made on all sides for the General welfare, combined to make it a work of so intricate and difficult a nature, that I think it is much to be wondered at, that anything could have been produced with such unanimity as the Constitution proposed."[80]

The men lapsed into silence, all thinking of the miracle of the United States and God's hand in it. Then Morris asked Washington about the progress being made on his carriage, and the two men chatted about paint and fabric choices for the vehicle like a couple of car buffs at an auto show. Spitz half listened to them and half sank into the calm of the summer day and the pleasant feeling of having spent the morning fishing and the afternoon with two incredible intellects. He couldn't have planned a more welcome day if he'd tried.

*Is this the message of today?* Spitz wondered. *Am I supposed to understand the way that peace follows war and rest follows work and recovery follows healing? And am I supposed to understand that no good thing on earth is ever finished? Good things require work.* It wasn't enough for the Americans to win the war; they had to win the peace, too, by learning to work together.

He sat for a while watching a robin foraging at the edge of the trees near the house, and then another thought occurred to him. *It's not enough for me to wake up after the stroke, either. I've got a lot of work to do. But I'll never get anywhere if I keep fighting myself, getting upset because I don't think I've done enough. It's a rhythm of rest and work. I can't expect it to happen all at once. Look at Washington. He started fighting in 1775. The war might have ended in 1781, but the treaty wasn't signed until 1783. Now it's 1787, and he's still fighting to put the country on the right course. Good work is never done. You have to learn to pace it and appreciate the path the journey requires, however difficult it may be.*

Mrs. Moore appeared on the porch to call the men to dinner, and they followed her to the dining room. There, Spitz saw Billy Lee standing in a corner. As soon as the men were seated, he disappeared to the kitchen. He and Dolly together served the first course, a fresh summer salad of greens and berries dressed with oil and wine and herbs. Dolly skedaddled back to the kitchen as soon as she'd set down the plates she carried, but Billy stood in the corner for the duration of the meal, wordlessly refilling drinks and eyeing the progress of the meal.

He cleared the empty plates alone and reappeared with Dolly to serve the entrees: butter-and-wine-poached trout with fresh parsley, thyme, and rosemary in the cavity. It was heavenly and tender and fresh. Jane Moore had paired it with tiny peas and yellow squash from her garden and hot wheat rolls handmade by Dolly. Morris and Spitz talked about their meeting and the fishing trip, and Mrs. Moore thanked them for the abundance of fish. "I have several more to use tomorrow, and pan-fried trout is always a fine breakfast," she said.

After the entrée, Billy again cleared the plates, and then he and Dolly served slices of a fresh berry tart heaped with fresh whipped cream. It wasn't as sweet as the desserts he usually ate, but it was flaky and juicy and perfect for summer. When the meal ended, Spitz was sure that he couldn't hold another bite.

"Would you gentlemen care for music?" Mrs. Moore offered. Morris and Washington agreed enthusiastically, and Spitz nodded. They followed her to the front parlor, where she opened the lid of a small, boxy harpsichord, sat, and began to play and sing a medley of songs, everything from simple country ballads to songs by Handel and Mozart. Her voice, though not extraordinary, was warm and low and pleasant. She played for nearly half an hour and then excused herself upstairs, wishing the men good night and leaving them a bottle of port and a tray of glasses.

When she had gone, Washington called for Billy to bring him his journal, and Morris picked up a volume of essays by Addison and Steele and began to read. Spitz went outside to the front porch, where he had left his pack and messenger bag, and he brought the bag inside and sat down across the room from Washington. As Spitz opened the bag to remove his journal and writing utensils, he saw Washington smiling fondly at him.

"I begin to think that I would recognize your luggage more readily than you," Washington said. "You have carried that bag since Great Meadows."

"I've had it since the trading post, actually," Spitz said.

"Can you not afford another?" Morris asked, wrinkling his nose. "I can smell the gunpowder across the room."

Washington and Spitz laughed. "To an old soldier, that smell is not entirely unpleasant," Washington chuckled.

Relieved that his old friend was not wholly under the sway of the foppish Morris, Spitz said, "I like the old bag. It holds a lot of memories."

Morris raised his eyebrows and retreated to his book. Washington accepted his journal from Billy with distracted thanks and began to write. Morris interrupted him to read an amusing essay aloud, with great flourishes of expression. So Spitz opened his calfskin journal and read his old entries in preparation to record a new one. He finished and then recalled his morning talk and afternoon conversation and the many quotes he wanted to record. Absently, he reached toward the floor, groping for his bag with its writing supplies while he kept his eyes on his journal.

Then his bag appeared right in front of him. Startled, Spitz looked up and saw Billy Lee, holding his bag where he could reach it easily. He took it, once again feeling that ever-present guilt he usually felt around Billy. "Thank you," Spitz said awkwardly.

Billy inclined his head. "You are welcome," he said softly, his head near Spitz's.

"But don't do anything else for me, please," Spitz said quietly, "because you're not free to refuse. I won't take advantage of your condition. You're a person, and you should be free."

Billy straightened up quickly and darted anxious eyes to Washington. He met Spitz's eyes and deliberately shook his head. "Thank you," he said. He looked as if he would like to say something else, but he turned and resumed his station at the back of the room.

Spitz could not imagine the life of Billy Lee—to be so close to such a great man, a man you perhaps respected and admired, a man who treated you kindly, but a man who did you wrong every moment you breathed. Had Spitz only made things worse by pointing out the discrepancy? He hoped not. But he could see for himself why Morris had called slavery a pestilential institution. It corrupted every relationship it touched.

Spitz retrieved his quill and ink and blotter from the bag and began to write.

**Mercy 10:** The colonies obtained a miraculous unity during tranquil deliberations that ended in voluntary consent largely due to the Christian beliefs and biblical principles the delegates commonly held. God's ambassadors and spokesmen, the clergy, paved the way, actively communicating with the citizens. Unification occurred with great speed, an undeniable miracle that was forced too strongly on the mind of George Washington to be suppressed.

**Sign 27**—Benjamin Franklin's affecting appeal to the delegates of the Constitutional Convention to seek the wisdom and guidance of God resulted in a miraculous change of hearts towards the process and its ultimate goal of constructing a document which all the states could ratify.

**Sign 28**—According to Washington, the miraculous crafting of the final constitutional document which the delegates sent to the states for their consideration demonstrated 'as visibly the finger of Providence, as any possible event in the course of human affairs can ever designate it.' [81] The remarkable manner in which 'the various and opposite interest which were... conciliated;... local prejudices... were... subdued, the diversity of opinions and sentiments which were... reconciled;... the sacrifices which were necessary... for the general welfare, combined to make it a work of so intricate and difficult a nature, that ... it is much to be wondered at, that anything could have been produced with such unanimity as the Constitution proposed'[82] –George Washington.

**Sign 29**—The difficult ratification process with its passionate debates for and against made the ultimate ratification by all states of the Constitution (as drafted by the convention delegates) truly remarkable.

**Mercy 11**—"The unparalleled perseverance of the Armies of the United States, through almost every possible suffering and discouragement for the space of eight long years, was little short of a standing miracle" [83]– George Washington.

**Sign 30**—"At once violent local prejudices ceased and a disciplined Army was formed. Men from different colonies with opposing habits; who were prone to quarrel with each other, instantly became one patriotic band of Brothers." [84]

**Sign 31**—'The singular Spirit of emulation which animated the whole Army from the first commencement of'[85] [the siege of Yorktown]. French officers and soldiers enthusiastically combined efforts with American officers and soldiers for the common cause.

Spitz looked at his record. This visit might be the last time he saw Washington, and he didn't know what would become of his carefully-kept journal once he stopped visiting the past. Even if he never saw

Washington again and never saw the journal again, he wanted to finish it. He wanted to record something else that wasn't exactly a sign. It definitely was a mercy, though. He wanted to record the character of the man he'd seen grow old before his eyes. He wanted to make a permanent record of the kind of man God had sent to America to lead it through its difficult beginning.

## The Beliefs and Principles Washington Advocated

*"Learning is not virtue but the means to bring us an acquaintance with it. Integrity without knowledge is weak and useless, and knowledge without integrity is dangerous and dreadful."*—General Nathanael Greene[86]

**Principle #1: Maintain a higher view** (Washington acknowledged his innate value).

Washington unlocked his potential by adopting the principle of believing in a better me. He maintained the high view and climbed the necessary steps of change to reach his summit. He developed profitable skills, sought mentoring and guidance, strove to be self-controlled, submitted to discipline and training, and remained a lifelong student who continually molded and shaped himself into a better person.

**Principle #2: Accept that all of life counts** (Washington saw the benefits of change).

All of Washington's life counted; even the difficult trials and mistakes. Through each step of change and through each hardship, Washington seemed to understand that it was all useful for good, preparing him for his ultimate role as a national servant leader. Embrace positive (though oftentimes painful) change, knowing that God uses change for valuable purposes. Conquer or die! Though Washington retreated to fight another day, he never gave up. Washington understood that victory waits on the other side of winter: the difficult circumstances we must endure that challenge and mold us. As we weather the cold and stormy troubles in our lives, we can maintain a higher view of ourselves, remembering that all of life counts, placing our hope and trust in the Lord, and allowing Him to reveal His encouraging work in and through our lives. If we persist in these habits while we embrace and respond to change along the way, we will eventually rise to the summit of our Mt. Life as conquerors.

*"We must resolve to conquer, or die; with this resolution and the blessing of Heaven, victory and success certainly will attend us."*[87]*—George Washington*

**Principle #3: Trust in the Lord** (Washington understood that God knows best!).

Rely on God. Washington believed that 'the all-wise disposer of events knows better than we do what is best.'[88] He maintained the view that God, as the 'author of every public and private good,'[89] constantly orders things for valuable purposes. Washington believed that 'providential aids can supply every human defect,'[90] and so he maintained a keen sense of trust in 'the invisible hand'[91] of God.

*"I do not think that any officer since the creation ever had such a variety of difficulties and perplexities to encounter as I have. How we shall be able to rub along till the new army is raised, I know not, Providence has heretofore saved us in a remarkable manner, and on this we must principally rely."—George Washington*[92]

**Principle #4: Recognize and acknowledge God's active involvement in your life** (see the signs, mercies, and interpositions of Providence).

George Washington sensed that God actively guided and protected him. He humbly submitted to the Lord's will, even when it seemed unfavorable. Washington recognized and acknowledged the many 'signal and manifold mercies and the favorable interpositions'[93] of Providence. He believed with all his heart that God established the United States according to His will. He viewed it a 'duty of all... to acknowledge the providence of Almighty God.'[94]

*"I did not let the Anniversary... [pass] without a grateful remembrance of the escape we had at the Meadows and on the Banks of Monongahela, the same Providence that protected us upon those occasions will, I hope, continue his Mercies, and make us happy Instruments in restoring Peace and liberty to this once favored, but now distressed Country."*[95] —George Washington

**Principle #5: Prayer is both important and powerful** (Washington prayed for strength, guidance, and encouragement).

George Washington called on all citizens to pray, giving thanks to God 'for the signal and manifold mercies and the favorable interpositions of His providence.'[96] When he felt lowest and most helpless at Valley Forge, he prayed for help. And on the day of his inauguration when he was lauded and honored, he prayed and led congress in prayer.

**Principle #6: Accept in faith the doctrine of providence** (Washington firmly believed in the doctrine of providence).

George Washington believed that a Supreme Being ruled the world and that He designed His every dispensation to answer some valuable purpose. Washington proclaimed that God's ways are wise, 'inscrutable, and irresistible,'[97] and he admonished others to 'acquiesce to the divine will' as a duty. Like Job, Washington acknowledged that God gives and has a right to take away. So he urged people to 'submit patiently to the decrees of the all-wise disposer of human events'[98] and 'never to repine at acts of providence, because they are always for the best.'[99] He warned that this world has no authority to controvert or scrutinize the will of heaven. He recognized that the 'author of every public and private good' is God. Washington believed that God's invisible hand conducts the affairs of men and that he had 'seen the divine Arm visibly outstretched for the deliverance'[100] of the United States of America.

*"The fortunate discovery, of the Intentions of Ministry, in Lord George Germains' Letter to Governor Eden is to be ranked among*

*many other signal Interpositions of Providence, and must serve to*
*inspire every reflecting mind with confidence. No man has a more*
*perfect reliance on the all-wise, and powerful dispensations of the*
*Supreme Being than I have nor thinks his aid more necessary."* [101]
*— George Washington"*

**Principle #7: Practice brotherly love for one another**
(Washington understood the scriptural principle that the most
excellent way is love).

The prospect of establishing civil and religious liberty induced
George Washington to enter the field of battle. He foresaw
that America would safeguard human rights. In this regard, he
wanted citizens to 'cultivate a spirit of brotherly affection and
love for one another,'[102] doing justice, loving mercy, and clothing themselves with the 'charity, humility and pacific temper of
mind, which'[103] he acknowledged were the characteristics of Jesus
Christ, 'the Divine Author' of Christianity; which he referred to
as "our blessed Religion." Washington further foresaw America
as an asylum for 'the oppressed and needy of the earth,'[104] a country that would diffuse 'happiness to all who wished to participate'
as citizens. George Washington envisioned Americans, 'possessed
of absolute freedom and independence,' as actors in 'a conspicuous theatre designated by Providence for the display of human
greatness and felicity.'[105] George Washington earnestly prayed and
desired that Americans would 'make wise and virtuous use of the
blessings'[106] God had placed before them. He believed in the practice of the Christian principle to love thy neighbor.

*"Believing, as I do, that Religion and Morality are the essential*
*pillars of Civil society, I view, with unspeakable pleasure, that har-*
*mony and brotherly love which characterizes the Clergy of different*
*denominations, as well in this, as in other parts of the United States;*
*exhibiting to the world a new and interesting spectacle, at once the*
*pride of our Country and the surest basis of universal Harmony."*[107]
*— George Washington*

**Principle #8: Avoid divisiveness, seek unity, and pursue noble actions:** E. Pluribus Unum, "one from the many."

George Washington believed that God 'directed the sword' during the Revolutionary War and that in peace He ruled in the councils of America's founding fathers. Washington believed that God cared for America in order to encourage Americans toward 'great and noble actions.' Washington believed that America therefore had to establish its national character and to guard against the deterioration caused by prejudices of local or state politics; that America must measure its 'honor, power, and true interests' 'by a continental scale;' and that every departure therefrom would weaken the Union.

*"The name of American, which belongs to you, in your national capacity, must always exalt the just pride of Patriotism, more than any appellation derived from local discriminations. With slight shades of difference, you have the same Religion, Manners, Habits and political Principles. You have in a common cause fought and triumphed together. The independence and liberty you possess are the work of joint councils, and joint efforts; of common dangers, sufferings and successes."* [108]
—*George Washington*

**Principle #9: Profit from dear-bought experience.**

Washington believed that we can profit from dear bought experience, saying, 'if the Roller will be of any use to the grain, I beg it may be applied.' [109] He also noted that part of wisdom is navigating the intricate paths of life, and he urged us to steer clear of rocks we have struck upon.

**Principle #10: Promote the knowledge and practice of true religion and virtue.**

George Washington believed 'that heaven itself has ordained' 'eternal rules of order and right' and 'that religion and morality are the essential pillars of civil society.' Washington espoused

Christian beliefs saying, 'You do well to wish to learn...above all, the religion of Jesus Christ.'[110]"To the distinguished character of Patriot, it should be our highest glory to add the more distinguished character of Christian.' [111]

*"The General hopes and trusts, that every officer and man, will endeavor so to live, and act, as becomes a Christian Soldier defending the dearest Rights and Liberties of his country."* [112] *— George Washington*

**Principle #11: Maintain a strong work ethic.**

George Washington encouraged his soldiers "to surmount every difficulty with a fortitude and a patience, becoming their profession, and the sacred cause." [113] In his private life, Washington made it an "unvaried rule, never to put off till tomorrow the duties which should be performed today." [114]

**Principle #12: Practice humility and avoid vanity.**

George Washington strove to avoid all types of self-glorification. He constantly pointed away from himself and toward God for all the glory and recognition. Washington did not believe it becoming to allow vanity to become a part of one's character.

## *Washington's Desire for America*

*"That Heaven may continue to you the choicest tokens of its beneficence; that your Union and brotherly affection may be perpetual; that the free constitution, which is the work of your hands, may be sacredly maintained; that its administration in every department may be stamped with wisdom and virtue; that, in fine, the happiness of the people of these States, under the auspices of liberty, may be made complete, by so careful a preservation and so prudent a use of this blessing as will acquire to them the glory of recommending it to the applause, the affection, and adoption of every nation which is yet a stranger to it."* [115] *— George Washington*

Yes, this list described his longstanding friend and hero—the faithful, humble, wise, courageous man who had acted as God's right arm to found the nation. If he never wrote another word in this journal and never saw it again, Spitz had at least paid tribute to the person who had taught him more about true liberty, real virtue, and honest faith than he had ever known before. He was imperfect, Spitz acknowledged, sending another uncomfortable glance toward Billy Lee, but Washington was humble and teachable and admirably a man's man. At the last hour of his life, he would mend his own wrong in an exemplary final show of humility by freeing his slaves. Spitz closed the book and packed his writing materials and his journal in his bag.

Washington looked up from his journal. "I bid you good night, Spitz. Shall I see you in the morning?"

"I doubt so, sir," Spitz said, "as I may leave early."

"Then I bid you farewell as well," Washington said. "I hope that our paths cross again soon. If I invite you once again to Mount Vernon, might I hope that you will accept?"

Spitz smiled ruefully. He knew that someday, he would pay a visit to Mount Vernon to see Washington for the very last time. He did not know now how he could bear to see him die. "Someday, sir, I will come, but I can't tell you when."

Washington chuckled. "I cannot say that your answer surprises me."

Spitz told Morris goodbye as well. He would never forget meeting the exuberant, contradictory founding father. Then he got his pack from the front porch and took it and his bag to the loft above the barn. Inside, the hay smelled sweet, nearly overpowering the smell of the horses below, a smell that didn't bother an old farm boy like Spitz.

He tossed his pack down and set his leather bag beside it. He unrolled his bedroll and lay down on it, watching the stars out the loft door. *I'm resting*, he breathed gratefully, *and I'm ready to stay as long as You like and get back to work whenever You're ready to send me.*

Spitz kept watching the stars until a few of them started to dance like the guests at a wedding, spinning in abandoned celebration. And then they came for him, including him in the dance, as he had known that they would. He closed his eyes and held out his hands to them.

# Chapter Twelve

*"With a mighty hand and outstretched arm; His love endures*
*forever."—Psalm 136:12*

*"Humble yourselves, therefore, under God's mighty hand, that he*
*may lift you up in due time." —1 Peter 5:6*

The noise of the helicopter was almost unendurably loud before Aspen put on the headphones with their speaker tube that made her feel like a television host at the Macy's Thanksgiving Day Parade. Bill wore a set, and so did their pilot and the guide. All of the sets connected so that the four of them could hear one another speak, although the pilot seemed naturally taciturn and the guide preoccupied.

It was the last day of the trip; Aspen and Bill would leave in the morning. Had Bill not promised to accompany her on this momentous journey, he could have enjoyed fishing on the Aikwa River near Timika or even in the Arafura Sea to the south near the port town of Amamapare. He could have played a round of golf at a championship course nearby at the Rimba Irian Golf Club. He could have sunbathed by the rainforest-style hotel pool while wait staff brought him fancy drinks with paper umbrellas and speared fruit, or he could have watched a cultural presentation including native dances by people who, the promoters implied, may have grown up among headhunters. The Indonesian province of Papua offered sport and luxury on par with tropical resorts in much more expensive places.

But Bill had chosen to fly with Aspen in this noisy helicopter to see the crumbling wreckage that marked the site where her parents had died. Aspen realized the sacrifice. She'd even offered him an out as they'd toured a client office near Timika that morning. "Listen, Bill, don't feel like you have to come with me. Our travel agent says that the guide is taking us to an American missionary; I'm sure I'll be perfectly safe. You shouldn't miss out on everything they're offering."

Bill had shaken his head, smiling. "I'm young, and I have a great job. I'll be here again in a few years. This afternoon, I want to be with you. It's important. And you're not talking me out of it."

Aspen, secretly glad that he would be with her, had only shrugged and agreed. Throughout these last few days, while they had toured work sites and shared dinners together, she had remembered her resolve on the airplane to tell Bill that she had changed her mind, but the words hadn't appeared whenever she was around him. *Coward,* she'd berated herself on her nightly return to her sumptuous hotel room. But the accusation hadn't strengthened her resolve. *Maybe we'll talk on the flight home,* she thought, although she'd seen firsthand Bill's propensity to sleep in the air.

Now he looked over at her as the helicopter soared crazily through the air and mimed holding a phone to his ear. "Did Angela leave another message for you?" he shouted over the noise.

Aspen nodded yes. "He can move his whole arm now and lift his head. He keeps trying to sit up, but he's not quite there."

"That's great," Bill grinned. "He'll be home before you know it."

"I hope so," Aspen shouted back, wincing at the noise.

She looked out the window at the rumpled landscape of low, tree-covered mountains, which looked like an adult version of the Appalachians. Everything was in similar proportions, only bigger. The trees were taller and thicker; the rivers were wider; the foothills rose faster; and the mountains towered higher. She could only imagine the size of the wildlife below. Two days earlier, they had seen a sixteen-foot saltwater crocodile, and yesterday she had seen a moth two inches wider than the length of her ink pen and had snapped a photo on her smartphone to prove it. This morning she had seen a dangerous, three-toed Cassowary nearly the size of an ostrich. Though the bird had been on exhibit behind a chain link fence, its heavy, sharp beak and prehistoric-looking claws had still been too close for comfort. *Nothing will be in cages down below,* Aspen thought grimly.

Bill followed her eyes and called, "We're flying lower than yesterday!"

Aspen nodded. "Thank goodness—I've seen enough mountains!" she shouted back.

Yesterday, Bill and Aspen had toured a massive, open-pit copper mine and two deep underground operations located high above the tree line, between 11,000 and 14,000 feet above sea level. As their prop plane had left Timika, following the Aikwa River north to the mountains, Aspen had marveled at the folds of green undulating before her. The hilly lowlands reminded her of background scenery in movies on Vietnam, only the ridges were more pronounced and the deep ravines more plentiful. Then the view changed, reminding Aspen of her flight to a college friend's wedding in Colorado. The same kind of high, brownish plateaus rose out of the low, green foothills and gave way to majestic, blue-grey mountains that dwarfed the Rockies. Thankfully, their pilot had skirted west around the highest elevations to land on a small company airstrip near the mines.

But Aspen was still grateful that today's journey took them northeast of Timika to a high plain sitting much lower than the glacier-peaked mountains they had seen yesterday. The wind buffeting the helicopter still made her stomach sink, though, and she was glad that she hadn't eaten much at lunch. She lifted her eyes to a fixed point in the distance, and the nausea subsided gradually. God, thank You for a clear day, she thought. Had the weather been bad, today's flight would have been scratched, and she would have had to return home without ever setting foot where her mother and father had been found.

After a forty-minute journey, during which Bill occasionally commented on the scenery or the morning discussions with their client, the guide waved at them and pointed down. "Dani village there," he shouted.

Aspen nodded at him and looked out the window he had indicated. Below her, small thatched huts and smoking fire pits circled an empty central space; a crude wooden fence encircled the whole of the village. Beyond the huts and beyond the fence grew garden plots green with sweet potato vines and bushes of every sort. From the air, the whole scene looked surprisingly like a diorama at a museum, as if she had traveled back in time before the invention of electricity or iron tools or the wheel. But even so, she saw the semblance of a neighborhood, one where the neighbors had all agreed to plant gardens instead of dig a swimming pool.

The helicopter descended closer to the village, and Aspen saw people craning their necks and shading their eyes to see it. Running through the village, across the plain, and then along a well-worn path embedded in the top edge of a deep ravine, the village children chased its shadow and waved happily. Aspen saw Bill waving back to them, though she was sure they couldn't see him from so high up. *What a nice guy,* she thought, smiling to herself.

The helicopter passed over the plain and up the ravine and kept moving north, toward the mountains. As it slowed and circled an outcropping among the foothills, Aspen's stomach clenched. The wind and the thin air of the higher altitude fought against the helicopter, even though the sky was blue and sunny. The blades absolutely had to catch air to keep them properly aloft, or they would have to turn back. Now she understood why the pilot had been so careful to log everyone's weight before takeoff. Aspen thought about the plane which had carried her parents into the fatal storm. She could only imagine how fiercely the wind would tear at a small biplane on the way to the Timika Airport if grey, swirling clouds lowered across the sky, pouring sheets of rain and aiming bolts of lightning at the craft.

Aspen could see the pilot comparing the land below to the map on his dashboard, and soon he descended onto a lightly treed, deserted plateau among the higher foothills. The guide waved out the window, and Aspen saw a plump woman waving up at the helicopter from the shelter of one of the trees. Several native people stood around her, waving, too. *They must have walked from the village I saw,* Aspen thought, remembering the expanse between the village and this foothill. *It must have taken them all day.*

She felt sorry for putting them to so much trouble, and she felt a spasm of panic about what she was about to see. She looked at Bill, her heart in her mouth, and he looked back at her and patted her hand on the seat. "It'll be okay. I'll be with you. You can do this," he encouraged her.

Aspen nodded and clenched her teeth as the helicopter bumped to the ground and powered down. The horrendous noise finally slowed and stopped, though Aspen's ears still felt like they were ringing. She took off her headset and left it on her seat as the others were doing, and then she clambered out of the helicopter.

The guide took them to the group of natives, saying, "Dani village— my village, and Martha, from Dani village." When the group from the helicopter reached the group from the village, the guide embraced the tallest native and grinned back at them. "My brother, Biak," he explained. He and the native men stood apart and began to talk rapidly in their own language.

The tribesmen wore little clothing, as Aspen had expected, but they wore no face paint or bone jewelry, like the men in photos she had seen online. Their skin was dark and their hair wiry, and their features blended the beauties of African and Asian features in a similar way to the Maori of New Zealand or Samoans or Fiji Islanders did. Looking between them and the guide, Aspen realized that the only physical difference between the men was the clothes they chose to wear.

The plump woman came forward and shook Aspen's hand with both of her own, smiling warmly. "I'm Martha Kaczmarek, with Wycliffe, and you must be Aspen. I've really been looking forward to meeting you."

"Aspen Spitzen," Aspen said, liking Martha instantly, "and this is my business partner, Bill Rawlins."

"Pleasure to meet you," Bill said, extending his hand and smiling warmly.

Martha shook hands with Bill and then turned back to Aspen. "I can take you to the crash site from here. It's just a few minutes' hike down the side of the hill. I have to tell you, though - I had a poke around on the way here, and there's not much left. How long has it been?"

"Seventeen years," Aspen said, wrapping her arms around her waist.

Martha nodded. "It's pretty well charred, and the jungle has taken a lot of what the fire didn't get."

Aspen nodded. "I used to dream about finding a last letter or something, but I know it's a long shot. I just need to see the wreckage, even if nothing is there for me."

Martha patted Aspen's shoulder. "I understand. Well, let's get started. We're going down the south side."

Martha led the way down the side of the mountain, and when the tribesmen and the guide saw her striding purposefully away, they loped after her, surrounding her protectively.

"How are you doing?" Bill asked Aspen as the two of them followed Martha and the men down the mountain.

"I'm okay," Aspen said, lifting her chin and forcing her arms away from her waist, clenching her hands determinedly by her side. "What's Wycliffe? She said she was with Wycliffe. Do you know?"

"It's an organization that translates Bibles," Bill explained. "I heard about them in church growing up; they have missionary translators in a lot of remote areas."

"So she translates Bibles?" Aspen said. "Do you think the people here can even read?"

"She probably teaches them," Bill guessed. "She learns their language and writes it down, most likely for the first time. Then she translates the Bible and teaches them what it says."

"They sure do seem to like her," Aspen said, watching the lean tribesmen carefully help plump, sweet-faced Martha down the mountainside.

"People usually like people who take an interest in them," Bill teased. "Of course, that doesn't always work, but it's a good rule of thumb."

Aspen smiled at the teasing and then concentrated on the rough terrain in front of her. The work of keeping her feet out of tangled tree roots and her hair out of low branches busied her for quite a few minutes. A few times, she accepted Bill's help past awkward rock outcroppings, blushing as she grasped both his hands in hers. And then ahead, through the trees, she caught a glimpse of rusted white and bright blue that stuck out from the greens and browns of everything else around. She drew in a sharp breath and held it, pressing her lips closed. She stopped still.

Bill turned back and saw her face. "I know. I saw it, too. It's really close."

Aspen didn't move.

"Come on, Aspen," Bill encouraged her. "It's just a short walk. Do you need help?"

Aspen started to shake her head, but then she nodded. Suddenly, after all of her dreaming and longing, approaching that plane was the last thing she wanted to do.

Bill held a hand out to her, and she took it, though the ground here was relatively smooth and free of obstacles. "I know it's rough for you. You're doing great," he said compassionately.

Aspen squeezed his hand. She couldn't speak, but she knew that without Bill, she would have turned around right there and run for the helicopter. Now, she made herself look straight at the wreckage and walk, noticing details as she neared it.

The nose of the plane had smashed to the ground and was still embedded in the dirt. The wing and tail sections had broken away from it, and the tail had separated from the wing. The metal had burned or rusted away in large, gaping holes, and underbrush had taken root around and inside the shell. The fire had charred beyond recognition the places where any passengers would have sat. The metal framework of the seats, rusted and bent, hung crookedly from the floor supports, their upholstery long gone. One wing crumbled into leaf loam twenty feet away, and the other stuck up at an angle.

Aspen looked at Bill, and he let go of her hand and motioned her toward the wreck. She walked forward alone and touched the upraised wing, which was cool in the thin mountain air. She ran her hand along it to the gaping hole in the cabin exposing the seat frame, and she touched that, too. Fire had consumed everything inside: seat covers and cushions, rubber flooring, cloth lining—it had even shattered and deformed the window glass.

She walked to the tail section and stuck her head inside the hollow cavity. A plastic first-aid kit toward the back had melted and fused to the metal. Jungle bushes grew in the space where light fell. The whole floor of the wreck from the wings to the tail had become a kind of planter, home to shade-loving flowers and shrubs. She could make out the bare, rusted sides of the metal cylinder arching over the growth. Then she felt a flurry of motion as something flew at her, shrieking, and escaped into the tree canopy above.

Aspen screamed and sank to her knees in fright, shielding her head with her hands. The sudden panic unlocked something in her, and she began to sob, covering her face with her hands. She felt soft, plump arms around her and knew that Martha had come to comfort her.

"Shh, it's all right. It was only a bat, and it's gone. It's all right, Aspen. You're okay," Martha murmured, stroking her hair and patting her back.

Aspen couldn't stop crying. Despite her brave words, she had really expected to find something here, some memento from her mother. Instead, she saw in the marks of fire and violent gravity how cruelly her parents had died. She was embarrassed to be falling apart like this in front of perfect strangers, one of whom was cradling her as if she were a toddler with a skinned knee. But the disappointment on top of the renewed grief was too strong. She felt like she would stay here forever, a monument to her lost parents, weeping in the jungle.

Then Martha's arms disappeared, and Bill's took their place. She turned and clung to him, sobbing into his shirt. "I'm so sorry, Aspen," he said softly. "I'm so, so sorry." He held her close and rubbed her back reassuringly, repeating his sympathy patiently and sincerely.

And though she didn't think it would ever happen, Aspen calmed, and her tears slowed. She let Bill go, and sniffed in ragged, jerky gasps. "Sorry," she choked out, wiping her tears with her filthy palms.

"Don't be," Bill said. He reached into his pocket for a travel pack of Kleenex, pulling three of them out and handing them to her. "I'd expected some kind of a reaction."

"I knew it," Aspen said, taking a deep, calming breath and letting it out. "I knew nothing was here."

"Do you want me to check one more time?" Bill offered. "I'm sure these guys would help."

Aspen shook her head. "I looked pretty thoroughly," she told him. "I don't see how anything could have survived through almost twenty years. There's nothing here."

Martha knelt down beside her and took her hand. "I wouldn't say that there was nothing here," she said, glancing back at the tribesmen who had accompanied her. She spoke to them in their rapid, fluid language, and one by one, they stepped forward, speaking to her. Martha translated for them.

"I was a little boy, almost a baby, and I got a box with toys and candy and a book. The people who gave it to me were kind to me. Other people come every year with a box. They were all kind. I kept the book, and Martha taught me to read it. I am a Christian now, like you." He nodded at her.

Another man said, "I got a box when I was a tall boy. It had colors and paper inside. The lady on this plane showed me how to use them," he said, jerking his head to the wreckage. "She was good. You look like her."

"You are like her," the guide said, and seeing them together, Aspen realized that the second man who had spoken was the brother the guide had embraced. "She gave us the first box. Martha brought the fourth box. Martha stayed. I know English. I have good job. I know Jesus, too." He grinned at her, and Aspen gave him a watery smile in return.

Martha squeezed the hand she held. "Aspen, your parents were the first people to come with Christmas boxes through the village where I serve. When I came from Wycliffe to translate for the Dani, I found copies of Scripture in Bahasa Indonesia, the language of Indonesia, all over the village. Those books were so unusual that nearly everyone kept them. Some of the men knew Bahasa from trading, and I taught them to read. Because of your parents, the whole village heard the gospel years before I finished the translation into their local language. I know it doesn't replace your mom and dad, hearing about the good they did, but I hope it helps a little."

Aspen nodded quickly. "It does. It helps some." Tears flowed again down her cheeks, and Bill handed her a fresh Kleenex.

Martha talked to Aspen about the work she had done and about the Dani she served. Bill asked her questions about the village structure and about the daily lives of the people. He included the tribesmen who had come with them in the discussion, using Martha as a translator. Aspen listened, her eyes straying continually to the wreckage behind them.

*It was harder than I could have dreamed, coming here and seeing this crash,* Aspen thought. *But I'm glad I came. I know now in my bones that nothing of them is here; so I can let this place go in peace. I can close this door in my soul. God, thank You for my job and the chance it gave me to see this place. Thank You for sending Bill to me to help me today, too. I couldn't have faced the disappointment without him. And God, I know that my parents are with You. Could You tell them that I love them and miss them? Could You tell them that I'll be all right?*

The sun began to decline over the trees, and Martha waved toward it. "I've got to leave soon so that we can all be in the village by nightfall."

"Of course," Bill said. "It was kind of you to come and talk to us."

"Thank you," Aspen said, putting her arms around Martha and hugging her. "Thank you for everything." *How else do you thank a stranger who held you and let you cry?* Aspen thought wryly. Martha had provided her comfort and kindness when she needed it most, and Aspen knew she'd never forget her.

Martha and the Dani tribesmen continued on foot down the south face of the mountain, but the guide led Aspen and Bill back up the way they had come. As Aspen picked her way over tree roots and around rock outcroppings, she watched Bill climbing ahead of her and thought of what she wanted to say to him. Every time he reached a hand to her to help her, her determination to speak grew, and her certainty about her choice firmed. Once they reached the summit, the guide waved at the helicopter pilot to start the machine again and walked ahead of Aspen and Bill to prepare for their boarding.

The deafening whine resumed, and the beating wash of the blades blew over Aspen with a force that felt almost like a giant, invisible hand holding her back, telling her that she wasn't done with her work on this mountain. Far enough from the helicopter that she could still hear herself think, Aspen reached forward and put a hand on Bill's shoulder. "Bill, wait," she called.

He turned around, frowning. "Is something wrong? Do you need to go back?"

"No," she said, squaring her shoulders and gathering her courage. "I just wanted to tell you something."

"Okay," he agreed, searching her eyes carefully.

"Thank you for coming with me today," she said.

Bill smiled. "I'm glad I was there. I'm only sorry we didn't find a message from your parents."

"I was disappointed about that," Aspen said, "but then I realized that they aren't there any more than they are in the graveyard in Virginia. And I thought that instead of looking back for a message from them, I ought to look around me at what's good in my life right now."

Bill smiled at her and reached for her hand. "Does this mean that you're changing your mind about me?"

Aspen took his hand and shook her head. "No—I've already changed it. You're a big part of what's good in my life right now, and I don't want to take you for granted. I just want you to know that I want to be around you every bit as much as you want to be around me."

Bill grinned and pulled her into a warm hug, and she reached her arms around him and leaned into his chest. *I'm living again, starting now,* she thought. *This moment, right here, is the beginning of something good.*

Feeling brave and exultant, she lifted her face to be kissed.

★ ★ ★

Angela's arm reached around Spitz's back, supporting him in a sitting position with his feet dangling over the side of the bed, and a physical therapist grasped his hands and braced her feet in front of him. She blew her long, wispy bangs out of her face impatiently and fixed Spitz with a steely glare. "On the count of three," she warned him; "one—two—three."

At the same time, Angela lifted while the therapist pulled, and Spitz tried to remember the muscles to use to stand up. The women held him upright on his weak legs as he focused his energy and flexed his back and thighs and calves for a count of five. Then Angela and the therapist eased him back to a sitting position.

"Great!" the therapist enthused, keeping hold of Spitz's hands. "Angela, gradually back off and let me see how he's doing sitting up on his own."

Angela's arm around him reminded him of the times he'd supported Washington, as well as the countless wounded soldiers he'd helped to hobble toward the field hospital in battle. She felt like a fellow soldier beside him. Her arm slid little by little away from him, and he felt his back wobble. But he concentrated on stiffening his spine and holding himself up. He managed for nearly a full minute, only occasionally swaying enough to prompt the therapist to steady him by his hands.

She smiled and squeezed his hands. "That's great, Spitz—really good job," she praised him. "Angela, let's help him lie back now."

Angela helped him balance upright while the therapist guided his legs around to the end of the bed, which was raised so that it felt kind of like a recliner. Once Spitz had started physical therapy, the orderly had helped him to dress in loose, cotton pajama pants under his hospital gown. Spitz felt more like himself in the new outfit.

The therapist guided Spitz through a few more exercises, pushing his control of hands and arms and feet and legs. She lifted and bent his legs for him, forcing flexibility back into his joints. Spitz worked with her as well as he could, happily accepting the soreness that meant his body was beginning to work again.

Then the fine motor skill exercises began. They were hard for Spitz, who felt increasingly frustrated that grasping and lifting gradually smaller balls and sticks should prove so hard for him. He wanted so badly to write Aspen a note, as she'd hinted she'd like. He would have liked better to talk to her, but his stubborn brain still refused to wake up his speaking apparatus.

Finally the therapist packed her equipment into the rolling cart she had brought to his room for the past few days. "Don't beat yourself up over the fine motor skills, Spitz," she said. "That and the talking are usually the last things to click. I've honestly never seen anyone progress this fast after a stroke. It's like as soon as your fingers moved, your body just jerked awake like Frankenstein's monster. 'It's alive!'" she joked, nudging him teasingly with her elbow.

Spitz's mouth stretched into a lopsided smile. He held out his hand for a high five, and she slapped it gently.

"Get some rest. Sleep heals; isn't that right, Angela?" the therapist said.

"It surely does," Angela agreed. "And you've worked hard enough to deserve a nice nap. Do you want to watch anything while you go to sleep?" Angela asked him, lowering the bed from the reclining position.

Spitz blinked twice before he remembered that his neck muscles worked. He shook his head no. The hospital didn't have the History Channel or the Discovery Channel. He'd pass.

"All right, Spitz—your Bible is right beside you," she said, pulling his covers up and tucking the Bible beside his hand. He turned his palm down and pressed it to the charred cover, grateful for the miracle of movement.

Angela noticed the movement and smiled at him. "You've had a great start to physical therapy this week, Spitz. You're remembering about rest and work and celebrating your accomplishments?"

Spitz nodded. He felt alive like he hadn't in years, tuned in to the present moment and aware of what he felt and thought and observed moment by moment instead of holding the present at bay while he obsessed over the past. He'd made great strides in returning to prayer as well, though he couldn't speak. He pretty much just kept up a silent, running conversation with God throughout the day.

Angela patted his hand. "I'm proud of you, and Aspen's proud of you, too, though she doesn't know how far you've come. I can't wait to see her face when she sees you!"

Spitz nodded and lifted his hand for another high five. Angela obliged him, grinning. Then she snapped off the lights as she left the room and closed the door behind her. Early afternoon sun streamed through his half-closed blinds, and Spitz watched the dust motes swirling in it, something he hadn't done in years. He patched together the strips of scenery outside that he could see around the blinds: gaunt, bare trees and iron-grey skies low with scudding clouds.

Today was the day Aspen was flying home with Bill. Today was the hardest day, when he knew that she was in danger in the skies while he lay here, helpless to help her and unaware of what was happening to her half a world away. Worry began to gnaw at the insides of his soul.

*I can't stop worrying about her,* Spitz confessed ruefully. *Every time I think about her on that plane, I just about go crazy thinking about Steve's crash and my trip to Timika to get his body. That memory is strong, and I don't know how to keep it away.*

The kind, patient voice that always answered him reassured him now. *Don't try to keep it away. Give it to Me. Tell Me about it.*

*I remember talking to the customs agent at the airport and signing papers to have the bodies transferred. The man looked at me like I was trying to smuggle exotic birds or native artifacts home—no sympathy at all when I was hurting so badly. I remember following him into the airplane hangar across the tarmac from the customs office. It was October when I left Virginia, and in Irian Jaya, it felt like June—warm, soft breezes and the smell of blooming flowers. I couldn't enjoy the flowers, though. I just kept thinking about the funeral home and the caskets I bought the day I left.* A tear flowed down Spitz's right cheek as he paused in his memories, the scent of lilies and green leaves tying the two discordant places together for him.

He felt wordless empathy and comfort flowing into him. When Spitz had walked across that tarmac seventeen years ago, he'd kept his eyes down. The tropical light blazing so close to the equator had seemed too bright to eyes that were red and stinging with grief, and his sorrow seemed to curve his spine and bow his head with premature age. He remembered his brown wingtips moving one after the other, heavy and spiritless. Now he invited God into that memory and pictured an arm around his back, holding him upright as Angela had during physical therapy and as he had done for Washington in the snow near the trading post. That arm was warm and comfortable and strong, and it connected to the sound of strong, firm footsteps beside him. You're not alone, they seemed to say.

*When we got to the hangar, the customs official showed me that the boxes contained remains and had me sign another form. We watched a forklift load the boxes into the cargo bay of the plane I'd be taking home. But the whole time I was around the boxes, I could smell the char in the air. I couldn't place it at first, and then I couldn't stop smelling it.* His tears ran down his face in small streams now, dripping off his jaw onto his hospital gown. He didn't care. His heart broke again at the smell of fiery death and the sight of those transport containers disappearing into the belly of the plane. *Can You imagine such a smell?*

*I can,* the voice mourned with him.

The response prompted Spitz to remember footage he'd seen on the History Channel of ovens at Auschwitz, their blasphemous smoke hovering low over the camps. An image flashed next across his mind of two towers smoking, burning, and falling, filling New York City streets with clouds of abominable ash. There followed in rapid succession a pen-and-ink illustration of Hus at the stake, flames wreathing his legs, a study Bible description of the idol Moloch belching flames through its yawning mouth as worshippers cast howling infants inside, and a bent woman in a sari falling onto a funeral pyre, the hands of her friends and family pushing her into the flames.

*I know that smell: sin and death and corruption ascending.*

Spitz shuddered. *How can You stand it?*

*Behold,* said the voice, *I am making all things new. In the place I am making for you, never again will there be any night. And a place where there is no darkness needs no lights from lamps or sun. The brightness of My glory is all the light anyone needs. No more burning, no more sacrifice, no more death or corruption staining the air: with Me, there is only light and life.*

Spitz sighed. *And even though You understand the pain of that memory, I still feel worried about Aspen. Is she going to be safe? Is the plane going to make it this time? What if the vision I saw of that huge wedding party was only wishful thinking? What if she's not going to make it?*

*The valley of the shadow of death,* the voice agreed, *is a terrifying place. And so I come with you through it. Aspen is in My hands, and nothing will happen to her that you and she cannot bear with My help. I hold you both in My hands. No one can take you from Me, not even you. I am with you. I am here.*

Spitz breathed deeply, sighing in his longing to know that Aspen was safe and reaching towards the comfort and companionship that was offered to him. He remembered Washington saying, "Lord, I believe—help thou mine unbelief." *Yes,* he thought, *yes—just so.*

Light enveloped him, sunlight and something beyond sunlight, surrounding him and lifting him gently from the room around him, sending him swaying and rocking down a river of light and silent, benevolent presence. The river bent and then circled, turning him faster and faster with no feeling of fear. Then it let him go, receding into a young spring sun ascending past the countless roofs and chimneys of a vast city murmuring and shimmering in happy anticipation. Spitz could feel the mood of the crowds around him, all triumphant and watchful, full of brotherhood and congratulation.

His pack was nowhere in sight, but his leather messenger bag hung across his chest, which once again boasted the buff-and-blue uniform of a Life Guard, complete with the solemn weight of the black helmet. Thankfully, his uniform looked much cleaner and smelled much fresher than he remembered. He stooped a little more and felt the same ache in his joints that marred his body now. Evidently his age in the past was catching up to his age in the present.

A firm hand clapped his shoulder from behind, and Spitz turned around to see three faces he recognized. "Paul Hawkins and Peter Sterling!" he exclaimed, "and you've brought Hurley with you, too!" Spitz shook hands with the men. Hawkins and Sterling had grown stouter and greyer since he'd last seen them, but Hurley looked as lean as ever.

"Mr. Spitzen!" Hawkins greeted him, beginning the round of handshaking that promised to continue for a while. "Hurley recognized you straightaway, and we hurried to give you good morrow. Annabella," he said, reaching behind him and presenting a thin, cheerful woman with several blue-eyed children clinging to her skirts and more crowded behind her, "here is Thomas Hurley's friend, the one we met at Yorktown. Children, this man guarded General Washington during the war along with Mr. Sterling's cousin, Mr. Hurley here. We may thank them both that our President is safe and sound, no harm to a hair of him, and ready to be inaugurated today."

*So I'm at Washington's inauguration!* Spitz realized. *This is New York, in April of 1789; so Washington is fifty-seven. And any minute, Washington will take the oath.* Excitement buzzed through him, lifting his spirits to join the holiday air around him.

Hawkins introduced all of his seven children to Spitz, who admired them all, and then Sterling followed suit with his shy wife Prudence and their five children. But Hurley topped them all. He and his tall, capable wife lined up ten children, two sets of twins among them. Older children held younger ones by the hand or carried them in arms.

Spitz forgot the names as soon as he heard them, but he congratulated Hurley on the sizeable brood. "It looks like you're not just raising cattle and sheep on that farm of yours," he joked.

Hurley only nodded solemnly and slowly said, "A-yep," laconic as ever in his New Hampshire accent, while his children smiled wanly as if they'd heard such comments time beyond measure.

"So you've all traveled to see the inauguration," Spitz said, looking around at the group. "That was quite a journey for the South Carolina contingent."

"'Twould be grievous neglectful of us to miss it or suffer our children to miss it," Hawkins declared. "They should see the hero of the war and the first leader of the nation it freed with their own eyes to tell their children and their grandchildren after them. Today marks the beginning of our country in earnest. No journey is too long for such a prize."

"Excuse me," a voice said, and Spitz felt a timid tap on his shoulder. "I see that you gentlemen wear the uniform of the Life Guard, and I have desperate need of your assistance. Are you both at liberty to aid me? The inauguration depends upon your swift, bold action."

"I cannot leave Abigayle wi' the children in such a throng," Hurley said, and then he nodded at Spitz. "Spitz will go along wi' you."

"Will you, sir? I cannot stress enough the importance of the task set me," the man pled.

"I'll help you," Spitz agreed. "What do you need me to do?"

"You see before you the impassable multitudes choking the streets," the man said, craning his neck around them. "I must reach the Masonic Lodge housed in the coffee shop at the corner of Water and Wall Streets. Your distinctive uniform and the gravity of its office will part a way where none will open before me."

"Say no more," Spitz said. He turned back and told his friends good-bye, and then he faced southeast toward the harbor, as the man indicated. "Coming through, folks," he boomed in his best field-drill voice, "part the way for inaugural business."

People fell back respectfully before him, and foot by foot, yard by yard, he won the way for his new companion to follow in his wake down Wall Street. Soon word spread up the road, and the crowd parted far enough ahead that Spitz and the man who trailed him could nearly jog. Soon they reached the door of the coffee shop, and the man produced a key to open the door.

Inside, Spitz sighed gratefully at the silence; the noise of the crowds outside had set Spitz's ears ringing. He removed his helmet, as the quick march through the crowds in the late April warmth had made him hot in his uniform.

"I am much obliged to you, sir. Allow me to introduce myself. I am Jacob Morton, Marshal of the inaugural parade and presiding master of St. John's Masonic Lodge, which meets in this coffeehouse." He began to rummage frantically through shelves as he spoke.

"Glad to meet you, Mr. Morton. I'm Stephen Spitzen," Spitz said. "Can I help you find something?"

"Oh, sir, I am sure to lay hands on it at any moment. Chancellor Robert Livingston, Grand Master of all Masons within the New York colony, just now requested to borrow the Lodge's Bible for use during the inauguration. Livingston asked me to retrieve the Bible with haste. The planning committee made meticulous arrangements, including Washington's extended parade from Mount Vernon to New York City. The details of the inaugural proceedings were carefully considered, but no one was asked to furnish a Bible for the swearing-in ceremony until

Washington arrived at the meeting hall at 11:00 a.m. and presented himself ready."

"That's a shame," Spitz said, recalling how Craik and Gist had looked at him awestruck when he produced a Bible in the middle of the frontier wilderness. Bibles were rare and precious in this time and place. "But all the other arrangements were in place?"

Morton raced across the room to another set of shelves and began looking through them. "We had determined how to decorate the Senate Chamber and arrange the furniture within the meeting hall. We had decided who would sit and who would stand and where. We outlined how to conduct the proceeding and even rehearsed it, but no one was assigned the responsibility of furnishing the Bible."

"And you have one?" Spitz said. "Are you sure it's here?" He looked around the coffee shop unhelpfully, aware that he didn't know where to begin to look.

"Sometimes members borrow the Bible for use at funerals, weddings, and special ceremonies," Morton conceded. "As guardian of the Bible, I recently lent it to a brother whose daughter was wed a fortnight past and trusted him to return it; alas that I failed to ensure its return before today!" Morton vented. Then he seized a large book from the shelf and clutched it to his chest, beaming victoriously. "I was uncertain if it had been returned. I know not what we would have done if it had not been here. Imagine," he proudly said, "our nation's first president will take his oath with his hand upon this very Bible. Today this holy book will become a national treasure."

"I'm glad you found it," Spitz told him, "shall we hurry it back?"

Spitz waited for Morton to lock the coffeehouse behind him and pocket the key, and then he resumed his crowd-clearing duties. The return trip was faster. They were now flowing with the pedestrian traffic and could easily assist one another as they parted and cut through the crowd. As they neared Federal Hall, Spitz noticed how people were crowding in the streets and sitting in the window casements of buildings, as if patiently waiting for a parade. Eager men, women, and children lined roof tops in every direction. Gaiety filled the air. But the crowd had left too little room in the streets for a procession of any size along Wall Street. He mentioned that fact to Morton.

"Fear not!" Morton called. "Washington will not pass this way. He is within doors already, and after the ceremonies he will process down Broadway to St. Paul's chapel, Trinity."

Finally they reached the entrance to the Federal Hall building again, Spitz leading Morton straight through the press of citizens that thronged around and against the hall angling for a view of the balcony, which stretched the entire width of the building. Spitz marveled at how close the people were to their president. There was a special kind of love and admiration between Washington and these first Americans, and no one thought of assassination, as later administrations would have to do after the attempts on the lives of other presidents. Spitz remembered once reading that there had been twenty assassination attempts over the years resulting in four presidents killed and two wounded.

Once Morton and Spitz passed through the outer doors and made their way inside Federal Hall, Morton took the lead, clearing Spitz past guards posted to keep the throng outside from swarming upstairs to the Senate Chamber and out onto the open-air balcony where the swearing in ceremony would be held. Spitz followed Morton across an airy entrance, up a grand, sweeping staircase, and down a hall to a spacious upper room, where he turned to Spitz and put out his hand.

"I thank you heartily for your assistance, Mr. Spitzen," Morton told him. "Please stay and observe the ceremony from here in the Senate Chamber. I fear it would be nearly impossible for you to find your friends now; neither can there be a suitable place remaining below among this crowd." Morton indicated a few rows of spindly gilt chairs with thin, flat, embroidered cushions—all taken by invited, distinguished guests. Spitz lifted a hand in farewell and stood to the side of the room, a place with a view out the portico. He began looking around for any chance acquaintance. He didn't see Martha Washington, but he saw across the room Henry Knox and Henry Lee, whom he recognized from the battlefield, and John Jay and John Adams, whom he recognized from his history books.

Morton appeared on the balcony, set the Bible down, and took his assigned standing position on the far side of the portico. His appearance must have prepared the people, for they immediately cheered as John Adams stepped outside. But when they spotted George Washington following closely behind, they exploded with joyous excitement.

Washington bowed several times to the multitude of upturned faces. Holding his hand over his heart, the General clearly felt the genuine affection the crowd lofted in his direction. Spitz had never witnessed such a sincere outpouring. The people were as authentic with their wholehearted welcome as the General was gracious in his humility.

Centered on the portico was an arm-chair reserved for the first U.S. president to use before swearing his oath, and Washington took the seat. Immediately other dignitaries began to fill the portico, taking their assigned positions and thereby freeing some space within the Senate Chamber, making it even easier for Spitz to see. When all had found their places, George Washington rose and stepped close to the outer railing, providing an unobstructed view for the crowd below. Near him, on a small table draped in red linen, lay a crimson velvet cushion. Waiting on the cushion for its moment in history was an opened Bible which seemed of a size fitting the occasion—large. Spitz glanced around. Everyone had now fixed his eyes on Washington.

Spitz saw the Secretary of the Senate, Samuel Otis, lift the opened Bible. General Washington placed his hand within it. Then Spitz heard the all-important question which has never changed, the president-sized challenge that all subsequent leaders of the United States have had to address. They have no other choice. "Do you solemnly swear?"

But George Washington did not simply answer the question and repeat the oath of office; he added four important words - four powerfully enlightening words. "I solemnly swear to faithfully execute the office of President of the United States and will, to the best of my ability, preserve, protect, and defend the Constitution of the United States." Then Washington reverently followed with the impromptu four additional words, "So help me God." Leaning over as he spoke these last words, Washington kissed the Bible. That kiss was his first official act as President.

A grand smile appeared on Spitz's face. That kiss meant more than intellectual assent to the doctrines of Christianity or lip service to a creed that did not hold Washington's heart. That one kiss signaled Washington's wholehearted love for the God of the book and utter dependence on His help to do the almost impossible job before him. *He means every word he wrote about Providence and the invisible hand. Seeing this moment crowning every other I've witnessed, how could I ever doubt again?*

Chancellor Robert Livingston, the administrator of the presidential oath, announced to the waiting crowd that the proceeding was finished. Livingston then shouted for all to hear, "Long live George Washington, President of the United States!" But the crowd amazingly roared back in unison, "God bless our President!"

Earlier Spitz had only thought that the crowd made much more noise than its size warranted; now he was sure of it. Then, overpowering their cadence, a thirteen-cannon salute fired from the nearby Battery. As the celebration continued outside Federal Hall, the President and the other dignitaries reentered the Senate Chamber to hear Washington's Inaugural Address, the address Spitz had read to Aspen the night he fell. He treasured the opportunity to hear it now with an un-jaded heart.

The Senate Chamber began to hum with quiet excitement as congressmen found their proper seats and greeted their fellows before this most important combined session of the House of Representatives meeting jointly with the Senate. Spitz found an unoccupied place along the back wall, where there was standing room only, and even that seemed crowded. He felt eyes on him and turned to his left, where a man much younger than he was stared at him, or more precisely at his distinctive uniform.

"Excuse me, sir, but you guarded him?" the man said quietly, nodding toward the front of the room where Washington greeted the congressional leaders.

"I did," Spitz nodded, "from Valley Forge to Yorktown."

"I served him, too, until Saratoga in '77, when he sent our division to Gates," the man said, adding, "I am Richard Wilkins."

"I'm Stephen Spitzen," Spitz returned. "Well done - Saratoga was a 'signal success'[116] and a 'powerful stimulus;'[117] it brought us the aid of the French in full force."

"Even if the price of French aid and thereby our liberty was my arm, I would say it was well worth it," Wilkins said, gesturing to his empty left sleeve, which was pinned to the shoulder. "Washington was a bold leader who understood his business. I knew when we marched to Saratoga that Washington severely depleted his own army to aid Gates; I only learned later that he had received news of Burgoyne's weakness and knew that Gates could thrash him with a few more men. There stands a true leader,"

Wilkins said, nodding to the front of the room, "who will weaken himself to strengthen the cause of liberty."

"He once said that 'Every dispensation of Providence [is] designed to answer some valuable purpose,'"[118] Spitz said warmly. "And after all his years of fighting in the Hudson Valley trying to throw Clinton out of the city, enduring one dispensation of Providence after another that seemed to spell defeat for him, it does me good to see him in New York. Now he's here as the President. What a triumph!"

Wilkins nodded. "Considering that he nearly lost the whole of New York to the treachery of Benedict Arnold, the triumph doubles."

"Did you ever see Arnold?" Spitz asked. He had read about Arnold: sympathetic accounts which put his treachery at the feet of his insolvent, alcoholic father as well as imprecatory diatribes which pictured him as a contentious, greedy goblin of a man who would sell his own mother to turn a profit. He wondered where between the two extremes the truth lay.

Wilkins frowned. "I did, and I served under him, too: not at Saratoga where he surely excelled, but later at West Point. After Saratoga, I left the ranks, not being able-bodied to fire a gun, but I reported to West Point for clerical work. I can still write," he said, holding up his whole right hand. "I served Washington and the other commanders until Arnold came. I thought he was only a fool, not seeing to repairs or strengthening the chain across the Hudson and sending more troops and supplies than we could spare here and there. Not until 'by a most providential interposition, Major Andre, Adjutant General of the British Army was taken'[119] did I know he'd turned his coat and blackened his heart."

"I can't imagine what Washington must have thought then," Spitz said. "He'd trusted Arnold, even after his court-martial." Arnold's mercenary side had surfaced in Philadelphia the summer after Valley Forge, when in order to spare the thrice-wounded general the rigors of combat, Washington had put Arnold in charge of the city the British army had only recently left. Hindsight showed Washington that Philadelphia, a Loyalist stronghold, was not the best place for a man whose vanity and pocketbook had both suffered at the hands of the Continental Congress. Though the court-martial had cleared Arnold, it also solidified his decision to betray the United States.

"I can tell you what Washington thought," Wilkins said. "He

thought that God preserved the nation by bringing Arnold's treason to light. I heard him say that 'the providential train of circumstances... [is] convincing proof that the Liberties of America are the object of divine Protection.'[120] By all rights, Andre should have got clean away to New York City carrying the plans to take West Point without a shot fired and after that, the whole state of New York."

Just then, Vice President John Adams, as president of the senate, convened the session, and Spitz and Wilkins fell quiet. They listened with solemn joy to Washington delivering his Inaugural Address, and Spitz heard again the words that he had questioned so bitterly what seemed like a lifetime ago.

"No people can be bound to acknowledge and adore the Invisible Hand which conducts the affairs of men more than those of the United States. Every step by which they have advanced to the character of an independent nation seems to have been distinguished by some token of providential agency; and in the important revolution just accomplished in the system of their united government the tranquil deliberations and voluntary consent of so many distinct communities from which the event has resulted can not be compared with the means by which most governments have been established without some return of pious gratitude, along with an humble anticipation of the future blessings which the past seem to presage. These reflections, arising out of the recent crisis, have forced themselves too strongly on my mind to be suppressed. You will join with me, I trust, in thinking that there are none under the influence of which the proceedings of a new and free government can more auspiciously commence."

This time, instead of seeing Washington through the lens of a doubtful and spiteful heart, Spitz saw his faithful friend as he truly was: a relentless warrior, an esteemed gentleman, and a firm believer in God. The Washington who stood tall and strong at the front of this Senate Chamber merely spoke the truth as he saw it. And as he spoke, Spitz saw Washington facing down the French at Great Meadows, dodging bullets and remounting horses as he gallantly delivered Braddock's orders, listening intently to the prophecy of an Indian sachem, praying silently at Valley Forge, rallying the retreat at Monmouth, and quietly accepting the comfort of God at Eltham.

Spitz turned his thoughts to heaven. *You really did build this nation. No one who was there could doubt it. Washington knew it, and now I do, too. I'll never doubt You again.*

The address ended, and Washington and the newly-formed congress left the chamber in solemn procession down Broadway to St. Paul's. Washington caught Spitz's eye on the way out and inclined his head in acknowledgement. Spitz recognized the expression in his eyes. It was the same look of grateful awe and exultation he had worn on top of that mountain in Ohio, looking west with dreams of freedom in his heart. Spitz and Wilkins pressed close behind the dignitaries, but they soon lost each other in the jostling mass of people. The crowd shunted Spitz back and sideways, and he fell so far back of the important guests that he lost all hope of even hearing the thanksgiving service at St. Paul's from the outside.

So he decided to make the best of the situation by finding a quiet place out of the way of the crowds to write in his journal. He turned around and walked down the next intersecting street he saw. The street followed a broad curve to the harbor, where raucous sea birds clamored to rival the crowds. There he found men at work loading and unloading ships, which Spitz supposed had to deliver goods no matter what celebration occupied the rest of the city.

Spitz found a quiet space between two piers and sat down on an unattended crate. He'd written in far more rough and crowded places in his journeys with Washington, and the sound of the water lapping against the harbor wall soothed him. Out towards the Atlantic, larger waves swelled and rolled, but the rise and fall of the ships around him showed a calm sea. The sun shone behind him onto the water in a thousand, thousand bright reflections.

He took his calfskin journal from the leather messenger bag and set his blotter and bottle of ink on an upturned crate next to the one on which he sat. He began to write, wryly smiling at the way these earlier New Yorkers carried on working around him without the slightest curiosity about what he was doing. *Some things don't change, I guess.*

Then he thought over the events of the day, beginning with his visit in front of Federal Hall with Hurley and Hawkins and Sterling and their families and ending in his conversation with Wilkins in the senate chamber before Washington's Inaugural Address. He began to write.

**Sign 32**—God provided a Bible for the inauguration, though the organizers had forgotten to arrange one.

**Sign 33**—The British attempt to split New England from the southern states was spoiled when Washington risked diminishing his manpower to strengthen General Gates, who engaged British General John Burgoyne at Saratoga. Providentially, American **reconnaissance intercepted British correspondence** revealing Burgoyne's distressed condition. Emboldened by the intelligence, the Americans pursued Burgoyne aggressively. Washington's selfless effort to assist Gates resulted in a **major victory** for the American Cause—a "signal success" [121] and "powerful stimulus" [122]

**Sign 34**—The victory at Saratoga providentially occurred just in time for Benjamin Franklin to use it to convince the **French government to declare their alliance officially** (providing troops and a naval fleet). "Every dispensation of Providence [is] designed to answer some valuable purpose,"—George Washington." [123]

**Favorable Interposition 13**—The Americans **discovered the treason of Benedict Arnold,** who was clandestinely planning to deliver the military post of West Point into British hands. "By a most providential interposition, Major Andre, Adjutant General of the British Army was taken,"[124] while carrying incriminating documents in Arnold's handwriting. "The providential train of circumstances... [is] convincing proof that the Liberties of America are the object of divine Protection,"[125] —George Washington.

Spitz blotted the entry carefully and with a sense of finality and gratitude, as well as irony. He'd counted thirteen direct interpositions of God's hand, one for each of the thirteen colonies. Then he reviewed the pages before this one, beginning with the entry of Washington falling into the Allegheny River. Time after time, God had spared and shielded

Washington from harm and saved the nation from destruction before its birth. When Washington suffered, as he did at Jack's death, he leaned on God for help. Now Spitz saw the way that Washington leaned on God for help in the hour of his greatest triumph, too.

He thought he saw in the pattern of Washington's life a way of being that seemed to balance freedom and responsibility, dependence and determination, and reverence and relationship in a beautiful dance. The way opened for him to grieve and to invite the mourning God into his grief, and then to celebrate and to invite the source of joy into his celebration. Spitz could see years ahead in which he lived with God not only as the author of his salvation and creator of the universe but also as his constant friend and confidante.

*I want to begin that life with You, no matter how long I have left to live. I want You to come with me every step of the way, starting now.* He looked at the Bible nestled into the messenger bag at his feet. He took it out and held it in front of him. *And if we're going to spend every day together, I suppose I've got to give You a chance to talk, too.* With a wistful smile, he remembered Aspen's suggestion along those lines on the night he had fallen.

Thinking of the passage Ed Campbell had read him from Revelation on the joy waiting at the end of time and thinking how well it fit what he had learned from his journeys to the past, he opened his son's Bible to the book of Revelation and flipped toward the end. Something caught his eye, a thin, shorter piece of paper in a different color, and as he turned back a few pages to examine it more closely, the lights on the sea gathered into a whirlwind that no one else saw and whisked him away from the harbor into the sky.

# Chapter Thirteen

*"Many are the plans in a person's heart,*
*but it is the LORD's purpose that prevails."*
*—Proverbs 19:21*

*"All this," David said, "I have in writing as a result*
*of the LORD's hand on me, and he enabled me to understand*
*all the details of the plan."*
*—1 Chronicles 28:19*

The bright whirlwind set Spitz very gently down in a wingback chair and withdrew tamely into a fireplace. Spitz looked around himself, lost until he saw the man in the opposite armchair.

"Albin Rawlins," Spitz said, relieved, "I thought I was going back to the hospital."

"You will return there soon, but not yet," Rawlins answered. "When I last saw you, I set you a task. Have you completed it?"

Spitz sighed. "If I'm here, I must have. So I won't be going to the past anymore. I'll miss it."

"You have lived in the past, Spitz," Rawlins observed. "Of course you will miss that time. It has been real to you. And I would hear of it, if you will tell me."

Spitz thought of the years and years he had lived in the past. They seemed too long a time to summarize easily. "How much do you already know?"

"I only know that you have observed General Washington closely, but not where or when or for how long," Rawlins told him. "Tell me all."

Spitz lifted the strap of the messenger bag off his chest and over his head and set the bag on his lap. He took out the calfskin journal and showed it to Rawlins. "This should help."

"It is much altered," Rawlins said wonderingly. Then he lifted his eyes to Spitz and added, "And so are you."

"I hope I am," Spitz said. "I feel that I am."

Rawlins leaned back in his chair. "Begin at the first. Where did you go when you left?"

Spitz chuckled at the memory of the trading post and how young and energetic he had been then. He described the place to Rawlins, and then he talked about the men inside and how angry they had been over the settlement massacre.

"They gave me guard duty, but I think it was more shoot-first-and-ask-questions-later duty," Spitz frowned. "I think that anyone else who saw Washington and Gist from the top of that hill would have shot."

"That is most certain sure," Rawlins said. "But you did not shoot, evidently."

"No, I raced down the hill and helped him out of the snow, though I didn't know it was him until I heard his name. He was so young back then," Spitz said.

"What a privilege was offered you!" Rawlins exclaimed softly. "You supported him in the snow and helped to save him."

"The whole time, I couldn't believe I had my arm around a future president," Spitz marveled.

"What did Washington make of the angry crowd within?" Rawlins asked.

Spitz laughed. "He told them to enlist in the militia instead of going off half-cocked. They didn't want to fight alongside Indian allies, but he stood up to them all. I'll never forget it. There were men in there two and three times older than he was, and he stuck to his guns. He was a sight to see."

"And what did you learn from that journey?" Rawlins asked.

"God saved Washington's life at least three times right before I saw him," Spitz said, thumbing backward through the book. "He could have been shot by a treacherous guide, scalped by a band of hostile Indians, or frozen in the Allegheny, but God kept him safe. It was a miracle."

"Good, good," Rawlins approved, "and have you come from there?"

"No, I went back to my hospital room. I kept going back there in between the trips to see Washington, and every time, I was getting better and better. You told me when I came here before that I was unresponsive in a coma. Well, now I can move and communicate again, though I'm still not strong and I can't quite write or speak yet. But they say it's a miracle how well I'm recovering. So I had my own miracle, too, like Washington."

"God is generous with His miracles, more generous than men imagine who do not wish to credit Him for them," Rawlins observed. "Perhaps the greatest miracle of all is when God changes the heart of a man or a woman. Despite all our efforts, we remain as helpless to change ourselves as we are to change anyone else. Only God can make things new."

Spitz nodded in agreement, for he knew in his heart that in more ways than one he was indeed a miracle in process.

"You said that you took several trips to see Washington," Rawlins prompted him. "At what point did you see him next?

"I went to Great Meadows, and I stayed from the end of May to the beginning of July," Spitz remembered, turning to that page in his journal and then looking up. "I was his aide-de-camp. I wrote letters for him and worked to build the forest road and fought at Fort Necessity. I was with him pretty constantly for six weeks."

Rawlins shook his head, smiling. "You would have come to know him quite well over six weeks. And what did you write at the end of that time?"

Spitz looked back down at the journal. "God gave Washington a high rank, higher than his age warranted. He helped him ally with Half King and beat the French spies at the battle of Jumonville Glen, and he wasn't wounded, even when the fighting was so close. I was terrified, but Washington charged straight ahead. And just when we were all close to starving, God sent beef cattle and sacks of flour." Spitz chuckled.

"Why do you laugh?" Rawlins asked, frowning.

"Oh, when they came I'd just worked a full day felling trees on starvation rations, and I was complaining to myself about the food. I wanted a cheeseburger—a kind of beef sandwich with cheese—and God sent beef on the hoof and flour for bread. It was a pretty direct answer to my grumbling," Spitz admitted sheepishly.

"But Great Meadows was a terrible defeat," Rawlins protested, "surely you wrote something about the battle."

"I did," Spitz said, looking down. "I wrote about the rain. The French and Indians had the upper hand, Rawlins, they outnumbered us by at least three to one, and it looked to be a slaughter. I didn't know how we were going to survive. But then the rain came back and stayed and damped everyone's powder. So the French offered us terms of capitulation. They didn't have to do that. They could have killed us all with bayonets and swords, or let the Indians do it with tomahawks." Spitz shuddered at a memory. "I saw plenty of that kind of work the next time I went back, to Braddock's expedition against Fort Duquesne."

"You followed Washington with Braddock?" Rawlins demanded. "But that ambush was a slaughter quite as bad as the one you feared at Great Meadows! How did you survive?"

Spitz shook his head. "I don't know. I don't know how Washington survived, either. He shouldn't have. He showed me his coat and hat with six bullet holes through them, but he didn't have a scratch on him."

"Marvelous," Rawlins murmured. "I have seen the hat and coat, but to have seen the fight that marred them—marvelous."

"And here's what I wrote about my time there," Spitz said, turning the page. "General Braddock offered to mentor Washington by making him an aide-de-camp after he resigned from the militia, and then he survived the massacre." Spitz looked up and frowned. "I can't believe I didn't write more than that. I don't feel like I'm doing justice to how bad things were and what a miracle it is that Washington and I survived."

"Tell me, Spitz," Rawlins asked hesitantly, "was it there that your grudge disappeared and your soul found peace?"

"No," Spitz admitted, "that wasn't until much later."

"Perhaps your resentment clouded your eyes to the miracles around you, even when you saw them occur," Rawlins suggested.

"I guess my heart just wasn't in it," Spitz said. "I could have written more if I hadn't still been angry."

Rawlins nodded in acknowledgement and then gestured to the book. "Continue, please."

Spitz turned to the next entry. His eyes grew wide with remembered eeriness and the consciousness of something holy happening. "I went to the survey trip in Ohio, and I climbed a mountain with Washington and saw him looking west and talked to him about independence. When we got back to camp, an old Indian chief came to us and prophesied over Washington." Spitz tried to describe the atmosphere of the encampment while the old chief spoke, as well as his own brush with the power of God afterwards, but he felt inadequate to the task.

"I believe you," Rawlins told him when he saw Spitz's frustration. "I have spoken to Doctor Craik about that evening, and he has impressed upon me the sense of reverence and utter certainty attendant on those words."

"But look here—I nearly forgot. Washington told me all about his life. I wrote about God giving him everything he needed to become the person he was: education, land, a profession, the connections of his relatives, and the notice of men in high places. Then the Davies sermon—Washington talked about that being one of the reasons for his sense of destiny. He felt that Davies was right. God saved Washington's life miraculously a number of times, most publically at Braddock's expedition, and Washington felt that he owed God a debt of service to the country to pay it back."

"He discharged any such debt tenfold over the course of his life," Rawlins declared. "No man has done more or could have done more in his place."

"Knowing about that sermon helped me understand his motives, though," Spitz mused. "He was never power-hungry. He wanted to do all he could from a sense of gratitude and a sense of destiny. I can't say I was surprised when the next time I saw him was at Trenton."

"Trenton," Rawlins mused, "I understand that the weather was insupportably bad there."

"It sure was," Spitz said. He described his early encounter with the Hessian guard and the patriot band and his long slog through the snow to meet Washington. "He was so sure that his surprise attack was ruined, but that false alarm worked in his favor, just like the snow and the hailstorm did, even though they looked like obstacles at first. And I wrote here about General Charles Lee getting captured; that was providential, because it secured Washington's place as the head of the army." Spitz paused. "I saw Lee some time later at Monmouth. He was insubordinate and disorganized. It was a good thing for the country that he didn't replace Washington then. Instead, Lee earned a humiliating court martial after Monmouth."

"We have been fortunate indeed in our leader," Rawlins agreed heartily. "Was Monmouth your next journey?"

"Nearly," Spitz answered, turning the page to the entry from Valley Forge. He described the terrible conditions and the bodies and sick men leaving on wagons to be treated far away, so that the well men wouldn't lose heart at seeing them. And he described his own unusual induction into the Life Guard.

"Something happened to me when I committed to stay with Washington as a Guard," Spitz remembered. "From that time on, I never left. Time sped up around me, but the other guards acted like I'd been there all along, serving my shifts just like them, even though I didn't know where or when I was when time slowed."

"Have you records from those times?" Rawlins frowned.

"Oh, yes," Spitz assured him. "Here's the one from Valley Forge. Baron von Steuben's arrival when Washington didn't even expect him was a miracle. He turned a bunch of different militias into one army. And then there was the run of shad when we were all so hungry. We sure were grateful for that fish, and catching them was a nice break from the Baron's drills. And then France promised to help with men and naval power and money—that reassurance put heart into everybody. We didn't feel so alone in our fight. Washington saw God's hand in all of it. He saw God's hand directing America and directing him personally."

"So it was here that you changed toward God," Rawlins assumed.

Spitz shook his head ruefully. "Something began to change in me the night I wrote all of those signs, though. Washington told me about losing his stepdaughter and father and brother, and he cried with me over Steve and prayed for me. I'll never forget that, as long as I live."

"A beginning is good," Rawlins acknowledged kindly.

Spitz turned the next page. "Monmouth was next. I helped Craik in the field hospital, carrying men he could help behind the lines."

"Monmouth was a signal victory," Rawlins said. "It must have provided a great deal of insight for you."

"A cannon ball just barely missed Washington right before the battle," Spitz read, looking up. "It threw dirt all over him and his horse, but he never flinched. It threw dirt all over me, too, though I sure noticed it! Craik reminded us all of the Indian prophecy then, because the officers were already worried about their General. And then Washington arrived at the front just in time to stop Lee's retreat and rally the men. A man who knew the ground well was providentially close by to help General Washington form a plan of battle right then. We had to hurry because the British were only fifteen minutes away. And during the battle, I saw Molly Pitcher!" Spitz said excitedly. "I learned about her in school when I was a boy."

"She was a courageous woman," Rawlins agreed. "I am glad to know that her nation does not forget her."

"I can't honestly say that it was from her gun, but drifting smoke for sure shielded General Washington from the eyes of the British. Sometimes they were within ten yards of him as he rode up and down the line encouraging men to press on, but he stayed right where he was. He was fearless." Admiration for Washington's courage glowed in Spitz. "I wrote about the Black Regiment, too, after a preacher from Tennessee territory told me about it. I had noticed preachers in the army before, but I hadn't known all he told me about the clergy sparking the fight for independence," Spitz said, remembering the cherubic face of the preacher resting from his work with the dying after fighting a full day on the left flank.

"You have heard, of course, what Horace Walpole said in reference to Dr. John Witherspoon when he heard news of the revolution: 'Cousin America has run off with a Presbyterian parson.'"[126]

Spitz smiled. "That quote is hilarious. It sounds like some rich family ashamed of the black sheep."

"That simile comes very near the truth," Rawlins said, "for pride of possession had more to do with the British fight for America than any good accrued to either party by the connection."

"I saw plenty of pride at Yorktown," Spitz remembered, "when Cornwallis wouldn't surrender his sword in person and when his men threw their arms down petulantly."

"So Yorktown was your next stop," Rawlins said, eyes alight, "the beginning of the end of the war."

"And the beginning of the end of my bitterness," Spitz agreed. "I arrived after most of the fight was over, just in time to give up my place in the Life Guards so that I could act as the messenger between Yorktown and Eltham while Jack was dying. I heard enough on my trips to Yorktown to understand what a great victory it was and how God orchestrated the whole thing, from arranging for the two arms of the French fleet to meet undamaged in Chesapeake Bay and send off the British navy, to Washington fooling Clinton and arriving in Virginia unsuspected to fight Cornwallis. And then there were the weather events—the fog and storms that shielded the trench diggers and the storm that prevented Cornwallis from retreating. And I heard from some southern soldiers about more things like that in the southern campaign, rivers flooding to delay Cornwallis so that he couldn't catch Greene and Morgan before they led him straight to where Washington could defeat him."

"And after that victory came a terrible tragedy," Rawlins said sadly. "Considering your particular history, to watch another man's son dying, especially the son of a man you loved and revered, must have been a nearly unendurable trial," Rawlins said compassionately. "I am sorry for it."

Spitz nodded, remembering the somber news of Jack's hopeless condition and Washington's grief at his death. He remembered his own grief and Washington's reminder of the comfort of God. He looked up at Rawlins, ashamed. "The truth is that every time I saw God do something miraculous for Washington, I was jealous that He didn't take the same care of my son. As much as I admired Washington, I resented him, because I thought that God was playing favorites."

"Then you saw him stricken, the same as you had been," Rawlins said thoughtfully.

"I realized then that God didn't take every pain from Washington. Washington suffered, too, but he clung to God and received comfort while I pushed God away and was bitter. I only hurt myself and Aspen with my anger; I could have turned to God and lived a very different life these past seventeen years," Spitz admitted.

"You have that comfort now," Rawlins told him, "I can see it in you."

"I do," Spitz said, "and I'm learning to reach for it more. I knew so much about God before the accident. I would have told you then that I was willing to die for Him. But I didn't know Him well enough to invite Him into my grief. When I was so torn up inside, I didn't know how to be the victorious Christian I felt I ought to be, the one my pastor described to me. So I tried to be strong and hide what I felt, but it only made me angry and resentful. Now I'm learning friendship with God."

"Have you come here straight from one deathbed to another, then?" Rawlins asked sympathetically.

Spitz shook his head. "I saw Washington twice more: once at Valley Forge during a break from the Constitutional Convention, and once at his inauguration in New York."

"Did you record those visits, too?" Rawlins asked.

Spitz handed him the book. "I talked to Gouverneur Morris and Washington about the progress of the convention. I think that God wanted me to learn that hard fights don't end all at once. You have a space to breathe, and then you come back fighting. Life is work and rest in rhythm."

"A valuable lesson," Rawlins said, perusing the book, "as is the one you noted here: God brought the delegates together during the convention. He brought the colonies together before the war; He brought the army together to fight it; and finally He brought the people of each state together to ratify the new constitution, one by one. Unity is His gift, especially when men remember to ask him for it."

"Just like Franklin's reminder to the delegates," Spitz agreed. "He was right. How could a mighty empire rise without Him? I know it's not the same thing, but I've been remembering what he said during physical therapy, when I've been learning to move all over again. The work I have to do right now is too hard and too important to attempt it without Him."

"And that is the lesson repeated to you at the inauguration, I see," Rawlins said. "Washington asked for help in the hour of his greatest triumph."

"Yes," Spitz agreed. "If Washington needed God's help then, I need it every day."

"I see that you heard about the victory at Saratoga and the treason of Benedict Arnold as well," Rawlins noted, holding up the journal. "Two momentous New York events remembered at the time of a third."

"God watched over America. He stopped Major Andre before he could get Arnold's West Point plans to Clinton. And he showed Washington how to support an important victory that would win us friends in Europe, even though another general would fight it," Spitz said.

"So you admit now that Washington was right in what he wrote?" Rawlins asked, though he evidently knew the answer. "You admit that God directly shaped America?"

"I noted in there thirteen times when I saw the hand of God move directly," Spitz answered, "and that's on top of dozens more signs and mercies that weren't as dramatic. I admit it freely; I was wrong before. After seeing what I did, I couldn't think anything else." He reached his hand to take his journal back from Rawlins, but Rawlins closed it and set it on his knee.

"I find that I have further need of your valuable notes, Spitz. Will you trust me that they will find the right hands in the right time?" Rawlins asked.

"I'll trust God that they'll end in the right hands," Spitz said, "though I would have liked to show them to Aspen and her children, when she has them."

"I understand," Rawlins acknowledged, and just then a knock at the door interrupted him. Billy Lee came into the room quietly and said in his smooth, deep voice, "Doctor Craik asks Mr. Rawlins and Mr. Spitzen to attend him now. The general nears a crisis." Tears still streamed down his face as he spoke, and Spitz felt for him again. What a complicated grief he had to endure; so tangled and marred was injustice and camaraderie in his life!

Lee withdrew, and Spitz saw Rawlins leave the calfskin journal on the table beside Lear's on their way out. He and Rawlins followed Lee up the wide staircase to a room on the second floor that seemed crowded with more people than it ought to hold. Spitz recognized Martha Washington, who was sitting at the foot of the bed, and the older version of Craik. There were attentive servants present and a few concerned visitors keeping a proper distance. By their actions, Spitz assumed the visitors were either family members or very close friends. Immediately surrounding Washington were Craik and the other two doctors, as well as Tobias Lear, who sat in bed with Washington and helped him to turn to the side.

Washington's face was pale, and he seemed drained of energy. His breaths came in long, rasping gasps and painful exhalations that seemed to scrape Spitz's own throat as he heard them. His heart ached with increasing intensity at seeing his friend in pain and struggling. Craik saw them enter and crossed to the rear of the room.

"He will not live out the day," Craik told them sadly. "If another hour remains to him, it will be a mercy."

"How could it be a mercy when he can't breathe?" Spitz whispered, agonized. "You're a doctor; can't you do anything for him? Can't you give him a tracheotomy so that he can breathe at least?" A tear fell down Spitz's face, and he scrubbed at it with the back of his hand, irritated at his helplessness.

Craik shook his head. "Your grief and your feeling for his agony bid you speak. But you must know that such a procedure would lengthen his life for only a few days, days filled with the risk of infection and the pain of the wound added to the pain of his illness, and days when he would be robbed of the power of speech. Surely you would not wish such a death on any man who was dear to you, as I know that he is."

Spitz shook his head wordlessly. His sorrow overtook him again.

"Death is not the worst enemy a man can face," Craik reminded him. "George has set his affairs in order, and those he loves surround him. He will pass decently and at peace into the arms of his Savior, and he is not afraid. Remember what he told me when I came: 'I die hard; but I am not afraid to go.'[127] I shall not rob him of such a fitting end with the clumsiest of the tools at my disposal."

His heart full of grief as he watched Washington, Spitz nodded. Washington turned his head just then and saw Spitz, and though he was too weak and ill to lift his hand or speak a superfluous word, he fixed Spitz with a look. Spitz knew that look. It was the one he had worn in the middle of a rough crowd of traders, at the outset of a lost battle, at the turn of a retreat, and at the mention of a hard negotiation. It was a look that echoed the same words he had spoken to Craik. It asked for no sympathy, only acknowledgement of his courage, determination, and faith.

Then the fierceness faded, and Washington's eyes moved to Martha, who was sitting at the end of his bed. Craik hurried to his side, his attention riveted. Washington looked tenderly at Martha, and his features relaxed into lines of peace and contentment. With Lear supporting him as he gathered strength and breath, Washington said with difficulty, "Tis well."[128]

After those words, Washington seemed to fall gradually and peacefully asleep. A few moments later, he exhaled his last breath, and the horrible, rattling gasps ceased forever, replaced by the loud sobbing of his nearest relatives and friends.

Spitz looked around him, torn. He did not belong to these people who knew one another and mourned Washington together. His grief, as overwhelming as it was to him, was a thing apart. Quietly he stepped back from the room and descended the staircase to the library alone, the reality of his loss becoming heavier and heavier to him as he walked.

He shut the door behind him, sank into the wingback chair by the fire, and cried. *Losing people you love never gets any easier, does it?* he prayed. *I need that comfort again. I don't know how to face my grief without losing myself in it or locking it away inside me again. I'm afraid of turning away this time, too. I'm afraid that I'm too weak to cling to You when I need You.*

The voice spoke to him, gentle and still. *It doesn't matter how weak you are. What matters is how strong I am. I will bear this pain with you; I loved him, too.*

Gradually, Spitz's heart calmed, and he wiped his tears away with a handkerchief he found in the pocket of his fancy coat. *Thank You,* he nodded. *I thank You for the peace, and I thank You for that last look from my friend. Thank You for that chance to say goodbye.*

The door opened again, and Rawlins stayed in the door frame in front of someone else. Spitz stood and turned to face him, curious about the person behind Rawlins.

Rawlins said, "I thought you might have come back here from a sense of courtesy towards Washington's family. But I am glad that you did not leave altogether. I want you to meet someone, Spitz, a distant relation of mine who has traveled like you, to help me with my work curating Washington's papers."

"I'd be glad to meet him," Spitz said, straightening his coat and tucking away the handkerchief in a pocket.

Rawlins stood aside with an air of expectation, allowing the young man to step forward, his hand outstretched to shake Spitz's. The young man had straight, dark hair that he wore cut short, not long in a queue like the men of this time, and his eyes were sea-green and piercing. He looked familiar to Spitz for some reason.

"I can't believe I'm meeting you," the young man said, grinning. "Mr. Rawlins told me what just happened, and I'm really sorry for your loss. But I've wanted to meet you my whole life, and I can't believe it's finally happened, especially here. How cool is this!"

The grin was infectious, and Spitz felt himself smiling despite the lingering ache in his heart. "Do I know you? You seem so familiar."

"What an apt word!" Rawlins said, pleased. "He is, indeed, familiar to you, though you have never previously met him. Allow me to introduce Aston Rawlins and to tell you that this man, who is a distant relation to me, is quite a close one to you."

"But we don't have anyone named Rawlins in the family," Spitz said, nonplussed.

"Not quite yet, but you will soon," Aston told him. "My mom's name is Aspen."

★ ★ ★

Aspen stepped off the hospital elevator with Bill, his arm around her affectionately. She couldn't wait to see her Papa again and congratulate him on his recovery. She also wanted to tell him her news. He would be so happy to know that she and Bill were dating. But more than anything, she knew that he wouldn't stop worrying until he saw her safe and sound again, and she wanted to give him that reassurance.

She rounded the corner and saw the nurse's station, where a familiar face brightened at the sight of her.

"Aspen, sugar, your Papa is going to be beside himself!" Angela said, coming around the desk to fold Aspen into a hug.

"I can't believe how well he's doing," Aspen said happily. "The whole time I was overseas, I kept getting your messages and just shaking my head. I never thought he'd be better so soon."

"I saved you a surprise for today. He's off the IV. He started swallowing yesterday when he woke up from his nap; so we've started him on soft food," Angela grinned.

Joy and relief bubbled up in Aspen. *He's almost well again—thank You for that.* "When can he come home, Angela?" Aspen asked. "He sounds so much better."

"The doctor and the physical therapist say that he needs another week here, and he'll need help at home to eat and to walk and some other things for a short time while he transitions. But you can hire an aide; we'll give you some resources."

"Another week!" Aspen exclaimed. "Next week is Thanksgiving!" She pictured herself and Bill and Papa together around the big farmhouse table in the dining room, sharing turkey and cranberry sauce. It was a sweet and welcome picture.

"Yes, next week," Angela said. "He'll be back with you in time to keep you company on Thanksgiving Day." Then she looked up at Bill and said mischievously, "Not that you've been that lonely lately."

Aspen laughed and blushed as she looked up at Bill, too. Bill grinned. "Hey, I'm happy to keep her company. I just had the great timing to show up when she was lonely enough to give me a second look."

"I probably would have given you a second look even if I wasn't that lonely," Aspen told him. "You are kind of cute, after all."

Bill hugged her and kissed the top of her head. "Thanks," he said, "you're kind of cute, too. Now let's go see your Papa."

Angela led the way and opened the door, but she let Aspen and Bill into the room ahead of her. The group found Spitz sitting up at the side of the bed, his feet resting on the floor. Aspen gasped to see him sitting up. The phone call updates hadn't fully prepared her to see the difference in her grandfather. She raced to him and threw her arms around his neck.

"Oh, Papa—I'm so glad you're better!" Aspen cried. "It's unbelievable how much better you look! And Angela says that you can come home next week!"

Spitz nodded and stretched his mouth into a lopsided smile.

"Look, Bill!" Aspen said excitedly, reaching for his hand and pulling him forward. "He's smiling and nodding. I didn't know you could do that, Papa!"

"He started recovering so fast that it was hard to remember all the things he'd learned all over again when I called you," Angela said. "But he's been working on one thing over and over with the therapist. Do you want to show her, Spitz?"

Spitz nodded and lifted his hand, palm up, to receive something. Angela produced a pen and paper and put the paper on the nightstand beside Spitz's bed. She carefully handed Spitz the pen, waiting for his fingers to close around it before she let go. He held it in a fist, like a child who hasn't been to school, and he frowned in concentration as he formed the letters with large, bold strokes. Then he looked up and gestured with his head for Aspen to come closer and see.

She let go of Bill's hand and moved forward a step. "I love you, Aspen," she read aloud. Tears of joy sprang to her eyes, and she sat beside Spitz on the bed and took his arm, leaning her head on his shoulder. "I love you, too, Papa. You wrote me a note, just like you promised. Thank you. I can't imagine how much work that took you."

He shook his head, and then he wrote something else. "It's worth it," Aspen read, sitting up and chuckling.

Bill came closer and sat in the visitor's chair across from Aspen and Spitz. "I'm sure it's worth it. You've probably got weeks of thoughts just pent up inside from when you couldn't speak. Now you can tell us all about them."

Spitz nodded and bent to write something else. When he finished, he eyed Bill and indicated that he should read it.

"Welcome to the family. Let's go fishing," Bill read aloud. He grinned and said, "Anytime you're up to it, Mr. Spitzen."

Spitz shook his head and wrote something else for Bill.

"Spitz," Bill read. He chuckled and looked up at Aspen. "He approves," he said, picking up her hand and holding it, "I get to use a nickname and everything."

They looked over at Spitz, who nodded, a satisfied expression on his face. Then he looked up at Angela and mimed holding on to something with both hands at chest height.

She nodded back at him. "All right - stand back, you two," she ordered. "We have one last thing to show you."

*What else could he have to show us?* Aspen wondered. She and Bill got up and stood at the foot of the bed, Bill standing behind Aspen with both his arms around her as they waited excitedly.

Angela pushed the visitor's chair far out of the way and retrieved a walker from the corner of the room by the door. She brought it to Spitz and then stood on the other side of him by the nightstand. "I'll jump in if I see you having trouble, but otherwise, you're on your own," she told him.

Spitz gathered his strength. Aspen saw him breathe deeply and then tighten his grip on the handles of the walker. With an almighty heave, he stood halfway to his feet and wobbled uncertainly for a moment. Then Angela put her arm around his back and helped him to stand the rest of the way. He looked up at her gratefully. Then she stood back, and he stood up straight.

Aspen gasped and started to clap, but her Papa looked around at her and shook his head. He wasn't finished yet. He swung the walker around to face them and took a hesitant step followed by a firm one. Then he took another and looked up, beaming at her and Bill.

They both clapped and cheered for him, Aspen laughing in joy to see him on his feet.

The door opened then, and Ed Campbell stuck his head inside. He took in the scene at a glance and broke into a grin. "Good to see you on your feet again, Spitz," he said.

"Come in," Bill told him, shaking his hand. "We're all celebrating in here."

"I remember you," Ed Campbell said, "I met you here a few weeks ago. I'm Ed Campbell."

"Bill Rawlins," Bill responded heartily, "and you'll remember my girl-friend, Aspen Spitzen, too; she's Spitz's granddaughter."

"Nice to see you again," Aspen said.

Campbell shook her hand next. "Aspen - so you're the young lady from the notes," he smiled

"What notes?" Aspen asked, puzzled. "Has Papa been writing some-thing with my name on it?"

"Not that I know of," Campbell said. "I meant the notes in the Bible over there."

Aspen froze. "What notes?" she repeated in a much different and much smaller voice.

"Well, they're stuck in all over the place, mostly towards the front and the back. You don't know about them?" he asked incredulously. No one else was moving; so he walked to the bed and picked up the Bible, bringing it to Aspen. He flipped through the pages until he found one stuck in the book of Numbers, picked it up, and handed it to her.

She was frozen in shock. She vaguely saw Papa sitting down in the visitor chair, Angela helping him. But Aspen was beyond reacting. In front of her was a note in her mother's unmistakable, loopy handwriting, with Aspen's name at the top and a row of hearts at the bottom underneath her mother's signature. She never thought she'd see such a thing again after the disappointment at the crash site in Indonesia, and here it had been all along, waiting in the Bible that nobody ever opened. She began to cry, and she handed the note to Bill. "Read it," she pled.

He cleared his throat and began reading, one arm still around Aspen as she clung to him.

"Dearest Aspen,

"I miss you so much, sweetie! I didn't think it was possible to miss a person this much, but it just goes to show you how the heart has depths you never suspect until you reach them. You're in the very deepest part of my heart, Aspen, and I love you with all of it.

"I know that you're being a good girl for Granny and Papa; I don't even have to ask. I hope that you're having fun out on the farm. Daddy says to tell you to ask Mr. Jordan next door to let you feed the horses. He'll probably let you ride one and play in the barn.

"You should see where I am right now, Aspen! It's at the top of a hill that's level, like a great, big table. A small village made of grass huts is in the middle of that table, and outside the village fence are gardens with sweet potato vines and big plants that look like elephant ears called taro. The children here are so sweet and so thankful for the gifts Daddy and I delivered. I've been playing with them all day and teaching them a few English words. It's been such fun!

But as much fun as I'm having here, I can't wait to come home to my sweet girl. I remembered a verse today and prayed it for you. You should read it yourself. Here's the address: Numbers VI: 24-26.

All the love in my heart,

Mom

In the silence that followed, Aspen cried silently. *Thank You for sav-ing that message and the other ones for me all these years. I can't wait to read them all. They're such a gift. They're a better gift than I could have imagined.*

A few moments later, Ed Campbell spoke up timidly. "I found that verse, if you want me to read it. She must have stuck it right where she was reading when she finished it."

Aspen nodded, not trusting herself to speak.

Campbell read aloud in his reedy voice, "The LORD bless thee, and keep thee: The LORD make his face shine upon thee, and be gracious unto thee: The LORD lift up his countenance upon thee, and give thee peace."

Aspen closed her eyes. Her mother had prayed these words over her far away and long ago. But hearing them now connected her to that time and to her dear, lost mother as if she whispered them in Aspen's ear right now. She thought of the words she had just heard. God had blessed her and shown grace to her and given her peace. All she could say in return was *Thank You.*

A new sound sent Aspen's eyes flying open. She was sure she'd heard her Papa's voice. She looked up at Bill. "Did you hear that?" she asked.

Bill, awestruck, nodded toward Papa and told Aspen, "Listen."

Aspen carefully watched her Papa in his chair across the room. He smiled and looked her in the eyes, a look full of contentment and joy. Then he opened his mouth and said, "'Tis well."

# *Epilogue*

*"Better is the end of a thing than its beginning, and the patient
in spirit is better than the proud in spirit."*
—*Ecclesiastes 7:8*

Aston Rawlins drove north on I-81 from Tennessee, relaxing in the scenery around him. He loved the heavily-wooded mountains shading away from velvet green right out the window to misty blue in the distance. This kind of land said home to him like nothing else did, and it felt like the right place to be on his birthday, especially a birthday as important as this one, his twenty-first.

His parents were making a special dinner for him and inviting some of his childhood friends to share it. He looked forward to seeing the familiar faces of people who would be genuinely happy to see him home from college for the weekend. And his parents had hinted that they had a special gift for him, too.

A few hours before the party, Aston pulled up in front of the family house, where he'd spent his entire life until college. There was a car in the drive that he didn't recognize. *Someone must have come early,* Aston figured.

On the porch, his father stood up from the swing, where he'd been reading a book. Bill came down the porch and met him halfway across the yard, sweeping him into a firm hug.

"It's good to see you, son," he said. "How was your drive?"

"It was good, Dad," Aston told him. "I just listened to music and watched the mountains."

The two men stood apart and grinned at each other. The grins were the same, and so were the sea-green eyes. They were almost exactly the same height. Bill threw an arm around his tall son's shoulders and led him inside. "Come say hello to your mother. She's been excited all day to tell you happy birthday."

"Is she in the kitchen?" Aston asked, sniffing hopefully in that direction.

"Not at the moment," Bill said, steering him left to the library. Through the glass doors, Aston saw a man in jeans and a button-down shirt with the sleeves rolled up sitting on a sofa across the coffee table from his mom. Bill opened the door and announced, "He's here."

"Happy birthday, Aston!" Aspen called cheerfully, sidling past the coffee table to reach him. She hugged him tight and then held him away from her. "I can't believe you're all grown up today. I miss my boy."

"Don't speak too soon," Aston joked. "I brought my laundry in the trunk."

"Grown men do their own laundry," Bill teased him. "Your mom will hand you the detergent, and then you're on your own, son."

Aston grinned and then looked at the man on the sofa, who stood up and put out his hand. "Mr. Pritchard," Aston said, "sorry to ignore you over there. Did I interrupt church business?"

"No, Aston, I came here for you. I've got my lawyer hat on today," Dave Pritchard said. Aston had known him his whole life; Pritchard and his father were both deacons together at the church Aston had attended since before he could remember.

Aston and his mom sat on one sofa, and his dad sat beside Mr. Pritchard on the other, the coffee table between them. Aston grinned nervously. "I'm so used to seeing you on the other end of a lawnmower that I forget you're a lawyer."

"Somebody's got to keep up the grounds," Pritchard joked.

Bill leaned back and grinned at his son. "I told you we had a present for you, and we need Dave here to deliver it for us."

"Actually, there are two presents," Aspen said, smiling up at her son. "One is from us, and the other is from Papa Spitzen."

Aston looked between his parents and the lawyer. "They must be some presents if you need legal representation. What are they?"

"We'll go first," Aspen said, taking Aston's hands in both of hers and holding them as she looked up at him. "You know that this farm has been in my family for generations. And you know that one day the whole thing will belong to you."

"Someone who will finally farm it," Aston said wryly.

"And who will do a great job after he gets his degree from agricultural college," Aspen said.

"Hey, it's UT; it's not like I'm going to a hick school. I know science," Aston said.

Aspen's eyes twinkled with the fun of the surprise. "Like I said—you'll do a fabulous job farming the whole six hundred acres for us once you graduate. But Daddy and I didn't want you to have to wait until we're gone before you had a piece of it for yourself."

Aston's eyes shot to his father, who nodded at him and laughed. "We're giving you the back forty free and clear to do whatever you want with it. That piece of Spitzen history belongs entirely to you as soon as you sign the paper. Dave, you want to do the honors?"

Pritchard pulled a deed from his briefcase and explained it to Aston point by point. Then he showed Aston the place to sign at the bottom. His parents had both already signed. He guessed that's what his mom had been doing before he came home.

Aston signed his name and then looked up at Aspen, eyes full of gratitude. "Thanks, Mom," he said softly. "Thank you both." He looked solemnly at Bill, who smiled at him.

"You deserve it, and I'm glad that you have it," Bill said. "Try out all that Amish farming you're so nuts about."

"I will, and you'll see how much better it works," Aston said confidently.

"I believe you," Bill told him, holding up his hands in surrender. "Now ask your mom about your other present."

Aston looked at her expectantly. *How could they top the land? That's all I've ever wanted. I can build a cabin and a stable out there and live on my own off the land. What else could they possibly think I'd want?*

Aspen rose and walked to a bookshelf behind her. Aston recognized the book she took from it, its cover charred and crumbling. She brought it back and handed it to him.

"You never got to know Papa Spitzen, but he loved you so much. He knew that the farm would come to you along with the house, but he wanted to give you something in particular that belonged to him."

"The family Bible," Aston said. He'd heard the stories about it growing up, how his grandfather and grandmother had taken it to Indonesia and died in a plane crash there and how his mother had found the messages from them years later. He'd heard how his great-grandfather kept it by his side while he was recovering from a stroke and carried it with him almost everywhere from then on.

"The Bible isn't all," Pritchard interrupted. "Your great-grandfather made his will with me, and he handed me a key that he said went with an antique desk. The desk is quite special, actually. It's an artisan copy of the one that George Washington used at Mount Vernon. And now it's yours, along with the key your grandfather gave me."

The key that Pritchard handed Aston felt small and fragile. He looked back at the desk, which had always seemed as if it belonged with a prosperous planter. Pigeonholes and drawers waited to be filled above the writing surface, which folded into place and locked. Aston could see the key in the lock, where it had been for as long as he could remember. Above the writing surface and drawers rose a tall, glass-fronted bookcase with old books in it. A key rested in that lock, too, a large one with an ornamental tassel.

Aston raised his eyes from the delicate key he held and looked from one parent to the next. "But it already has two keys. Why do I need another one?"

Bill shrugged. "I don't know. Maybe it's a replacement for the one that locks the fold-down writing table."

"I never knew he gave you a key, Dave," Aspen said to Pritchard. "He didn't mention it to me when he told me he was leaving Aston the desk and the Bible."

"I'm sure Aston will figure it out," Pritchard said kindly. "Now if you folks will excuse me, it's Saturday, and I hear a lawn downtown calling my name."

The Rawlins family stood and thanked him for coming over on a weekend. He left the house and then drove away, waving to them and honking by the cattle guard across the drive that marked the end of the lawn and the beginning of the fields. The family waved back and then closed the door.

"Why don't you take some time with your gifts?" Bill suggested. "Mom and I will go and work on your birthday supper, and you can come and talk to us when you're done."

"You're eaten up with curiosity over that spare key; I can just see it," Aspen agreed. "Figure it out and let us know."

"Thanks, guys," Aston said. "Thanks for everything. I can't wait to start work on the land. It's the best present ever."

His parents hugged him and left, walking toward the kitchen with their arms around each other. Aston liked seeing them together like that, happy with each other.

He went back to the library and closed the glass doors behind him. Then he removed both keys from the desk and tried the new key in both locks without success. So he replaced the original keys and opened the bookcase. Methodically, he removed all of the antique books inside, placing them carefully on the coffee table. When the shelves were empty, he checked the back and the sides for secret compartments. He found none.

He replaced all of the books in the bookcase and locked it again. Next, he opened the writing surface with the key that had been standing in the lock and folded it down. He opened all of the drawers and looked inside, finding nothing but ordinary office supplies that hadn't been used in years. He emptied the drawers and examined them one by one, and then he took them completely out and examined the empty spaces where they belonged as well as the empty spaces of the pigeonholes. Nothing moved, and no tiny lock appeared to receive the tiny key.

Aston carefully replaced all of the office supplies in the drawers and then put the drawers in the spaces where they fit. He moved his hands along the inside panels and pressed different points along the writing surface. Nothing happened. He closed the writing surface again and began to run his hands along the outside front of the desk. Then he moved to the left side, running his hands up and down the wood to feel for any irregularities. And as he ran his hand up the wood veneer on the left panel, it moved upward slightly. Excited, Aston pressed the wood more firmly and slid the veneer entirely upward over the panel of veneer above it.

And behind the lower veneer, he saw a rectangle of darker wood with a crevice running right around it and a miniature keyhole in the top center. He steadied his hand, fit the key into the lock, and turned. It clicked and sprang open enough for Aston to pull it the rest of the way.

Inside was an unbelievably old and stained calfskin journal. He sat on the floor right by the secret compartment and opened it. The first page read: "Signs, Mercies, and Interpositions of the Invisible Hand." He began to read. He found bullet points describing events in someone's life. Then he saw the name Washington and pieced some of the other events and names together. This journal was about the life of George Washington. Aston went back to the beginning and started over.

He read through each of the bullet points, noticing candle wax on the page about Trenton and what he was pretty sure was blood on the entry for Monmouth. The whole journal still smelled like old leather and gunpowder.

After the last bullet point, Aston saw entries in a different handwriting, as if the journal had traded owners. The new handwriting told a story of a man out of his time, a man brought to meet George Washington after he challenged God. That man was his great-grandfather, Papa Spitzen, and Aston read, fascinated, the story he saw there of Papa's answer and his repentance. When Aston was done, he pondered. *Could it have been true? Could Papa have gone back in time like that? Did he really write those bullet points after battles in the American Revolution?*

He discounted the possibility immediately. *People don't time travel; that's all science fiction,* he told himself. He flipped through the journal again, and four pieces of old parchment paper fell out; each one had been folded and still bore the broken remains of a wax seal. He carefully picked one up and unfolded it. The handwriting was thin, elegant cursive, the kind that belonged on fancy wedding invitations. At the top of the first document, Aston read, "GENERAL ORDERS, Head Quarters, Freehold (Monmouth County)," followed by the date: June 29, 1778.

Aston's hand began to tremble as he read through Washington's congratulation of his troops for their victory. "The Commander in Chief congratulates the Army on the Victory obtained over the Arms of his Britanick Majesty yesterday and thanks most sincerely the gallant officers and men who distinguished themselves upon the occasion and such others as by their good order and coolness gave the happiest presages of what might have been expected had they come to Action."[129] At the bottom of the yellowed page, he read the signature of George Washington. Aston turned the page over in wonder.

He discovered, much to his surprise, that in the same handwriting as the signature, George Washington had written a personal note on the other side of the official orders. The note was addressed to a Doctor Craik, acknowledging a prior correspondence from Craik and concurring with his esteem and appreciation of the Guard in the exercise of their duty with the medical units during the occasion of the Battle of Monmouth. Aston's eyes widened as he continued to read. "I, along with you, acknowledge Life Guards Spitzen, Zylstra, Grayson, and Gloege for their brave and distinguished conduct."

Aston noticed that the next paragraph took on a friendlier and more intimate tone. "James, I was most satisfied to find Spitz listed among the Guard for particular commendation. I have offered to advance him by some means, which honor he has always gently refused, and now he must accept in the course of his duties. You know that the man deserves some recognition for his personal faithfulness to me over the course of some years, as well as his recent instance of particular bravery, and you know as well that I always pay my debts. Do join me at supper tonight. You, too, have labored long and well tending to the wounds and fevers of this army, and I wish to thank you."

Aston's eyes lingered over his grandfather's surname in the list of guards to be honored, and then they strayed to his grandfather's nickname, Spitz, in the personal note. *Could that Guard really be Papa Spitzen?* Aston quickly glanced through the other documents. They were all personal letters from George Washington. The first offered condolences, encouragement, and admonishment to stay the course and persevere through adversity and loss. It was addressed to Guard Spitzen at Valley Forge. The next letter referenced faithful service at Trenton and included an invitation to Mount Vernon at the conclusion of the war. The last letter noted the distinguished service of a patriot at Yorktown and of a true friend during the waning days of Jack Custis. Aston paused in thought. *Could Papa Spitzen really have been a personal friend of George Washington?* Again he pushed back the notion that somehow his great-grandfather had traveled back in time. *It's impossible; don't be silly.* But he was still boy enough for curiosity to overpower his rational explanations.

Aston replaced the letters in the journal, locked the journal in the drawer and sealed it with the veneer, and went to the coffee table, where he had left the family Bible his mother had handed to him.

Buzzing with anticipation, Aston sat in the wingback chair by the dying fire in the hearth and put the Bible in his lap. *This is crazy. Nothing is going to happen when I open this Bible,* he scolded himself. *I should just put it away and go talk to my parents in the kitchen.*

Then another, more hopeful voice contradicted him kindly. *But what if something does happen, something wonderful?*

Aston hesitated. And then he opened the book.

# Afterword

*"Then the man in linen with the writing kit*
*at his side brought back word, saying, "I have done*
*as you commanded."—Ezekiel 9:11*

"On Washington's resignation of the presidency, one of the first employments of his retirement as a private citizen was to arrange certain letters and papers for posthumous publication. With this view he wrote to General Spotswood, in Virginia, to select a young man of respectable family, good moral habits, and superior clerkly skill, to copy into a large book certain letters and papers that would be prepared for such purpose.

"Now, these letters and papers were by no means of an official character; neither did they come within the range of recollections of the Revolution or the constitutional government; they were more especially private, and could with propriety be termed *Passages, Personal and Explanatory, in the Life and Correspondence of George Washington.*

"General Spotswood selected a young man named Albin Rawlins, of a respectable family in the county of Caroline, and well qualified for the duties he was to perform. He soon after arrived at Mount Vernon, and entered upon his employment.

"The letters were delivered to Rawlins by the chief in person, were carefully returned to him when copied, and others delivered out for copying. As the duties of the clerk lasted for a considerable time, very many of the most interesting and valuable letters that Washington ever wrote or received were copied into the *Rawlins' Book.* While we repeat that these letters were not of an official character, we must observe that they were written to and received from some the most illustrious public men who flourished in the age of Washington, and shed more light upon the true character of the men and things of that distinguished period than any letters or papers that ever were written and published.

"Washington postponed the arrangement for publication of his private memoirs to the last; all such matters lay dormant during the long and meritorious career of his public services. It was only when retired amid the shades of Mount Vernon that he thought of self, and determined in his latter days that nothing should be left undone to give to his country and the world a fair and just estimate of his life and actions.

"A portion of the letters of the Rawlins' Book were of a delicate character, seeing that they involved the reputation of the writers as consistent patriots and men of honor. *These letters are no where to be found.* But, although the veil of mystery has been drawn over the *lost letters of the Rawlins' Book* that time and circumstance can never remove, our readers may rest assured that there is not a line, nay, a word, in the lost letters that Washington wrote, that, were he living, he would wish to revoke or blot out, but would readily, fearlessly submit to the perusal and decision of his countrymen and the world.

"During the agitation of the public mind that grew out of the subject of the lost letters... it was contended that the rumors were groundless; that there were no such letters. Faithful to our purpose... to give in these *Recollections* only of what we saw, and only of what we derived from the undoubted authority of others, we do not hesitate to declare, and from an authority that can not be questioned, that there were such letters as those described as the *Lost Letters of the Rawlins' Book.*"[130]

*George Washington Parke Custis*
*Son of Jack Custis, adopted by George Washington*

# Endnotes

1. Peter A. Lillback and Jerry Newcombe, *George Washington's Sacred Fire* (Bryn Mawr, PA: Providence Forum Press, 2006), 685.

2. John Alexander Carroll and Mary Wells Ashworth, *George Washington: Completing the Biography by Douglas Southall Freeman, Vol. 7: First in Peace* (New York: Charles Scribner's Sons, 1957), 7:623

3. George Washington Parke Custis, *Recollections and Private Memoirs of Washington* (New York: Derby and Jackson, 1860; Bridgewater, VA: American Foundation Publications, 1999), 473-474.

4. Lillback and Newcombe, *George Washington's Sacred Fire*, 174.

5. Ibid., 47.

6. James D. Richardson, *A Compilation of the Messages and Papers of the Presidents 1789-1897, Vol. 1* (New York: Bureau of National Literature, 1897), 1:51.

7. Ibid., 1:54-55.

8. Ibid., 1:56-57.

9. Ibid., 1:64.

10. Douglas Southall Freeman, *George Washington: A Biography, Vol. 1: Young Washington* (New York: Charles Scribner's Sons, 1948), 1:318.

11. George Washington, speech at headquarters at Middle Brook to Delaware Chiefs, May 12, 1779, in *The Writings of Washington from the Original Manuscript Sources: Vol. 15*, ed. John C. Fitzpatrick, (Charlottesville, VA: University of Virginia Library Electronic Text Center, 2007, http://etext.lib.virginia.edu/Washington/), 15:53.

12. Library of America ed., *George Washington Writings* (New York: Literary Classics of the United States, Inc., 1997), 20-22.

13. Freeman, *George Washington: A Biography*, 1:317.

14. Library of America, *George Washington Writings*, 48.

15. Freeman, *George Washington: A Biography*, 1: 411 and Library of America, *George Washington Writings*, 373.

16. George Washington to Robert Orme, Mount Vernon, March 15, 1755, in *The Writings of Washington from the Original Manuscript Sources: Vol. 1*, ed. John C. Fitzpatrick, (Charlottesville, VA: University of Virginia Library Electronic Text Center, 2007, http://etext.lib.virginia.edu/Washington/), 1:107.

17. George Washington to John Augustine Washington, Fort Cumberland, May 14, 1755, in Ibid., 1:123-124.

18. George Washington to John Augustine Washington, Fort Cumberland, July 18, 1755, in Ibid., 1:152-153.

19. George Washington to Mary Washington, Fort Cumberland, July 18, 1755, in Ibid., 1:150-152.

20. George Washington to John Augustine Washington, Fort Cumberland, July 18, 1755, in Ibid., 1:152-153.

21. George Washington to Governor Robert Dinwiddie, Fort Cumberland, July 18, 1755, in Ibid., 1:148-150.

22. George Washington to Robert Jackson, Mount Vernon, August 2, 1755, in Ibid., 1:155-156.

23. Custis, *Recollections and Private Memoirs*, 374-375.

24. George Washington to John Augustine Washington, Fort Cumberland, July 18, 1755, in *Original Manuscript Sources: Vol. 1,* ed. Fitzpatrick, 1:152-153.

25. Douglas Southall Freeman, *George Washington: A Biography, Vol. 2: Young Washington* (New York: Charles Scribner's Sons, 1948), 75.

26. Ibid., 2:103.

27. Ibid., 2:210.

28. Reverend Samuel Davies, sermon, "Religion and Patriotism the Constituents of a Good Soldier", Virginia Militia Company, Hanover County, VA, August 17, 1755, in *Original Manuscript Sources: Vol. 1,* ed. Fitzpatrick, 1:153 (note).

29. Custis, *Recollections and Private Memoirs,* 302.

30. Ibid., 303.

31. Reverend Samuel Davies, sermon, "Religion and Patriotism the Constituents of a Good Soldier", Virginia Militia Company, Hanover County, VA, August 17, 1755, in *Original Manuscript Sources: Vol. 1,* ed. Fitzpatrick, 1:153 (note).

32. Custis, *Recollections and Private Memoirs,* 304.

33. Ibid.

34. Mark A. Beliles and Stephen K. McDowell, *America's Providential History: Including Biblical Principles of Education, Government, Politics, Economics, and Family Life* (Charlottesville, VA: Providence Foundation, 1989), 162.

35. Ibid., 568.

36. Ibid., 575.

37. Ibid., 575-76.

38. Ibid., 143.

39. George Washington to Landon Carter, Valley Forge, May 30, 1778 in *The Writings of Washington from the Original Manuscript Sources: Vol. 11,* ed. John C. Fitzpatrick, (Charlottesville, VA: University of Virginia Library Electronic Text Center, 2007, http://etext.lib.virginia.edu/Washington/), 11:492.

40. George Washington to Landon Carter, Valley Forge, May 30, 1778, in Ibid., 11:494.

41. Shakespeare, Henry V, act IV, sc. iii, 60-62.

42. George Washington to the Secretary of War, Philadelphia, September 8, 1791, in *The Writings of Washington from the Original Manuscript Sources: Vol. 31,* ed. John C. Fitzpatrick, (Charlottesville, VA: University of Virginia Library Electronic Text Center, 2007, http://etext.lib.virginia.edu/Washington/), 31:360.

43. Custis, *Recollections and Private Memoirs,* 275.

44. Ibid., 191.

45. Ibid., 191-192.

46. Ibid., 201-202.

47. Ibid., 222.

48. Ibid., 222-223.

49. George Washington to Lord Stirling, English Town, June 27, 1778, in *The Writings of Washington from the Original Manuscript Sources: Vol. 12,* ed. John C. Fitzpatrick, (Charlottesville, VA: University of Virginia Library Electronic Text Center, 2007, http://etext.lib.virginia.edu/Washington/), 12:124.

50. Custis, *Recollections and Private Memoirs,* 224.

51. Ibid.

52. Ibid., 305-306.

53. Douglas Southall Freeman, *George Washington: A Biography, Vol. 5: Victory with the Help of France* (New York: Charles Scribner's Sons, 1952), 5:29.

54. Custis, *Recollections and Private Memoirs*, 222.

55. Beliles and McDowell, *America's Providential History*, 118.

56. Ibid., 141.

57. Custis, *Recollections and Private Memoirs*, 214.

58. Wikipedia.org s.v. Battle of Kings Mountain, http://en.wikipedia.org/wiki/Battle_Of_King%27s_Mountain.

59. Wikipedia.org s.v. Battle of Kings Mountain, http://en.wikipedia.org/wiki/Battle_Of_King%27s_Mountain.

60. George Washington, General Orders at Headquarters at New Windsor, January 6, 1781, in *The Writings of Washington from the Original Manuscript Sources: Vol. 21*, ed. John C. Fitzpatrick, (Charlottesville, VA: University of Virginia Library Electronic Text Center, 2007, http://etext.lib.virginia.edu/Washington/), 21:63.

61. George Washington to Comte de Rochambeau, New Windsor, February 26, 1781, in Ibid., 21:298.

62. Beliles and McDowell, *America's Providential History*, 166.

63. Ibid.

64. Wikipedia.org s.v. Battle of Guilford Court House, http://en.wikipedia.org/wiki/Battle_of_Guilford_Courthouse.

65. Wikipedia.org s.v. Battle of Kings Mountain, http://en.wikipedia.org/wiki/Battle_Of_King%27s_Mountain.

66. George Washington to Thomas McKean, Mount Vernon, November 15, 1781, in *The Writings of Washington from the Original Manuscript Sources: Vol. 23*, ed. John C. Fitzpatrick, (Charlottesville, VA: University of Virginia Library Electronic Text Center, 2007, http://etext.lib.virginia.edu/Washington/), 23:343.

67. George Washington, The Last Will and Testament of George Washington, Mount Vernon, July 9, 1799, in *The Writings of Washington from the Original Manuscript Sources: Vol. 36*, ed. John C. Fitzpatrick, (Charlottesville, VA: University of Virginia Library Electronic Text Center, 2007, http://etext.lib.virginia.edu/Washington/), 36:286 (notes).

68. Wikipedia.org s.v. Gouverneur Morris, http://en.wikipedia.org/wiki/Gouverneur_Morris.

69. Douglas Southall Freeman, *George Washington: A Biography, Vol. 6: Patriot and President* (New York: Charles Scribner's Sons, 1954), 6:98.

70. George Washington to Major General John Armstrong, New Windsor, March 26, 1781, in *Original Manuscript Sources: Vol. 21*, ed. Fitzpatrick, 21:378.

71. George Washington to Lucretia Wilhemina Van Winter, Mount Vernon, March 30, 1785, in *The Writings of Washington from the Original Manuscript Sources: Vol. 28*, ed. John C. Fitzpatrick, (Charlottesville, VA: University of Virginia Library Electronic Text Center, 2007, http://etext.lib.virginia.edu/Washington/), 28:120.

72. George Washington, Circular to the States, Headquarters at Newburgh, June 8, 1783, in *The Writings of Washington from the Original Manuscript Sources: Vol. 26*, ed. John C. Fitzpatrick, (Charlottesville, VA: University of Virginia Library Electronic Text Center, 2007, http://etext.lib.virginia.edu/Washington/), 26:484-485.

73. George Washington to Bushrod Washington, Philadelphia, July 10, 1787, in *The Writings of Washington from the Original Manuscript Sources: Vol. 29*, ed. John C. Fitzpatrick, (Charlottesville, VA: University of Virginia Library Electronic Text Center, 2007, http://etext.lib.virginia.edu/Washington/), 29:310-311.

74. George Washington to Marquis De Lafayette, Mount Vernon, May 10, 1786, in *Original Manuscript Sources: Vol. 28*, ed. Fitzpatrick, 28:420-421.

75. George Washington, Farewell Orders to the Armies of the United States, Rock Hill near Princeton, November 2, 1783, in *The Writings of Washington from the Original Manuscript Sources: Vol. 27*, ed. John C. Fitzpatrick, (Charlottesville, VA: University of Virginia Library Electronic Text Center, 2007, http://etext.lib.virginia.edu/Washington/), 27:224.

76. Ibid., 27:223.

77. George Washington to the President of Congress, headquarters near York, October 19, 1781, in *Original Manuscript Sources: Vol. 23*, ed. Fitzpatrick, 23:241.

78. Beliles and McDowell, *America's Providential History*, 171.

79. George Washington to Marquis De Lafayette, Philadelphia, July 10, 1787, in *Original Manuscript Sources: Vol. 29*, ed. Fitzpatrick, 29:508.

80. George Washington to Catherine Macaulay Graham, Philadelphia, July 10, 1787, in Ibid., 29:316.

81. George Washington to Marquis De Lafayette, Philadelphia, July 10, 1787, in Ibid., 29:508.

82. George Washington to Catherine Macaulay Graham, Philadelphia, July 10, 1787, in Ibid., 29:316.

83. George Washington, Farewell Orders to the Armies of the United States, at Rock Hill near Princeton, November 2, 1783, in *Original Manuscript Sources: Vol. 27*, ed. Fitzpatrick, 27:223.

84. Ibid., 27:224.

85. George Washington to the President of Congress, headquarters near York, October 19, 1781, in *Original Manuscript Sources: Vol. 23*, ed. Fitzpatrick, 23:241.

86. Wikipedia.org s.v. Nathanael Greene, http://en.wikipedia.org/wiki/Nathanael_Greene.

87. George Washington, General Orders, headquarters at New York, August 14, 1776, in *The Writings of Washington from the Original Manuscript Sources: Vol. 5*, ed. John C. Fitzpatrick, (Charlottesville, VA: University of Virginia Library Electronic Text Center, 2007, http://etext.lib.virginia.edu/Washington/), 5:437.

88. George Washington to William Pearce, Philadelphia, May 25, 1794, in *The Writings of Washington from the Original Manuscript Sources: Vol. 33*, ed. John C. Fitzpatrick, (Charlottesville, VA: University of Virginia Library Electronic Text Center, 2007, http://etext.lib.virginia.edu/Washington/), 33:375.

89. Richardson, *Messages and Papers, Vol. 1*, 1:52.

90. Ibid.

91. Ibid.

92. George Washington to John Parke Custis, Morris Town, January 22, 1777, in *The Writings of Washington from the Original Manuscript Sources: Vol. 7*, ed. John C. Fitzpatrick, (Charlottesville, VA: University of Virginia Library Electronic Text Center, 2007, http://etext.lib.virginia.edu/Washington/), 7:53.

93. Richardson, *Messages and Papers, Vol. 1*, 1:64.

94. Ibid.

95. George Washington to Colonel Adam Stephen, New York, July 20, 1776, in *Original Manuscript Sources: Vol. 5*, ed. Fitzpatrick, 5:313.

96. Richardson, *Messages and Papers, Vol. 1*, 1:64.

97. George Washington to the Secretary of War, Philadelphia, September 8, 1791, in *Original Manuscript Sources: Vol. 31*, ed. Fitzpatrick, 31:360.

98. George Washington to Henry Knox, Head Quarters, September 12 1782, in *The Writings of Washington from the Original Manuscript Sources: Vol. 25*, ed. John C. Fitzpatrick, (Charlottesville, VA: University of Virginia Library Electronic Text Center, 2007, http://etext.lib.virginia.edu/Washington/), 25:150 (notes).

99. George Washington to William Pearce, Philadelphia, June 21, 1795, in *The Writings of Washington from the Original Manuscript Sources: Vol. 34,* ed. John C. Fitzpatrick, (Charlottesville, VA: University of Virginia Library Electronic Text Center, 2007, http://etext.lib.virginia.edu/Washington/), 34:217.

100. George Washington to the Legislature of New Jersey, Trenton, December 6, 1783, in *Original Manuscript Sources: Vol. 27,* ed. Fitzpatrick, 27:261.

101. George Washington to Reverend William Gordon, New York, May 13, 1776, in *The Writings of Washington from the Original Manuscript Sources: Vol. 37,* ed. John C. Fitzpatrick, (Charlottesville, VA: University of Virginia Library Electronic Text Center, 2007, http://etext.lib.virginia.edu/Washington/), 37:526.

102. George Washington, Circular to the States, Headquarters at Newburgh, June 8, 1783 in *Original Manuscript Sources: Vol. 26,* ed. Fitzpatrick, 26:496.

103. Ibid.

104. George Washington to Lucretia Wilhemina Van Winter, Mount Vernon, March 30, 1785, in *Original Manuscript Sources: Vol. 28,* ed. Fitzpatrick, 28:120.

105. George Washington, Circular to the States, Headquarters at Newburgh, June 8, 1783, in *Original Manuscript Sources: Vol. 26,* ed. Fitzpatrick, 26:484-485.

106. George Washington to the Ministers, Elders, Deacons, and Members of the Reformed German Congregation of New York, New York, November 27, 1783, in *Original Manuscript Sources: Vol. 27,* ed. Fitzpatrick, 27:249.

107. George Washington to the Clergy of Different Denominations Residing in and near the City of Philadelphia, Philadelphia, March 3, 1797, in *The Writings of Washington from the Original Manuscript Sources: Vol. 35,* ed. John C. Fitzpatrick, (Charlottesville, VA: University of Virginia Library Electronic Text Center, 2007, http://etext.lib.virginia.edu/Washington/), 35:416.

108. George Washington, Farewell Address, Mount Vernon, September 19, 1796, in Ibid., 35:219-220.

109. George Washington to William Pearce, Philadelphia, March 27, 1796, in *The Writings of Washington from the Original Manuscript Sources: Vol. 34,* ed. John C. Fitzpatrick, (Charlottesville, VA: University of Virginia Library Electronic Text Center, 2007, http://etext.lib.virginia.edu/Washington/), 34:507.

110. George Washington to Delaware Chiefs, Headquarters at Middle Brook, May 12, 1779, in *Original Manuscript Sources: Vol. 15,* ed. *Fitzpatrick,15:53.*

111. George Washington, General Orders, headquarters at Valley Forge, May 2, 1778, in *Original Manuscript Sources: Vol. 11,* ed. Fitzpatrick, 11:343.

112. George Washington, General Orders, headquarters at New York, July 9, 1776, in *Original Manuscript Sources: Vol. 5,* ed. Fitzpatrick, 5:245.

113. Douglas Southall Freeman, *George Washington: A Biography, Vol. 4: Leader of the Revolution* (New York: Charles Scribner's Sons, 1951), 4:565

114. Custis, *Recollections and Private Memoirs,* 473-474.

115. George Washington, Farewell Address, Mount Vernon, September 19, 1796, in *Original Manuscript Sources: Vol. 35,* ed. Fitzpatrick, 35:217-218.

116. George Washington, General Orders, headquarters at Wentz's, Worcester Township, October 18, 1777, in *The Writings of Washington from the Original Manuscript Sources: Vol. 9,* ed. John C. Fitzpatrick, (Charlottesville, VA: University of Virginia Library Electronic Text Center, 2007, http://etext.lib.virginia.edu/Washington/), 9:391.

117. George Washington, General Orders, headquarters at Towamensing, October 15, 1777, in Ibid., 9:377.

118. George Washington to Lund Washington, headquarters at Middlebrook, May 29, 1779, in *Original Manuscript Sources: Vol. 15,* ed. Fitzpatrick, 15:180.

119. George Washington to Major General William Heath, Robinson's house, September 26, 1780, in *The Writings of Washington from the Original Manuscript Sources: Vol. 20*, ed. John C. Fitzpatrick, (Charlottesville, VA: University of Virginia Library Electronic Text Center, 2007, http://etext.lib.virginia.edu/Washington/), 20:88-89.

120. George Washington, General Orders, headquarters at Orangetown, September 26, 1780, in Ibid., 20:94.

121. George Washington, General Orders, headquarters at Wentz's, Worcester Township, October 18, 1777, in *Original Manuscript Sources: Vol. 9*, ed. Fitzpatrick, 9:391.

122. George Washington, General Orders, headquarters at Towamensing, October 15, 1777, in Ibid., 9:377.

123. George Washington to Lund Washington, headquarters at Middlebrook, May 29, 1779, in *Original Manuscript Sources: Vol. 15*, ed. Fitzpatrick, 15:180.

124. George Washington to Major General William Heath, Robinson's house, September 26, 1780, in *Original Manuscript Sources: Vol. 20*, ed. Fitzpatrick, 20:88-89.

125. George Washington, General Orders, headquarters at Orangetown, September 26, 1780, in Ibid., 20:94.

126. Dave Kopel, "The Religious Roots of the American Revolution and the Right to Keep and Bear Arms," http://davekopel.org/Religion/Religious-Roots-of-the-American-Revolution. pdf, 12/11/12.

127. Lillback and Newcombe, *George Washington's Sacred Fire*, 685.

128. Carroll and Ashworth, *George Washington, First in Peace*, 7:624.

129. George Washington, General Orders, Headquarters, Freehold (Monmouth County), June 29, 1778, *Original Manuscript Sources: Vol. 12*, ed. Fitzpatrick, 130.

130. Custis, *Recollections and Private Memoirs*, 436-437.

# UP *and* IN

## Seven Keys to Unlocking Your Potential

*Steve Kubicek* | www.upandinbook.com

*Up and In* is an inspiring, self-mentoring resource based on the encouraging stories of a successful corporate executive, ordained deacon, and speaker. With gentle humor, uplifting anecdotes, and inspiring quotes woven throughout, *Up and In* takes readers on a rich, rewarding, and meaningful journey of reflection, discovery, and transformation. Resplendent with simple truths and powerful personal testimony, timeless Scripture and timely insights, Up and In presents an exceptional collection of 42 daily readings designed to encourage, challenge, renew, and uplift. An inventive, inspiring, and invaluable resource, *Up and In* has garnered high praise, including: "one of the most encouraging books that I have read...practical and filled with pearls of wisdom"; "a great personal resource"; "a breath of fresh air." Uplifting and affirming, *Up and In* addresses such issues as: uncovering true worth and potential; confronting damaging thinking and habits; developing the tools to rebound from setbacks; outlining the path for discovering significance and more. With the deft touch of a true storyteller and an unmistakable faith, author Steve Kubicek created a book that is anything but an ordinary self-help guide: with its conversational, inviting, and warm tone, *Up and In* is part good friend/trusted confidant/wise-mentor-in-a-book, part road map to a meaningful life, part inspiring companion—and wholly enriching. Moving and motivational, thoughtful and thought-provoking, Up and In is an extraordinary—and extraordinarily valuable—resource.

Hardcover: 978-0-98484-260-5
Paperback: 978-0-98484-261-2

*"Searching for success? Significance? No matter what your walk of life or your station in life, this book will make your life better. Read it. Apply it. Reap the benefits. Now."*

**—DAVID B. GILLOGLY,** Former President/COO, Express Personnel Services

STEVE KUBICEK, author of *Visibly Struck*, www.visiblystruck.com, has more than thirty years of U.S. and international sales and marketing experience. As a successful Fortune 500 corporate executive, Kubicek oversaw billions of dollars in annual sales. His passion is to inspire, mentor, and motivate. Steve believes that lessons of experience are precious gifts to be shared for the encouragement of others, www.stevekubicek.com.